Oliver Dyer

General Andrew Jackson

Hero of New Orleans and Seventh President of the United States

Oliver Dyer

General Andrew Jackson
Hero of New Orleans and Seventh President of the United States

ISBN/EAN: 9783744728782

Printed in Europe, USA, Canada, Australia, Japan

Cover: Foto ©Raphael Reischuk / pixelio.de

Geo. Wilson

GENERAL ANDREW JACKSON.

GENERAL ANDREW JACKSON *Frontispiece*

General Andrew Jackson

HERO OF NEW ORLEANS

AND

SEVENTH PRESIDENT OF THE UNITED STATES.

BY

OLIVER DYER,

Author of "Great Senators of the United States," "Character Sketch of Henry W. Grady," "Life and Writings of George Bancroft," etc.

WITH ILLUSTRATIONS BY H. M. EATON.

NEW YORK:
ROBERT BONNER'S SONS.
1891.

Press of
The New York Ledger,
New York.

GENERAL ANDREW JACKSON.

CHAPTER I.

HEROES—CHILDHOOD OF A HERO.

ANY boy or any man, however poor and humble, or however rich and exalted, wants to be a hero. Every girl and every woman, however lowly and obscure, or however fashionable and fortunate, wants to be a heroine and have a hero for her lover and husband; and the bride who marries for love thinks she has him—at least, until the honeymoon has passed. Any boy or man, any girl or woman, who has this volume in hand and is reading these words, feels the force of the truths they express, and longs to be a hero or heroine, aspires to do something grand and noble, and would gladly win a place among the illustrious men or the honored women of the world.

Because every human being thus wishes to become great and good and noble, according to his or her standard of greatness, goodness and nobleness, there is not a boy or girl, not a man or a woman who does not sympathize with the struggles and the triumphs of heroes and heroines, and love to read the history of their lives. And so I am encouraged in the hope that everybody who sees it will enjoy the reading of the life-story which I am about to tell them of one of the greatest heroes who ever lived in this world, and who is known to history and to fame as Andrew Jackson, Judge Jackson, Senator Jackson, General Jackson, President Jackson, Old Hickory Jackson.

This celebrated hero was born in poverty and obscurity. It is doubtful if there is a boy or a girl who will read this story of Andrew Jackson's life who is as poor as he was in his childhood, or who is encountering as great obstacles as he encountered, or suffering hardships and privations as bitter as those which he suffered. But, fortunately, poverty, obstacles, hardships and privations are not the worst things which can befall a child of destiny. They are, in fact, more likely to be blessings than misfortunes.

> "Cast the bantling on the rocks,
> Suckle him with the she wolf's teat;
> Wintered with the hawk and fox,
> Power and speed be hands and feet."

The old stories of Romulus and Remus suckled by a wolf and Cyrus the Great by a goat, are symbolic representations of the great truth that exposure and hardship and danger are sometimes the best things which can be provided for young immortals. It was certainly so in the case of our poor boy, Andrew Jackson; and because he lived his life, and fought his fight, and conquered fate, and blazed a path from poverty and obscurity to greatness and renown, this land for which he fought and which he loved so well, has been a better land for poor boys and poor girls, and is now a better land for every struggling boy or girl, for every toiling man or woman, than it would have been had Andrew Jackson not thus lived and fought and conquered. And now let us read the story of this poor boy's life, and see how it was that he became the idolized hero of his native land.

Andrew Jackson was born near the Waxhaw settlement, in what is now Union County, North Carolina, on March 15, 1767, nine years before the Declaration of Independence was given to the world. His father died a few days before Andrew was born. In obscurity had he lived, and in obscurity was he buried. Mrs. Jackson, with her fatherless little boys, rode to the graveyard in the wagon that carried her husband's rude coffin.

The bereaved widow was left without a protector and in absolute poverty. Obliged to abandon her desolate and squalid home in the wilderness, she took refuge, with her two little sons, Hugh and

Robert, in the house of a hospitable friend, and there awaited the birth of her third child.

It was a pitiful case. Andrew's father (after whom the new-born infant was named) had come from Carrickfergus, in the north of Ireland, two years before (1765), inspired by the hope that he would be able to make a home for his family in the American wilderness. Being too poor to buy land, even at the low price at which it was then sold, he built a cabin on land that was not his own, and set at work to chop and plough out a farm for himself. But dying prematurely and suddenly, he left his little family without a home, and they were compelled (as stated above) to seek refuge with friends who had come from their native land with the Jacksons.

A pitiful case it was, most certainly; but our little germ of a hero had got into the world; and when we think of it, there was much in that. Without that, nothing would have been possible for him; with that, God willing, everything was possible. Yet when we look back to those far-away days, and in imagination gaze upon that little child born in poverty so squalid and in obscurity so dense, it seems well-nigh miraculous that such a poor little creature should have come to fill so large a space in the world's history—should, in fact, have become the hinge on which his country's destiny was to swing for many years. When the *Mayflower* was launched she was as obscure as Andrew Jackson was in his infancy. The *Mayflower* might have sailed the seas for years, carrying merchandise, without impressing her name upon the minds and the hearts of mankind. It was the freight she carried and the use she performed on her memorable voyage in 1620, which gave her immortality. She was then freighted with the embodied principles of religious and political liberty, and was the instrument for transplanting them to a soil where they could take root, and grow beyond the fondest dreams of their advocates; and for these reasons her name became as imperishable as the incarnated principles which she brought to the shores of the Western World. As with ships, so with babies; whether they win an immortality of fame depends on the freight of principle and character they carry on the voyage of life, and the uses to which their lives are devoted. Owing to his mother's religious teaching and example and her ardent patriotism, our Waxhaw boy, as we shall see, though as obscure as the *Mayflower* was at her launching, was freighted with the principles which that little vessel brought across the ocean, and through the passionate development of these principles in him and the heroic deeds he performed in maintaining them, his name, like that of the *Mayflower*, became invested with immortality.

The widow Jackson, like most women of Scotch-Irish blood, was a strong, capable and thrifty woman, an excellent housekeeper and a wise and affectionate mother. Her maiden name was Elizabeth Hutchinson. Her father's family, in the old North of Ireland home, was as poor as her husband's. But she and her sisters were fairly educated, according to the standard of education in those primitive times, and were brought up by pious, God-fearing parents "in the nurture and admonition of the Lord." They were weavers of linen. It is said that sometimes they worked all night at their looms in order to earn enough to keep the wolf from the door. It is not unfrequently the fortune of such obscure, faithful, God-fearing women to be the mothers of heroes.

When little Andrew was three weeks old, Mrs. Jackson left her temporary home and took up her abode with another family of friends and relatives, where she lived as housekeeper for several years. Her two elder boys worked on neighboring farms. Andrew grew apace. He was the idol of his mother's heart. Mrs. Jackson was a devout woman and a habitual and prayerful reader of the Bible. The incidents narrated in the sacred Word, of the consecration of children, in their early infancy, to the service of God, had made a deep impression on her mind. In her heart she consecrated her baby boy to God's service, and resolved that, Providence permitting, he should be a minister of the Gospel. In her devout and simple faith, which believed all things and hoped all things, she could say, with Hannah of old: "For this child I prayed; and the Lord hath given me my petition which I asked of Him: therefore, also have I lent him to the Lord; as long as he liveth he shall be lent to the Lord."

Although Mrs. Jackson's fond hopes were not to be realized, her indulgence of them was providential. They elevated and hallowed her intense maternal love, and filled it with a reverence which caused her son's childhood to be enveloped in a spiritual atmosphere that carried airs from Heaven in its bosom.

His nature was extraordinarily receptive of religious influences, and he breathed them in from infancy. He loved and reverenced his mother with passionate devotion. Her religious habits; her daily reading of the Bible; her praying on her knees at his bedside; her custom of having him read the Bible, and pray at her knee with her hand resting lovingly on his head—all these sacred influences entered deeply into his soul and staid there forever. Although in after years they sometimes seemed to be buried deep under less benignant influences, they nevertheless were there, doing their silent work; and as in childhood and youth and early manhood they had a powerful influence in the development and formation of his character, so in old age they blossomed anew and shed a halo of genial glory over the closing period of his life.

Many babies were born in the year 1767, some of which were surrounded by influences that seemed to predestine them to greatness; but how few of them can now be called by name, except by the assiduous students of history! On July 11, 1767, when Andrew Jackson was within four days of being four months old, a boy baby was born in Braintree, Massachusetts, that was to become closely associated with some of the most important events of his life. As those two babies were rocked, so widely apart, in their North Carolina and Massachusetts cradles, only the eye of Omniscience could foresee the coalescences and the collisions that were to occur between them. The Massachusetts baby, afterward known as John Quincy Adams, was to pass through comfort, high social position, institutions of learning, the cabinets of diplomacy and the courts of Europe, to meet, at last, in the envenomed contests for the Presidency of the United States in 1824 and 1828, that North Carolina baby who, meantime, had come up through partisan warfare in the Revolution, through poverty and bitter struggles for an education and a profession, through fighting with wild beasts, Indians, Spaniards, British and foes innumerable, to a commanding position in the admiration and affection of his countrymen. As this narrative goes on, it will be interesting to note how the wide-swirling current of events slowly but constantly brought these two babies, destined to become such shining stars in the political firmament, first into friendly contiguity and then into resounding collision.

There was another baby born that same year (1767) that was to have vastly more influence on Andrew Jackson's life than the Massachusetts baby. On what day, or in what place, this influential baby was born, I do not know. It was a girl baby, and was subsequently known as an intelligent, vivacious, lovely brunette, named Rachel Donelson. Her father, John Donelson, was a noted surveyor in Virginia, and it is probable that Rachel was born in that colony. How strangely the currents of human lives are mingled! A man, at that time yet unborn, was to perish by Andrew Jackson's hand, for uttering insulting words in the presence and hearing of the lovely brunette, Rachel Donelson, of whom much will be said as this story goes on.

As Andrew Jackson increased in years and stature, he learned to ride, to hunt, and to do a good deal of hard work of the kind that fell to the lot of all the boys of that region. In the days when the Persian Empire was at the height of its power and glory, the sum of a Persian boy's education was to ride on horseback, to shoot arrows, and to speak the truth. Andrew Jackson's education was like that of the Persian boy, except that he handled a rifle instead of a bow, and shot bullets instead of arrows. He could ride as well as any Persian, and he always spoke the truth. During a few months of each year, he was sent to school in a log school-house, where he was taught by rough, poorly educated, itinerant teachers. He took to his books kindly, and learned to write a fine, clear hand. His only failure was in his spelling; to the end of his days he never mastered the orthography of the English language; nor, in truth, did many of his contemporaries. It seemed as though the only way in which the majority of our Revolutionary worthies could escape being bad spellers was never to spell at all.

Andrew was tall for his years, rather loose-jointed and not robust. He had sandy hair and piercing blue eyes. He was free in his manners, looked people squarely in the face, had an air of dauntless resolution, and became more and more the pride of his mother's heart.

In 1848, I went to Washington as a reporter in the United States Senate. James K. Polk, a disciple and personal friend of Jackson's, was then President. Old Hickory had left Washington, at the close of his second term, in 1837, only eleven years before. The city was full of people who knew him personally, thousands of whom idolized him and hundreds of whom hated him. I had been intensely interested in his life from childhood, and I eagerly listened to everybody who would talk to me about him. I ransacked their memories for facts, for stories, for anecdotes, and made notes thereof, with the intention of some day writing the old hero's life.

I heard enough about Andrew Jackson from his personal friends and his personal enemies in Washington to fill several volumes. Some of his friends were old men from North Carolina whom he had appointed to office while he was President, and who professed to be related to him either on his father's or his mother's side. Their pretensions may have been founded on fact, for Andrew Jackson was not a man to pass over an honest and capable relative or friend to give office to a stranger, under the hypocritical assumption of a degree of public virtue which was never possessed by any man so basely mean as to forget in the day of triumph the friends who stood by him in the battle and helped him to win his victory. According to the testimony of these old men, who were familiar with the legends of Old Hickory's youth, the boy Andrew Jackson—or Andy Jackson as he was called—was a sprightly, fun-loving imp, whose propensity to boyish mischief was irrestrainable. He was fond of all athletic games, especially running, jumping and wrestling. He was also fond of horseback riding and hunting. As a wrestler, he depended on his grit more than on his strength. No matter how often he was thrown by more muscular boys, he would always demand "one more trial," until, by his tireless persistency, he would obtain a victory over a boy larger and stronger than himself. Mr. Parton, whose extensive and comprehensive "Life of Andrew Jackson" is a store-house of facts and anecdotes, gives the testimony of an old school-mate of Andy Jackson's who says:

"I could throw him three times out of four, but he would never *stay throwed.* He was dead game, even then, and never *would* give up."

Andy's courage was so marked, it made a lasting impression upon the minds and memories of the inhabitants of the neighborhood. He was a leader of the brave boys of the settlement, and was ever ready to defend the weak and to defy the strong. He had a terrible temper, but his wrath was easily appeased as soon as opposition was overcome and victory had perched upon his banner. In all these respects, the old adage, "The boy is father of the man," was absolutely true in the case of Andrew Jackson. To the end of his days he was a leader among the bravest of the brave, a defender of the weak, a defier of the wrong and strong. His courage and his fortitude were, as we shall see by and by, so lofty and so unconquerable as to seem to be superhuman. In 1834, William Cobbett, well known in his day as a brave British soldier, a member of Parliament and a writer of distinction, wrote a life of Andrew Jackson, in which he calls, him "the greatest and bravest man now living in this world, or who has ever lived in this world, as far as my knowledge extends."

As years went on and Andrew's character developed, Mrs. Jackson's fond hope that her favorite boy would become a preacher of the Gospel increased in strength and deepened in intensity.

To see Andrew in a pulpit, expounding the Word of God and warning sinners to flee from the wrath to come, was the highest object of her ambition, the consuming desire of her heart. She toiled, scrimped and schemed for that end, managed to send Andrew to some of the best schools then accessible, and would probably have accomplished her purpose of making him a clergyman had not over-ruling circumstances of a stern and terrible nature interfered with her plans. But her efforts had been in the direct lines of Providence, and, to a degree beyond computation, had begun to prepare her boy for a career which was to be altogether different from a clergyman's. The gospel which Providence was to call Andrew Jackson to preach was the gospel of patriotism; his church was to be the military camp; his pulpit was to be his war-horse, and his doctrine was to be thundered from the mouths of cannon.

One cannot help considering what the result would have been if the fond mother's wishes had been realized, and the brave, passionate, indomitable, uncompromising Andrew Jackson had become a preacher of the Gospel. As far as one can judge, he would have been a commanding pastor. His flock could have taken no middle course—would not even have been permitted to look at forbidden pastures through the fence. He would have sharply separated the goats from the sheep and driven the goats to Hades and the sheep to Heaven "without mitigation or remorse." No neighboring clergyman, no wandering preacher from afar would have been permitted to poach on his parish. He would have taken care of his own saints and provided for his own sinners. He would have given the devil no peace. But, as has already been intimated, Providence was preparing quite another arena for Andrew Jackson to display his powers in; an arena for which his nature pre-eminently fitted him.

CHAPTER II.

THE BOY SOLDIER.

Andrew Jackson was nine years old in the year (1776) in which the Declaration of Independence was adopted and published. His brother Hugh was fifteen, and his brother Robert was twelve years old. The next year, 1777, a baby was born near Richmond, Va., that was to thwart some of Andrew Jackson's dearest hopes and to incur his bitter enmity. That baby was afterward known and passionately loved, and is still admired and loved, as Henry Clay.

In 1779 a boy baby was born in Ireland that, by the swirling current of events, was to be brought in sharp and far-sounding collision with the Carolina boy. That Irish baby boy was afterward known by the honored and celebrated name of General Sir Edward Pakenham.

In 1780, Charleston was captured by the British, and Lord Cornwallis swept through the Carolinas, marking his path with devastation. The country was laid waste, and the inhabitants were driven to the woods and the swamps for refuge. The Waxhaw settlement lay in the path of the British army. Hugh Jackson was already a trooper in the regiment of Colonel William R. Davie, who subsequently became Andrew Jackson's ideal soldier. Hugh Jackson, though well grown for his age (nineteen), could not stand the hardships of partisan warfare. After fighting bravely at the battle of Stono Ferry, he died of exhaustion. The brave boy had the true Jackson grit, which never gave up so long as the vital principle remained.

In that same year (1780), a baby boy was born that was afterward known as Charles Dickinson. I do not know the place of his birth. There are legends that he was a marvelously beautiful babe; in after years he was certainly a marvelously handsome man. As his mother kissed his dimpled hand, she had no premonition that it was to become the most expert hand in the use of a pistol known to that day and generation. How little a mother knows, as she kisses her baby boy's hand, with what it may in time be stained! The hand now reddest with a human brother's blood was once a baby's innocent, dimpled hand. Fortunately for her peace, Mrs. Dickinson could not foresee that her son's confidence in his mastery of the pistol was to lead him to insult the lovely brunette, Rachel Donelson, in order to provoke the chivalric Andrew Jackson to come within his weapon's deadly range.

In the spring of 1780, a camp of militia was formed near the Waxhaw settlement, for the purpose of protecting the patriots against the hostility of the Tories who sided with the British. Militia have never been noted for taking precautions against surprise, and the Waxhaw militia were not different in this respect from other soldiers of their kind. In May (1780), the dashing Colonel Tarleton, who worked so much woe to the patriots of the Carolinas, surprised the camp and dispersed the militia, who left over a hundred of their number dead and a hundred and fifty wounded. Such terror did Tarleton's name and conduct inspire, the inhabitants fled to the forests for safety; Mrs. Jackson fleeing with them in company with her two sons, Robert and Andrew.

Tarleton swept on his devastating way, not pausing to note the ruin he had wrought, and after he disappeared, the frightened inhabitants returned to their desolated homes. An appalling scene met their view. The bodies of the dead lay unburied, the wounded were suffering without any ministering hand to assuage their agonies. The work of burying the dead and caring for the wounded was at once begun by the returned fugitives. The old Waxhaw Church was turned into a hospital. Mrs. Jackson and her two boys became nurses of the wounded, and were assiduous in their ministrations to the helpless men, who died day after day despite all that could be done for them. On Andrew Jackson, the sympathetic, fiery-hearted boy of thirteen, the effect of all this ravage and destruction and suffering and death was profound. It burnt into his soul. As he tenderly ministered to the wants of the wounded, and day after day saw the dead buried in their rude graves, he hungered to avenge their wrongs. His patriotic passion set his child's heart aflame, and pulsated in every drop of his fiery blood. It is related of him that while afterward passing a few months in the family of a distant relative, he used to be sent to the blacksmith shop with broken household utensils and farm implements to have them repaired. He never came home without some deadly weapon that he had rudely fashioned at the shop, with which to smite the British. Once he fastened a scythe to the end of a long pole, and on reaching home he began with great fury to cut down the weeds that grew about the house, exclaiming, in his wrath:

"Oh, if I were a man, how I would sweep down the British with my grass-blade!"

In the summer of 1780, Robert Jackson, aged fifteen, and Andrew, aged thirteen, became regular partisan troopers, donned their hunting-shirts, slung their guns across their shoulders, mounted their horses and joined the Patriot forces. It is impossible not to think that a boy only thirteen years old would be of but little service in such rough work as the Patriot troopers were called upon to perform. But Andrew Jackson was a phenomenal boy. In describing General Sumter's successful attack on the British at Hanging Rock, on July 30, 1780, Bancroft says:

"Among the partisans who were present in this fight was Andrew Jackson, an orphan boy of Scotch-Irish descent, whom hatred of oppression and love of country impelled to deeds beyond his years."*

In order to understand Andrew Jackson's seem-

* Bancroft's History of the United States. Vol. v, 383.

ingly incredible boyish achievements, we must remember the training he had received in his mother's home and at his mother's knee. Under the influence of this training, he had come to believe in God's superintending Providence with absolute faith; and by a superintending Providence he understood a Providence that would superintend Andrew Jackson. His predominant characteristics were such as unwavering trust in God rapidly develops in ardent young natures that are predisposed to faith in the Divine. It is well known that elevated and ardent spiritual affection quickens and strengthens and matures all the faculties of the mind to a marvelous degree. Andrew Jackson's mental faculties were thus quickened, strengthened and matured. He was under the domination of trust in God, love for his mother and his native land, and hatred of his country's foes. This triple combination of strenuous affections, kept in full play by the circumstances which environed him, gave the boy the courage, the fortitude, the endurance and the sagacity of a man. All the legends of those days testify to his zeal, his energy and his efficiency. His chance had come to gratify the dearest wish of his heart, to help "sweep down the British with his grass-blade," and he was vigilant to make the most of his opportunities.

Raid after raid upon the country near the Waxhaw settlement kept the people in constant alarm, and compelled them again and again to flee to the woods and the swamps foi refuge. Colonel Davie and the other partisan leaders could do but little to protect them against the numerous detachments of British troops aided by the malignant Tories. The wrath of the Patriots against the Tories burned at white heat, and their hatred was rancorously reciprocated by the allies of the British. The most cruel civil war raged throughout the Carolinas. The passions of the inhabitants became so inflamed that kind-hearted Christian men enacted the part of fiends.

In August, 1780, General Gates was defeated at Camden, S. C., by Lord Cornwallis. That was a crushing blow to the Patriots. It filled the Tories with exultation. They became still more active, rancorous and brutal: and the Whigs (as the Patriots were called) defended themselves with corresponding animosity and ferocity. The effect of this horrible contest on the malleable, the growing, the forming nature of Andrew Jackson was powerful and lasting. Patriotism became a religion with him, and hatred of his country's foes a frenzy; and we shall see how, thirty-five years afterwards, when his opportunity came, he poured forth all this, in one terrific blast of doom, upon the finest British army that ever stepped upon American soil.

Things finally came to such a pass in the Waxhaw region that, whenever one of the American soldiers wanted to spend a night at home, special arrangements had to be made to defend his dwelling and save him from capture or death. On a certain occasion, Captain Sands, one of the Patriot officers, wishing to visit his family, a guard was sent to protect him. Andrew Jackson was one of the guard. The men were so exhausted by long-continued marching and watching, that they all fell asleep by midnight; but one of them, who was restless in his slumber, heard a noise, and, going out of doors, saw a band of the enemy stealthily approaching the house. Andrew Jackson was lying next the door. The man who had discovered the approach of the enemy, seized the sleeping boy by the hair, and cried: "The Tories are upon us!" Instantly, the boy was wide awake. Springing through the door, with the rest of the guard gathered in a group behind him, he challenged the approaching foe. No reply being given, he discharged his musket at the enemy, who returned the fire, mortally wounding the restless man who had given the alarm. Fortunately, another band of Tories, unknown to the first assailants, came up from an opposite direction and opened fire on the house. This caused the first band to halt. Little Andrew, with the instinct of a commander, took advantage of their confusion to withdraw the guard into the house, from which the Patriots kept up a brisk fire. At a critical moment, a bugle call was heard, which indicated that a company of Patriot troopers were advancing to the rescue of the beleagued guard. This caused both bands of Tories to hasten away, and the guard passed the remainder of the night in peace. It was afterward learned that the bugle call was sounded by a neighbor who heard the firing, and, suspecting that Captain Sands's house was attacked, took that method of rendering him the only efficient aid he could give.

Lord Rawdon, whom Cornwallis had left in command at Camden, hearing of the activity of the Waxhaw Whigs, sent a detachment of troops to the aid of the Tories in that region. Forty Whigs, among whom were the two Jackson boys, assembled to make preparations to repulse the British. They were betrayed by their Tory neighbors, surprised and put to flight. Eleven of the forty men were taken prisoners. The rest were hotly pursued by the British. The Jackson boys rode different ways. Andrew galloped by the side of his cousin, Lieutenant Thomas Crawford, one dragoon close behind them, and others not far off. The fugitives plunged into a swampy field, which Andrew succeeded in crossing, but Lieutenant Crawford was overtaken, wounded and compelled to surrender.

Robert Jackson escaped unharmed. In the course of the day, the brothers found one another. They passed a sleepless night. In the morning, being nearly famished, they quit their hiding place and went in search of food. Leaving their horses and arms behind them, safely hidden in the woods as they thought, the boys crawled stealthily to the nearest house, which was that of their wounded and captured cousin, Lieutenant Crawford. They supposed they were unobserved, but they were mistaken. A Tory of the neighborhood had discovered their hiding-place, had found their horses and arms, and procured the assistance of a party of dragoons. Before the boys had a suspicion of danger, the soldiers had surrounded the house and cut off all chance of escape. The brave lads were prisoners.

The soldiers rushed into the house with the ferocity of demons. The rude dwelling was occupied only by a young wife, her infant children and the two famishing boys, but the soldiers acted as though they were carrying an armed fortress by storm. They broke to pieces the crockery, glass and furniture; they emptied the beds, and tore all the clothing to rags, not sparing garments belonging to the baby carried in Mrs. Crawford's arms. While the destruction was going on, the officer in command of the party ordered Andrew Jackson to clean his high, muddy cavalry boots. Take notice of the little fellow's dignified response to the officer's bullying command.

"Sir," said the brave boy, "I am a prisoner of war, and claim to be treated as such."

The officer, in a rage, drew his sword and aimed a furious stroke at the child's head. Andrew threw up his left hand, which broke the force of the blow and probably saved his life; but he received a deep cut on his hand and another on his head. Both wounds were severe, and he carried the marks of both all the days of his long life. When one contemplates the circumstances in which that captured, unarmed American lad, only thirteen years old, with slashed hand and cloven head, and his hunting shirt stained with his dripping blood, unflinchingly and defiantly stood his ground against his brutal British assailant, the heart is stirred with inexpressible emotions, and one feels that there was a boy for all the boys in the world to admire and for every girl in the world to love.

Finding it impossible to make Andrew clean his boots, the officer turned to the elder brother Robert and ordered him to clean them. Animated by Andrew's example and indignant at the officer's brutality, Robert likewise refused to perform the menial service; whereupon the martial Briton felled him to the earth by a blow of his sword upon the head.

It is impossible to estimate the influence which such barbarities had upon the mind and the heart of our high-spirited young hero. He not only saw such brutalities with his own eyes and experienced them in his own person, but he heard of worse ones that were perpetrated in different parts of the country—the murder, for instance, of Colonel William Ledyard, the gallant defender of Fort Griswold, in Connecticut. On September 7, 1781, Fort Griswold, defended by Colonel Ledyard with only one hundred and fifty-seven militia, was attacked by eight hundred British troops. The defense was so gallant that two hundred of the enemy were slain before the fort was captured. Major Bromfield, the commander of the British force, on entering the captured fortress, asked:

"Who commanded this fort?"

"I did, sir, but you do now," Colonel Ledyard replied, at the same time handing the officer his sword.

Major Bromfield seized the sword, plunged it to the hilt in Colonel Ledyard's bosom, and the gallant American fell dead at his British murderer's feet.

The patriotic people of the Carolinas were writhing under the insolence of British armies in which every soldier was licensed to plunder and every officer outlawed peaceful citizens at will.

"Tarleton and his corp set fire to all the houses and destroyed the corn from Camden down to Nelson's ferry; he beat the widow of a general officer because she could not tell where Marion was encamped, burned her dwelling, laid waste everything about it, and did not leave her a change of raiment. The line of their march could be traced by groups of houseless women and children, once of ample fortune, sitting round fires in the open air."*

The unspeakably revolting conduct of British officers which Andrew Jackson witnessed and heard of convinced him that of all brutes the British brute is the most brutal. He had not yet learned, he had had no opportunity to learn, that of all brave, honorable and noble men, the brave, honorable and noble Briton stands high among the very bravest, the most honorable and the noblest of mankind. Of this truth Andrew Jackson was entirely ignorant. He saw only the most odious traits of the British character, and they excited in him nought but feelings of indignation, wrath, hatred and vengeance. As Hannibal, in his childhood, swore eternal enmity to Rome on the altar of his country's gods, so Andrew Jackson, in his childhood, swore eternal enmity to England on the altar of his young heart. His own personal wrongs were burnt into his soul and forever remained vivid in his memory. Long years afterward, even when he was President of the United States, in recounting the outrage perpetrated upon him by the British officer whose boots he refused to clean, he sometimes took hold of the finger of a sympathizing listener and laid it in the deep wound made by his assailant's sword.

When the soldiers had satiated their rage for

* Bancroft v, 402.

destruction upon the household effects of the helpless and hapless Mrs. Crawford, Andrew Jackson was ordered to mount his horse and guide some of the dragoons to the house of a noted Whig of the vicinity, named Thompson. Weak from starvation and loss of blood, suffering from his wounds, and threatened with instant death if he failed to guide the soldiers aright, this dauntless boy nevertheless resolved to save his friend Thompson. In order that the reader may work himself up to something like an adequate conception of this boy's character, let him think of all the boys of thirteen that he knows, or ever knew, and imagine any of them in the strait in which this thirteen-year-old Carolina boy now was, and then consider what the result would have been. But, as I have said, Andrew Jackson was a phenomenal boy; and now observe with what sagacity he planned, even in the terrible and distracting circumstances in which he was placed, to save his friend Thompson.

Andrew surmised that if Thompson were at home, he would have some one on the lookout for danger, and a horse ready for flight. In order that Thompson might be put on his guard, the sagacious boy, instead of leading the dragoons on the direct road to his friend's abode, led them by a roundabout route which brought them in sight of the house while still half a mile distant. On coming in sight of the dwelling, Andrew saw Thompson's horse, saddled and bridled, standing by a rack in the yard. The dragoons also saw the horse, and inferring therefrom that Thompson was at home, they dashed forward to seize their prey. Andrew's heart seemed to rise in his throat at the thought that his stratagem would not save his friend, after all. But while the dragoons were still several hundred yards from the house, the boy's heart was made glad by Thompson's bursting from his door, leaping upon his horse and riding directly into a foaming creek, swollen with recent rains, that rushed and roared along near his dwelling. The dragoons did not dare attempt to cross the raging creek. Thompson, seeing their timidity, gave a shout of defiance and galloped into the woods.

Mr. Parton, to whom the reader is indebted for the anecdote just related, tells us that the elation caused by the success of Andrew's stratagem was soon swallowed up by misery. With their wounds undressed, weak with hunger and the loss of blood, the Jackson boys, with their cousin Crawford and twenty other prisoners, were ordered to mount and begin their weary march to the chief British depot at Camden, in South Carolina, forty miles distant. It was indeed a dreadful journey to them all; but worst to these boys, sick and sore from fresh wounds. Amos Kendall says in his "Life of Jackson" that not an atom of food, nor a drop of water was allowed them on the way. Such was the brutality of the soldiers that when the miserable Jackson lads tried to scoop up a little water from the streams which they forded, to appease their raging thirst, they were ordered with threats to desist.

At Camden, the prisoners were placed in a small inclosure around the county jail. There were two hundred and fifty prisoners in all shut up in that yard, without beds, medicine or attendance; without any means of dressing their wounds or assuaging their pain. Their only nourishment was a small daily ration of inferior bread.

"They were robbed even of a part of their clothing, besides being subject to the taunts and threats of every passing Tory. The three relatives, it is said, were separated as soon as their relationship was discovered. Miserable among the miserable; gaunt, yellow, hungry and sick; robbed of his jacket and shoes; ignorant of his brother's fate, chafing with suppressed fury, Andrew passed now some of the most wretched days of his life."

The small-pox broke out among the prisoners, a disease still terrible, but which in those days, when no rational mode of treatment had been discovered, struck terror to all who were exposed to it, and filled the hearts of its victims with despair. In the prison pen at Camden, the ravages of the disease were attended with every conceivable horror. The sick were not separated from the well; the festering corpses of the dead were tardily removed from the inclosure, The emaciation of the prisoners and the wretched condition of their systems, invited the fatal attacks to which their lack of vitality caused them speedily to succumb.

"For some time Andrew escaped the contagion. He was reclining one day in the sun near the entrance of the prison, when the officer of the guard, attracted, as it seemed, by the youthfulness of his appearance, entered into conversation with him. The lad soon began to speak of that of which his heart was full—the condition of the prisoners and the bad quality of their food. He remonstrated against their treatment with such energy and feeling that the officer seemed to be moved and shocked, and what was far more important, he was induced to ferret out the villainy of the contractors who had been robbing the prisoners of their rations. From the day of Andrew's remonstrance the condition of the prisoners was ameliorated; they were supplied with meat and better bread, and were otherwise better cared for." *

From an aperture in the fence surrounding their inclosure, some of the prisoners witnessed the battle of Hobkirk's Hill, between the armies of General Greene and Lord Rawdon, on April 25, 1781. General Greene had superseded General Gates in the command of the Revolutionary forces in the South, and great things were expected of him. He advanced to drive Lord Rawdon out of Camden, but having outstripped his artillery, he halted on Hobkirk's Hill for it to come up. The suffering prisoners hailed the appearance of the American army with rapture. They had no doubt of Greene's success, and to them his success meant liberty and home; and to some of the more sick and despairing it meant life itself. Rawdon had only nine hundred men to Greene's one thousand three hundred. Owing to the superiority of his force, the American commander had no idea that he would be attacked, and failed to take proper precautions against a surprise. But Lord Rawdon did not choose to wait in Camden for Greene's artillery to arrive. He sallied out on

* Parton I, 91.

the morning of April 25th, took the Americans by surprise, drove them from their advantageous position, and put them to disastrous rout. Through a knot-hole in the fence surrounding the prison, Andrew Jackson saw this battle, or rather this rout, and learned lessons of war from it which he never forgot. He learned that danger lurks in every relaxation of precaution or discipline, and that the army which strikes the first blow in a battle has the inspiring influence of attack on its side, and, if skillfully handled, gains an advantage which it is always difficult and sometimes impossible even for a superior opposing force to withstand. What splendid use he made at New Orleans of these lessons in war which, while a boy, he studied through his knot-hole at Camden, will be seen further on. Just now the brave boy had a battle close upon him more desperate than that of New Orleans; a battle, indeed, of life and death.

CHAPTER III.

THE LITTLE HERO'S STRUGGLE FOR LIFE—DEATH OF HIS MOTHER—ANDREW'S FORLORN CONDITION.

After General Greene's defeat, the Jackson boys, still suffering from their wounds and despairing of escape fron their imprisonment, began to show symptoms of the small-pox. Before they were quite prostrate, their mother, who had long been scheming and striving for their exchange, reached Camden with an order for their release. In exchange for thirteen British soldiers, she received her two boys, her nephew (Thomas Crawford) and four of her Waxhaw neighbors. When this devoted mother saw her sons, she scarcely knew them, so wasted were they with wounds, starvation and disease. Robert could not sit on horseback unsupported. Andrew was reduced to a skeleton, but the fire of his eyes was not dimmed, nor his dauntless spirit subdued.

Determined, if possible, to get her boys home at once, Mrs. Jackson procured two horses, one of which she rode herself, and placed her son Robert on the other. He was held in his seat by his companions. Last of all walked Andrew, without shoes, without a hat, wearing nothing but shirt and trousers, both ragged. How this wounded, diseased, emaciated lad of fourteen, with the small-pox fever raging in his veins and about to prostrate him, could have had the grit, the fortitude and the endurance to make that weary journey of forty miles on foot, is beyond human comprehension, unless we ascribe the phenomenon to the sustaining power of his trust in God. But he had the grit, the fortitude and the endurance to accomplish such a marvel, even when a boy; and he had the same characteristics in a more marked degree when he became a man, and he had the corresponding trust in God, also. When these forlorn wayfarers were almost in sight of their home, a cold and driving rain set in, which chilled both of these fevered boys to their marrow. They reached home well-nigh exhausted. Two days after Robert Jackson died, and Andrew was raving in delirium. He had a narrow escape from death. After a desperate struggle, his mother's admirable nursing saved his life, but he did not fully recover for many tedious months.

Long before his strength returned, harrowing rumors spread through both Carolinas to the effect that hundreds of American prisoners, among them many of Mrs. Jackson's relatives and neighbors, were perishing of hunger and disease in the Charleston prison-ships, a hundred and sixty miles distant. Inspired by her success in the exchange of her sons, Mrs. Jackson set out for Charleston, accompanied by two other women, with intent to procure, if possible, the release of her friends and relatives. It is known that those noble and devoted women reached the prison-ships, carrying joy and hope to despairing men.

Andrew Jackson never saw his mother again. At the house of a relative near Charleston, she was seized with the ship-fever, of which she died after a short illness. She was buried on the open plain near by, in an unmarked grave—a grave which Andrew Jackson could never find, though in after years he sought for it with the energy and persistency which his filial devotion inspired.

For this wise and resolute mother, Andrew Jackson cherished to his life's end an unparalleled veneration. So far as the record of his life shows, he was but little given to the shedding of tears; but once, on a memorable occasion, he shed them on his mother's account. During his candidacy for the Presidency in 1828, the floodgates of vituperation and slander were opened upon him. So malignant was party animosity, that not only himself, but his wife, and even his mother were assailed with vindictive falsehood. During the campaign, his wife once found him in tears. In response to her looks of surprise and sympathy, he pointed to a paragraph reflecting on his mother, and said:

"Myself I can defend; you I can defend; but now they have assailed even the memory of my mother!"

He loved to speak of his mother's firmness, of her good sense, of her capacity and of her compassionate heart. He loved to quote her maxims concerning the conduct of life, especially one: "Never to injure another, nor to accept from another an injury unredressed." Often in the heat of argument, when he was at the height of his renown, he would quote some homely saying, with the remark: "*That* I learned from my good old mother."

How little that "good old mother" knew what

the result of her maternal faithfulness was to be! How little she dreamed that, in her lowly sphere, and in her humble, pious way, she was training for a great career the hero of the age! In truth, she had imparted to her son what was of far more value than the learning of the schools, than the acquisitions of commerce. From her he had learned to believe in God, in the Bible, in virtue, in the sacredness of woman's purity and love, in everything which gives strength to character, nobility to human nature, and honor and dignity to life.

> "Happy he
> With such a mother! Faith in womankind
> Beats in his blood, and trust in all things high
> Comes easy to him."

To Andrew Jackson may be applied, in all their fullness and power, the words that Carlyle puts in the mouth of his favorite character: "My mother, with a true woman's heart, and fine though uncultured sense, was in the strictest acceptation Religious. * * The highest whom I knew on earth I here saw bowed down, with awe unspeakable, before a Higher in Heaven; such things, especially in infancy, reach inwards to the very core of your being; mysteriously does a Holy of Holies build itself into visibility in the mysterious deeps, and Reverence, the divinest in man, springs forth undying from its envelopment of Fear."

When he heard the news of his mother's death, Andrew Jackson was in the fifteenth year of his age. He was surrounded by worn-out, suffering, disheartened neighbors, who had begun to despair of their country's struggle for liberty; he was an orphan; he was homeless; he was destitute; he was broken in health and emaciated by disease; his heart was desolate from the loss in quick succession of all the members of his family. Was there ever a more pitiful case? So far as ordinary human observation can see or foresee, there never was a more pitiful case. But Providence knew what it was about, and saw that this desolate orphan boy's situation was full of glorious promise. Heroes are not brought up in boudoirs, nor nourished with sugar-plums.

What a calamity it would have been if a committee of the supposed wisest men then in the world had been apppointed to supersede Providence in training Andrew Jackson for the career he was to achieve. The committee would have done everything for the boy; Providence compelled him to do everything for himself. He who does a little for himself, gains more than he who has much done for him. To overcome obstacles, to triumph over difficulties gives one self-reliance, and strengthens and ennobles his character; whereas, a habit of depending on what others do for him, lessens one's reliance and weakens and degrades his character. In the light of these truths, it is possible for us to see that what seemed the worst features in this orphan boy's case, were, in fact, its best features. Moreover, in this boy there were elements of character which, if properly developed, could triumph over all misfortunes and surmount all obstacles.

CHAPTER IV.

THE SECRET OF ANDREW JACKSON'S CAREER AND POWER.

Some of the incidents of Andrew Jackson's life are so incredible, some of his exhibitions of mental, moral and spiritual power so transcend belief, it is necessary to give an exposition of his character in order that the reader may be prepared to understand how these seemingly impossible events could come to pass. It is a familiar fact that, when Andrew Jackson was President of the United States, although he was frequently opposed by a great preponderance of the intellect, scholarship, genius and commercial power of the Union, he nevertheless came out of every contest victorious. It is also a matter of history that during General Jackson's military career, he repeatedly held in check and reduced to subjection whole regiments of mutinous troops, simply by the force of his will and the overpowering majesty of his presence. And as the story of his life goes on, it will be seen that he did other things more wonderful still.

We already have a key to the character of the man who could do such incredible things. We have seen that the overruling attributes of Andrew Jackson's nature were reverence and faith in God; he was also honest, truthful and chaste, and his mother's teaching and influence developed and exalted those natural traits until they became spiritualized and ennobled to a transcendent degree.

There are two pillars on which the edifice of civilized society mainly rests. One of these pillars is integrity, the other is chastity. To man it is given to uphold integrity; to woman it is given to uphold chastity; and all that the ungodly world demands is that each sex shall stand by and uphold its own pillar. But here was a boy, a man, a hero, who, as to both of these sustaining pillars of society, was immaculate from his boyhood to his grave. There is ample and convincing evidence of this. More than forty years ago, in Washington, when talking with a banker who knew General Jackson intimately, I asked him if the general was in fact as scrupulously honest as he was said to have been. "Honest!" he exclaimed, "Why, sir, everybody that knew him knew that he was honest. A promissory note, or any piece of commercial paper, with Andrew Jackson's name on it, *was legal tender,* sir, wherever that name was known!" Mr. Parton has collected a mass of testimony on this point, among which is the declaration of an old neighbor of the general's, who said: "As for Jackson's own part, law or no law, he would pay what he owed; he would do what he said he would." A gentleman living in Tennessee went to Boston in 1838 to raise a large sum of money. The Boston bankers declined to let him have it, although his securities were backed by many of the best commercial names in Tennessee. They told him, however, that if he could get General Jackson's endorsement on his paper, they would let him have all the money he wanted. "Why!" exclaimed the Tennesseean, in surprise, "General Jackson isn't worth a tenth as much as any one of the gentlemen whose names I have." "No matter," was the reply; "*General Jackson always protects his paper and we'll let you have the money on the strength of his name.*" The general's endorsement was procured, and so was the money, "on the strength of his name"—a name that was never dishonored.

The evidence with regard to Andrew Jackson's purity of character and his chivalric conduct toward women is overwhelming. On this point, Judge Overton, of Tennessee, who was intimate with him from Jackson's early manhood, says, in an article on the subject: "In his singularly delicate sense of honor, and in what I thought his chivalrous conception of the sex, it occurred to me that he [Jackson] was distinguishable from every other person with whom I was acquainted."*

Colonel Benton, in his "Thirty Years in the U. S. Senate," page 738, says of General Jackson: "There was an innate, unvarying, self-acting delicacy in his intercourse with the female sex, including all womankind." The Honorable Nicholas P. Trist, for a time President Jackson's private secretary, says: "There was in him a womanly modesty and delicacy as respects the relation of the sexes. * * * This chaste tenderness toward the sex was constantly manifesting itself, and in a manner so unstudied, so perfectly spontaneous, as to show that it was as natural to him as to breathe." †

During the reception given to President Jackson

* Parton's Life of Jackson, I, 151. † Ibid. III, 602.

at Cambridge, after Harvard College had made him a Doctor of Laws, some beautiful little girls came up to salute him. Josiah Quincy, a political enemy of Jackson's, who witnessed the scene, wrote of it thus: "He took the hands of these little maidens, and then lifted them up and kissed them. It was a pleasant sight—one not to be omitted when the events of the day were put upon paper. This rough soldier [Jackson], exposed all his life to those temptations which have conquered public men whom we still call good, *could kiss little children with lips as pure as their own.*"* (The italics are mine.) On such statements by Judge Overton, Colonel Benton, Mr. Trist and Josiah Quincy, I am willing to rest the case, without calling any more witnesses.

It has been said that "integrity, chastity and reverence are the three traits of human character which are most pleasing to God." I do not pretend to be in the secret of God's preferences; but it is no secret that integrity and chastity are the moral bed-rocks on which human character rests; and Andrew Jackson's integrity and chastity were immaculate. It is an accepted truth and fact that exalted reverence—"the divinest in man," as Carlyle says—quickens, deepens and strengthens all the other qualities and faculties, and gives a man such *confidence in himself* as nothing else can bestow. Andrew Jackson's reverence exceeded that of any man of his time, or of any time, so far as the observations of phrenologists and the developments of his character can determine.

* Figures of the Past, page 367.

A man of excessive reverence, if he is a Christian, has implicit faith in God; if he is an infidel, he has implicit trust in his star, his fate, his destiny; and whether Christian or Infidel, he has a satisfying and sustaining belief in himself. That is the kind of man that Andrew Jackson was. Of all the men of whom I have any knowledge he had the most faith in God and in himself. Throughout all his life he was sustained by a comforting assurance that God and Andrew Jackson constituted a combination that could not be overcome by human power. Consequently he never "lost his head;" he never quailed before any degree of danger; no amount of suffering and disaster, and of seemingly utter dissolution of opportunity could overcome his fortitude. His favorite adjuration, "By the Eternal," was an outcome of his reverence, being to him equivalent to "In the name of the Eternal." When, on hearing, on the afternoon of December 23, 1814, that the British army had come within eight miles of New Orleans, he said, "By the Eternal, they sha'n't sleep on our soil!" the sentiment of his heart was that, "In the name of the Eternal," he that very night would deal the invaders a staggering blow; and, "By the Eternal," he did it.

In addition to the elements of character already specified, Andrew Jackson's combativeness, destructiveness, secretiveness, cautiousness and other animal organs were very large: so were his firmness, hope, conscientiousness and self-esteem. It is not difficult to understand that such a combination of extraordinary mental, moral and spiritual qualities endowed him with a character which, practically considered, was of that unconquerable kind, solid and firm as Gibraltar, that Emerson defines as "centrality, *the impossibility of being displaced or overset.*" It was in vain, therefore, for men whose characters were so defective they could be displaced and overset, to contend with Andrew Jackson. He might have been destroyed, but while he lived he could not be vanquished. Like Milton's angels, such character as his,

> "Vital in every part, ...
> Cannot, but by annihilating, die."

There is another factor in the character and career of Andrew Jackson which should be kept in view, and that is, the race from which he sprang. He was of Scotch-Irish lineage.

Owing to some inscrutable dispensation of Providence, the Scotch-Irish combine nearly all the opposing extremes of character. Of all the descendants of Adam, they are among the most zealous advocates of the Gospel of Peace and the most belligerent of the children of God; among the most ferocious and the most tender-hearted; the most courageous and the most cautious; the most impetuous and the most canny; the most dashing and the most strategic; the most exacting and the most generous. They are noted for pugnacity, tenacity, veracity—for fight, grip and truth. They excel in bringing things to pass and in husbanding results. They are thrifty, accumulative; they get and they keep—"keep the Ten Commandments and everything else they can lay their hands on," as the Rev. Dr. John S. MacIntosh, a distinguished Scotch-Irishman, says of them. Politically, socially and religiously—to borrow a phrase from another eminent member of the race, the Hon. William Wirt Henry, of Virginia—the Scotch-Irish are distinguished for "stern integrity, high sense of duty, hatred of tyranny and devotion to God."

The names of eminent and prosperous members of this race are thickly sown through American history, among which are the names of Charles Carroll, of Carrollton, Thomas Jefferson, Patrick Henry, John Paul Jones, Andrew Jackson, John C. Calhoun, Thomas H. Benton, John Marshall, James Madison, James K. Polk, Robert Fulton, Horace Greeley, Robert Bonner, Abraham Lincoln, Ulysses S. Grant, Robert E. Lee and Stonewall Jackson. The list might be extended to thousands, but let these names suffice. And when, in addition to the delineation of his character already given, it is understood that of all the Scotch-Irishmen known to history, Andrew Jackson possessed, in the most exuberant fullness, the best characteristics of the race, and had just the right field to display them on, it will be easy to believe that incidents so extraordinary as to seem incredible often occurred in his unparalleled career, the narrative of which will now be resumed.

CHAPTER V.

FROM YOUTH TO MANHOOD—FROM THE WAXHAWS TO NASHVILLE.

On the 19th of October, 1781, Cornwallis surrendered at Yorktown to Washington and Rochambeau. This virtually ended the war; but the British held possession of Charleston until December, 1782, when they sailed away, to the great joy of the inhabitants of the Carolinas. During that year (1782), several babies were born that were to collide with Andrew Jackson and more or less affect his career. On January 18, 1782, Daniel Webster was born in Salisbury (now Franklin), New Hampshire; on March 14, Thomas H. Benton was born in Hillsborough, N. C.; on March 18, John C. Calhoun was born in the Calhoun settlement, Abbeville District, S. C.; on October 9, Lewis Cass was born in Exeter, N. H.; and on December 5, Martin Van Buren was born in Kinderhook, N. Y. Seventeen hundred and eighty-two was a great year for babies that were to become famous. Andrew Jackson and his Massachusetts contemporary (John Quincy Adams) were now youths of fifteen, and Henry Clay was a boy five years old. All these babies, and the boy of five, and the youths of fifteen, who were born so far apart and under such different circumstances, were to have their threads of life woven together on the loom of Providence in strange ways and after strange patterns. The lovely brunette, Rachel

Donelson, now fifteen years old, had gone with her brave father through awful perils of flood and forest, to the wilds of Western Tennessee. But the remoteness and obscurity of her residence did not save her from having the threads of her own life fatefully woven into this many-patterned web. And the handsome baby boy, Charles Dickinson, was to find his way to far Western Tennessee, and to have his life-threads woven into the same fabric; and they were to give it a crimson stripe not pleasant for human eyes to look upon.

There is but little authentic information concerning Andrew Jackson's life during the next three years. Kendall says that a low fever hung about him long after his recovery from the small-pox, and kept him weak and dispirited. But weak as he was, he had the spirit to resent a threat of chastisement made by one Captain Galbraith. "Before you lift your hand to strike me," said the brave lad, "you had better prepare for eternity." The irate Galbraith did not lift his hand to strike the boy.

Andrew lived several months with a saddler, named Joseph White, and during that time he worked in the saddler's shop as regularly as his health permitted. He became a school-teacher before he was seventeen years old, and was successful in his vocation; especially in preserving order among the half-civilized and vivacious youths of the Waxhaw region. In 1785, at the age of eighteen, he went to Salisbury, N. C., to study law in the office of Spruce McCay, a noted lawyer of that day. He was admitted to the bar in 1787, a few weeks before he reached the age of twenty-one. That was the year in which the National Constitutional Convention was held. The Constitution of the United States was adopted in 1788. What is now the State of Tennessee was then Washington County, N. C. This vast region was divided into three judicial districts, the westernmost of which was called the Western District, and had Nashville, then a small village of log cabins, for its capital.

Andrew Jackson practised law in his native region and contiguous localities, for several months with fair success. About all that is remembered of this part of his career is that he conducted a lawsuit in a characteristic way; that is, he made a personal fight of it, and usually won by his grit and his strategy rather than by means of his legal knowledge. In 1788, John McNairy, a relative of the Jacksons, was appointed Judge of the Western District of Washington County, N. C. (now Tennessee). Andrew Jackson was appointed Solicitor and Public Prosecutor, and a young friend of his—Thomas Searcy—was appointed clerk of the court. These were not very desirable appointments. The salaries were small. Nashville was hundreds of miles distant, beyond the Alleghany Mountains, and the route to it lay through an unbroken wilderness, swarming with Indians who cherished a fiendish hatred of the whites, and murdered them whenever they could get an opportunity.

But the spirit of adventure was strong in the lawyers of that day. Their characters had been formed amid the strife by which the country had been scarred for many years, and they welcomed danger with stern joy. So the newly-appointed

Judge, the Prosecuting Attorney and the clerk of the court, prepared themselves to carry law and justice into the wilds of Western Tennessee. They were accompanied by a score of neighbors, loaded with household utensils and farm implements, and with a plentiful supply of fire-arms and ammunition. They rendezvoused at Morganton, in the western part of North Carolina, then the starting-point for "the great West," and set out for Jonesboro, a hundred miles distant. They made the journey in five days. Jonesboro was then a "settlement" containing about sixty log cabins, and a new log court-house. Judge McNairy's party was detained at Jonesboro many weeks, waiting for the formation of a company and the organization of a guard strong enough to brave the perils of the wilderness. Meanwhile, the court was organized and the trial of cases was begun in the new log court-house. Andrew Jackson took part in these trials, and soon distinguished himself in a characteristic manner.

In the trial of a case which attracted a crowd to the court-house, young Jackson (then twenty-one) was opposed by a lawyer of much experience, named Colonel Waightstill Avery. Colonel Avery, who was at the head of the legal profession in the backwoods, treated Jackson in such a contemptuous way, that the young man's blood, never too placid, glowed with fiery indignation. He wrote a note of expostulation to Colonel Avery, but the next day the offensive conduct was repeated. Andrew Jackson opened a law book which lay on the table before him, and on one of the blank leaves wrote a challenge to his insulting opponent, demanding speedy satisfaction. Several years ago, one of Colonel Avery's descendants sent that challenge, yellow with the age of nearly a hundred years, to the New York *Ledger* for publication. I then examined the document with much interest. The hand-writing was firm, clear and handsome—good enough for anybody; but the orthography and punctuation were not in accordance with the present prevailing standards. Here is the challenge:

"August 12, 1788.

"Sir When a mans feelings & charector are injured he ought to seek speedy redress: You rec'd a few lines from me yesterday, & undoubtedly you understand me. My charector you have injured; and further you have Insulted me in the presence of a court and a larg audiance I therefore call upon you as a gentleman to give me satisfaction for the same; and I further call upon you to give me an answer immediately without Equivocation and I hope you can do without dinner until the business is done; for it is consistant with the charector of a gentleman when he injures a man to make a speedy reparation; therefore I hope you will not fail in meeting me this day from yr. Hbl. st.

ANDW. JACKSON.

"COLL. AVERY.

"P. S. This Evening after court is adjourned."

This challenge, although it was dashed off on the spur of the moment and in a spasm of rage, exhibits the thoughtful, logical and canny traits of character which were always paramount in Andrew Jackson's conduct, no matter how great the fury to which his temper was aggravated. The challenge shows that he had good cause for his action; that his character had been injured; that he had previously written a note to the aggressor; that notwithstanding his note he had been insulted before the court and a large audience. The challenge demands "an answer immediately, without equivocation," and alluringly suggests that the challenged party "can do without dinner until the business is done," because "it is consistent with the character of a gentleman, when he injures a man to make a speedy reparation." How very polite, logical and reasonable.

In that age and in that region, a man who declined a challenge to mortal combat could not hold up his head in the community; he was ostracized; he was despised; he was sometimes shunned by his own kindred as a coward who had brought disgrace upon the family. Therefore Colonel Avery unhesitatingly accepted the challenge of his young antagonist. The belligerents met that same day, after sunset, in a small hollow near Jonesboro, which is stlll pointed out as the scene of the duel. Fortunately, neither party was injured. After an exchange of shots, Jackson, whose wrath was always easily appeased after "the right thing had been done," expressed himself satisfied and shook hands with Colonel Avery.

After reading the account of this duel, it would not be unnatural for a person of hasty judgment to wonder where Andrew Jackson's enormous reverence and intense religious nature were at this juncture. But when said person of hasty judgment remembers that in bygone times religious men used to fight duels on slight provocation, and even burned other Christians at the stake for a difference of opinion, he will be able to understand that Andrew Jackson's enormous reverence and intense religious nature were not quiescent on that occasion, but strenuously stood by him, and enabled him to look into the muzzle of his antagonist's pistol without a tremor. The religion of an era seldom rises above the social and political standards of the era. When it was believed to be the duty of a Christian not to keep his word with an infidel; when it was believed to be right to hang, drown or burn women accused of witchcraft; when personal combats were the fashion among the chief supporters of the church; when it was believed to be right to burn people at the stake for differences of opinion; when slavery was predominant in the government and in the commerce of the United States, the religion of the time was readily adjusted to those low moral and political conditions. Let us not be unreasonably severe in our condemnation of the conduct of those who lived in comparatively barbarous ages; but let us rejoice that the barbarous customs of those ages (except within narrow limits) no longer oppress mankind.

The duel had a profound influence on the fortunes of Andrew Jackson. His conduct excited the admiration of the people among whom his lot was cast, and won the respect of his professional brethren. Thenceforth, no member of the bar ventured to treat him with discourtesy, and he became the admired leader of the younger portion of the community. A proof of his genius as a born leader of men, and as one who instinctively knows just what to do in the hour of danger, when others lose their self-possession, was given while he was in Jonesboro, several years afterward. The account of the incident is from the pen of an eye-witness, Colonel

Isaac T. Avery, who was a son of the Colonel Waightstill Avery with whom Jackson fought the duel. He says:

"I was at Jonesboro court, at one time, when every house in the town was crowded. About twelve o'clock at night a fire broke out in the stables of Rawlings, the principal hotel-keeper in the place. There was a large quantity of hay in the stables, which stood in dangerous proximity to the tavern, court-house and business part of the town. The alarm filled the streets with lawyers, judges, ladies in their night-dresses and a concourse of strangers and citizens. General Jackson no sooner entered the street, than he assumed the command. It seemed to be conceded to him. He shouted for buckets, and formed two lines of men reaching from the fire to a stream that ran through the town; one line to pass the empty buckets to the stream, and the other to return them full to the fire. He ordered the roofs of the tavern and of the houses most exposed to the fire to be covered with wet blankets, and stationed men on the roofs to keep them wet. Amidst the shrieks of the women and the frightful neighing of the burning horses, every order was distinctly heard and obeyed. In the line up which the full buckets were passed, the bank of the stream soon became so slippery it was difficult to stand. While General Jackson was strengthening that part of the line, a drunken coppersmith named Boyd, who said he had seen fires at Baltimore, began to give orders and annoy persons in the line.

"'Fall into line!' shouted the General.

"The man continued jabbering. Jackson seized

a bucket by the handle, knocked him down, and walked along the line giving his orders as coolly as before. *He saved the town!*"*

In the latter part of September, 1788, a large party started from Jonesboro for Nashville. It is reported that in a great degree they owed their escape from the perils of the wilderness to the vigilance of young Jackson. On one memorable occasion he saved the party from massacre. They had marched a night and two days without a longer halt than an hour, in order to reach a place where it was supposed they would be safe from the attacks of their Indian foes. The entire party, worn out with their long march, and supposing themselves to be beyond danger, fell asleep soon after eating their suppers. Only one man kept awake, and that man was Andrew Jackson. He sat leaning against a tree, smoking his corn-cob pipe. After awhile his attention was attracted to the hooting of owls in the surrounding woods. It struck him that there were too many owls, and that there was something queer in the quality of their hoots. His keen and practiced ear soon recognized, in the hooting of the owls, the signals of savages who were surrounding the camp. He cautiously awoke his friend Searcy, and called his attention to the signals. Then he quietly aroused some of the more experienced woodsmen who, on hearing the hootings, agreed with him that they were Indian signals. What is to be done? was the appalling question which at once arose. Fortunately, there was a young man there who was always

* Parton's Life of Jackson, I, 162.

inspired by the genius of courage and leadership when that question arose in the hour of peril. He at once took command. By his direction, every sleeper was quietly awakened. Silently, and in perfect composure, he made every needful preparation, and then the whole party stole away in the darkness. They traveled all night, and escaped the toils in which the savages would have environed them, had it not been for Andrew Jackson's vigilance and his ready resources in the hour of danger. A party of hunters, who reached the abandoned camp an hour after the fugitives had left it, and went to sleep by the still burning camp-fire, were attacked by the savages before morning, and all of them killed but one man.

The emigrants (that was what those who went west over the mountains in those days were called) reached Nashville late in October, 1788. As the long train approached the village, they were received with enthusiasm by the isolated inhabitants, to whom they brought letters from friends and relatives, and among whom in fact were not a few of their own kin. People of our times, who are not exposed to the isolation and the dangers which were the lot of frontier settlers in the last century, cannot realize the joy and gladness which news from relatives, and reunion with friends, brought to their hungry hearts. The little group of inhabitants in Nashville were in a hostile country, surrounded with myriads of alert, revengeful and merciless savages. Men did not dare go to their work in the fields without being armed and in readiness to meet the stealthy attacks of their wily foes. When men met on the highway and stopped to converse, they stood back to back, with cocked rifles in hand. No man dared stoop to drink from a spring unless he had a comrade on guard. Girls never went berrying without the attendance of armed men. Think of that, ye young men and maidens who now go berrying and picnicking without a thought of fear! Try to put yourselves in the place of those Tennessee boys and girls who picked berries and made love in the very shadow of death! But such a life had its compensations. Every girl's lover was a hero, ready to meet death for her dear sake. And she knew it; and what could any girl of spirit accept as a substitute for such heroic devotion? And those Tennessee girls were all girls of spirit. They were heroines, worthy of the devotion of their heroic lovers; and in their descendants there still abide the qualities which a hundred years ago made Tennessee renowned for the bravery of its inhabitants.

To those brave inhabitants of the frontier settlements, eternal vigilance was not only the price of liberty, but of life itself. The least relaxation of vigilance was sure to be followed by the death of some of their number. Hence, in addition to other pleasant considerations, the arrival in an isolated settlement of a party of newcomers, comprising many brave and well armed men, was like the arrival of a relieving force to a weak and beleaguered fortress. So there was joy in Nashville, and the newly arrived emigrants were welcomed with a hospitality that was limited only by the meager resources of the village.

Log-cabins were at once "raised" for the accommodation of the newly arrived families. The unmarried men were gladly welcomed to the cabins of the settlers. The addition of a fighting member to a household was a valuable acquisition under circumstances in which the safety of a family depended on its fighting power. In such a community, a young man like Andrew Jackson would be in great request. He considered himself fortunate in finding a home with the Widow Donelson. Her husband, Colonel John Donelson, a sturdy and prosperous pioneer, had built himself a block-house of unusual size and strength, and furnished it with more than ordinary frontier comfort; but he was slain while surveying a piece of woodland some distance from the village. Mrs. Donelson's married daughter Rachel, and her husband, Lewis Robards (a Kentuckian), were living with her; but she was glad to have such a chivalric young man as the new Solicitor, whose appearance indicated that he could be depended upon in the hour of danger, take up his abode under her roof.

This choice of a boarding-place, which seemed to be a trivial matter, was in truth and all unknown to the parties concerned, one of the most important steps which Andrew Jackson ever took. It brought to him the greatest misery as well as the greatest happiness of his life; it embroiled him with many of his fellow-citizens; it occasioned envenomed feuds; and in one conspicuous case it led to the death of one of his foes under circumstances peculiarly tragic and memorable. And it was the little hand of the lovely brunette which unconsciously mixed this cup of mingled bliss and woe for the young Solicitor and Prosecuting Attorney from the Waxhaw settlement in North Carolina.

CHAPTER VI.

THE RIGHT MAN IN THE RIGHT PLACE.

In taking up his abode in Nashville, Andrew Jackson planted himself in exactly the right spot for the fullest and most beneficent development of his natural capacities and aptitudes. A better place for him could not have been found, nor could a better man have been found for the place. At that time, and for many subsequent years, Nashville furnished fitting opportunities for him to make his natural qualities of the greatest possible use to his fellow-citizens.

In the first place, as has already been said, the settlement was perpetually beleaguered by Indians, who never let an opportunity for wreaking vengeance on the whites pass unimproved. For many years, a fortnight did not elapse in which at least one white person was not killed in the neighborhood of Nashville, by the Indians. But these red savages were not more dangerous than the white ones who infested the settlement. Even in our own times, remote frontier settlements are cursed with too many red-handed ruffians who have fled from justice and the executioner. But the robbers and murderers who nowadays figure on the fringe of civilization are not to be compared in numbers or ferocity with those who helped to render life precarious and to make it a burden to honest people in the frontier settlements seventy-five or a hundred years ago.

In these latter days scientists have discovered that there is a universal tendency, as silent and as sleepless as the law of gravitation, for every form of life to revert back to its original low condition. This tendency is called atavism. The moment that educating, refining, elevating influences are withdrawn from any creature, that forsaken creature begins to deteriorate. For instance, if a herd of the finest bred cattle were to wander off into some region uninhabited by intelligent men, the cattle would begin to retrograde; and they would go on deteriorating, generation after generation, until they had sunk to the original condition in which the first breeder found his lank, bony, uncouth stock a century or more before.

Human beings are subject to this same tendency to retrogression and degradation. Indeed, atavism, where it has full play, affects man more than any other creature. When civilizing, refining, elevating and religious influences are withdrawn from men for a long period of time, a large percentage of them sink to a level with savages, sometimes to a level with wild beasts, and become worse than wild beasts; become fiends—brutes with enough human cunning left to make their brutality all the more horrible and formidable. In the light which this great law of nature sheds upon the subject, it is easy to understand the conditions in which Andrew Jackson was placed in Nashville a hundred years ago. For twenty years, during Indian wars and the war of the Revolution, fighting and killing had been one of the industries and duties of the people living on the confines of civilization. Lawlessness had become a habit with thousands of men who under more propitious circumstances would have been law-abiding citizens. "As the husband so the wife is," sings the poet; and, it may be added, so are the sons and daughters. Women and children who live in the bonds of daily domesticity with ruffians, themselves become ruffianized, and the entire family circle sinks into a state of lawlessness and brutality.

One of the most annoying of the minor phases of the lawlessness of the times was the contempt which a large portion of the community felt for the sacredness of contracts. They never kept an agreement; they never paid a debt, never responded to any obligation whatever, unless it suited their convenience to do so. To ask one of them to pay a just debt was, in his opinion, to insult him; or, as he would probably put it, it was a reflection upon his honor. More than forty years ago I was told of an amusing incident which occurred in Eastern Tennessee, about 1805, which illustrates that phase of business life in those days. A trader in Knoxville, who dealt in all manner of goods and notions, including books and stationery, sold a settler a Bible on credit. The customer seemed a little ashamed of his purchase, and explained his conduct by saying he wanted the book for his "old woman." Evidently he did not read the Bible himself, and not being imbued with its spirit, he failed to pay for it. After a long time, the bookseller sent him a dunning letter which touched his "honor," and he wrote back to his creditor, in substance, as follows:

"SIR,—Your insulting letter has come to my hands. I cannot allow such an insult to pass. Therefore I demand of you such satisfaction as one gentleman is always entitled to from another, under such circumstances."

The bookseller being a plucky man, as any one who survived in that region had to be in those times, accepted the challenge and wounded his debtor, who, after recovering from his wound, paid for the Bible like a Christian.

Into this environment of bloodthirsty savages, of sensitive, fighting debtors, of vagabonds and cut-throats, Andrew Jackson, in October, 1788, came as a *Deus ex machina*—a God who sets all things straight and right. On his arrival at Nashville, there was but one other lawyer in the Western District of Tennessee, and he was retained by the delinquent debtors to help them avoid paying their debts. The young solicitor let it be known that he was ready to take the side of honesty and justice. He belonged on that side by nature. As we have already learned, he hated debt, and would pay whatever he owed, no matter to what inconvenience the payment put him. As soon as the traders, and others who had claims due, learned that a lawyer had come to Nashville who would undertake to collect their claims, they flocked to his office. In the course of a month he had issued seventy writs. At first, the debtors treated his proceedings with indifference. They had had everything their own way so long, that they imagined themselves to be securely intrenched in their own dishonesty. They supposed that the preponderance of public sentiment was on their side. And so it had been, previous to Andrew

Jackson's advent; but he changed the face of affairs. It had also been supposed to be impossible for a creditor to collect a debt which the debtor did not choose to pay; but Andrew Jackson ordered it otherwise.

The law-defying debtors soon began to feel the Solicitor's grip. As, one after another, they came in contact with him, they discovered that he was a man who could not be, who would not be trifled with. There was something so lionlike in his presence, something so overmastering in his demeanor, that, with his piercing eyes looking into theirs, they found their lawless courage dying out of their hearts—"oozing out of their finger-ends." Still, they were not inclined to surrender without striking a blow for their liberty to defy the law and their right to disregard their pecuniary obligations. Something must be done to stem this torrent of legal procedure, and show that frontier lawlessness could maintain its "honor." As all attempts to intimidate the young lawyer came to naught, efforts were made to wheedle him, but it was found that his cunning was equal to his courage. Efforts were made to evade him, but no one whom he proceeded against could escape his clutch. It is even said that plots were formed to silence him by assassination, but if such plots were formed they all miscarried. He marched straight on. The debtors had to pay, or flee beyond his jurisdiction. The greater part of them paid, and the remnant fled. Jackson's proceedings purified the financial atmosphere of the settlement; the moral tone of the village was elevated and strengthened; honest men breathed more freely; business men felt that they could no longer be cheated or browbeaten out of their just dues. The young Solicitor was hailed as a public benefactor; and as years went on he monopolized a large part of the civil practice in the courts of Western Tennessee.

Being Public Prosecutor (District Attorney), as well as Solicitor, it became Andrew Jackson's duty to suppress the lawlessness which was so general, and to bring the offenders to justice. This part of his practice was not only exciting, but dangerous. Scores of desperate men were in the habit of openly defying the courts and insulting the judges on the bench. The moral tone of the community was so low as to such matters, and the belligerent customs of the people were so barbarous, that offences which would now excite horror in Nashville, or in any enlightened community, were then looked upon as trivial. If men fought with deadly weapons, it was expected that both parties would be wounded, and one of them killed. What did men fight for, if not to wound or to kill? The idea of fighting with deadly weapons without adequate results, was looked upon with contempt. When men fought only with the weapons with which nature supplied them, they used all their natural weapons—hands, feet, claws and teeth. They pummeled each other; they kicked each other; they stamped on one another; they gouged and bit one another. If a man lost an eye, or an ear, or a part of his nose in a rough-and-tumble fight, it was looked upon as a natural consequence of the skirmish; and the eye-gouger, the ear-biter, the nose-mangler was not considered blameworthy by the fighting portion of the community. Among these people, the biting off of a part of a man's ear or nose, "in fair fight," so far from being looked upon as a misdemeanor, was not even thought to be a breach of etiquette.

It must not be supposed that all the inhabitants of the settlement relished such barbarous customs. On the contrary, a majority of the people disrelished them exceedingly, and longed to have a stop put to them. Andrew Jackson was the man to satisfy these civilized longings. Regardless of his personal safety, he assailed the violaters of the law with all the legal weapons he possessed; he brought them to the bar for trial; he had them convicted, sentenced and punished. On one occasion, a formidable gang of ruffians who had long defied the law, having been indicted at Jackson's procurement, came into court in a blustering manner and insolently refused to be tried. Quick as lightning, Jackson drew his pistols from his saddle-bags, covered the ringleaders with them, and called upon the law-abiding citizens in the court-room to stand by him and have the law respected and enforced. Brave men instantly responded to his ringing call, and rallied to his side. The ruffians, awed by his commanding attitude, wilted before the consuming blaze of his eyes. They surrendered, were tried, convicted and punished in accordance with their ill deserts.

On another occasion, a stalwart, raging bully and ruffian, who was determined to thrash and maim Jackson, began by trampling on his toes so as to provoke him to offer resistance, and thereby give the aggressor a seeming reason for putting his detestable purpose in execution. It is needless to say that his effort to provoke Andrew Jackson was completely successful. He provoked him not only to resistance but to unspeakable rage. Seizing a rail from the top of a fence close at hand, and using it as a battering-ram, Jackson dealt the ruffian a blow with the end of it in the pit of the stomach which doubled him up and felled him to the earth. The enraged young man trampled on the brute and then permitted him to rise. He made a feint to attack Jackson, but quailed before the power of his eye. Physically, he was much larger than Jackson and had twice his strength. But—

> "Though so tall to reach the pole,
> Or grasp the ocean with my span;
> I must be measured by my soul,
> The mind's the standard of the man."

In bodily capacity the bully far outmeasured Jackson, but in the measurement of soul the young hero towered above him like Chimborazo above an ant-hill. And that towering soul was ablaze with just indignation, and the bully's vulgar, brutal courage shriveled when brought within the flame of a great soul on fire.

CHAPTER VII.

YOUNG JACKSON'S ADVENTURES—HIS MARRIAGE.

It did not take many years for the inhabitants of Western Tennessee to learn that two things could be always and absolutely depended upon, namely: the integrity, and the courage of Andrew Jackson. These being the qualities most useful to the inhabitants of that primitive region, their possessor, of course, advanced to the front rank in the respect and esteem of his fellow-citizens. He was the pride of the settlement; "the man," to use a phrase of that time, "on whom they bragged." The Western Judicial District of Tennessee comprised an extensive region, which was an unbroken wilderness, except within the immediate vicinity of sparse settlements. The wilderness was intersected by rivers and cut up by streams which a few hours' rain would turn into impassable torrents. Through this wilderness Andrew Jackson, in the discharge of his duties, was obliged to travel with frequency, sometimes in company with his neighbors or with strangers, and sometimes alone. Every furlong of the wilderness path was beset with dangers. The savages were so numerous, so alert, and so wily, it required the greatest vigilance, sagacity and promptness of action to escape their snares, their arrows and their tomahawks. But Andrew Jackson was a born Indian fighter. He was more cunning and more wary, as well as more brave and more brainy than any Indian that ever lay in ambush for a victim. The savages knew every ford by which the rivers were crossed, and it was near these fords, or on the paths leading to them, that they most frequently sought to entrap and murder white travelers. Many a party of whites fell into their snares, and it was seldom that the ambushed parties escaped either partial or total destruction. But they could never entrap Andrew Jackson. Whoever traveled with him got through safe; and when he traveled alone he foiled all the attempts of his savage foes to ambush him or take him at a disadvantage. His eye was so piercing and far-seeing, his ear was so acute, that his eyes and his ears gave him all the safeguard he needed. He sometimes passed days and nights without daring to shoot game or light a fire lest the crack of his rifle or the sheen of the flames should betray his presence to the savages. Mr. Parton has collected a great number of anecdotes and incidents which illustrate the remarkable courage, sagacity and self-possession of young Jackson:

"One lonely night passed in the woods was very vividly remembered by Jackson. He came, soon after dark, to a creek that had been swollen by the rains into a roaring torrent. The night was as dark as pitch, and the rain fell heavily. To have attempted the ford would have been suicidal, nor did he dare to light a fire, nor even let his horse move about to browse. So he took off the saddle, and placing it at the foot of a tree, sat upon it, wrapped in his blanket, and holding his rifle in one hand and his bridle in the other. All through the night he sat motionless and silent, listening to the noise of the flood and the pattering of the rain drops upon the leaves. When the day dawned he saddled his horse again, mounted, swam the creek, and continued his journey.

"On his way home from Jonesboro Court, with only three companions, he reached the river Amory one evening at the point where it gushes out of the Cumberland mountains, and saw on the opposite bank the small, smouldering fires of a party of hostile Indians. Jackson, assuming the command, directed his comrades to abandon the road at different points, so as to leave no trace behind, and then led them into the mountains along the banks of the stream. All night they traveled, guided only by the noise of the waters, and, at dawn of day, came to the edge of the river with the intention of crossing. The March rains had made it a rushing flood; and the nearness of the enemy rendered the keeping of their powder dry a matter of the utmost importance. So, instead of plunging in, in the usual style of the backwoods, they made a raft, upon which they placed all their effects, except their horses, which were to swim over afterward. Jackson and one of his companions jumped upon the raft and pushed off, leaving two others upon the bank with the horses. Rude oars had been rigged to the sides of the raft, at which the two men tugged away, with their backs toward the head of the stream. The men on the shore perceived that the raft was carried swiftly down the stream, and cried out to Jackson to return. He, not aware of his swift downward progress, did not heed their outcries, but strove with all his might

to gain the opposite bank. At length, discovering that the raft was nearing the edge of a fall, he attempted to return. He strained every muscle and nerve in his efforts to bring the soggy and lumbering craft to the shore he had left, along which his two friends were running to keep abreast of him. In vain. The raft was already rushing toward the fall with accelerated and accelerating swiftness, when Jackson tore one of the long oars away from its fastening, and bracing himself in the hinder part of the raft, held out one end of the oar to the men on shore. Luckily, they caught it, and were able to draw them in to the bank.

"Then his comrades reproached him for not returning when they had first called out. His reply was very characteristic, and explains much in his remarkable career:

"'A miss is as good as a mile. *You see how near I can graze danger.* Come on, and I will save you yet.'

"He did so. They resumed their march up the stream, spent a second night supperless in the woods, found a ford the next morning, crossed, continued their journey, and saw the Indians no more.

"Once, as he was about to cross the wilderness, he reached the rendezvous too late, and found that his party had started. It was evening, and he had ridden hard, but there was no hope of catching up, unless he started immediately and traveled all night. With a single guide he took the road, and came up to the camp-fires just before daylight; but his friends had already marched. Continuing his journey, he was startled, when daylight came, to discover the tracks of Indians in the road, who were evidently following the travelers. Equally evident was it to the practiced eyes of these men of the woods that the Indians outnumbered the whites. They pressed forward, and paused not till the tracks showed that the enemy were but a few minutes in advance of them. Then, the guide refusing to proceed, Jackson divided the stock of provisions equally with him, saw him take his way homeward, and kept on himself toward the Indians, resolved at all hazards to save or succor his friends. At length he came to a place where the Indians had left the path and taken to the woods, with the design, as Jackson thought, of getting ahead of the white party and lying in ambush for them. He pushed on with all speed, and reached his friends before dark, just after they had crossed a deep, half-frozen river, and were drying their clothes by their camp-fires. He told his news. The march was instantly resumed. All that night and the next day they kept on their way, not daring to rest or halt, and reached toward evening the cabins of a company of hunters, of whom they asked shelter for the night. The boon was churlishly refused, and they marched on in the teeth of a driving storm of wind and snow. They ventured to encamp at length. Jackson, who had not closed his eyes for sixty hours, wrapped himself in his blanket and slept soundly till daylight, when he awoke to find himself buried in snow to the depth of six inches. The party of Indians meanwhile had pursued unrelentingly, until reaching the huts of the inhospitable hunters, they murdered every man of them, and, satisfied with this exploit, left the travelers to complete their journey unmolested."*

Jackson's bravery and self-possession carried him through everything. He continually showed that his character was of that kind heretofore defined as "centrality, the impossibility of being displaced or overset." It is an old and time-honored adage that "Discretion is the better part of valor." A coward does not distinguish between discretion and cowardice, and under the pretense of acting with discretion, he yields to cowardice. It is doubtful if there ever was a man who had more discretion than Andrew Jackson had; but it was the discretion of a hero, not of a coward. It was the discretion which does not flee from danger, but impetuously attacks danger and overcomes it. He instinctively knew that the best way to avoid danger in desperate cases is not to flee from it, for the bullet enters the coward's back as readily as it pierces the brave man's breast. His discretion was of that peerless kind which comes from the perfect balance and complete control of all the faculties which enter into the constitution of a hero's character. We must remember, however, that what would be discretion in him might be rashness in another. An eagle can safely undertake what it would be folly for a gander to attempt.

At the end of chapter fifth it was stated that the seemingly trivial act of Andrew Jackson's going to board with the widow Donelson was, in fact, one of the most important steps he ever took; that it

* Parton's Life of Jackson, I; 142-3-4.

brought him the greatest happiness and the greatest misery of his life and led to tragic results. The time has now come to narrate these indicated events.

It will be remembered that Mrs. Donelson's married daughter Rachel—the baby girl born in Andrew Jackson's natal year, and the beautiful brunette of after years—with her husband, Lewis Robards, was living with her mother when Andrew Jackson took up his residence under the widow's roof. Robards was a shiftless, cross-grained, shallow-brained man, who had no affection for his lovely and amiable wife, whom he had often ill-treated, and on one occasion deserted. Ample and conclusive evidence has been given that Jackson was always the most chivalric of men in his behavior to women. It has also been shown that the unparalleled reverence, tenderness and chastity of his nature, combined with his affection and veneration for his mother, made all women sacred to him. The contrast between his treatment of Mrs. Donelson and her daughter, and the disrespectful way in which Robards behaved toward them, was apparent even to the dull apprehension of the ill-mannered husband and son-in-law. He saw that he was at great disadvantage in comparison with the young stranger, and he resented his sense of humiliation as a personal outrage upon himself. He tried to pick a quarrel with Jackson, but in vain. I never read or heard of any other instance in which it was impossible to pick a quarrel with Andrew Jackson. It is surprising that the fiery young man should have held himself under restraint in this instance, nor could he have done so had not his chivalry been the master of his temper. It was impossible for Andrew Jackson knowingly to do anything which could possibly injure the reputation of a woman or expose her name to calumny. He knew that if, under the circumstances, he should fight Robards, it would be injurious to Mrs. Robards and also to Mrs. Donelson. So he magnanimously refused to resent the impertinence of Robards, and went to board with another family.

Robards finally deserted his wife and returned to Kentucky, where he sought to obtain a divorce. In those days, Kentucky belonged to Virginia, and in Virginia a divorce could not be obtained unless the legislature first passed an act permitting the plaintiff to bring his suit in the court having jurisdiction of the case. Robards made the necessary application to the legislature, his petition was granted, and it was reported that he had obtained his divorce in due form. After an investigation on the part of Mrs. Robards' friends, the fact of divorce was accepted beyond question. Eighteen months afterwards, in 1781, Mrs. Robards and Andrew Jackson were married. Subsequently, it was discovered that there had been a hitch and delay in the action brought by Robards, and that he did not get his divorce at the time he was supposed to have obtained it: that in fact, he did not obtain it until several months after the marriage of Mrs. Robards with Jackson.

When this unpleasant information was verified, as it soon was, the new-married pair found themselves in a dilemma. In the eye of the law their marriage was not legal, and it was necessary that the marriage ceremony should be re-performed. This was done, and everybody seemed to be satisfied. It too often happens that a marriage which the newly wedded pair hail as a paradisiacal oasis in the desert of life, turns out to be only a delusive and tantalizing *mirage*. It was not so in this case. The marriage was looked upon as a fortunate one for both the wife and the husband. Mrs. Jackson was a favorite in society; handsome, vivacious, amiable; she was a notable housekeeper, possessed rare executive ability, and idolized her husband. Jackson's commanding position in the community is known to the reader, and so is his admirable and dazzling character. That he loved his wife with chivalric devotion was a matter of course. He was pre-eminently that kind of a husband. He gave her a place alongside his mother in his affection and respect. Those two women, his mother and his wife, were enthroned in the innermost sanctuary of his brave, loyal, loving heart. But for his spouse, the beautiful and captivating Rachel, he cherished that tenderness of love, that overmastering and everlasting loyalty of devotion, which can be given to a wife only by a man who has never profaned his affections, and to whom the chosen of his heart is as sacred as his God. Let these overruling and far-reaching truths be remembered, that the reader may clearly understand and justly appreciate the cause and the circumstances of a terrible tragedy that was to follow.

CHAPTER VIII.

REPRESENTATIVE IN CONGRESS—UNITED STATES SENATOR—BACKWOODS MERCHANT—JUDGE OF THE SUPREME COURT OF TENNESSEE.

In January, 1796, a convention assembled at Knoxville to form a State constitution for Tennessee. Jackson was one of the delegates, of which there were fifty-five in all. When the convention had been organized, a committee consisting of two members from each county was appointed to draft a State constitution. Jackson was one of the committee. He suggested Tennessee as the name of the new State. The constitution which was adopted would now be considered intolerably conservative, but then it was looked upon as so radical that the Federalists opposed the admission of Tennessee into the Union. Rufus King, a fossil federalist, led the opposition to its admission; Aaron Burr, a rank and leading democrat, was Tennessee's chief advocate.

The State was admitted into the Union in the following June. Its population entitled it to only one Represenrative. In the ensuing fall election, 1796, Andrew Jackson was elected Tennessee's first Representative in the Congress of the United States.

The journey from Nashville to Philadelphia, then the seat of the Federal Government, was made on horseback, and it usually took six weeks to accomplish it. It would be interesting to know what were the thoughts of the Honorable Andrew Jackson, as

—now a prosperous gentleman and the honored Representative of the State of Tennessee in the Federal Congress—he rode eastward, over the mountains he had crossed westward only eight years before, an almost penniless young man. He was now twenty-nine years old. Up to this time his life had been passed in what might be called an environment of Christian barbarism. Many of the Waxhaw people and a large percentage of the inhabitants of Western Tennessee, though devoutly religious, were always ready, like the Boanerges, to call down fire from Heaven to consume those who crossed their path, or, like the Apostle Peter, to cut off an offender's ear when the unsanctified portion of their nature was aggravated. Andrew Jackson had been a leader in this contentious and belligerent society from his boyhood and was saturated with its spirit. His arrival in Philadelphia early in December, 1796, was his first emergence from the wild civilization of the backwoods. He then, for the first time, came in contact with the usages of cultivated society. Then, for the first time, he took part in legislation with men who were his superiors in parliamentary experience, and the transaction of public affairs. It would be gratifying to know what Philadelphia society thought of him, and what he thought of Philadelphia society: but the record is blank as to such matters. The only glimpse we get of him is given by Albert Gallatin * who years afterwards recalled Jackson as "a tall, lank, uncouth-looking personage, with long locks of hair hanging

* Hildreth's History, IV, 692.

over his face, and a cue down his back tied in an eel-skin; his dress singular, his manners and deportment that of a rough backwoodsman."

He took his seat in the House of Representatives on December 5, 1796, in the second (or short) session of the Fourth Congress. It was not an eventful session. The most notable part of it was that it was the last session of Congress to which Washington addressed his annual speech.

Andrew Jackson was already imbued with, in fact was native to the political principles on which the Republican party, under Thomas Jefferson, was founded. These principles, after a long percolation through the filter of events, came out, thirty-two years afterward, as the foundation principles of the Democratic party that was established on the first election of Old Hickory to the presidency, in 1828. Andrew Jackson hated a Federalist by instinct, and the Federalists instinctively returned his hatred. The poor boy of the Waxhaw settlement, who had literally fought his way, on his own merits, from poverty and obscurity to competence and fame, loved every poor man who honestly tried to do his duty manfully. It was impossible, therefore, for him to sympathize with the Federal aristocrats who were friendly to England, who had opposed the admission of Tennessee into the Union, who distrusted the people and looked coldly upon everybody outside of their own perfumed party. On the other hand, the only feelings with which the Federalists could contemplate Andrew Jackson, were akin to those which well-fed door-yard fowls experience when they see a magnificent young eagle coming up the horizon. The fowls instinctively know that there is not room or prerogative for both them and the eagle in the same door-yard.

The honorable member from Tennessee did not set his political light under a bushel; he let it shine on all within the House of Representatives. The committee on President Washington's annual address to Congress prepared a report which embodied a warm eulogium on both the President and his administration. Jackson was opposed to some of the sentiments enunciated in the report, and, when it came to a vote, he, with eleven others, voted against it. It took a good deal of nerve to do such a thing, as the action of the dissenting Representatives was sure to be misrepresented and ascribed to feelings of personal ill will against Washington. But Andrew Jackson was never known to hesitate, on account of probable ill consequences to himself, in the discharge of what he believed to be his duty.

It is regrettable that Jackson did not take a broader and more appreciative view of Washington's administration; it is easy, however, to understand why he did not. The course of events had brought the Government of the United States into seeming friendship with that of Great Britain, and into hostility to France, the recent ally of the colonies in their struggle for independence. Those who remember the spirit of everlasting hatred of England that was engendered in Andrew Jackson's heart during that struggle for independence, will not wonder that it was impossible for him to look with favor on an administration which, in the phrase of that day, "was constantly drawing nearer to England."

Jackson had come to Philadelphia mainly for the purpose of procuring payment from the government of the expenses incurred by Tennessee (then a Territory) three years before, in an expedition against the Indians. The danger to the whites was so imminent, that the governor—General John Sevier—could not wait two months for an authorization from the government at Philadelphia. In order to save the Tennessee settlements from destruction, he had to move at once. The expedition was successful; but the government, not having authorized it, refused to pay the expense of it. This was a great hardship on the Tennesseeans who had served in the expedition, many of whom had been wounded and worn down by toil and privation, and needed their pay to meet pressing demands. When Jackson presented the claim, it was strongly opposed. It was thought that granting money to pay the claim would be a very disastrous precedent, and lead to unauthorized expeditions against Indians in all the Territories. There was a good deal of common sense in this view of the matter, but Jackson was able to bring forward still more common sense to support his side of the question. He was opposed by debaters of greater experience, and more eloquent than himself; but they lacked his earnestness and pertinacity, his familiarity with the subject and his overpowering personality. He believed that the claim was just, and that it was his duty to press it to a victorious issue. Animated by these convictions, he stripped the question of all irrelevant considerations, sheared right down into the heart of the matter, and there hitting the nail squarely on the head, he drove it home and clinched it. He won his case. The claim was allowed, and the sum of $22,816 was voted to pay the Tennessee Indian fighters.

When Congress adjourned on the 3rd of March, 1797 (John Adams being inaugurated President, and Thomas Jefferson Vice President the next day), Jackson went home. He was received by his fellow-citizens with enthusiastic demonstrations of affection and respect. They gratefully recognized the benefit he had conferred on them by securing from the government the payment of their claims for service against the Indians. The distribution among the needy families of the settlements of nearly twenty-three thousand dollars in cash gave comfort to thousands who otherwise would have felt the stings of want for many months. So highly were Jackson's services appreciated, and so great was his popularity, that when a vacancy occurred in Tennessee's representation in the United States Senate, nobody but the Honorable Andrew Jackson was thought of for the place. The governor appointed him to fill the vacancy, and in December, 1797, having returned to Philadelphia, he took his seat in the Fifth Congress as a Senator of the United States.

When Andrew Jackson took his seat as a Senator of the United States, he was but a few months past the age (thirty years) at which one must have arrived to render him eligible to the United States Senate. There was so little business to transact during the first part of the session that the situation became intolerably irksome to the energetic Senator from Tennessee. An embassy, consisting of John Marshall, C. C. Pinckney and Elbridge Gerry, had been sent to France by President Adams, to adjust if possible the threatening difficulties between the two countries, and Congress was not in a mood to do anything until dispatches had been received from the embassy. The dispatches did not come, and Congress idly waited for them four months. When the dispatches finally came, they were so alarming that Congress prepared for war with France, and its action was approved by a majority of the people. While Congress was waiting, Senator Jackson, aided by his colleague in the Senate and the Representative from Tennessee, persuaded the Administration to send a commission to the Cherokee Indians in Tennessee, for the purpose of buying from them all the land which that tribe would sell. The commission made a successful negotiation with the Cherokees, whereby Tennessee was relieved for many years from further trouble with them.

Senator Jackson sympathized strongly with France and with the French revolutionists, and with everything which was republican and progressive. There are traditions that he used to become furious at the tardy transaction of the public business, and with members of Congress who favored what he thought to be anti-American measures and principles. It is even said that sometimes his anger would be so great that he could not articulate for several moments at a time, and that to the aristocratic Federalists, who were devotees of deportment, he was not a pleasant antagonist. He won the friendship of Aaron Burr, Edward Livingston, and other leading democrats; and his relations with them had an influence on his subsequent career. Becoming utterly wearied out by the do-nothingness of the Senate, in April, 1798, he obtained leave of absence for the remainder of the session, went home, resigned his office, and took his place as a private citizen for the first time since his twenty-first year.

It was time he relinquished the public service and attended to his private affairs, which had become embarrassed on account of his long absences from home. He owned so many large tracts of wild land, on which he had to pay taxes, that he was what is called "land poor." While serving in Congress, he had mingled a good deal in Philadelphia society, and had made the acquaintance of some of the merchants of that city. In this way he had learned what large profits were made on merchandise bought in Philadelphia and taken to the West for sale, notwithstanding the enormous expense of transporting the goods over the mountains and through the wilderness. He sold several thousand acres of his western land for nearly seven thousand dollars, to David Allison, a prosperous merchant in Philadelphia, of great reputation as a shrewd business man and financier. Allison paid for the land by giving three promissory notes on long time, the last note not coming due for about six years. Allison's credit was so good that Jackson, by indorsing the notes, was able to buy merchandise with them in Philadelphia. This merchandise he sent to Pittsburg in wagons; then by flatboats down the Ohio to a convenient point, and thence, on pack-horses, through the wilderness, to Nashville.

He opened a store in a block-house, near his residence at Hunter's Hill, two miles from his subsequent abode which became so widely known as the Hermitage. The Indians and many white men of that day were such adroit and persistent thieves that precautions had to be taken to prevent them from purloining such articles as they could easily hide about their persons and carry away undiscovered. To meet this emergency, a small window was cut in one end of the block-house, and Indians and notoriously light-fingered white men who wanted to trade with the merchant were required to stand outside and do their buying and bartering through that aperture.

By the time his new business had got fairly under way, the Legislature of Tennessee elected him Judge of the Supreme Court, an office which was considered next to the governorship in dignity and importance. The governor's salary was $750; the judge's $600. Jackson had not expected the office; he did not want it; he accepted it with reluctance, and only in deference to the principle (of which he was an advocate) that a citizen should neither seek nor decline office. As he had to hold court in different parts of the State, his duties took him from home so much that his judgeship was disastrous to his private interests. There are no authentic records with regard to the manner in which he performed the duties of his office, but there are many legends and anecdotes concerning his adventures while he was a Judge of the Supreme Court. One of the five noted babies born in 1782—Thomas H. Benton—now grown to be a youth of seventeen, gives this interesting glimpse of the famous Judge, as he appeared on the bench:

"The first time I saw General Jackson, was at Nashville, in 1799; he on the bench, and I, a youth of seventeen, back in the crowd. He was then a remarkable man, and had his ascendant over all who approached him; not the effect of his high judicial station; nor of the senatorial rank which he had held and resigned; nor of military exploits, for he had not then been to war; but the effect of his personal qualities, cordial and graceful manners, hospitable temper, elevation of mind, undaunted spirit, generosity and perfect integrity."

The testimony is unanimous that General Jackson was the most distinguished-looking man of his time in America; also that he was one of the most elegant and graceful, whether on horseback at the head of his troops, or in a drawing-room surrounded by ladies; moreover, that he was invincibly just, inflexibly upright and chaste as ice. Such a man might be a stern judge, but he could not fail to be a firm and a just one. Mr. Benton says that General Jackson "was a remarkable man, *and had his ascendant over all who approached him.*" This is as great a power in a judge, as it is in a military chieftain. It enables a judge of indifferent legal ability to do what a weak man, however professionally accomplished he may be, cannot do on the bench, especially when he has such fighting lawyers and litigants to deal with as Judge Jackson had. It was seldom that anybody ventured to dispute his decisions or to cavil at his rulings. Besides, his invincible love of justice, in combination with his fearlessness in the performance of his duty, and his penetrating intellect, gave him clear perceptions as to the vital issues in the cases which came before him for trial. He was quick to see the pivotal fact or principle on which a case turned; and this enabled him to keep the lawyers to the point, to strip a case of all irrelevant considerations and drive it rapidly to a conclusion. For these reasons he could dispose of more cases in a day than any other judge of whom I have any knowledge, and the parties to the suits always got substantial justice; which, of course, was an intolerable grievance to those who were in the wrong.

Mr. Benton, in the article from which the above extract is taken, refers to solecisms in style and errors in grammar which were made by Judge Jackson. It was customary, during the embittered political contests in which General Jackson was subsequently the central figure, for his enemies to try to cast ridicule upon his "literary style." But the pedants never could gain the sympathy of the people for such attacks. The people then, as now, looked at the real substance and heart of things. They knew that Andrew Jackson's terrible experiences during the tender years when boys are usually laying the foundation for a literary style, had developed characteristics in him which were worth more to his country than all the literary style which the universities can confer. And as a matter of fact, Jackson's style in writing, like his style in fighting, was just the style which fitted the time in which he lived. It struck right at the core of things. It accomplished his purpose. If, now and then, a sentence did not stand straight on its legs, it was never broken-backed, it never sprawled, it did not even wobble. He was at his best in his addresses issued to his armies. In these, his burning thoughts came forth in fit burning words, often with fiery emphasis, and sometimes with a commanding clarion blast as inspiring to his troops as his heroic demeanor in battle.

CHAPTER IX.

FRONTIER LIFE A HUNDRED YEARS AGO.

One of the stories told of Judge Jackson illustrates his coolness and his readiness of resource at a critical moment. As he was riding along an unfrequented country road in his gig, a ruffian, upon whom a few years before he had inflicted a heavy sentence, suddenly sprang out of a clump of bushes, covered the judge with a loaded pistol and ordered him to dismount from the vehicle. Seeing there was no alternative, he dismounted.

"Now dance," said the ruffian, still covering him with his pistol.

The judge had on heavy boots. Looking at them he quietly said:

"I can't dance in these boots. I must get my pumps; then I'll dance for you."

As he thus spoke, he stepped to his valise that was strapped behind the gig and began to open it.

"All right," said the ruffian, with his pistol still pointed at the judge's head.

He had no sooner spoken than Judge Jackson whirled upon him with a cocked pistol in his hand, and his eyes flashing lightning. The ruffian was so taken aback that he lost his nerve, and also "the drop," which, up to that moment, he had kept on the judge. Knowing that if he made the slightest movement, the judge would put a bullet through his brain, he stood trembling before him, without making any defense.

"Throw down your pistol," said Judge Jackson.

The ruffian obeyed.

"Now dance," said the judge.

The ruffian danced.

"Keep on dancing," said the judge, when the fellow began to slacken his efforts from fatigue. And he kept the weary wretch dancing until he fell to the ground with exhaustion. The judge then picked up and discharged the man's pistol, threw it down beside him, re-entered his gig and drove off, leaving his assailant lying helpless by the roadside.

On another occasion two wagoners attempted to make Judge Jackson dance in the road. In those days wagoners were a numerous and influential class. They were rough men, fond of rude fun, and were not respecters of official personages. One of their favorite pastimes was to make people whom they met on the road dance for their amusement. Two of them meeting the judge, ordered him to get out of his gig and dance. He resorted to the same ruse which he had practiced in the case of the ruffian. Pretending to go for his slippers, he opened his valise and suddenly confronted the wagoners with a pistol in each hand. The playful wagoners were dumbfounded. The judge compelled them to dance until they were exhausted, and then gave them a moral lecture which was probably far more tiresome to them than the dancing, but which the contiguity of the lecturer's pistols caused the auditors to listen to with seeming respect.

Jackson's unparalleled readiness of resource in

emergencies, which would have been insurmountable by other men, was shown on a memorable occasion. It was at Clover Bottom, on the day of the annual horse races. It was customary, on that day, for the landlord of the small tavern to set a long table in the open air, at which hundreds of guests could be accommodated. Several races had been run, and an intermission was had for dinner. The long table was filled, Jackson at the head of it, and on each side was a vast and dense multitude. Suddenly, a disturbance arose at the lower end of the table, and soon Jackson learned that an attempt to kill a particular friend of his named Patten Anderson was on foot.

"They'll finish Patten Anderson *this* time, I *do* expect," said some one in the crowd.

Jackson sprang to his feet. He must get to the side of his friend at once. But how could he do it? To force his way through the dense crowd was impossible. Every second of time was of incalculable importance. In such a case, Andrew Jackson's will would find a way. It did find a way. Springing upon the table, he rushed down its whole length, crying in his most clarion tones: "I'm coming, Patten!" As he neared his friend, he put his hand in his coat pocket behind. In Tennessee, in those days, when a man under such circumstances put his hand in his coat pocket behind, it meant that he was reaching for his pistol. Jackson had no pistol; but he had an old-fashioned steel tobacco-box with a stiff spring, which he snapped as he approached. The snap of the spring sounded like the click of a pistol when it is cocked.

"Don't fire!" cried one of the by-standers, as Jackson came down the table like a cyclone. The hostile crowd heard the cry, looked up, saw the coming cyclone, and—vanished, leaving Anderson unharmed.

People of this age, living in communities where fighting is looked upon by all with disfavor and by many with disgust, should not judge the inhabitants of the extreme West in the days of Andrew Jackson, by our standards. It is ungracious, it is ungrateful for people who reap harvests from fields which they now till without fear, to criticise with ungenerous severity the lives and conduct of the men who, constantly surrounded by danger and in the perpetual presence of death, reclaimed those fields from the wilderness. Let any man of spirit imagine how *he* would have behaved if he had lived in that country in those times, and been surrounded by Indians thirsting for his blood, and had encountered ruffians bent on biting off his ears or his nose, or on gouging out his eyes, or determined to stab him to the heart with a hunting-knife, or to put a bullet through his head! In such a community, where the law of the survival of the fittest reigns supreme, a man must fight, or he isn't fittest, and will not long survive. In such a community, instead of its being a disgrace to fight in defense of one's rights or life, it is an honor, a distinction, a certificate of character. In such a community, as the celebrated Colonel David Crockett used to say: "A man's willin'ness to fight is a proof of his innercence."

In those wild days even ministers of the Gospel had to fight, in order to hold their own against the bullies and the ruffians who sometimes attempted to disturb and break up religious meetings, especially during revival seasons. The Reverend Peter Cartwright, the celebrated frontier preacher and revivalist, who was a giant in size and strength, gives some thrilling accounts in his autobiography of the physical encounters he had with aggressive ruffians. On one occasion, when a gang of ruffians attempted to break up a revival meeting, he put himself at the head of a band of stalwart members of the church militant for the purpose of defending the tents of Zion. Here is the way the God-fearing, but not man-fearing, old preacher concludes the story (the italics being mine):

"I threw myself in front of the friends of order. Just at this moment the ringleader of the mob and I met; he made three passes at me, intending to knock me down. The last time he struck at me, by the force of his own effort he threw the side of his face toward me. *It seemed at that moment I had not power to resist temptation, and I struck a sudden blow in the burr of the ear and dropped him to the earth.*"

Dear old Peter's inability to resist temptation at that critical moment turned the scale in favor of the Gospel. The rowdies were driven off, the revival went on gloriously, and many precious souls, incarnated in the bodies of wild western converts wearing hunting-knives and pistols, were garnered into the fold of the church.

On another occasion, a certain Major L., taking umbrage at Cartwright's plain preaching, assailed him with profuse vituperation and challenged him to a rough-and-tumble fight. To his great dismay, the Reverend Peter accepted his challenge. Choking with rage and profanity, the major yelled:

"If I thought I could whip you, I would smite you in a moment."

"Yes, yes, Major L.," Peter quietly replied; "but, thank God, you can't whip me; but don't you attempt to strike me, for if you do, and the devil gets out of you into me, I shall give you the worst whipping you ever got in your life."

Major L. did not attempt to strike the brave old man, who "whipt him with his gaze," then turned on his heel and leisurely walked away.

The oft-told Russell Bean adventure was one of the most thrilling incidents in Andrew Jackson's experience as a judge. Bean was one of the most desperate ruffians in Tennessee. He seldom hesitated to commit any act of brutality to which his passions prompted him. He even cut off a babe's ears, close to its head, for the purpose of avenging himself on the infant's mother, who was his own unfaithful wife. A warrant having been issued for Bean's arrest for a breach of the law, he refused to be arrested and defied the sheriff. As he was armed with a pistol and a hunting-knife, the sheriff did not dare to grapple with him. Judge Jackson was holding court. The sheriff reported the case to him, saying that Bean was in front of the court-house and threatened to shoot anybody who attempted to arrest him. Authorities differ as to the details of what then occurred; but the majority agree that the judge waxed wroth and volunteered to serve as one of the *posse* summoned to capture Bean. Cocking his pistol, which was then and there a portion of the paraphernalia of justice, he led the way to the court-yard, where Bean was blustering and threatening to shoot anybody who came within ten feet of him. Judge Jackson walked straight toward him, pointing his pistol directly at the ruffian's head and transfixing him with his eye. For an instant, Bean attempted to rally. But his nerve was not equal to the crisis, and stammering, "There's no use, Judge; I give in," he put up his weapons and suffered the sheriff to lead him away. It is said that Bean's explanation of his sudden collapse was that when he caught Judge Jackson's eye, he "saw shoot in it, and that there wasn't shoot in nary other eye in the crowd."

Amos Kendall, in his Life of Jackson, tells a characteristic and thrilling anecdote, which Mr. Parton quotes. In the fall of 1803, while Judge Jackson was on his way from Nashville to Jonesboro' where he was about to hold a court, a friend who met him on the road informed him that a combination had been formed against him, and that on his arrival at Jonesboro he might expect to be mobbed. Jackson was then sick with intermittent fever, which had so weakened him that he was scarcely able to sit on his horse. He spurred forward, however, and reached the town, but so exhausted that he could not dismount without help. Burning with fever, he retired to his room in the tavern and lay down on a bed. A friend soon came in and said that in front of the tavern, were Colonel Harrison and a regiment of men who had assembled for the purpose of tarring and feathering him. His friend advised him to lock his door. But that was not Andrew Jackson's way.

Enfeebled as he was, he rose suddenly, threw his door wide open, and said, with that appalling emphasis which won him so many battles without fighing:

"Give my compliments to Col. Harrison, and tell him my door is open to receive him and his regiment whenever they choose to wait upon me, and I hope the colonel's chivalry will induce him to *lead* his men, not follow them."

Nothing more was heard of the colonel or of his men. Judge Jackson recovered from his fever, and held his court as usual, without molestation.

CHAPTER X.

FINANCIAL DISASTERS.

While Judge Jackson was so faithfully serving the public on the bench, his private affairs, owing to his frequent absences from home, were disastrously neglected; moreover, heavy financial burdens were unexpectedly laid upon his shoulders. In 1798 and 1799 there came a great commercial crash, which swept away hundreds of fortunes based on credit and impoverished thousands of business men.

Among those who failed was David Allison, the Philadelphia merchant, to whom Jackson sold his wild land. It will be remembered that Allison paid for the land with his notes on long time; that Jackson indorsed the notes and bought merchandise with them. The failure of Allison threw the payment of the notes upon Jackson. It was a terrible blow. He met it, as he always met danger or trouble, without flinching, and with a resolute purpose to perform his duty at whatever cost to himself. The notes had to be paid in Philadelphia, in hard cash; and paid they were, every one of them on the day it became due.

The payment of these notes was only accomplished after a struggle which almost wrung the life out of Jackson's resources, and left him in a state of painful pecuniary embarrassment. Being so constantly absent from home, he could not give personal supervision to his store; his partner and his assistants were inefficient, and the establishment became an extra burden and expense to him. I will dismiss this storekeeping business by stating that, after several years of unsatisfactory experiment, Jackson finally sold out his interest in the store to his partner, General John Coffee, taking the general's notes for the purchase price, which notes were never paid. Thus ended Andrew Jackson's career as a frontier merchant. It often happened that his debtors failed to pay him; and so long as a man was honest and did his best, Andrew Jackson had not the heart to distress him by enforcing payment. But, although many people failed to pay him, he paid everybody. In this respect he was strongly contrasted with some of his illustrious contemporaries who lived in debt, were harrassed by debt all their lives, and died in debt, leaving a legacy of shame to their children. "Who has not seen," exclaims Emerson, in his Essay on Prudence —"who has not seen the tragedy of imprudent genius, struggling for years with paltry pecuniary difficulties, at last sinking, chilled, exhausted and fruitless, like a giant slaughtered by pins."

There is no part of Andrew Jackson's life which the young men of this country can contemplate with more profit than that in which his struggles with financial disasters are described. But few, probably none of those who read this narrative, will be called upon to fight their country's battles in the field, but it is highly probable that many of them will have occasion to struggle more or less with pecuniary embarrassments and financial misfortunes; and in such struggles they cannot find a better guide or model than Andrew Jackson.

Clearly perceiving the magnitude of his embarrassments, and also perceiving clearly the only way in which he could retrieve himself, in 1804 Jackson resigned his judgeship, took the management of his affairs into his own hands, and set at work with characteristic energy and sagacity to rebuild his shattered fortunes. He sold his house and farm at Hunter's Hill and twenty-five thousand acres of wild land, paid all his debts with the proceeds, opened a new farm and established a new residence, the Hermitage. Under his personal supervision his affairs at once began to be prosperous. He devoted himself to agriculture and stock-raising. From Virginia he brought a famous race horse, Truxton, that was the progenitor of a long line of highly valued descendants. According to the testimony of his neighbors he was a skillful and in many respects a model farmer. Nothing which could conduce to the success of his farm was overlooked or neglected. Everything was attended to at the right time and in the right way.

In addition to his own superior qualifications, he had a loving, competent, devoted helpmeet in his wife. Mrs. Jackson was celebrated throughout Western Tennessee as one of the most energetic and skillful housewives of her day; and it was the very life of her life to work with and for her idolized husband. Her "woman's sphere" is worthy of the careful consideration of the women of this day, and also of the men. She lived in what is called a double log-house; that is, two log-cabins placed end to end or side by side, with communicating doors. There was a log annex to this house for the accommodation of guests. Near by, and at various convenient localities on the farm, were cabins for the accommodation of the negro servants and the slaves. Over the "home department" of this little kingdom Mrs. Jackson reigned as queen. She attended to all manner of duties—knitting, spinning, butter-making, cooking, sewing. She made her own dresses, superintended the preparation of clothing for the slaves, and in her husband's absence she looked after outdoor affairs; was proud of her clear, ever-flowing spring; was a good judge of horses, cattle and sheep; in short, was competent and ready to oversee with energy, tact, kindness, skill and judgment, every variety of domestic functions, and bring them all to successful issues.

It is probable that many a man, on reading this description of Mrs. Jackson's domestic competency and faithfulness, will say to himself: "Would to heaven that I had such a wife!" To that man perhaps it would be advisable to say: "Would to heaven that your wife had such a husband as Mrs. Jackson had!" Remember what the poet says: "As the husband, so the wife is." Andrew Jackson was a model husband. He loved his wife with chivalric devotion. As Mr. Parton says, thirty-seven years he kept pistols in perfect readiness for any man who breathed a word against her name. During all their married life he treated her with the respect, the delicacy, the tenderness, the courtesy, the adoring affection of an ardent lover. In his imagination he idolized and glorified her, until, in the words of Carlyle, "to him she was indeed a morning star; her presence brought with it airs from heaven." And the man who thus loved and cherished his wife was a hero, a king of men. What wonder, then, that his wife loved and idolized him in return, and found her chief joy in being his true helpmeet.

It is a truism that the love of a poodle is not to be despised; and, in truth, poodles are thought much of now in some quarters; but the devoted love of a grand old lion, and the consciousness that his courage and strength are perpetually at our service, would give such satisfaction and delight, especially to woman, as the love of many poodles could not bestow. And he or she who will look intelligently at this matter may understand something of the felicitous domesticity of the Jackson household, in that double log-cabin and on that prosperous farm. When the minds, hearts and souls of a married pair are conjoined in perfect conjugal union, the masculine and feminine natures so supplement and reinforce one another that each flows out, in its own functional way, to the performance of its duties as naturally and harmoniously as the heart and lungs perform their respective and different but equally necessary functions.

Since the disaster in the Garden of Eden, no earthly paradise has been secure against the machinations of the devil. The Jackson paradise was not exempt from the common perils of paradises. That handsome boy baby, whose hand was to become so skillful with the pistol, now grown to manhood, was rapidly nearing the culmination of his earthly destiny, and threatened to work irretrievable woe to the happy husband and wife who dwelt at the Hermitage.

CHAPTER XI.

PLOTS TO GET RID OF JACKSON—THE DICKINSON DUEL.

Before he resigned his judgeship, Andrew Jackson was elected a major-general of the Tennessee militia, and was thenceforth known as General Jackson. He made this appellation so famous and so dear to the hearts of his countrymen that only his subsequently acquired nickname, "Old Hickory," could supersede it. Even after his election to the Presidency of the United States he was seldom called President Jackson. He was General Jackson or Old Hickory to the end of his life. The Tennessee major-generalship was one of the most coveted offices in the State, and Jackson's election to it was another proof of the high esteem in which he was held by his fellow citizens.

General Jackson's successful and honorable career in Tennessee had excited the jealousy of ambitious rivals who coveted the honors so freely lavished on him. It was not unnatural that his intolerable success should have exasperated his defeated competitors. One cannot entirely withhold his sympathy from those who were so poignantly afflicted by the general's rapid rise to distinction and his monopoly of honors. Their jealousy and their hatred were aggravated by the general's temper, which Colonel Benton says "refused compromises and bargaining, and went for a clean victory or a clean defeat in every case. Hence," Colonel Benton adds, "every step he took was a contest; and, it may be added, every contest was a victory."

Considering all the circumstances of the case—including the sanguinary disposition of nearly every man who had achieved any degree of distinction in that belligerent age and in that fighting community—it is not surprising that there were hundreds of men in Tennessee who would have been glad to hear of General Jackson's death. When people very much want a man to die, it is not impossible for them to find plausible ways and means for helping him to pass from this world of sorrow into another and a better world. General Jackson's enemies, knowing what a terrible man he was in a contest, and how ready his friends were to stand by him, proceeded with caution and cunning. They knew how he idolized his wife; they had not forgotten that, owing to misinformation, he had unwittingly married her several months before Robards had obtained his divorce, and therefore was obliged to have the marriage ceremony re-performed. They seized upon these facts as a means of annoying General Jackson. They magnified the facts; they misrepresented them; they tortured them into the most vilifying calumnies. The general was profoundly affected by these venomous attacks upon the woman whom he respected as one of the purest of mortals and adored as the paragon of her sex; the woman who was *his wife*, and therefore sacred to him, and whom, according to his convictions, he was bound by every human and divine consideration to defend against her calumnious enemies.

Having brought things to this pass, General Jackson's enemies sought, and supposed they had found, a way to expedite his departure from this world. In the latter part of the year 1805, there was a young lawyer in Nashville, twenty-five years old, named Charles Dickinson, who had the reputation of being "the best pistol shot in the world." According to all accounts, Dickinson deserved his reputation. At all events, he was the best pistol shot in Western Tennessee. This young lawyer was "the marvelously beautiful baby" born in 1780, now grown to manhood. He was in sympathy with some of General Jackson's most malignant enemies. Inasmuch as he spoke disrespectfully of Mrs. Jackson, in a public bar-room, it is probable that he was himself embittered against Jackson. The fact that Dickinson had spoken disrespectfully of Mrs. Jackson was communicated to the general. Mr. Parton's statement about pistols kept in readiness for thirty-seven years by General Jackson for anybody who spoke disrespectfully of his wife, will recur to the reader's mind. No one will have any difficulty in imagining the effect upon his fiery nature of the report that Dickinson had publicly used insulting language about Mrs. Jackson. He immediately took Dickinson to task. Dickinson denied all recollection of having said anything disrespectful about Mrs. Jackson, and added that if he had in fact done so, he did it while he was drunk and irresponsible. This pacified the general for a time; but rumors were circulated that Dickinson had repeated his sneering innuendoes; and at last he made an insulting remark about Mrs. Jackson in her own presence and hearing.

This unfortunate occurrence, which was to have a tragic and fatal issue, took place on the Nashville race-course, where one of General Jackson's horses was outrunning its competitors. Mrs. Jackson, seeing her husband's horse coming in far ahead of its rivals, clapped her hands and exclaimed:

"O, he is running away from them!"

Dickinson, who was standing near Mrs. Jackson's carriage, said to an acquaintance, in a tone of voice loud enough to be heard by her:

"Yes, and a good deal as his owner ran away with another man's wife."

Such a gratuitous and wanton insult to a lady was, of course, unpardonable. Mrs. Jackson told her husband of it. To the surprise of his friends, who knew with what readiness General Jackson avenged an insult to his wife, he behaved with exemplary coolness and forbearance. The truth was, the general's almost preternatural sagacity divined the intentions of those who were plotting to destroy him; and while he had no intention of faltering in the discharge of what he believed to be his duty, he was resolved that he would make no false step. Besides, he was held in check by his own celebrity and high position. A man who has arrived at nearly forty years of age, who has been a Representative in Congress, a Senator of the United States, and Judge of the Supreme Court, and is a major-general of the military organization of his State, cannot speak and act with the reckless freedom with which a young man may behave who is just starting out in the world.

The truth of the deplorable events which followed has never been, and probably never will be, completely revealed to mortal minds. In such matters there is always much which is known only to the hearts of the chief actors, and it is this unknown quantity which usually determines and controls the course of events. As to this affair, suffice it to say that General Jackson verily believed there was a conspiracy to kill him, and that Dickinson was the instrument selected for that purpose. If he could be provoked to challenge that renowned dead-shot, his doom would be sealed. So far as known, no human being could cope successfully with Dickinson on "the field of honor," if the weapons were pistols. And if he were challenged he would have the right to name the weapons, and would, of course, choose pistols. He always fired instantly, with the quickness of lightning, and he never missed his aim.

In spite of all exertions on the part of well-intentioned friends to pacificate the differences between Jackson and Dickinson, they grew worse and worse. It being apparent that, if the foreshadowed duel should be fought on the ground that General Jackson was fighting in defense of his wife and to punish a man who had wantonly and personally insulted her, he would have public sympathy on his side, persistent and artful efforts were made to deprive him of that rightful advantage. Other persons and other matters became mixed up in the affair. It seemed as though some secret, malign influence was at work to render a reconciliation impossible.

When Paul, after his shipwreck on the Island of Melita, laid a bundle of sticks on the fire, "there came forth a viper out of the heat and fastened on his hand." The fomenters of the strife between Jackson and Dickinson constantly laid sticks on the fire, knowing that out of its heat only vipers of hatred and vengeance could come. And finally, in May, 1806, General Jackson sent Dickinson a challenge. The challenge was immediately accepted, but Dickinson demanded a delay of a week, in order that he might procure a dueling pistol, which would enable him to shoot General Jackson with a nicety and precision which would gratify his fastidious artistic taste in such a matter. He knew that the duel would be a celebrated one; and as he expected to be the sole survivor, he wished to have his part in the deadly business performed in a way which would win the enduring admiration of his friends.

General Jackson protested against the delay demanded by Dickinson, and offered him the choice of his own pistols, in order that the alleged reason for delay might be obviated. But Dickinson, being the challenged party, had the right to dictate terms, and he would not consent to an earlier meeting. So it was arranged that the duel should be fought at seven 'o'clock on the morning of May 30, 1806, at Harrison's Mills, on Red River, in Logan county, Kentucky—a long day's ride on horseback from Nashville.

Rumors of the impending duel spread through the country, but the time and place were kept secret. The excitement was intense and universal. It is probable that not an individual who heard of the coming conflict had the least doubt as to the result. General Jackson was looked upon as a doomed man —as good as dead already. Neither Jackson nor his second (General Thomas Overton, an old Revolutionary soldier, who had had much experience in dueling) had much if any doubt as to what the result would be. That Dickinson would fire quicker than General Jackson could, and that his shot would be unerring, both Jackson and Overton conceded. That being the undoubted truth, what was to be done? A serious question truly. The two generals studied the problem long and thoroughly. The conclusion which they finally came to was that General Jackson should receive Dickinson's fire, and take his chance of surviving and of being able to return the shot. It is doubtful if, under such circumstances, any man except Andrew Jackson could have come to such a conclusion, and abided by it, and awaited the crisis with cheerfulness. But that old chieftain, whose sympathetic tenderness was so great that he could not hear a lamb bleat on an inclement night without getting out of his bed, and going forth into the storm and bringing the suffering little creature into the house and putting it in a warm place on the hearth, had the resolution and fortitude of a god,

"And a heart for any fate."

Early on Thursday morning, May 29th, the duelists, accompanied by their seconds and their surgeons, set out for Harrison's Mills. Dickinson, who was the first on the road, had several young friends in his party, who went along to see him shoot General Jackson. They made a picnic of the trip. Along the route, Dickinson gratified his friends by giving them proofs of his skill with the pistol. He shot four bullets into a space that could be covered by a silver dollar; he severed strings by which cucumbers were suspended in the sun to ripen; indeed, he performed wonders with his artistic pistol, and amazed his friends by what seemed to them the superhuman accuracy of his fire. All this was not merely done for sport; there was a purpose in it. It was arranged that General Jackson's attention should be called to some of these proofs of his adversary's deadly skill, for the purpose of shaking his nerves and breaking him up. It was supposed, and not without reason, that a man riding all day along a road sown with proofs of his coming doom, would be disadvantageously affected thereby. It is probable that anybody but Andrew Jackson would have had his nerves shaken by such an experience, but his nerves were danger proof.

How strange, how unfathomably strange are the workings of the human heart! One reason—the chief reason—why General Jackson rode so calmly to the dueling-ground, was because he was sustained by his trust in a superintending Providence. He believed that he was performing a sacred duty in defending his wife against her calumnious detractors, and was sure that Heaven would smile upon his conjugal devotion. Nevertheless, he was keenly alive to the danger to which he was going. He was one of those thoughtful and prudent Christian soldiers who, while trusting in God, always keep their powder dry. He spent the hours of his ride to the dueling-ground in serious consultation with his friend and second, General Overton. They re-examined the whole ground, analyzed the situation thoroughly, and became as well prepared for the approaching emergency as was possible under the circumstances. The antagonists were to stand twenty-four feet apart, facing each other, with their pistols pointing downward. When the word was given, they were to fire as quickly as they pleased. As Jackson had come to the conclusion to receive Dickinson's fire, Overton's only hope was that, by some fortuitous circumstance, the general might be able to stand upon his feet long enough to give Dickinson a return shot. It seems, however, that General Jackson himself had no doubt as to what *he* should do, inasmuch as, years afterward, in conversation upon the subject, he said to a friend:

"I should have hit him, if he had shot me through the brain."

The parties arrived near the place of meeting, on Thursday afternoon, and took up their respective quarters at log taverns about a mile distant from each other. In after years, Jackson's landlord used to tell his guests that the general ate a hearty supper, conversed pleasantly, and smoked his pipe with a relish before he went to bed; that he was in equally good humor in the morning, and rode off gayly to the dueling-ground. To one of his friends, who asked him how he felt about the issue of the duel, the general replied:

"Oh, I'm all right; I shall wing him, never fear."

Both parties arrived punctually on the ground,

which was in the midst of a forest. The twenty-four feet were measured off, and the principals took their places. Dickinson was one of the handsomest young men of his day. His friends said he never looked more handsome or more noble than when he stood there, under the great forest trees, awaiting the word to fire. According to the testimony of all parties, and especially that of General Overton, Jackson looked like a demi-god. His tall form was erect, his countenance calm, stern, resolute. The majesty of his presence was overwhelming; as the appearance of a man, whose heart was fearlessly braving the consciousness that in all probability his last few moments of life had come, well might be.

General Jackson wore a loose frock coat buttoned over his chest. It is reported that Dickinson told his second on which button of that coat his bullet would strike. It was a button, as he supposed, directly over Jackson's heart. In a few moments all the forms of the *duello* had been complied with. The combatants had saluted each other with the courtesy of the drawing-room; both said they were ready, and instantly General Overton, who had won the right to give the word, gave it in a loud and shouting tone. True to expectation, Dickinson fired instantly, and hit the very button of Jackson's coat that he had indicated. Overton saw the puff of dust which followed the stroke of the bullet, supposed that General Jackson was fatally hit, and looked to see him fall. But he did not fall. A grimmer expression spread over his countenance, but he stood erect. He raised his pistol and took deliber-

ate aim at his adversary. Dickinson was thunderstruck, and exclaimed: "Great God! have I missed him?" falling back from his position as he spoke. "Back to your place!" yelled Overton, placing his hand on his pistol. Dickinson stepped back and stood erect, with his side toward Jackson, and looking away from him. Jackson took aim, and pulled the trigger with deliberation. No explosion followed. The trigger had stopped at half-cock. Re-cocking his pistol, Jackson again took aim and fired. A ghastly pallor overspread Dickinson's face; he tottered; he staggered; he was about to fall, when his friends caught him in their arms and laid him on the ground. He was shot through the lower part of his body. He was removed to his quarters at the tavern. His wound was mortal. He died at nine o'clock in the evening of that day.

General Jackson, his surgeon, and General Overton at once left the ground. When they had gone some way towards the place where they had tied their horses, the surgeon, happening to look down, saw that blood was running into Jackson's shoes, and exclaimed:

"General Jackson, are you hit?"

"Oh, I believe that he has *pinked* me a little, but say nothing about it *there*," pointing to the tavern.

On examination, the surgeon found that Dickinson's bullet had broken a couple of ribs and grazed the breastbone. The bullet had gone to the very spot at which Dickinson aimed; but at that moment, a puff of wind blew Jackson's loose frock-coat a little to one side and saved him from probable instant death. The wound, though not fatal, was a bad one; hut it did not flurry him, and it was only by accident that his surgeon discovered it. The general mounted his horse with a little assistance, and rode to his tavern. A negress was churning near the door, and learning from her that "the butter had come," he asked for a drink of buttermilk. She gave him a quart mugful, which he drank at one draft. His wound was then dressed. Immediately after the surgeon got through dressing the wound, General Jackson sent to inquire after his antagonist's condition, and offered any aid which he or his surgeon could render him. He received word that no aid could be rendered to the wounded man by any one; but he continued his polite attentions to Mr. Dickinson's party until they were no longer required. General Jackson sedulously concealed the fact that he was wounded, giving as a reason for his precautions that he did not wish Dickinson to know of his wound, because, as he used frankly to say:

"Dickinson considered himself the best shot in the world; he was certain that he would kill me at the first fire, and I didn't want him to have the gratification of even knowing that he had touched me."

The duel occasioned intense and wide-spread excitement. General Jackson's enemies utilized it to the utmost for the purpose of making headway against his popularity, and, if possible, of depriving him of the admiration and affection which the people of Tennessee had so long felt for him. For a time they made some progress. But it was vain to fight against Andrew Jackson. No matter what faults he had, no matter what mistakes he made—(and who has not faults, who does not make mistakes?)—his magnificent qualities and his vast usefulness to his fellow-citizens always brought them back to their allegiance to their favorite hero.

CHAPTER XII.

BURR'S CONSPIRACY.

In the midst of the excitement about the Dickinson duel, Aaron Burr arrived in Nashville, on his secret expedition against Louisiana and the Spanish possessions in Texas.

Burr began his treasonable plottings while he was Vice-President of the United States, and when his term expired, on March 4, 1805, he had already woven a network of conspiracy which reached from New York to New Orleans, from Philadelphia to St. Louis. In this network were entangled many influential persons, only a few of whom were let into the secret of Burr's ulterior designs. Jonathan Dayton, ex-United States Senator from New Jersey, was one of his chief confederates. Senator John Smith, of Ohio, was deep in his confidence, and so was the British Minister at Washington, who supposed it would be agreeable to his government to have the Union dismembered, and held out to Burr hopes of aid from Pitt, then Prime Minister. The majority of Burr's dupes supposed, in a vague sort of way, that he was preparing for an expedition against Mexico and other Spanish possessions in America. At that time the Spanish possessions in America were looked upon as lawful prey by the inhabitants of the Western and Southern States, and the sentiments of Northern and Eastern people were not so strongly tempered with a sense of national obligations as to make them actively antagonistic to the schemes of filibusters. In every part of the country, and especially in the West and Southwest, there were numberless adventurers destitute of property and of the means of earning a livelihood, discontented with their lot, ambitious of distinction, weary of the monotony of peaceful life, and eager to engage in any enterprise which promised to give them opportunities to gratify their lawless aspirations and better their condition. Such men were easily deluded into becoming the dupes and accomplices of Burr and his co-conspirators.

Nor were disunion sentiments then unknown; it is shown by evidence now accessible that they were not uncommon. In truth, but very little love for the Union had been developed, and the physical conditions of the country were adverse to the growth of a national spirit. The different sections of the country were separated by vast ranges of mountains, and by wildernesses stretching for hundreds of miles and swarming with hostile savages. It took weeks, and in some cases months, for the inhabitants of widely separated regions to communicate with one another. Steamboats, railroads, telegraphs were then unknown. A traveler can now go from San Francisco to St. Petersburg or Constantinople sooner than he could then go from Philadelphia to New Orleans, and a message can now be sent around the world in less time than it could then be sent from Boston to Cambridge, from New York to Harlem, or from Washington to Georgetown. It is difficult, perhaps it is impossible, for us of this generation to appreciate in all its force the effect which such a state of things had upon the minds and the affections of the people into whose keeping the destiny of the United States was then given. New England and the Southwest, the Seaboard States and the trans-Alleghany States, in many respects were foreign to one another. The interests of one section were, or were supposed to be, hostile to the welfare of other sections. For the most part, the inhabitants were poor, burdened with debt, and a prey to discontent; and it is a habit of discontented people to charge their misfortunes upon the government, and to imagine that their condition would be bettered by a revolution, or by such a reformation of the government as would lead to a fundamental readjustment of their political relations.

It would be unjust for us of this day to condemn with too great severity any lack of patriotism or laxity of principle exhibited by the American people with respect to these matters a hundred years ago. Despite all theories to the contrary, men are governed in worldly affairs by what they believe to be most conducive to their worldly interests. Whatever is hostile to those interests they will oppose; whatever is favorable to them, they will support. A hundred years ago, the great need of the inhabitants beyond the Alleghanies was an outlet for their commerce, whereby their products could reach the marts of the world. That outlet—and it was the only one—was the Mississippi river. "That outlet," as General Jackson said in his address to his troops in 1812—"that outlet blocked up, all the fruits of the Western man's industry rot upon his hands; open, and he carries on a commerce with all the nations of the earth." The mouths of the Mississippi were in the possession of Spain, whose rulers interposed obstructions to Western commerce which were intolerable to the inhabitants of Kentucky, Tennessee and the whole trans-Alleghany country. The United States Government could not or would not do anything to remove these obstructions, and the Western people naturally resolved to take the redress of their grievances into their own hands. Their plan for redressing their grievances was a radical one—a plan of the true "wild Western" kind. They proposed to wrest the mouths of the Mississippi from the Spaniards, take possession of the whole country, unite the conquered territory with their own, form a trans-Alleghany Union and assume that independent station among the nations of the earth to which nature and their own achievements would entitle them.

Fortunately, the spirit of disaffection, which for years had been growing more and more ripe, was allayed in 1795, when the Federal Government, by a treaty with Spain, acquired the right of deposit at New Orleans, for three years, which temporarily relieved Western commerce of the intolerable impositions to which it had been subjected by the Spaniards. Then, too, for the first time, the Western people caught a glimpse of the national dignity and material advantage which the Federal Union conferred upon them. They clearly saw that it was respect for the growing power of the United States which caused Spain to grant the right of deposit—a right which the court of Madrid would never have accorded to a feeble trans-Alleghany republic. From that time Union sentiments rapidly increased in the West; but owing to constant quarrels between Americans and Spaniards, the deep seated hostility to Spain grew stronger and stronger from year to year. Even, when by the cession of Louisiana to France in 1800, and its purchase by the United States in 1803, all restrictions on Western commerce were removed, the desire of the trans-Alleghany inhabitants to avenge themselves on Spain survived in full vigor. Hence Burr's alleged design to seize all the Spanish territory east of the Rio Grande, and if possible to conquer Mexico, excited no effective disapprobation west of the Alleghanies. The desire to "extend the area of freedom" was as strenuous in the people of that region, in 1806 and 1807 as it was in their descendants forty years later, when, in 1846 and 1847, they enthusiastically rushed to the contest for that same territory under the lead of General Taylor and General Scott.

In New Orleans the situation was favorable, not only to Burr's schemes of conquest, but also to his treasonable plans for disunion. The French and Spanish inhabitants of that city, and indeed of Louisiana, hated the Government of the United States, and longed for the restoration of the Territory either to France or Spain. Governor Claiborne was odious to the people, and General Wilkinson, the commander of the department, was despised by them. Monsieur Laussat, who had been the French prefect at New Orleans, and remained there for a time to protect French interests, in writing to his government, thus speaks of those two men:

"It was hardly possible that the government of the United States should have made a worse beginning, and that it should have sent two men (Messrs. Claiborne, Governor, and Wilkinson, General,) less fit to attract affection. * * * They have on all occasions, and without delicacy, shocked the habits, the prejudices, the character of the population."

Wilkinson was in the pay of Spain and also one of Burr's most trusted accomplices. Judge Prevost, of the Superior Court at New Orleans, was Burr's stepson. James Brown, Secretary of the Territory, was one of Burr's henchmen. Many of the leading citizens were leagued with Burr, and it was believed that the inhabitants of the city and of the Territory could be depended upon to abet any movement which could relieve them from subjection to the hated government of the United States. Daniel Clark, the richest man in the Southwest and Louisiana's first representative in Congress, was supposed to be in favor of the movement; but becoming alarmed, he, for the purpose of shielding himself, on September 7, 1805, wrote Wilkinson a letter indicating that he was not in the secret, and expressing horror at the idea of a plot for dissolving the union of which he professed to have recently heard. "The tale," he wrote, "is a horrid one if well told. Kentucky, Tennessee, the State of Ohio, the four territories on the Mississippi and Ohio, with part of Georgia and Carolina, are to be bribed, with the plunder of the Spanish countries west of us, to separate from the Union."

Burr had influential accomplices all through the West. Harman Blennerhasset, a comparatively wealthy Irishman, who had created a sort of frontier paradise on an island in the Ohio river, a short distance below Parkersburg, became one of Burr's most enthusiastic dupes, and his wife shared his folly. Burr's daughter Theodosia, the wife of ex-Governor Alston, of South Carolina, accompanied her father to the island in the Ohio, and cast an irresistible spell over Mrs. Blennerhasset. The enthusiastic Irish pair indulged in the wildest dreams. Burr was to be Emperor of Mexico; Blennerhassett was to be one of his high officers and stand near the throne of Aaron the First, and Mrs. Blennerhassett was to be maid-of-honor to the imperial Princess Theodosia. It was not long before those deluded people were rudely awakened from their romantic dream to find themselves the laughing-stock of the public and bankrupted in fortune.

Burr's visit to Nashville was made for the purpose of furthering his designs. Thousands of Tennesseeans were ready to engage in an expedition against the Spanish possessions. Hardly any American living west of the Alleghanies would have withheld his sympathy from such an expedition. Andrew Jackson certainly would not. The building of flatboats was then an important industry in the west. General Jackson and Colonel Coffee had facilities for building them at Clover Bottom, on Stone's river, an affluent of the Cumberland. Burr had bargained with them to build five boats for him, in which his Tennessee followers could float down the Cumberland and the Mississippi to their destination. His avowed object was the occupation and peopling of a vast tract of land on the Washita river, the title to which he professed to have purchased from the representatives of the original Spanish grantees. He did not disguise the fact that the enforcement of his rights would probably cause a collision with the Spanish authorities; that such a collision would bring on war, and that Burr would improve the occasion to conquer Mexico, become emperor of that country, and bring it into friendly alliance with the United States. To further such a scheme, General Jackson was willing to build boats at a profit. He had not the slightest suspicion that Burr was plotting treason. But in November, 1806, while Burr was in Kentucky, Jackson was warned that he was planning a dissolution of the Union. This caused a violent and total change of feeling on the general's part. He wrote a warning letter to Governor Claiborne at New Orleans, and another to President Jefferson, offering the services of his division of militia, "In the event of insult or aggression made on our government or country FROM ANY QUARTER."*

Burr returned to Nashville December 14, 1806, and called at the Hermitage. General Jackson was not at home. Mrs. Jackson received him coldly; so did Colonel Coffee. On December 19th it was rumored that a proclamation by President Jefferson denouncing Burr had been received in Nashville. On December 22nd Burr left Clover Bottom, in two unarmed

*Parton I, 319.

boats carrying a few of his deluded followers. Among his dupes was a young man named Stokely D. Hays, a nephew of Mrs. Jackson's, about seventeen years old, by whom General Jackson sent a letter to Governor Claiborne. The young man's father, Colonel Hays, was an old friend of Burr's. Having become reduced in his circumstances, he had acceded to a proposition made by Burr to take his son Stokely under his protection, provide for his education and give him a start in life. In afterwards narrating the circumstances which induced him to accompany Burr, young Hays said:*

"In the winter of 1806-7 the Colonel [Burr] came to Nashville, and sent for me when at school near there, and on meeting him he claimed the promise which had been made to him on his first visit—but stated he was going by way of the Mississippi, and that I must accompany him, and that he had seen my father and obtained his consent; that he received me as a son, and I must consider him in the character of a father. I observed to him that I must see and consult my friends before I gave my final consent. On advising with them, some doubt of Mr. Burr's object was suggested, but he having pledged his word of honor that he had nothing in view hostile to the best interests of the United States, I determined to go with him. Mr. C. C. Claiborne was at that time Governor of Louisiana, and an old friend of my father's, and had requested him to permit me to go to New Orleans as his private secretary. To him General Jackson wrote a letter, and

* Parton I, 321.

gave me to deliver, urging it on me, in the most earnest manner, to leave Burr, if at any time I should discover he had any views or intentions inimical to the interests or integrity of the government."

It would take a very prejudiced mind to see in this transaction any evidence of General Jackson's sympathy with Burr's treason. But Mr. Henry Adams, in his recently published history * presents this incident in a way which he doubtless hopes will turn it into evidence against Jackson's patriotism. In fact, Mr. Adams, in his sketch of this conspiracy, seems to have resolved to make it appear that General Jackson was cognizant of and in sympathy with Burr's treasonable designs, and in order to carry out his purpose he does not hesitate to indulge in felonious innuendoes and repeated indirect falsifications of the historic record. As an example of his method, his use of the young Hays incident will now be given:

"Without further hindrance," Mr. Adams says, "Burr then floated down the Cumberland River, taking with him a nephew of Mrs. Jackson, furnished by his uncle [General Jackson] with a letter of introduction to Governor Claiborne,—a confidence the more singular because Governor Claiborne could hardly fail, under the warnings of General Jackson's previous secret letter, to seize and imprison Burr and every one found in his company. Thus, by connivance, Burr escaped from Nashville three

* History of the United States of America During the Second Administration of Thomas Jefferson. Vol. I, 290.

days after the news of the President's proclamation had arrived."

It will be observed that Mr. Adams has no authority for saying that General Jackson gave young Hays "a *letter of introduction* to Governor Claiborne." Hays does not authorize such a statement. He says that Jackson wrote a letter to Claiborne and gave it to him [Hays] to deliver. That is not the way one speaks of a letter of introduction given to himself. Moreover, it is evident that young Hays did not need "a letter of introduction" to Claiborne. The Governor was intimate with the young man's family, and had requested his father to let him come to New Orleans as his (the Governor's) private secretary. The fair inference is that the letter which General Jackson wrote was a letter of warning and explanation to Claiborne. This inference is strongly supported by the fact that when the General gave the letter to Hays to deliver, he "urged it on" the young man, "in a most earnest manner, to leave Burr if at any time he should discover" anything treasonable in his conduct or his intentions. All of this information Mr. Adams withholds from his readers; and over and over again he resorts to the same method for the purpose of unfairly making what he imagines to be a point against General Jackson.

Mr. Adams had all the facts before him. They are given *in extenso*, and with great fullness of detail, in Mr. Parton's comprehensive "Life of Jackson, to which Mr. Adams repeatedly refers, and of which he sometimes makes use. Many attempts were made by General Jackson's enemies, especially during his campaigns for the Presidency, to make his countrymen believe that he was privy to Burr's treason. But although it was easy to show, what the general never denied, that he was Burr's personal friend, and that after Burr's trial and acquittal he disbelieved the charges of treason that had been made against him, it was impossible to convince the American people that General Jackson ever sympathized with any attempt whatever to dismember the Union, or that he would ever have winked at any scheme involving treason to the flag which from his childhood he was ever ready to defend with his life.

To return to Burr, whom we left floating down the Cumberland. He had been gone but a short time when the President's proclamation was published in Nashville, and caused a prodigious excitement. Burr was burnt in effigy in the public square; General Jackson called out the militia; volunteers offered their services; the people of Western Tennessee were ablaze with patriotic fervor and ready to turn out *en masse* in defence of the Union. But the excitement soon died out. Burr's chief accomplices deserted him. General Wilkinson was eager to catch and shoot him, in order to save himself from exposure and disgrace—perhaps from death. Burr's nerve failed him, and ignominiously deserting his dupes, he fled, disguised in the coarse attire of a Mississippi boatman. His arrest, his trial at Richmond, and his acquittal followed in due course. Burr was a born traitor and conspirator; but he was so deficient in that grand executive ability which is indispensable to him who would overthrow governments and carry out schemes of conquest, and was so destitute of even that low grade of honor and principle which sometimes binds thieves together, that his treasonable projects lacked all power of cohesion and disintegrated at the first shock of exposure.

CHAPTER XIII.

THE WAR OF 1812—GENERAL JACKSON IN THE FIELD AND IN HIS GLORY.

War was declared against Great Britain by the Government of the United States on June 12, 1812. The declaration had been anticipated for many months. As early as the preceding February, Thomas H. Benton (one of the babies of 1782), then a lawyer, thirty years of age, living in Nashville, received intelligence from Washington which convinced him that the declaration of war would be made in a few months. Benton was on General Jackson's military staff, was ambitious for military glory, and was animated by intense and lofty sentiments of patriotism. The news from Washington was accompanied by an act of Congress, authorizing the President to accept organized bodies of volunteers to the number of fifty thousand, to serve for one year, and to be called into service when an emergency should require it.

This news and the act of Congress fired Benton's brave and patriotic heart. He saw that here was a probable opportunity to gratify his thirst for military glory in the most legitimate way, by helping to repel an arrogant and aggressive foe from the shores of his native land. That very hour, he mounted his horse and rode to the Hermitage, where he had long been a favored guest with both the master and the mistress. Colonel Benton told the story of this ride and of its consequences, in the House of Representatives, forty-three years afterward (1855), when General Jackson's sword was presented to Congress. It was a cold, wet day, and the ride was long and difficult, over the miry roads of early spring. Benton reached his general's log house about twilight, and found him sitting alone before the fire, with a lamb and a child between his knees.

"He started a little," says Benton, "called a servant to remove the two innocents to another room, and explained to me how it was. The child had cried because the lamb was out in the cold, and begged him to bring it in, which he had done to please the child, his adopted son, then not two years old."

The impetuous Benton lost no time in communicating the news and his project for action. He knew very well that Jackson could raise volunteers enough for a general's division, and urged him to issue the call. Before leaving his office, Benton had drawn up a plan for the organization of three regiments, to be commanded by John Coffee, William Hall and Thomas H. Benton. If these three regiments should be in good condition for service at the outbreak of war, the Administration, in the urgent need that would then exist for troops ready to take the field, would gladly accept their services, although, as Benton knew, Jackson was out of favor with the Administration. He had come in collision with the Government at the time of Burr's trial; he had also had controversies with agents of the Government (especially with one Silas

Dinsmore, an Indian agent), which had caused a good deal of trouble. So far as Jackson was known at Washington, he was known as a man who was always ready to take the responsibility of carrying out his own plans without regard for red tape. For these reasons Benton was somewhat apprehensive that the Administration would hesitate to confer military power on General Jackson; hence his prudential proceedings. Benton laid his plan for the organization of the three regiments on the table. To use his own language, General Jackson "was struck with it, adopted it, acted upon it." A call was promptly issued; companies were formed. In a few weeks, more than three thousand men were enrolled, and there was a general drilling of soldiers and furbishing of arms throughout the western part of Tennessee.

All turned out very nearly as Colonel Benton had anticipated. The news that war with Great Britain was declared on the twelfth of June, reached Nashville in eight days. On the twenty-fifth of June, which was about as soon as the business could be accomplished, General Jackson offered to President Madison, through the governor of Tennessee, the services of his division of twenty-five hundred volunteers. The offer was most cordially accepted. The Secretary of War wrote that the President received the tender of service by General Jackson and his troops "with peculiar satisfaction," and "in accepting their services, the President cannot withhold an expression of his admiration of the zeal and ardor by which they are animated."

Everybody in Tennessee seemed to be delighted

with the result of the movement. Governor Blount publicly thanked General Jackson and his division for the honor they had done the State of Tennessee by coming forward so promptly to the service of their country.

The War of 1812 began with the bold and judicious but ill-conducted attempt upon Canada, which ended in shame and disaster. The surrender of Detroit by General Hull and subsequent military miscarriages covered our arms with disgrace. Besides, the failure of the Canada expedition left the British forces free to attempt the capture of New Orleans, which, it had long been supposed, would be among their first objects. General Wilkinson, a conspicuously incompetent officer, still commanded at New Orleans, but the place was wholly unprepared for defense.

In October, 1812, a despatch came from Washington to the Governor of Tennessee, asking him to detach fifteen hundred of the Tennessee troops to re-enforce General Wilkinson at New Orleans. The governor at once issued the requisite orders to General Jackson, who, in his turn, named the 10th of December, 1812, for the troops to rendezvous at Nashville, armed and equipped for winter service.

The address which General Jackson issued to the troops was well calculated to kindle their enthusiasm. He appealed to their patriotism, to their pride and to their interest. He told them that Nature herself had committed to the people of the Western country the defense of the lower Mississippi, "the only outlet" for their produce.

The Mississippi "blocked up, all the fruits of the

western man's industry rot upon his hands; open, and he carries on a commerce with all the nations of the earth. At the approach of an enemy in that quarter, the whole Western world should pour forth its sons to meet the invader, and drive him back into the sea."

The troops, however, needed no words of exhortation to increase their zeal. When the day appointed for the rendezvous came, more than two thousand men presented themselves for inspection, bringing their own arms and ammunition, and wearing every sort of costume, more or less resembling military uniform. The majority were attired in hunting shirts, with such other garments within their reach as seemed best adapted to winter wear. It so chanced that the day (December 10, 1812) appointed for the assembling of the troops, was one of the coldest ever known in Western Tennessee, and the ground was covered deep with snow. The quartermaster, the late Major William B. Lewis, in view of a possible cold snap, had provided a thousand cords of wood for the use of the troops, which he supposed would last them until they had embarked on board the flat-boats on which they were to descend the river to New Orleans. *It was all burned the first night.* General Jackson and the quartermaster were out all night, seeing that the men were sheltered and warmed, that drunken men were brought near a fire, and that sleeping sentinels should not freeze to death on their posts.

About six o'clock in the morning, after having thus tramped through the camp all night, General Jackson entered a tavern in Nashville. It happened that one of those pestiferous creatures constituting the class of chronic grumblers, who had passed the night comfortably in bed, was finding fault with the authorities for having assembled such a large body of troops without suitable accommodations. He was loud in his denunciation of the officers who, he said, had the best accommodations in town, while the men were exposed to the terrible inclemency of the weather.

"You infernal scoundrel," roared the general, "*sowing disaffection among the troops!* Why, the quartermaster and I have been up all night making the men comfortable. Let me hear no more such talk, or I'll ram that red-hot andiron down your throat!"

There was "no more such talk." I have italicized one of the general's wrathful sentences to call attention to his unsleeping canniness, even when he was most enraged. "Sowing disaffection among the troops" was an offense of such a serious nature that it might have justly been punished with a red-hot andiron in the throat of the offender, even though the disaffection was sown in the isolation of a bar-room.

Fortunately, such cold periods in the latitude of Tennessee are as brief as they are sometimes severe. In a day or two the weather was warm enough, and in a few days the little army was ready to begin the descent of the Cumberland. On one of these days of waiting, there was a grand review of the troops by the governor, who complimented their general highly upon their appearance and discipline. The general wrote in response a letter which, glowing as it is, truly expressed his own feelings and those of the volunteers, the flower of the young men in the western counties.

"We have changed the garb of citizens for that of soldiers," said he. "In doing this, we have none of us changed our principles; for let it be recollected, as an invariable rule, that good citizens make good soldiers. The volunteers have drawn their swords for no other purpose than that of defending their country against the hostile attacks of their enemies, the British, and their barbarous allies, the Indians. * * We hope that your Excellency shall never blush for the honor of Tennessee. Your Excellency will not call it presumption when the volunteers say that it is their full determination to return covered with laurels or die endeavoring to gather them in the bloody field of Mars."

On the seventh of January, 1813, the boats at length were ready. The foot-soldiers went on board, and the fleet began the descent of the Cumberland River, while Colonel Coffee, with the mounted regiment, set out on his march across the country, with orders to join the infantry at Natchez.

The commander-in-chief was in the highest spirits. From his early youth he had taken a peculiar interest in military affairs and in military men. His heart swelled with pride and confident expectation as he saw the boats glide from the shore. One of his last actions was to write to the Secretary of War, informing him that he was in command of two thousand and seventy volunteers, the choicest citizens of Tennessee, who had "no constitutional scruples" about executing the will of their government, and would rejoice to place the American eagle "on the ramparts of Mobile, Pensacola and Fort St. Augustine," thus "effectually banishing from the Southern coast all British influence."

It was in this spirit, and with his heart fired with the memory of British brutalities perpetrated in the Waxhaw settlement long years before, that Andrew Jackson started on his first warlike expedition.

The flotilla descended the Cumberland to the Ohio; and then went down the Ohio to the Mississippi, and thence continued on its way southward. For thirty-nine days they floated upon those winding rivers, the whole heart of Western Tennessee going with them. On the morning of February 15, 1813, after traversing a distance of more than a thousand miles, the fleet came to at the levee of Natchez, where they were to meet the mounted men of the command. It was cheering to learn that Colonel Coffee and his men were encamped near by.

At Natchez, General Jackson received a letter from General Wilkinson, commanding at New Orleans, informing him that no enemy had yet appeared in the waters of the South. Wilkinson further said that he had received no orders respecting the Tennessee troops, and did not know the purpose of the Administration in sending them southward. At New Orleans he had neither barracks nor provisions for such an increase of force, and he therefore requested General Jackson to wait at Natchez for further orders.

Wilkinson seemed to be more anxious for himself than for his country. He gratuitously informed General Jackson that he should not think of yielding up his command, "until regularly relieved by superior authority." General Jackson assented to the suggestion that his troops should remain at Natchez, and added that his command should be kept in instant readiness to move.

Accordingly, the troops disembarked at Natchez, and went into camp five miles from the town, where their officers kept them steadily drilling, and, in all other ways known to them, preparing for efficient service. At that season of the year the country about Natchez is one of the most pleasant in the Southwest, and as both officers and men felt the need of further drill and preparation, all were content with the delay, which they hoped would be but brief, and prepare the way for a glorious campaign by and by.

Two weeks passed pleasantly away, the troops daily improving in soldierly arts. But although the men were happy under the novel restraints and congenial labors of the camp, their general was becoming impatient. Natchez was then a six weeks' journey from Washington, even for a rapid messenger. Nevertheless General Jackson wrote to the Secretary of War on the 1st of March to offer the services of his command in a new sphere. The defeats of the Northern troops weighed heavily upon all patriotic minds, and so he wrote:

> "Should the safety of the lower country admit it, and government so order, I would with pleasure march to the lines of Canada and there offer my feeble aid to the army of our country, and endeavor to wipe off the stain on our military character occasioned by the recent disasters."

This idea so fired General Jackson's mind that,

when another week had passed without orders and the hot weather was beginning to affect unfavorably the health of the troops and no indications of an enemy appeared in the South, he wrote again to the Secretary of War, assuring him that, on his return to Tennessee, he could raise three thousand men, who would engage for a year if he could tell them that their destination was Canada.

Two weeks more passed away and the month of March was nearly at an end. The men had been waiting and drilling for six weeks, subsisting chiefly upon the provisions they had brought with them. The sick list lengthened every day, and the troops themselves now shared the impatience of their commander.

At length, on a Sunday morning near the end of March, came an express bringing a ten-line letter from the Secretary of War, General John Armstrong.

It is doubtful if so much discouragement and dismay were ever before or since compressed into ten lines of writing as the Secretary's letter contained. It was written six weeks before, and should have reached the troops before they had gone beyond the boundaries of Tennessee. It read thus:

"Sir: The causes of embodying and marching to New Orleans the corps under your command having ceased to exist, you will, on receipt of this letter, consider it as dismissed from public service, and take measures to have delivered over to Major-General Wilkinson all the articles of public property which may have been put into its possession. You will accept for yourself and the corps the thanks of the President of the United States.

No language can adequately express General Jackson's amazement on reading this order to dismiss two thousand men at a point five hundred miles from their homes—five hundred miles of nearly unbroken wilderness—without pay, and unprovided with any other means of performing so difficult a journey. On the instant he made up his mind that he would never dismiss his troops, most of whom were young men specially confided to his care by parents and friends, until he had conducted them to the public square of Nashville, where they had been enrolled into the service of their country. He sent for Colonel Benton, who still served as aid and secretary to the commander-in-chief, though himself at the head of one of the regiments. He showed Benton the order of the Secretary of War, and at the same moment announced his determination to disregard it. Colonel Benton is our authority as to what ensued. General Jackson dashed upon paper the draught of a letter he wanted written to the Secretary of War, which he gave to Colonel Benton to copy and arrange. "It was very severe," Benton records; "I tried hard to get some parts softer, but it was impossible." The general then summoned what he called a "council" of the field-officers. Their advice he did not ask, but merely informed them of his intention to march the troops back to Tennessee. and issued the requisite orders. Every officer was clear in the opinion of the absolute necessity of taking the troops home as an organized body, since it was known that the savages had been greatly excited by the declaration of war, and the homeward path lay through the Indians' country.

There was not in the camp one dollar of public money. There were a hundred and fifty men on the sick-lists, fifty-six of whom were utterly helpless and would have to be carried in wagons. Upon inquiry, the commander found that the wagons would each cost ten dollars a day coming and going, and a considerable number of them would be required. The men had received no pay since leaving home. Their clothes, and particularly their shoes, were worn out. Even the officers had made no provision, either of money or goods, for such an emergency. In these circumstances, General Jackson took the responsibility. To the teamsters, the farmers and the merchants of Natchez he pledged his whole estate for the goods they were to furnish. He personally indorsed every draft, although his property, at the time, was far from being sufficient to cover the expenditure.

Five days were passed in preparation. On the last day, a dispatch arrived from the Government which ought to have accompanied the order to dismiss the troops. Owing to some error never explained, this second dispatch was started on its way several days after the first. The new dispatch directed General Jackson's troops to be paid off, and to be allowed pay and rations for the homeward journey. About the same time came a letter from Genaral Wilkinson urging General Jackson to encourage his troops to enlist in the regular army. In this effort to obtain recruits for the regular army, occurring simultaneously with the dismissal of his own forces, General Jackson thought he had discovered a clew to the outrageous treatment of his troops. He distrusted and despised Wilkinson, and ascribed to him the desire to get a rival general shelved, and to have his own forces augmented by the gobbling up of that rival's brave soldiers. In his reply to Wilkinson, he said:

"These brave men, at the call of their country, voluntarily rallied round its insulted standard. They followed me to the field. I shall carefully march them back to their homes. It is for the agents of the Government to account to the State of Tennessee and the whole world for their singular and unusual conduct to this detachment." This letter gives little indication of the wrath of General Jackson at Wilkinson's suggestion. But when a recruiting officer was detected lurking about the camp, *he* was made to understand how the general felt, by an immediate notification that if he attempted to seduce one of the volunteers into enlisting in the regular army, he should be drummed out of the camp in the presence of the whole corps.

CHAPTER XIV.

THE MARCH HOME—GENERAL JACKSON WINS HIS NICKNAME OF "OLD HICKORY."

The homeward march began, with the fifty-six helpless men in eleven wagons. Those who could sit a horse were mounted on the horses of the officers. General Jackson had brought with him three of his own excellent horses, but gave them all up for the use of the sick men, himself performing the whole distance on foot. A march of five hundred miles, to save his sick comrades from suffering, was nothing to the man who, as a wounded, diseased and emaciated boy of fourteen, had made that terrible march of forty-miles from Camden to his home, while the small-pox fever was raging in his blood. General Jackson seldom, perhaps never, appeared to greater advantage than he did on this long and toilsome journey; for he was called upon at every moment to exercise one of the strongest of his instincts—to care for those who were dependent upon him in critical emergencies—which never failed to call forth all the fortitude and tenderness of his nature. To see the commanding officer marching gayly along, chatting with officers and men, and encouraging the sick with his cheerful words, had a magical influence on the whole corps. The sick men improved every day, and even those who had seemed marked for a wayside grave reached their homes in good health.

"'Where am I?' asked one young trooper who had been lifted insensible and apparently dying into a wagon, on coming to consciousness. "On your way home, my brave boy," the general cheerfully and affectionately answered. The young soldier began to improve from that hour, and reached home in good health.

It was on this journey from Natchez to Tennessee that General Jackson acquired his nickname of "Old Hickory." Mr. Parton says: "One of the officers who marched with him informed me that it arose out of the impression of toughness which the general's pedestrian alertness made upon the men. From 'tough' he became 'as tough as hickory,' and long before they reached home he was familiarly called by the famous nickname, 'Old Hickory,' which he retains to the present hour."

The day's march averaged eighteen miles, and they accomplished the distance in something less than a month. On the twenty-second of May, the troops were drawn up in the public square of Nashville, about to depart for their homes. A beautiful stand of colors was presented to them by the ladies of East Tennessee, made by their own skillful hands. On the white satin, eighteen stars were embroidered in orange, with two sprigs of laurel lying across them. Besides a glowing inscription to the volunteers, the ladies had wrought representations of war-like objects, such as arms, cannon-balls, drums, colors and axes, all so harmoniously arranged as to excite universal admiration. The general in command was deeply touched, and wrote to the ladies an eloquent letter of acknowledgment.

At this time, Andrew Jackson's popularity was at the highest point it had yet reached. It was more than popularity, for his treatment of the soldiers had been truly paternal, and the affection which his soldiers bore him excited a similar feeling in the homes of all the western counties. Only one thing marred for a time the happiness of his triumph. The numerous drafts that he had given for transportation and supplies were returned protested, the Government claiming that they were given without authority of law. It happened, however, that Colonel Benton was going to Washington on business of his own. He explained the whole transaction to the Secretary of War, and told him that as those volunteers represented every substantial family in Tennessee, and the whole State stood by the commanding general, Tennessee would be lost to the Administration if he were left responsible for the drafts. This touched the Government in a vulnerable and sensitive spot. The Administration could not afford to lose the support of Tennessee, and so Colonel Benton's argument prevailed. The Government assumed the expenses, and thus saved General Jackson from ruin.

Soon after Colonel Benton had done this great service for his esteemed commander, General Jackson, impelled by what to him was a stern sense of duty, acted as the second of a dear young friend in a duel with Jesse Benton, Colonel Benton's brother. Jesse Benton naturally saw only his own side of the question. He gave his brother an exaggerated account of the affair, in which the conduct of General Jackson was described in a way which made

Colonel Benton furious. Misunderstanding after misunderstanding followed, and provocation after provocation was given, until the feud culminated in a street fight between General Jackson and his friends and the Bentons and their friends. General Jackson was terribly wounded by Jesse Benton, who fired a huge pistol, loaded like a blunderbuss, at him as he was facing Colonel Benton. A large slug shattered General Jackson's left shoulder, a ball entered the upper part of his left arm and sunk to the bone, while another ball splintered a board partition at his side. He fell across the entry of a tavern, where he lay bleeding and nearly insensible until the fighting ceased. As soon as possible he was carried to a room in the Nashville Inn, and all the doctors in the town were gathered around him. They succeeded, when life was nearly extinct, in staunching the flow of blood. The arm was so badly injured that all the physicians present but one recommended immediate amputation.

"I'll keep my arm," said Jackson.

No attempt was made to extract the ball from the arm, and the horrid wounds in the shoulder were dressed in the simple manner of the Western country, with applications of slippery-elm and other native products. Mrs. Jackson used to tell her friends that, before the bleeding could be stopped, two mattresses were soaked through. General Jackson lay for nearly three weeks, before he could sit up in a chair while the bed was made.

Soon after the occurrence of this terrible affray, Colonel Benton left Nashville and went to Franklin in Tennessee. A short time afterward, he was appointed lieutenant-colonel in the regular army, in which he served to the end of the war. He then removed to Missouri, which, as is well known, he represented for thirty years in the Senate of the United States. In the first volume of his "Thirty Years in the United States Senate," at page 737, Colonel Benton makes a final allusion to his unfortunate collision with General Jackson, in these touching words:

"His [Jackson's] temper was placable, as well as irascible, and his reconciliations were cordial and sincere. Of that, my own case was a signal instance. After a deadly feud, I became his confidential adviser; was offered the highest marks of his favor, and received from his dying bed a message of friendship, dictated when life was departing, and when he would have to pause for breath."

"To err is human; to forgive, divine."

CHAPTER XV.

MASSACRE AT FORT MIMS—THE CREEK WAR—GENERAL JACKSON TAKES COMMAND.

For many days after the affray with the Bentons, General Jackson lay in his room at the Nashville Inn seemingly at the point of death. At the end of the second week he could scarcely lift his head from the pillow, and the wounds in his shoulder were only beginning to heal. No one supposed that he could serve again in the field during the war. Indeed, it was not thought there would be any particular occasion for his services in that part of the country, but that proved to be a great mistake.

Through the eloquence and artifice of Tecumseh, the most warlike of the tribes which then occupied Florida, Georgia and Alabama, had ranged themselves on the side of the British, who directed their movements from Pensacola, with the assistance and cordial sympathy of the Spanish governor of Florida. Let these facts be remembered; and let it not be forgotten that the horrible massacre at Fort Mims, which began the Creek War, was the direct result of British and Spanish efforts to strike terror to the hearts of American settlers by means of Indian atrocities.

Fort Mims, on Lake Tensaw, in Southern Alabama, was merely a log stockade, an acre or two in extent, which Samuel Mims, an old resident of the Indian country, had hastily erected on the first vague alarm of an Indian rising. According to frontier custom, in time of danger, the inhabitants of the country far and near poured into the stockade to the number of more than five hundred, of whom one hundred were women and children. Each family, or group of families, built its log-hut within the inclosure, and all awaited the onset of the Indians. As time passed and no Indians appeared, the people, as usual in such cases, grew careless and incredulous of danger. Major Beasley, the commander of the garrison, did not believe the Indians had any intention of attacking the fort, and all the officers shared his incredulity. Discipline was relaxed; precautions against surprise were disregarded; the inmates of the stockade gave themselves up to amusement and jollity.

On August 29 (1813), two negro slaves, who had been stationed to watch cattle a few miles distant, rushed, breathless, into the fort and said they had seen a band of painted Indians lurking in the woods. A party was sent out to reconnoiter, but found no trace of Indians. The negroes were sentenced to be whipped for giving a false alarm, and one of them was punished. The owner of the other believed his slave had told the truth and objected to his being whipped; whereupon the commandant ordered him and his family to leave the fort, which they fortunately did. This fatuous hallucination was on the eve of being dispelled. On the very next morning (August 30), a thousand Creek warriors, under the command of their most renowned chief, the half-breed Weathersford, lay in ambush within striking distance of Fort Mims, awaiting their chieftain's signal to attack. Precisely at noon, when the drums of the garrison beat for dinner, the gates being wide open, and all the men unarmed strolling to their several quarters for the mid-day meal, Weathersford gave the signal, and the savages rose from their ambush and rushed upon the inclosure. Then arose the terrible cry, so often heard in those days on the exposed frontiers, "*Indians!*" "*Indians!*" The thousand Creeks came on like a tempest of destruction. Within the stockade there was a rush of women and children to the log-huts and of men to the gates and the port-holes. Major Beasley, brave soldier that he was, was one of the first to reach the main gate, but he was too late to close it. The savages dashed forward, struck down the commander, and ran over his body into the fort. The situation was appalling; but the garrison was composed of brave men, and they behaved as brave men should in circumstances so terrible. They made a heroic defense of more than five hours, and would have beaten off the foe, if the Indians had not succeeded in setting fire to the stockade and its cluster of cabins. In a few minutes after the conflagration burst out, further defense was impossible, and then a hideous massacre began, which was too horrible for detailed description.

When the sun set on that August evening, of the five hundred and fifty-three persons who were living in the stockade in the morning, all so incredulous of danger from their savage foes, four hundred lay dead upon the ground, scalped and mangled. Not one white woman nor one white child escaped. Weathersford tried to save the women and children, but his warriors encircled him with uplifted tomahawks and he was forced to let them glut their vengeance to the full. The few white men who by desperate powers broke away, wandered for days in the wilderness and reached places of refuge almost starved. One faithful negro woman, who had received a bullet in her breast, seized a canoe on Lake Tensaw, in which she paddled fifteen miles, and bore the first news of the massacre to Governor Claiborne of Louisiana.

In this terrible way began the Creek War of 1813. The massacre occurred at the time when it could do the greatest amount of harm, when the magnificent crops of that fertile land were nearly ready for the harvest. Every plantation was abandoned in the belt of country between Tennessee and the Gulf of Mexico, and all the white inhabitants sought safety in forts and stockades.

Fort Mims was about four hundred miles distant from Nashville, and the dreadful tidings reached the village in eighteen days. There could be no question in Nashville as to what was to be done. Every out-lying settlement in Tennessee was in peril, and Nashville was never known to lose its head in such a crisis. A public meeting was immediately called. The man who should have taken the lead in that meeting was lying half dead in his room, within hearing of the speakers' voices. No one supposed it would be possible for him to enter the field against the Indians, and the universal conviction of his helplessness produced a sad and depressing effect. A committee was appointed, of which Colonel Coffee was a member, to confer with

Governor Blount and General Jackson; after which the meeting adjourned to reassemble on the following day, which was Sunday.

The committee, to the great surprise and the still greater joy of its members, found that General Jackson by no means regarded himself as a non-combatant. Shot almost to death as he had been, with his wounds still festering, and so weak he could hardly raise his hand to his head or his head from his pillow, that unparalleled character of his asserted itself—that character which Emerson defines as "*the impossibility of being displaced or overset.*" The terrible news from Alabama did not dismay him. It gave him new life; it brought healing to his wounds; it augmented his strength; and he took it entirely as a matter of course that he should have command of the troops and lead them against the savage enemy who had disturbed or menaced the peace of Tennessee for twenty years.

The committee reported on Sunday morning that the governor was in favor of calling out the entire strength of the State against the Creeks. The committee regretted what they called "the present temporary indisposition of our brave and patriotic General Jackson;" but added that there was no doubt of his being able to command the freemen of Tennessee by the time they could assemble at the rendezvous.

The Legislature empowered the governor to put four thousand men into the field, and besides guaranteeing their pay and subsistence, voted three hundred thousand dollars for the first expenses. Fayetteville, eighty miles south of Nashville, was appointed as the place of rendezvous, and October 4th as the day. The fourth of October would be exactly a month from the day when General Jackson received his wounds. Prostrate as he was, he was superior, in such an emergency, to any dozen other men in the State. He at once assumed control of the campaign, and, as usual with him, he began by issuing an address to the volunteers.

"I regret," said he, "that indisposition, which from present appearances is not likely to continue long, may prevent me from leading the van; but I indulge the grateful hope of sharing with you the dangers and glory of prostrating those hell-hounds who are capable of such barbarities."

He did not precisely lead the van. Nine days after the arrival of the news of the massacre, he dispatched Colonel Coffee, with five hundred mounted men, to Huntsville, in Alabama, to give assurance to the frontier of coming protection. Every village through which Colonel Coffee passed increased his force, and on the fourth of October he crossed the Alabama line with thirteen hundred mounted men, every man riding his own horse and carrying his own weapons. And still the men kept coming in. "Volunteers," as he wrote back to his commanding officer, "are flocking in every hour."

The day soon came when the commanding general himself had to move toward the rendezvous. He could not yet mount a horse without powerful assistance. His left arm was closely bound and in a sling. He was unable, therefore, to put it in a coat-sleeve, and during the whole period of his military service, he could not carry an epaulet on his left shoulder. In point of flesh, he was the merest shadow of a man. His stomach would retain so little food that he was in danger of dying from inanition. His wounds were so sensitive that the least wrench or jar afflicted him with agony. But his dauntless spirit was unimpaired. He was sustained during the agonizing journey of nearly ninety miles by that invincible determination and fortitude of his, in which he seems to have excelled all men known to history. Several times during his first two days' ride, members of his staff had to take him aside and sponge him from head to foot with whiskey.

Weak and wounded as he was, he was ahead of most of his troops, for he reached Fayetteville on the seventh of October, to discover that less than half of the men ordered to gather there had arrived. He received, however, favorable news from Colonel Coffee, who was thirty miles nearer the seat of war.

It had been expected that the Indians, aided by the British, would capture Mobile; but the Spanish governor of Florida, who claimed that Mobile belonged to Spain, and who expected that it would be restored to that power, did not wish to have the place destroyed. For this reason Mobile was spared, and the Indians were turned northward for the purpose of devastating the country clear to the Ohio. Hence, Colonel Coffee (who only knew what was going on, without having the slightest idea of the cause) was able to inform his commander that the Indians, instead of attacking Mobile, as was expected, were making their way northward toward the settlements of Tennessee. , This was delightful news to the sick and grim Old Hickory. He replied that he was glad to learn that the Creeks were going to save him the pain of traveling. "I must not be outdone in politeness," he added, "and will, therefore, endeavor to meet them on the middle ground."

A week was passed at Fayetteville completing the preparations for an advance, the general daily gaining a little in health and strength. Then, at one o'clock, on the eleventh of October, a dispatch was received from Colonel Coffee, who was still posted at Huntsville, saying that the Indians were approaching him. The order was given instantly to prepare to march. Before three o'clock the troops started, and reached Huntsville at eight o'clock the same evening—six miles an hour for five hours, incredible as it may seem. But this is a positive statement of a dispatch written in General Jackson's name; and it must be remembered that the troops were frontiersmen and the very flower of the population. The alarm proved to be a false one, but the march united the army thirty-two miles nearer the scene of action.

And now began the serious difficulty of this eight months' struggle in the wilderness. When General Jackson joined his forces to those of Colonel Coffee, and pitched his camp on a bluff of the Tennessee river, he was a hundred and fifty miles from any adequate supply of provisions. He had with him twenty-five hundred men and thirteen hundred horses, a force that requires for a week's subsistence two hundred barrels of flour, twenty tons of meat, sixty tons of provender and many wagon-loads of miscellaneous stores. Already Colonel Coffee, in his eight days' advance movement, had swept the surrounding country of the supplies it could furnish. On this bend of the Tennessee, the government contractor had engaged to deliver a thousand barrels of flour, a week before, with a proportionate supply of meat, and he had done all that in him lay to keep his word. But his flour and his meat were on a bend of the Tennessee, three hundred miles above, where the flat-boats, in the low tide of water then prevailing, would not float.

It was in meeting such difficulties as these, even more than in actual conflict, where he was unmatchable, that Andrew Jackson showed his extraordinary powers—powers never surpassed and only equaled by those of Cæsar. With calmness and rapidity he set to work to procure the indispensable provisions. He sent his trusty quartermaster, Major W. B. Lewis, to Nashville, to stay there and take charge of the vital business of supplying his army. He sent Colonel Coffee and seven hundred mounted men on a foraging expedition, while he kept the infantry drilling from morning to night. He wrote burning letters to men in East Tennessee, to the Governor of Tennessee, to the Governor of Georgia, to all the Indian agents among the friendly tribes, to friendly Indian chiefs, to the general in command at New Orleans, to a great number of friends in various parts of his own State, saying to all of them in substance, that there was no obstacle in the way of his annihilating the Creek power, except the lack of a steady supply of provisions for about six weeks.

He kept his secretary, Major John Reid, writing and copying the whole week.

"There is an enemy," the general wrote, by his secretary's hand, "whom I dread much more than I do the hostile Creeks—I mean the meagre monster *Famine*. I shall leave this encampment in the morning direct for the Ten Islands, and yet I have not on hand two days' supply of bread-stuffs."

At the last moment his meagre store was increased, by Colonel Coffee's raid, to a sufficiency for about four days. He marched, therefore, at the time appointed, having first delivered to the troops an address as well calculated to inspire prudence as courage. He called to their minds the Indian mode of fighting, and urged them not to be deceived by their arts, nor alarmed by their ill-sustained attacks. He urged them to be vigilant, and yet not to be terrified by shadows. "Our soldiers," he said, "will lie with their arms in their hands, and the moment an alarm is given they will move to their respective positions, without noise and without confusion." The camp was then broken up, and he directed his course toward the heart of the enemy's country, relying upon raids and victory, and upon them alone, for food enough to keep his men alive.

He was running a great risk, which he felt more acutely than any man of his command. Rash and impetuous as he sometimes seemed, he was in reality a very prudent person. It was instinctive with him to be sure of his ground before taking an irretrievable step. On this occasion he was not sure of his ground, and he made a choice of evils. He instinctively knew, as has already been said, what philosophers have stated with much verbosity, that the highest discretion does not consist so much in evading danger as in meeting it with skill and resolution. In the present terrible exigency he thought that a bold advance was better than a retreat, which might have brought a fearful disaster upon the southern counties of Tennessee. In two days, his corn being nearly all gone, he halted for a day while a raid of two hundred men went in quest of a supply, and brought in a considerable amount, besides twenty-nine Indian prisoners, the late owners of the corn.

Cheered by this success, he kept on his way for a week, and reached the river Coosa. Here certain news reached him of the presence of a large Indian force at Tallushatches, thirteen miles distant. At daybreak the next morning, with a thousand mounted men and some friendly Indians, Colonel Coffee was encircling that Indian camp and preparing for an assault upon it, the horses having been left a safe distance in the rear. The Creeks were completely surprised, but they rallied and fought as long as one Indian remained alive; or, to use the language of Colonel Coffee, "they fought as long as one existed. * * * Not one of the warriors escaped to carry the news—a circumstance unknown heretofore."

Two hundred Indians were killed, and eighty-four women and children taken prisoners. Five white men were killed, and forty-one wounded, none mortally. The Indian captives were taken to the settlements and treated kindly; General Jackson himself adopting one of the boys, whom he reared in his family and apprenticed to the trade of harness maker.

If Indians had been all that General Jackson had had to contend with, he would speedily have vanquished them, but that foe that was more to be dreaded than savages, was close upon him.

CHAPTER XVI.

GENERAL JACKSON'S DESPERATE FIGHT AGAINST FAMINE—THE INDIANS CRUSHED—JACKSON MADE A MAJOR-GENERAL IN THE REGULAR ARMY.

Four days after Colonel Coffee's battle at Tallushatches, during which time the troops had been erecting a fortification or depot which was named Fort Strother, it was General Jackson's turn to encounter the Indians. News came that a camp of a hundred and fifty friendly Creeks, thirty miles down the Coosa, at a place called Talladega, had been suddenly surrounded by a thousand hostile Indians, cut off from their supply of water, and so closely hemmed in that escape was impossible. One wily Indian chief, dressed in the skin of a large hog, made his way through the hostile lines, and came into camp, twenty-four hours later, breathless and exhausted, to tell his story to General Jackson. It was a crucial moment for the general, for his army was close to starvation, and he was again obliged to choose one of two perilous and possibly fatal risks. Again his courage and his instinctive genius for the performance of heroic and desperate deeds were equal to the terrible emergency, and again he decided to advance.

Without any certainty of being able to subsist his troops, and leaving his sick behind him with four days' supply of food, he hastened forward with all his available force, and promptly arrived where his men could hear the exultant Creeks howling around their expected prey. Adopting the familiar Indian tactics of surrounding the enemy, the Tennesseeans closed upon them. After a short but most decisive battle, the Indians fled, leaving two hundred of the flower of their nation dead upon the field. Colonel Coffee and his horsemen pursued them four miles, "killing and wounding as they ran" two hundred and ninety-nine in all. "Very few got clear without a wound," adds Coffee. Jackson lost fifteen men killed, and eighty-six wounded, most of them slightly with arrows.

The joy of the rescued Creeks, who had been expecting an assault that very day, was indescribable, for they knew nothing of Jackson's approach until the battle began. As soon as they had satisfied their raging thirst, they gathered round the commanding general, testifying their gratitude by expressive gestures and joyful cries. The little corn which they had left, the general bought and distributed among his hungry men and hungrier horses, that had begun this march of thirty-two miles with only one day's supply of food.

There was no time to be lost, if they meant to escape starvation. The dead being decently buried and the wounded placed in litters, the army marched back to Fort Strother, where the sick had been left. General Jackson had fully expected, and with reason, that an abundant supply of food would reach the fort in his absence. Not an ounce had arrived, and the little which he had left behind him was nearly all consumed, even his own private stores, which he had told the surgeons to draw upon if necessary for the comfort of the sick and wounded men. All had been consumed except a few pounds of biscuits, which he immediately caused to be distributed to the most needy applicants. Major Reid reports that the general tried to make a jest of his acute disappointment. He and his staff went to the slaughtering-place and selected from the refuse a quantity of tripe for their supper. A few starving cattle were still left, upon which the men subsisted for a few days, the general and his staff eating nothing but tripe without seasoning of any kind. In these distressing circumstances, General Jackson did not omit to send a polite message to the ladies of East Tennessee, that their colors had been borne in the thickest of the fight, tied around the person of Captain Deaderich.

"In return," he wrote, "I send you a stand of colors (although not of such elegant stuff or magnificent needlework) taken by one of the volunteers, which I beg you to present to them as the only mark of gratitude the volunteers have it in their power to make. With his own hand he slayed the bearer."

And now began General Jackson's long contest with Famine—an enemy, as he said, far more formidable than the Creeks. He struggled with it for ten terrible weeks, during which he could make no effective movement against the foe, whom he could have totally destroyed in ten days if he had had an adequate supply of provisions. Sometimes his army was reduced to extreme destitution, when a trifling supply would alleviate the situation for a few days. It cannot be justly said that the scarcity was due to the fault of any man, but wholly to natural obstacles—the wilderness, the distance and the wet season. More than once there was a formidable mutiny of the idle troops, which the general met with a happy blending of persuasion, tact and firmness.

His force consisted partly of militia and partly of volunteers, between whom there was some degree of rivalry and jealousy. The militia having resolved to start for home at a certain set time, General Jackson, learning their intention, stationed the volunteers, early on the morning the militia were to start, across the road along which they would have to march, and took his place at the head of the force. The militia, finding the lion-like general, backed by the volunteers, barring their way, quietly retired to their quarters. Shortly afterward, the volunteers resolved to abandon the camp and go home. Then the general called on the militia to help him block the game of the volunteers, which they did with a relish. Finally both militia and volunteers became incurably infected with the spirit of discontent and mutiny, and terrible scenes occurred.

On one occasion, when a large body of troops had got ready to set out on their homeward march, General Jackson seized a musket, and placing himself in their front, swore "by the Eternal" that the first man who took a step in advance should die. It is said that his countenance, on such an occasion, appalled the most courageous man. There was in it the majesty of a god, the ferocity of a tiger, the

determination of fixed fate. Every lineament was stamped with invincible power, and his eyes blazed with a fire that no other eyes could look upon without blenching. The mutinous soldiers, confronted by such a terrible apparition, hesitated, wavered, retired. It was afterward discovered that the musket which the general had seized for the occasion was so damaged it could not be fired. But it was the man, not the musket, that the mutineers feared.

Force was not the only means used by General Jackson to keep the troops in the field. He addressed to them the most passionate entreaties. "Wagons are on the way," he once said to them; "a large number of beeves are in the neighborhood and detachments are out to bring them in. If supplies do not arrive in two days, we will all march back together."

If he had said three days he might have kept the troops, but unfortunately he had miscalculated by four-and-twenty hours. At the end of the second day, when no provisions had arrived, he was obliged to fulfill his promise. "If only two men will remain with me," he passionately declared, "I will never abandon the post." One hundred and nine men were willing to remain. He left them in charge of Fort Strother, and himself marched northward with the rest of the troops, on the explicit understanding that, as soon as they had satisfied their hunger and procured supplies, they would return to Fort Strother and march upon the foe. They met the provision train the next day and satisfied their hunger; but the mania to return home was not satisfied, nor could it be overcome. Terrible scenes took place between the general and the troops, who appeared to be held to their duty only by the force of his invincible will and the irresistible domination of his courage and character. The soldiers marched southward, but with discontented minds, and there was still a long contest before General Jackson deemed it best to exchange these dissatisfied troops for new regiments from Tennessee.

And now still greater discouragements arose. The men who returned home, in order to justify their abandonment of their general, gave such doleful accounts of the situation, and such harrowing descriptions of the hardships of the service, as appalled their fellow-citizens and effectually checked volunteering. Even Governor Blount became discouraged, and wrote to General Jackson, advising him to give up the enterprise and return home.

And so it had come to this: the godlike courage and fortitude of one man alone stood between the Indian hordes of the South and the defenseless settlements to the north of them. And that man was physically a wreck. His wounds had not yet healed. He could not get his left arm into his coat-sleeve. For weeks he had not had sufficient food, and the little he had had was unwholesome. He was tortured by acute dyspepsia. He was afflicted with a chronic diarrhœa, accompanied by pains so acute that the only way he could obtain relief was to have a sapling partially cut and bent down so he could lean over it, with his abdomen pressing the wood and the ends of his fingers resting upon the ground. So emaciated and feeble was he, it is a wonder that he was able to sit upon his horse or even to stand upon his feet. But his indomitable soul triumphed over his wasted body. The fire of his eye was not dimmed, the majesty of his demeanor was not impaired. His fortitude was as enduring as his courage was unconquerable. That character of his —"the impossibility of being displaced or overset" —now shone forth in all its incomparable and quenchless luster.

General Jackson was not the only brave man in the army. It is not probable that there was a coward in the entire force. It was not courage but fortitude that was lacking. Fortitude is *persistent* courage—courage which is so sustained by conscience and a lofty sense of duty that it never gives up. The troops who abandoned the enterprise were brave men. If they could have got within reach of their foes, there would have been no lack of courage among them. Every man of them would have fought like a hero. But fortitude they did not possess in sufficient measure to stand the strain, and so the greater part of them abandoned their general, who at last permitted them to return to their homes. But he stayed on. Under the terrible, the seemingly hopeless circumstances in which he was placed, any other man would have hailed the advice of Governor Blount as a godsend, and under its cover would have gladly gone home. But General Jackson met it characteristically, by writing the governor such an eloquent, circumstantial, logical and convincing reply that Governor Blount's enthusiasm was reawakened, the patriotism of the people was stirred to its depths, their courage was reanimated, volunteers came forward, and when the spring opened amazing exertions were put forth to collect and transport the requisite provisions. It took many weeks for these movements to come to such a head as to relieve General Jackson. Meanwhile, in January, 1814, although he had but nine hundred undisciplined and disaffected troops, he planned a raid upon the Indians which he executed with characteristic daring and skill. On December 22nd and 24th he fought the battles of Emuckfau and Enotachopco, inflicting heavy loss on the savages. At the beginning of the battle of Enotachopco a panic occurred among the raw troops, which threatened the destruction of the army. In this terrible emergency General Jackson exhibited those heroic qualities for which he was so renowned. Major Eaton, in describing the general's conduct on that occasion, says:* "But for him everything must have gone to ruin. On him all hopes were rested. In that moment of confusion he was the rallying point even for the spirits of the brave. Firm and energetic, and at the same time perfectly self-possessed, his example and his authority alike contributed to arrest the flying and give confidence to those who maintained their ground. Cowards forgot their panic, and fronted danger, when they heard his voice and beheld his manner; and the brave would have formed round his body a rampart with their own. In the midst of showers of balls, of which he seemed unmindful, he was seen performing the duties of the subordinate officers,

* Parton I, 495.

rallying the alarmed, halting them in their flight, forming his columns, and inspiriting them by his example."

This successful raid over, the troops whose time was about to expire were sent home, and General Jackson waited weary weeks for reinforcements and provisions. At last, fresh troops began to arrive, and among them, on the sixth of February, came the Thirty-ninth regiment of United States soldiers, six hundred strong, under command of Colonel Williams. This was an important acquisition. By the end of February, the general had five thousand troops, within two days' march of Fort Strother, waiting till twenty days' rations could be accumulated, to march on the foe and strike a finishing blow. Prodigious exertions were made to hasten the transport of provisions. Over the miry forest roads of March, four barrels of flour made a heavy load for four horses. Although the general had five hundred men at work improving the last thirty miles of the road to Fort Strother, it required a whole week for a wagon train to perform one journey of sixty-four miles; and not one wagon brought more than sixteen hundred pounds of food. All the sick and disabled men were sent home, and the teamsters were forbidden to convey anything not strictly indispensable; not even whiskey, which was then generally considered indispensable to men in the field. There was such a weeding out of non-combatants that there was only one man left in camp who could beat the ordinary calls on the drum, and this one drummer performed the whole duty.

The most inflexible discipline was enforced. On March 14, 1814, John Wood was shot for insubordination and assault upon an officer. This severity had a happy effect on the army, but years afterwards, during his presidential campaigns, Jackson was fiercely assailed for it. But as Professor Sumner* says, "party newspapers during a presidential campaign are not a fair court of appeal to review the acts which a military commander in the field may think necessary to maintain discipline. Jackson showed in this case that he was not afraid to do his duty, and that he would not sacrifice the public service to curry popularity."

At length, about the middle of March, 1814, after six weeks of the most intense exertion, the supplies were gathered at Fort Strother, and an advance movement became possible.

Fifty-five miles to the southward, the Creeks had assembled nearly the whole of the effective warriors of their tribe, with their women and children. It was on a bend of the Tallapoosa, called Tohopeka, "The Horse-shoe," from its shape. It contained about a hundred acres of land, mostly covered with the primeval woods. Across the neck of this bend the Indians had built a log breast-work of great strength, pierced with two rows of port-holes. The construction of this breast-work showed that the savages had had the aid of soldiers accustomed to build such fortifications. At the bottom of the peninsula, near the river, were their wigwams, and the shore was fringed with a great number of canoes.

* Sumner's life of Jackson, 35.

The Indians had had plenty of time to complete this fortification, and with the aid of the British they had made it strong. It was defended by something less than a thousand warriors, and in the wigwam village there were about three hundred women and children.

It required eleven days of intense exertion for Jackson's army of two thousand men to march the fifty-five miles of pathless wilderness which lay between Fort Strother and the Horse-shoe Bend. But when he had reached the place, he perceived at the first glance that the Indians had merely, as he said in one of his letters, "penned themselves in for destruction." He first sent General Coffee to cross the river two miles away and take a position opposite the line of canoes, to prevent the escape of the Indians. This, Coffee promptly did, and sent his swimmers over, who cut the canoes loose and brought them across the river. Colonel Coffee used them to send over a number of troops to attack the savages in the rear. Thus the ferocious Creeks were assailed in front by General Jackson and behind by Coffee, and the men seconded their efforts with the most splendid gallantry.

After the first heroic assault the battle resolved itself into a long, slow massacre, which lasted from two o'clock in the afternoon until dark. As in the former battles so in this, not one Indian asked for quarter, nor would accept his life, because they had been assured by their prophets that if spared they would be subjected to a death of torment. Upon counting the dead, five hundred and fifty-seven bodies of the red men were found within the peninsula, two hundred more, it was thought, lay at the bottom of the river, and there were many in the woods who had perished of their wounds while attempting to escape. Jackson's loss was fifty-five killed and one hundred and forty-six wounded, of whom more than half were friendly Indians. Ensign Houston, afterwards senator from Texas, lay within the bend, after the battle, with two balls in his shoulder and fearful wounds in his thigh.

In this battle the power of the Creeks was broken forever. The leading chiefs all surrendered. Weathersford himself, mounted on his matchless gray horse, known far and near for its speed and endurance, rode into General Jackson's camp and gave himself up. He was tall, straight, fearless and majestic, and was the greatest Indian warrior of his time, as well as the most chivalric and romantic. In truth, he was more like a knight of olden time than a savage of his period. He commanded at the capture of Fort Mims, and although he sought, as has been stated, to save the white women and children from destruction, he got no credit for his humanity and was held responsible for the whole horrible massacre. Owing to the rancorous hatred of him by the entire white population of the South, it was a hundred chances to one that if he came into their power he would be slain on sight. Yet, for the sake of the suffering women and children of his tribe, he boldly rode to the door of General Jackson's tent and surrendered himself unconditionally. He was immediately surrounded by officers and soldiers who cried: "Kill him! Kill him!" General Jackson commanded silence, and, in his emphatic way, said: "Any man who would kill as brave a man as this would rob the dead!" He then invited the chief into his tent, and took him under his protection.

Weathersford induced the remnant of the Creeks to accept the terms of peace which General Jackson proffered, although one of the conditions was that half their lands should be ceded to the government of the United States.

The victorious general and his troops enjoyed a triumphal reception at Nashville, in which the entire population took part; and soon after, on May 31, 1814, *The National Intelligencer*, of Washington, contained the following announcement:

ANDREW JACKSON, *of Tennessee, is appointed Major-General in the Army of the United States, vice* WILLIAM HENRY HARRISON, *resigned.*"

Words cannot express the gratification which this appointment gave to General Jackson.

CHAPTER XVII.

THE NEW ORLEANS CAMPAIGN—FORMIDABLENESS OF THE BRITISH EXPEDITION AGAINST NEW ORLEANS—THE DEFENSELESS CONDITION OF THE CITY.

As soon as General Jackson's acceptance of a major-generalship in the United States army reached Washington, he was assigned to the command of "the Southern divison of the army," as it was called, although there were but three half-filled regiments in the "division." He was ordered to stop on his way to the Southern coast, at Fort Jackson, long enough to conclude a treaty with the Creeks. After a rest of only three weeks, he started on the enterprise which, after many trials, disappointments and harrowing mortifications, was to end in the almost incredible triumph at New Orleans.

After concluding the treaty with the Creeks, on the 9th day of August, 1814, General Jackson turned his attention to the proceedings of the British at Mobile, Alabama, and Pensacola, Florida. Mobile was in possession of the Americans; Pensacola, of the Spaniards. A British fleet had anchored in the bay of Pensacola; a British force had taken up its residence in the town. From this vantage-ground the British were able to send emissaries among the Indians with gifts and promises, which induced hundreds of the savages to join the invaders and threatened devastation to the southern country and massacre to the inhabitants. General Jackson requested authority from Washington to invade the Spanish territory and drive the British from Pensacola. The administration complied with his request, and the Secretary of War sent him the requisite order, but owing to some fatality, it did not reach him for six months, when the war was ended.

It is not surprising that General Jackson was left without orders or aid from Washington. That city was captured on August 24, 1814, by the British under General Ross; the President and his Cabinet fled for safety beyond the reach of pursuit; and the Government was utterly demoralized. It was more than a month before President Madison recovered from the nervous shock which was occasioned by the circumstances of his flight.

The non-receipt of orders from Washington left General Jackson in a sore dilemma. Immediate action, involving not only critical military operations but still more critical diplomatic considerations, was imperative. If he could not obtain orders from the government, he must either content himself with fatal delay or else take the responsibility of acting without orders. He took the responsibility and acted. Divining that the British were going to attack Mobile, he hastened thither. The British did attack Mobile, or rather Fort Bowyer, situated on Mobile Point, thirty miles down the bay. As the safety of the town depended upon the ability of the garrison in Fort Bowyer to beat off the British fleet and repel the attack of any land force that should be sent against the fort, General Jackson did everything in his power to meet the enemy successfully at that point. The attack was made on the 15th of September, 1814, and was gallantly repulsed by Major Lawrence, to whom the defense of the fort had been intrusted. This defeat of the British ruined their prestige with the Indians, who at once began to desert them and sought to make peace with the terrible Jackson. This victory also gave the inhabitants of the Gulf States confidence in General Jackson, and in their ability, under his invincible leadership, to defend their homes against their previously dreaded foes.

General Jackson was resolved, as he said, "to rout the British out of Pensacola." After prodigious exertions, on the first of November, Jackson had assembled a force of about four thousand troops, consisting of General Coffee's little army of twenty-eight hundred Tennesseeans, the garrison of Mobile, a body of mounted Mississippians, and a small number of Creek Indians. With this force he made an impetuous but wary dash upon Pensacola, "routed out the British," brought the Spanish governor to terms, and made him his steadfast and admiring friend. He then hastened back to Mobile. He supposed that the British forces routed out of Pensacola, and the British fleet driven from Pensacola Bay, would renew the attack on Mobile. He waited ten days for them, and then learned that the British land force and their Indian allies, under the command of Colonel Nichols, had been landed by the fleet at Appalachicola, where they were hard at work fortifying their position. He at once sent a body of troops and friendly Creeks, under Major Blue, against them. After some hard fighting, the Indians were driven into the interior of Florida, and Colonel Nichols was forced to abandon the peninsula.

Mr. Adams (see chapter 12, Vol. viii of his history) seeks to undervalue and belittle this energetic and successful campaign against the British and Indians in Florida. He assumes, with rare military opacity, that the campaign was all a mistake; that General Jackson should have left the British and Indians in peace and gone directly to New Orleans. Such a course would have been equivalent to Alexander's leaving Egypt and Syria unconquered before he entered upon his conquest of Asia. But Alexander knew better than to commit such an act of folly, and so did General Jackson. Professor Sumner agrees with Alexander and Jackson. He says: *

"This energetic action against Pensacola, which a timid commander would have hesitated to take, although the propriety of it could not be seriously questioned, was the second great step in the war in the Southwest. If the Creeks had not been subdued, Mobile could not have been defended. If Pensacola had not been captured, New Orleans could not have been defended three months later."

General Jackson, having pacificated Florida and made everything secure in that quarter, was now able to devote all his energies to the defense of New Orleans. Leaving Mobile in command of General Winchester of the regular army, and Fort Bowyer

* Sumner's Life of Jackson, 38.

in command of its defender, Major Lawrence, he ordered General Coffee to move by easy marches toward New Orleans, and on the 22d of November, accompanied only by his staff, he himself started for that city. The roads were in a frightful condition; the distance was one hundred and seventy miles. The little party rode leisurely, averaging seventeen miles a day; and on the 2d of December, General Jackson and his staff arrived within a few miles of New Orleans, where they made a brief halt for breakfast.

If General Jackson, on the second day of his journey from Mobile to New Orleans (November 24, 1814), had been aware of the magnificent naval spectacle which was visible on that day in Negril Bay, at the western end of the island of Jamaica, twelve hundred miles distant from New Orleans, it might have caused him to accelerate his pace. At that time and place, the British expedition against New Orleans, which was to sail the next day (November 25), had a grand final review. It seems as though the magnitude of this expedition was never realized by the American people. It was so utterly defeated by General Jackson and his small force of militia and volunteers, that the public mind has never seemed able to grasp its magnitude and its power. The fleet comprised forty-eight armed vessels, many of them of the most formidable character. Some of the ships carried eighty guns; others carried seventy-four; others carried fifty, forty, thirty-eight guns. In addition to these men-of-war, there were bomb vessels and transports in great numbers. The naval officers in command were veterans of great skill and experience, some of whom had achieved renown. Admiral A. J. Cochrane commanded the fleet. Among the captains was Sir Thomas Masterman Hardy—the gallant Hardy, "Nelson's Hardy," as he was called, who commanded the *Victory*, Lord Nelson's flagship at Trafalgar, and to whom the dying but victorious hero said: "Kiss me, Hardy; I am content." Ten thousand troops were on board the vessels, and about the same number of sailors and marines. Among the troops were some of the most renowned regiments in the British army; all of them were thoroughly brave and disciplined soldiers, and they were commanded by officers equal to any in the world.

On the 25th of November, 1814, this vast and formidable expedition set sail for New Orleans. Not a man in it had the slightest doubt of its success: officers and men were alike exhilarated as with the foretaste of assured victory, and the British government shared their confidence. Favorites of the government had been appointed to fill the civil offices in Louisiana. The British collector of the port of New Orleans and his five handsome daughters were on board one of the vessels; "the collector," as a facetious writer of the day said, "hungry for the honors and the spoils of office, and the daughters eager for Creole husbands. Thus happily were blended business and romance, masculine avarice and feminine tenderness, with military ardor and ambition for fame, in this remarkable expedition, which longed for the solace of the 'beauty and booty' it expected to find, to seize, and to enjoy in New Orleans."

After taking possession of New Orleans, the British forces, under the command of Sir Edward Pakenham, the Duke of Wellington's brother-in-law, and one of his most trusted subordinates, were to ascend the Mississippi, reducing the country to British domination as they went, until they met a co-operating British force launched from Canada and coming down the Mississippi, when the two armies were to be united and hold the whole western portion of the country, or as much of it as they might choose to hold, in subjection to the British crown.

Of the approach of this powerful expedition the government of the United States, the people of New Orleans and General Jackson, were entirely ignorant. But General Jackson was thoroughly convinced that some British force was coming from somewhere to attack New Orleans. So was Edward Livingston, and a few other American patriots. Of the inhabitants of New Orleans, then numbering about twenty thousand, the majority were of foreign blood—French and Spanish. The Americans, about eight thousand in number, were such people as are usually found in remote frontier localities. Some of them were thoroughly honorable men; others were of that class who are honorable when honor and honesty are the fashion; and many belonged to the class of adventurers and desperadoes who, being beyond the pale of the law, are naturally hostile to the government which enforces the law.

This heterogeneous population was at variance. The French and the Spaniards were distrustful of one another and of the Americans; the Americans hated and distrusted the people of foreign blood, and had bitter feuds among themselves. The governor and the legislature were at loggerheads, and whatever one party proposed the other opposed. As the people did not wish to be put to the trouble and expense of defending the city, they refused to believe that the city was in danger. But their sense of security received a severe shock by revelations made to the governor by Jean Lafitte, a noted smuggler, who was at the head of a colony of smugglers and pirates on the bay of Barataria, formed by the island of Grand Terre, forty miles south of New Orleans. This was the Lafitte who has figured in countless stories and novels as "Lafitte, the Pirate," or "Lafitte the Pirate of the Gulf." As a matter of fact, he was never at sea but twice in his life; once when he came from France, his native country, to Louisiana, and again when he attempted to return, on which occasion he was drowned. Lafitte was a loyal citizen, though not a law abiding one; and when the British, under the mistaken notion that he was a pirate of great resources and power, sought to bribe him to enter their service and co-operate with an approaching British expedition in the conquest of Louisiana, he pretended to listen favorably to their proposals, but at once sent their written offers to Governor Claiborne, and also to a member of the Louisiana Legislature. The governor immediately laid the documents before a council of officers of the army, navy and militia. The council refused to believe in the genuineness of the documents, and came to the conclusion that Jean Lafitte was simply intriguing to get his brother Dominique out of the calaboose, where he was confined for certain serious "irregularities." Governor Claiborne, General Villeré, of the militia, and Edward Livingston, the leading spirits among the Americans, did not coincide in the opinion of the council. They believed that the documents were genuine, that Jean Lafitte told the truth, and that New Orleans was menaced by serious danger. Lafitte's letter to the governor and the accompanying British documents were published broadside in the New Orleans newspapers, both English and French, and occasioned a profound sensation. A public meeting was called, fiery speeches were made, committees were appointed, and the entire population was aroused to action.

But bickering, jealousy and strife continued. There was no one in whom the people could or would trust sufficiently to accept him as their leader and obey his orders. Owing to this deplorable state of affairs, which grew worse and worse for many weeks, the efforts to prepare the city for defense were neutralized, and it looked as though the approaching British would be justified in their belief that New Orleans would fall an easy prey to their powerful armament. And so it would, had not the one man able to defend the city come to its rescue.

CHAPTER XVIII.

EFFECT OF GENERAL JACKSON'S ARRIVAL AT NEW ORLEANS—PROCLAMATION OF MARTIAL LAW.

Yes, the one man in all the world who, under the circumstances, could defend New Orleans, was close at hand. He came at the very nick of time; at the moment when faction had done its worst, and when the population was well nigh in a state of disintegration. He came bearing the spell of the national authority, and crowned with the prestige of continuous victory over enemies savage and civilized.

On the morning of December 2, 1814, as stated in the previous chapter, General Jackson, with his staff of six worn and travel-stained officers, was within an hour's ride of New Orleans. One who saw them on the road describes the chief of the little party as tall, gaunt and yellow, but very erect on his horse, with a countenance expressive of energy and decision, and a presence which inspired confidence and showed him to be a born leader of men.

The toilsome ride of seventeen days was not favorable to his malady, which required, above all things, rest and genial food. The whole party had almost worn out their clothes in hard service. The general had on a small leather cap, a short blue cloak, and high dragoon boots, all much discolored and worn. Nevertheless, even the passers-by on the lonely road, long expectant of his arrival, did not need to be informed, when they saw him, that General Jackson had come.

The party stopped for breakfast seven miles from the city, at the villa of J. K. Smith, a merchant of wealth and liberality. The table was covered with Creole dainties, of which, however, it was observed that the chief partook of nothing but a bowl of the exquisite hominy of the region, as white as snow and more delicate than rice. On diet similar to this, taken frequently and in small quantities, he went through the whole of this arduous and exciting campaign.

General Jackson did not linger long at the table. Looking at his watch, he reminded his companions that the day was advancing and they must be getting on. At this point they left their exhausted horses and performed the rest of the journey in carriages, alighting at the abode of Daniel Clark, who had been the first Representative of Louisiana in the Congress of the United States.

In the large drawing-room of this spacious mansion General Jackson was received by Governor Claiborne, Nicholas Girod, the Creole Mayor of New Orleans, by the military and naval officers of the vicinity, by the members of the legislature and others. Among them was his old friend and comrade, Edward Livingston, then fifty years of age and in the maturity of his powers. In a somewhat ornate address the governor welcomed the general and his staff and placed the entire resources and manhood of Louisiana at his disposal, to enable him, as he said, to become what the people of the city were already beginning to call him the Savior of New Orleans.

General Jackson made a brief reply, to the effect that he had come to defend the city, and was fully intent upon doing it. "I will drive the enemy into the sea," he quietly said, "or perish in the attempt." He called upon all the citizens to rally round him, to lay aside all differences, all prejudices of race, all party feeling, and unite as one man for one object, to save the city of New Orleans from the dishonor and spoliation of an insolent and ruthless foe.

As most of the gentlemen present understood little English, Edward Livingston, who was master of both languages, translated the general's address into French, and in doing so gave it the tone, the elegance and the epigrammatic point which are so captivating to French ears and minds. It produced a truly electric effect. Every countenance expressed relief and confidence, for there was something in the calm and resolute demeanor of the general, despite his gaunt and yellow countenance, his emaciated form and his helpless left arm, that gave assurance to them all that the man for the hour had come.

It is doubtful if there was ever a more striking illustration of the truth of Emerson's aphorism, "The hero conquers by his presence; *because his arrival changes the face of affairs*," than was given by the result of General Jackson's arrival at New Orleans. The influence of heroism, like that of sunlight, is recognized by every one who comes within its presence, without regard to condition or nationality. Frenchman, Spaniard, American; the honest citizen, the vagabond, the cut-throat—all felt the spell of the hero's presence. As a spring gushing from far up the mountain-side runs down into and fills receptacles below it with its pure waters, so General Jackson's brave, truthful, reverent, patriotic, self-reliant nature ran down into the minds and hearts of those below him in character, filled them with his own heroic spirit, and, while the spell of his influence lasted, made patriots and heroes of them all.

The reception over, General Jackson and his staff were conducted to the building, which had been selected for his headquarters, 106 Royal Street, one of the few brick houses of the city, which was standing little changed at a recent date. The flag of the United States was unfurled from a window in the third story, notifying the people that General Jackson had assumed the command. From that hour there was no more factious controversy, no heated arguments for special plans, no distrust and no divided allegiance. There was now but one plan: to assist General Jackson in defending the city; and there was no strife, except a generous emulation to give him the most prompt and efficient aid.

Major A. L. Latour, in his spirited and graphic history of the defence of New Orleans, in which he took an honorable part, says: "The energy manifested by General Jackson spread, as it were, by contagion, and communicated itself to the whole army. I shall add, that there was nothing which those who composed it did not feel themselves capable of performing, if he ordered it to be done. It was enough that he expressed a wish, or threw out the slightest intimation, and immediately a crowd of volunteers offered themselves to carry his views into execution." Truly "The hero conquers by his presence."

As soon as General Jackson had taken possession of his office, he appointed a new aide-de-camp, Edward Livingston, who served in that capacity to the end of the strife, and rendered invaluable assistance of many kinds.

To horse again. The uniformed companies of the city were drawn up on parade, awaiting review by the commanding general. These companies consisted of five or six hundred men of various equipments and costumes, merchants, lawyers, clerks and others. They made an excellent impression upon the general, who then for the first time saw something of the picturesque aspect of military life. He complimented them warmly upon their appearance and drill, and made minute inquiries as to the history and organization of the companies.

The new aide-de-camp, at the end of the review, invited the general home to dinner, an invitation which was promptly accepted. It chanced that Mrs. Livingston had invited a few ladies to dinner that day, and as Mr. Parton tells us, she received the announcement of the honor intended her with a good deal of alarm, for she knew little of General Jackson except his recent fame as a great Indian fighter.

"What shall we do with this wild general from Tennessee?" whispered the ladies to one another, as they sat awaiting his entrance. But when he came in, perfectly composed, an erect, bronzed figure, in uniform of coarse blue cloth and yellow buck-skin, his high boots flapping loosely, he seemed to the ladies the very ideal of the veteran warrior. He gave them one of those magnificent bows for which he was afterward noted, and behaved with a mingled grace and dignity that astonished the ladies as much as it delighted them. What surprised them most was "the society tone" of his conversation. He begged the ladies, as he rose to take his leave, not to give themselves the least concern about the safety of the city. "I am confident," said he, "of being able to defend it." When he was finally out of hearing, and the ladies found themselves alone, they gathered round the hostess, saying:

"Is this your backwoodsman? Why, madam, he is a prince!"

As soon as he returned to his quarters, General Jackson had a long conference with the engineers in the city, among whom was Major A. L. Latour of the regular army, afterward the competent historian of the defense. The whole Delta was carefully gone over by the aid of maps and plans. All the possible approaches were explained and considered, and the readiest way of defending each was determined upon. In the course of a few hours, the work to be done was ascertained and assigned, and measures were taken to enlist the co-operation of the whole mass of slaves who could be spared from household labor. The commanding general also laid before the conference of engineers his own simple plan of defense, which was to put every possible obstruction in the way of the enemy's approach, and to attack him instantly, wherever and in whatsoever force he might effect a landing.

The next morning, the general set out in a barge, with his staff and the engineers, to make a personal inspection of the vulnerable points on the lines. This tour lasted six days. Upon his return, he made an extensive tour of inspection around the broad bays, which are called Lake Pontchartrain and Lake Borgne, by means of which vessels of light draught can sail within nine miles of the city. When he had completed these surveys, his confidence in his ability to defend the city was considerably increased, and he had little fear of a surprise. On Lake Borgne, too shallow for large vessels, there was a fleet of six gunboats, carrying twenty-three guns and one hundred and eighty-two men, under the command of Lieutenant Ap Catesby Jones, and upon these he relied chiefly for the first news of the enemy's approach.

Let us now enumerate the troops upon which he could rely for the defense of the city. On his return from his second tour of inspection, December 14, he had under his command eight hundred regulars, newly raised, but sufficiently armed; the volunteer companies of the city, about five hundred in number; two regiments of State militia, about half armed and little acquainted with military duty; a battalion of free colored men, about four hundred in number, making a total little exceeding two thousand troops actually in the city. Anchored in the river were two vessels of war, a small schooner named the *Carolina*, and a ship the *Louisiana*, neither of them manned. Captain Patterson and a few other naval officers were at hand, rendering zealous and skillful service, and ready for any task the general might assign them. This was the force actually present in the city on the 14th of December, 1814.

General Coffee with his little army from Pensacola, had been for three or four weeks struggling along over roads nearly impassable, streams swollen beyond fording, and with forage so scarce that he feared to lose all his horses by mere starvation. Three hundred men, out of his three thousand, were sick with fever, dysentery and exhaustion, but he was moving slowly toward the Mississippi River, and reached it finally at Baton Rouge, one hundred and thirty miles above New Orleans. General Carroll also was floating down the river from Tennessee, with two thousand volunteers, and one musket for every ten of them. Happily, on the way he overtook a flat-boat load of government muskets, which enabled him to put a weapon in the hands of every soldier, and to give them a kind of drill every day, on the roofs of their flat-boats. They owed this good fortune to the intelligent and patriotic zeal of a Natchez merchant, Mr. Thomas L. Servoss, who had been to New York on business and learned something of the formidable preparations of the enemy against New Orleans. Full of a sense of the danger, he urged the captain of the flat-boat carrying the muskets to hasten along without stopping to trade at the river towns, and thus the boat reached the lower Mississippi in time to arm General Carroll's regiments.

Two thousand Kentuckians were also descending

the Mississippi, with a few rifles among them, but pitifully destitute of blankets, tents and equipage. General John Adair, indeed, informs us that all they had in the way of equipage was "a cooking kettle to every eighty men."

Such, then, were the means at General Jackson's disposal, on the 14th of December—twenty-five hundred miscellaneous and inexperienced troops in the city, four thousand more within ten days' march, six gun-boats on Lake Borgne; two armed, unmanned vessels anchored in the river; a small garrison of regular troops at Fort St. Philip, at the well-known bend of the Mississippi; another small body at a fortified post between the two lakes. Most of the able bodied men, black and white, in the Delta, were laboring to obstruct the bayous. The citizens generally, being all vigorously employed, were full of confidence and resolution.

On the 16th of December, public confidence was still further strengthened by the proclamation of martial law. This converted New Orleans into a camp and all the citizens into soldiers. Rigorous military discipline was enforced, and the entire population was brought under its iron rule. One overmastering mind now controlled everything and everybody. Every one seemed to feel the grip of the Jacksonian hand upon his shoulder. The effect was electric and universal. All timidity vanished; all discord was harmonized; all rivalry was effaced. Public confidence rose to the highest pitch. General Jackson was believed to be absolutely invincible, and this universal belief was equal to a reinforcement of many thousand men. Verily, "The hero conquers by his presence; because his arrival changes the face of affairs."

Immeasurably fortunate it was that such confidence was reposed in General Jackson, for dangers were close at hand which nothing but such confidence in the commanding general could enable the defenders of New Orleans to face unflinchingly.

CHAPTER XIX.

ARRIVAL OF THE BRITISH—CAPTURE OF THE AMERICAN GUN-BOATS ON LAKE BORGNE—PICKETS AND SENTINELS CAPTURED.

Let us now see how it has fared with the formidable expedition that was so confidently advancing to the capture of New Orleans.

On December seventh, 1814, after a prosperous sail of fifteen days, the British fleet made Ship Island, forty-five miles from General Jackson's head-quarters, and cast anchor as near the entrance of Lake Borgne as the pilots dared to venture. It had not been intended to attempt the ascent of the Mississippi River, which, indeed, without steamers, would have been impossible. The plan was to get the attacking army across Lake Borgne and Lake Pontchartrain, spacious but shallow bays, supposed by the English to be wholly undefended.

Here the agreeable part of this expedition ended. It was a picnic no more. For all hands there was nothing now but a deadly conflict with the difficulties and perils either not foreseen at all, or foreseen most imperfectly.

As the greater ships could go no farther, three days were spent in transferring the troops from the larger to the smaller vessels, with the supplies they needed for immediate use; an operation that tasked severely the resources of the fleet and the endurance of the men. At length, December thirteenth, these lighter vessels deeply laden, thirty in number, hoisted anchor and entered Lake Borgne, all hands still counting upon taking the city by surprise.

This delusion was soon dispelled. The lookouts reported six ugly-looking gun-boats lying at anchor in one of the lake passes, evidently prepared for resistance. Admiral Cochrane gave the signal for the large vessels to come to anchor and the smaller ones to chase, which was done; but Lieutenant Jones, commanding the gun-boats, hoisted sail in a leisurely way, and soon led the pursuers to a part of the lake where, one after the other, they ran aground.

It was now evident that nothing farther could be done against New Orleans until the attacking party had absolute control of Lake Borgne. Either the American gun-boats must be taken, or the expedition must seek access by another pathway. Admiral Cochrane did not hesitate a moment, but proceeded in the British method of taking the bull by the horns. He collected fifty men-of-war's boats, placed a small cannon in the bow of most of them, and called for volunteers. At daybreak the next morning, the fleet of boats, with twelve hundred men on board of them, got under way and rowed toward the gun-boats, which were then about ten miles distant. It was a calm, breathless day. Owing to the dead calm, it was impossible to make sail; so nothing remained for Lieutenant Jones but to anchor his vessels in line and await the attack of this formidable force. The gun-boats made all the resistance possible for an hour and forty minutes. Several of the English boats were sunk; others were injured and obliged to abandon the fight. After an hour's fierce exertion, a large number of the English boats succeeded in reaching and grappling the American vessels, and while the British marines kept up a rapid fire of musketry, the sailors, cutlass in hand, leaped upon the decks of the American boats and overpowered their crews by the weight of numbers.

The severest conflict was on board the vessel of Lieutenant Jones, which was somewhat larger than the rest of the American fleet. Captain Lockyer, who commanded the British, observing that it bore the pennant of the commodore, placed himself alongside and sprang on board the vessel, followed by his crew. A desperate fight ensued. The Americans, though outnumbered, fought with the traditional valor and prowess of American seamen; but the British were equally brave, and in much greater force. Captain Lockyer received several wounds; but soon he was joined by sufficient numbers to overpower Lieutenant Jones and his resolute men. This was the last of the gunboats to surrender. Captain Lockyer reported his loss to be seventeen killed and seventy-seven wounded. On the American side the loss in killed and wounded was sixty, and among the wounded were all the gun-boat commanders, except one.

The English were now masters of Lake Borgne. Their victory over the gun-boats had been so complete that not a man escaped to tell the tale. The firing had been heard, however, by inhabitants of the desolate shore, and the news had reached General Jackson in a few hours.

The British fleet again weighed anchor, hoping to sail within easy reach of New Orleans without further opposition. But before they had been many hours on the voyage, the larger ships began to run aground. One after another they stuck fast in the mud and could go no further. The troops on board of them were transferred to smaller vessels, and as these stuck in their turn, the operation of transferring the troops to still smaller vessels was repeated, until, toward the close of the day, the lightest vessel in the fleet had run aground, and New Orleans was yet forty miles distant. A portion of the soldiers were then transferred to the small boats, and the voyage was continued by means of oars. The situation now became distressing. Drenching rains poured down during the day, and at night benumbing frosts forbade sleep. Some of the negroes who yielded to drowsiness after the troops landed on Pine Island, froze to death in their sleep. After due consideration of all the circumstances environing the situation, it was determined to collect the whole army on Pine Island, preparatory to crossing over to the main land.

It would be difficult to imagine a more dismal place than this low, swampy island, with only a few acres of firm ground at one end of it. A British officer, who accompanied the expedition and wrote a history of its adventures, described Pine Island as "the abode of wild ducks and apparently the winter resort of torpid alligators." To this miserable island the British army was gradually brought, in the course of the next five days. The sufferings of the troops from fatigue, cold, wet and hunger, were well nigh unendurable, yet not a murmur or complaint was heard. From General Keane, who was then in command of the army, to the youngest drummer, all indulged in the confident hope of soon finding rest and luxury in the opulent city of New Orleans.

It seems also that some renegades from the city reached Pine Island, who assured the British officers that New Orleans was practically defenseless. The principal people, they said, had long ago abandoned the city, and those who remained would welcome the coming of the British troops. They expatiated also upon the immense wealth gathered in the town, which, in the course of a day or two, would become the easy prey of the British army.

It required five days of heroic exertion and endurance before the last of the troops reached Pine Island. Another day was spent in organizing the force into battalions and brigades, and in preparing an advanced corps of sixteen hundred men. It was not until the morning of December 22nd, that this select band of pioneers embarked once more on board the boats, now headed for a bayou leading out of Lake Pontchartrain to a point about ten miles below the city. This bayou, which was then called the Bayou de Catiline, is now known by the name of Bienvenue. The approach was exceedingly well chosen—was, perhaps, the best which that amphibious region then afforded. At midnight the fleet of boats cast anchor near the entrance of the bayou. There, a day or two before, two British spies had discovered a picket of eight white men and three mulattoes, posted by general Villeré, of the Louisiana militia, for the sole purpose of keeping a lookout for the enemy's approach. In order that the approach of the British might not be made known to General Jackson, it was necessary to capture this picket without letting one man escape; and as every man on the post was sound asleep, the operation was performed with the greatest ease. This capture accomplished, the flotilla resumed its course, and about nine o'clock landed safely, without discovering one other sign of human life, at the head of the bayou Bienvenue.

The ground now occupied by the advance corps of sixteen hundred men, was little better than a vast swamp, covered with tall reeds, and with a few trees growing along the banks of the bayou; but here it was that the troops were expected to remain until the boats could return to Pine Island and bring up the remainder of the force. But now, as we are told by the British narrators, the American renegades, who were serving them as guides, repeated their assurances that the city of New Orleans was defenseless, and that the British soldiers had but to show themselves to be joined by the great mass of the population. Moreover, the situation was extremely unpleasant, and the position incapable of defense if attacked by an enemy familiar with the region. The commanding officer, therefore, determined to advance and to work his way, with the assistance of his native guides, across the marsh to the narrow strip of cultivated land a mile wide which borders the Mississippi River.

As soon as this resolution was formed, the boats were dismissed and the advanced corps entered upon a difficult march of several hours, sometimes wading, sometimes leaping a wide ditch, sometimes obliged to halt and throw across a deep place a rough bridge. Gradually the marsh became firmer, groves of orange trees presented themselves, and finally two or three houses appeared in view. As soon as they came in sight of a house, a rush was made to surround it, capture the inmates, and so prevent an alarm. They succeeded in this vital object, except in a single instance. "One man," says a British officer, "contrived to effect his escape."

This one man was no other than young Major Gabriel Villeré, the son of General Villeré, upon whose plantation the British came to a halt. From that moment the troops became careless about their prisoners, and the British officers endeavored by covering as much ground as possible with their small force, to give a magnified idea of their number. Quickening their pace, too, they soon struck the main road leading directly to the city, only eight miles distant. Protected now, as they thought, by the Mississippi on one side, and on the other side by the marsh from which they had just emerged, they deemed it an excellent place to halt, dine and encamp for the night. They had no thought of an attack by the Americans. It had become an adage in the British armies that "The Americans never attack." The events of the war thus far had inspired the British with contempt for the American commanders. So General Keane resolved to refresh his worn-out soldiers with food and rest, and capture New Orleans at daylight the next morning.

The invaders had a merry dinner, and the afternoon was passed in repose; nevertheless, every precaution was taken against surprise, and things were so ordered that the entire force could be at once rallied to repel an attack. The evening meal was still more merry. One of the British chaplains, (the Rev. George Robert Gleig,) who wrote under the name of "The Subaltern," has placed on record a pleasing account of the manner in which he and his comrade passed the first hour of the evening.

"My friend and myself," he says, "had been supplied by our soldiers with a couple of fowls, taken from a neighboring hen-roost, and a few bottles of excellent claret borrowed from the cellar of one of the houses near. We had built ourselves a kind of a hut by piling together in a conical form a number of large stakes and broad rails torn up from one of the fences, and a bright wooden fire was blazing at the door of it. In the wantonness of triumph, too, we had lighted some six or eight wax candles, a vast quantity of which had been found in the storerooms of the chateaux hard by, and having done ample justice to our luxurious supper, we were sitting in great splendor and in high spirits."

This was very pleasant indeed, and the whole camp presented similar scenes of comfort and hilarity. However, "one man contrived to effect his escape," young Major Villeré, as before remarked. He was confined in a room of his father's house. He was in an agony of apprehension as to the fate of New Orleans, unless news of the enemy's approach could be carried to General Jackson. He was a splendid young Creole—brave, patriotic and a famous athlete. He was so surrounded by British officers and soldiers that it seemed as though any attempt to escape would certainly be fatal. Nevertheless, he resolved to make an effort to break from his captors and carry the news of their proximity to his commanding general. Suddenly he leaped through the window of the room in which he was confined, ran across the yard full of red-coats, cleared a picket fence at a bound, and made for the woods. Colonel Thornton, comprehending the consequences of his escape, shouted to the soldiers: "Catch him, or kill him!" But they neither caught nor killed him. He reached the woods, though pursued by forty or fifty of the troops. Many were his adventures during the next few hours, which in after years he loved to relate to his friends on the piazza of the very house in which he had been captured and from which he escaped. Of one of those incidents the gallant major could never speak without tears. Being closely pressed by his pursuers, he was about to climb a large live oak for the purpose of concealing himself in its branches, when his attention was attracted by a low whine at his feet. He looked down and saw his favorite setter crouched on the ground, and piteously and appealingly looking up at him in a way which expressed the dog's deathless devotion to his master. A great pang smote his heart, for he at once saw that the affectionate setter must be killed, or that he must be captured. Had it been only a question of his own personal safety, he would have spared the dog and accepted capture. But the fate of New Orleans was at stake, and to secure the city's safety the setter must die. Seizing a club, he killed the faithful dog, concealed the body, climbed the tree, and was not discovered, although his pursuers swarmed around him. They pressed on in pursuit of him, and when their voices could no longer be heard, he came down from his hiding place and continued his flight. Luckily, he overtook a friend, who was also hurrying toward the city with the news. Together they obtained a boat, rowed across the river, procured swift little creole ponies, and finally reached General Jackson's headquarters at half-past one in the afternoon, about half an hour after the British troops had come to a halt eight miles below.

CHAPTER XX.

GENERAL JACKSON LEARNS THAT THE BRITISH HAVE ARRIVED—"WE MUST FIGHT THEM TO-NIGHT!"—HIS TERRIFIC NIGHT ATTACK.

On arriving at General Jackson's headquarters, Major Villeré and his companions were at once shown into the general's presence. Major Villeré told his story, and General Jackson learned that the British were at the Villeré plantation, only eight miles from the spot where he stood, whereupon he said, with prodigious emphasis:

"By the Eternal, they shall not sleep on our soil!"

He then pointed to the sideboard, in the polite fashion of the time, took a sip of wine with them, and then turning to his staff, uttered the well known words:

"Gentlemen, the British are below. We must fight them to-night."

There spoke the hero, *the fittest man.* The triumph of the terrible New Orleans campaign was there and then made sure.

General Jackson prepared and dispatched orders to every corps in and near the city, directing them to break up their camps and march to the positions assigned them, all of which were just outside the city on the road to the Villeré plantation. He sent for Commodore Patterson of the navy, and requested him to get the little *Carolina* ready to weigh anchor and drop down the river. These preliminaries arranged, he had an hour at his own disposal, for some of the troops were three or four miles distant. This interval he improved by taking a few tablespoonfuls of boiled rice and half a cup of coffee, the only food he tasted that day. Having finished this repast, he lay down on a sofa in the office and dropped into a doze. What other man could have slept on such an occasion? The old hero knew that a little sleep was necessary to enable him to go through the coming ordeal, and "By the Eternal," he took it, and it was the last sleep he had for seventy hours.

A little before three o'clock he mounted his horse, rode to the lower part of the city, and took his stand on the site of the present Branch Mint building, then occupied by Fort St. Charles, one of the primitive defenses of the city. Before the gates of the fort he reined in his horse and remained until every corps had passed by to its appointed station, each halting a moment to receive precise orders as to its position at the rendezvous. Behind the general were his six aides-de-camp. The troops that passed him were these: 66 marines; 22 artillery men, with their two six-pounders; two regiments of regular troops, 796 in number; the uniformed companies of the city, numbering 287 men; a battalion of 210 colored troops; 18 Choctaw Indians; General Coffee's Tennessee brigade of mounted riflemen, 563 men; a local mounted rifle company, 62 in number; and 107 mounted Mississippians. Total, 2,131.

The old people of New Orleans, as long as they

lived, loved to relate the events of that afternoon, particularly the departure of the troops. The windows were filled with ladies, who waved their handkerchiefs as the men marched by, and they recognized husbands, fathers and brothers. During the excitement of the departure, every face wore an expression of cheerful confidence, but when at last all had gone, and no uniformed men were seen in the streets, no riding by of aids, no drill in the public squares, no sound of bugle or drum, then the women and children and old men left behind, realized all the seriousness of the situation. A band of ladies, who were sewing for the soldiers, sent a messenger to General Jackson, asking what they were to do in case the city was attacked.

"Say to the ladies," was his reply to the messenger, "not to be uneasy. No British soldier shall enter the city as an enemy, unless over my dead body."

By four o'clock the last corps had passed by the general, who, however, still lingered in front of the old fort. He was apparently waiting for something. He occasionally cast a look toward the *Carolina*, still anchored in the stream. He attached much importance to the part she was to play in the coming event. It was not until he saw her at last hoist her anchor and float down the rapid stream, that the commander-in-chief, followed by his staff, rode down along the levee road by which the troops had gone.

Those who saw General Jackson as he thus rode to battle, never forgot the spectacle. He was one of the finest horsemen that ever sat in a saddle. His heart was on fire with patriotism, and his soul was aglow with the joy of coming conflict. The long awaited hour had come when, with an army under his own command, he was to meet the foe that from boyhood he had yearned to encounter. With his patriotic mind thus inspired, with his resolute soul thus animated, he rode to meet the invaders as the conqueror rides, with the light of battle on his brow and the assurance of victory in his dauntless heart. As one of his contemporaries said: "A great silence enveloped him, and his companions looked upon him with awe."

He arrived about half-past four at the Rodriguez canal, which formerly cut the plain between the Cypress swamp and the river. This line was two miles from the British pickets, and the orders were not to go beyond it, and to avoid everything which could attract the enemy's attention.

At five o'clock, while there was still a little daylight, Inspector-General Hayne, of South Carolina, with a hundred horsemen as an escort, made a rapid reconnoissance of the British position, and then as rapidly returned. He estimated their strength at two thousand. He had the pleasure of reading a printed bill stuck upon many of the plantation fences, which read as follows:

"Louisianians! Remain quiet in your houses. Your slaves shall be preserved to you, and your property respected. We make war only against Americans.

"JOHN KEANE, *General Commanding.*
"A. J. COCHRANE, *Admiral.*"

A negro was overtaken by the horsemen with

printed copies of this proclamation in his pocket, in Spanish and in French. By the time the inspector-general returned it was quite dark, and the British watch-fires, blazing freely all over the narrow plain, revealed their position to the American forces as conveniently as if they themselves had ordered the illumination. By six o'clock, General Jackson had issued his final orders. Coffee, with his rifle-men and the other mounted men, was to march across the plain to the Cypress Swamp, turn down toward the enemy, and keep them close to the river. When this movement was in a good state of forwardness, and the *Carolina* had come to anchor opposite the British camp and close in shore, the rest of the troops were to march directly and rapidly upon the enemy. The signal of attack was to come from the *Carolina*. Not a shot was to be fired, nor a sound uttered, until the first gun of her broadside was heard.

It required nearly an hour for the commodore to get his little vessel anchored just where he wanted her, and even that scarcely gave General Coffee time enough to perform his five-mile march, dis-mount his men and get near enough to respond to the signal.

All this elaborate and long-continued preparation was completed without in the least alarming the British pickets. Their whole army had enjoyed an ample and even a luxurious repast. Some of them, as we have seen, were seated in their huts sipping the claret taken from the neighboring houses, in the light of half a dozen wax candles. Some of the men were already asleep; others were preparing for their beds. To quote again the language of "The Subaltern:"

"We were sitting in great splendor and in high spirits at the entrance to our hut, when the alarm of an approaching schooner was communicated to us. With the sagacity of a veteran, Grey instantly guessed how matters stood. He was the first to hail the suspicious stranger, and on receiving no answer to his challenge, he was the first to fire a musket in the direction of her anchorage. But he had scarcely done so when she opened her broadside, causing the instantaneous abandonment of fires, viands and mirth throughout the bivouac."

Thus the attack was begun. The broadside of grape and canister from the *Carolina*, laid prostrate upon the plain, as some authorities give it, a hundred British soldiers. She continued to fire into the darkness with cannon and musketry, without knowing aught of the effect of her fire, and ceased only when the flash and noise of the battle showed that no enemy was within her reach. For the space of ten minutes after she began the attack, General Jackson withheld the word for the troops near him to advance. Then he gave it, and each corps marched down toward the foe; while General Coffee was still making his way across the plain, not near enough yet to join in the strife.

No one can relate the events of this memorable night. For two hours, there was a nearly continuous, confused combat. All sorts of mistakes were made. Men rushing forward to take prisoners found themselves captured. At one time the horses attached to the pieces of artillery, terrified and wounded, overturned one of the cannon into a ditch and created a scene of confusion that threatened serious consequences. Major Eaton describes the commander-in-chief as dashing into the midst of the tumult, with the cry, "Save the guns, my boys, at every sacrifice!" The presence of the general calmed the marines engaged, who, with the assistance of another company, drew the guns out of danger. Early in the fight, Coffee's hunting-shirted Tennesseeans reached the scene of conflict. Their skill in such irregular combats and the deadly fire of their long rifles enabled them to drive the British who were opposed to them from their position. But the darkness was so dense that neither the Americans nor the British knew what was going on, except in each company's immediate neighborhood. Both sides fought gallantly. During the engagement, the second division of the English troops arrived and re-enforced the advanced corps. Soon after, the fog from the river became so dense as to compel the suspension of aggressive movements. By ten o'clock, all of the American troops who could be found had been withdrawn from the field and were spread over the plain a mile or two from the scene of conflict. The British, too, had withdrawn some distance below, leaving the actual field of battle in possession of the dead. General Keane officially reported his loss at 46 killed, 167 wounded, 64 prisoners and deserters; total, 277. The American loss was: killed, 24; wounded, 115; missing, 74; total 213.

When General Jackson gave the order to withdraw the troops, his intention was to renew the battle at daylight, and to this end he sent a dispatch to the city, ordering the men who remained in and about New Orleans to join him instantly. But, toward midnight, British deserters brought certain information that General Keane had been strongly re-enforced.

General Jackson was as cautious as he was brave, and at critical times he was as prudent as he was resolute. It did not take him long to see that it would be rash to risk the campaign upon a fight in the open field, between twenty-five hundred raw troops without bayonets, and some thousands of British veterans, well-armed and vigorously commanded.

It was ordered, therefore, at the conclusion of a midnight council on the field, to march back at day-break to the old rendezvous behind the Rodriguez canal, there make the best line of defense possible, and await the enemy's advance.

So far as its consequences can be estimated, General Jackson's speedy attack on the invaders was enormously successful. It gave them an exaggerated idea of the number of his men and of his readiness to repel any attack they could make on New Orleans. It in fact paralyzed their movements for a period which enabled him to construct the famous line of breast-works that insured his triumph when the decisive struggle came.

There was only a mile of firm ground between the river and the swamp. The two men-of-war remaining at their anchorage below the canal, could render the enemy's advance certainly difficult, perhaps impossible. If the worst came to the worst the levee could be pierced and the plain flooded. To mask the contemplated movements, Colonel Hind's dragoons were to retain a position between the two armies and do their utmost to veil the movements designed.

While the general and his officers were settling this plan, the troops were standing in the open field, tired out with long marches and penetrated with the chill of the foggy night. Permission was given to light fires. In twenty minutes the whole plain was lighted up by hundreds of watch fires, every squad of men having their own, and thus conveying to the foe an impression that the American army was far more numerous than it really was.

The fires were welcome, indeed, to General Coffee's men, few of whom came out of the battle with a whole garment. Many of them were shivering in their shirt-sleeves, having thrown away their hunting-shirts.

The Rodriguez canal, as it was called, was nothing but an old mill-race, extending across the plain where it was narrowest. It was now partly filled up and grown over with grass. It had been originally cut for the purpose of obtaining water-power when the river was high, but there was now no water in it. Soon after dawn, of December 24, the main body of General Jackson's army was in position behind this canal, and, a little later, wagon-loads of intrenching tools, besides carts and wheel-barrows, began to arrive from the city. They had been sent for soon after midnight. Now, December 24, 1814, began the formation of the memorable "Lines" of General Jackson on the

Delta of the Mississippi, which defended the city of New Orleans. The tools were distributed as fast as they arrived.

"Here," said Jackson, as he looked down upon the scene, "here we will plant our stakes, and not abandon them until we drive those red-coat rascals into the river or the swamp!"

CHAPTER XXI.

GENERAL PAKENHAM ARRIVES IN THE BRITISH CAMP WITH REINFORCEMENTS—HIS VIGOROUS MEASURES.

Before dark, on December 24th, General Jackson's Lines were raised to an average height of four or five feet, and were supposed to be thick enough to resist a cannonade; and so they were, except where a few cotton bales had been used in their construction. The two pieces of artillery, saved the night before by General Jackson's intrepidity, were placed in position to command the high road. There was no sign of the enemy during the day. No alarm interrupted the work for a moment; because, early in the morning, the *Carolina* from her anchorage opposite the British camp, and the *Louisiana* from an excellent position a mile above, completely paralyzed the foe. The vessels not only commanded the road along the levee, but also the entire breadth of the plain. Not a regiment could be formed within the range of their guns. The British troops were, in fact, besieged. They could do nothing while the daylight lasted but crouch close under the levee, or lie at the bottom of ditches, or find shelter behind huts and houses, or retreat beyond the range of a fire which they could not endure and could not silence.

This was the day before Christmas. It was the day on which, at noon, in the city of Ghent, the treaty of peace was signed between Great Britain and the United States. It was precisely at noon when one of the secretaries of the American commissioners announced to a group of invited guests at their quarters that the peace had been signed. Soon after, Mr. Gallatin, Mr. Clay and the other commissioners entered and confirmed the joyful news, which rapidly spread over Europe. A few evenings after, when the news was announced in the theatres of Paris, the people rose and cheered the United States. If there had then been an Atlantic cable, the men of these two contending armies would at once have become friends. General Jackson and General Keane might have dined together at the hospitable abode of Major Livingston. Indeed, Admiral Cochrane had said, before leaving his ship, that he should eat his Christmas dinner at New Orleans. "If he does," said General Jackson, on hearing of the remark, "I shall have the honor of presiding at the meal."

Christmas dawned upon a scene of cheerful activity in the American Lines below New Orleans. The men were at work as soon as they could see, and continued their labor with animated hope and gay alacrity all day long; and they were assisted by the floating laborers from the city, by the sailors and slaves; the horses, also the mules, the oxen, and whatever creatures could lift, draw or carry, were all employed in strengthening the American position against an attack which might come at any moment. General Jackson had established his headquarters in a roomy mansion-house two hundred yards behind the Lines, from an upper window of which, above the trees which surrounded it, he surveyed the situation with the aid of an old telescope lent him by an aged Frenchman. The men had the feeling of working under their commander's eye.

"May I go to town to-day, General?" asked the son, sixteen years of age, of Edward Livingston. He had been complimented with the title of captain, and had worked assiduously with the rest of the young men of the city.

"Of course, Captain Livingston," replied General Jackson, "you *may* go. But *ought* you to go?"

The boy made no reply. He blushed, saluted, and went back to his place in the works.

In the British camp, three or four miles away, Christmas morning broke gloomily, indeed. There was discouragement and discontent, for the position of the army was felt to be erroneous, and many of the officers thought it beyond rectification. But in the course of the morning an event occurred that completely restored their former confidence. This was the arrival in camp, to take the supreme command, of Major-General Sir Edward Pakenham, and with him, at the head of a numerous and capable staff, Major-General Samuel Gibbs. The troops greeted General Pakenham's arrival with enthusiastic cheers, and began at once to cast about for the means of enjoying a Christmas dinner. To some of the officers who had lost comrades in the recent action, the repast had little in it of hilarity or festivity.

If for a few moments they could forget their situation, a round shot from the little *Carolina* reminded them of their situation and of what they had to do. She managed to elevate her single twelve-pounder to such a degree, and to fire with such accuracy, that a spent ball occasionally struck the side of the barn in which these officers were dining. Once they were alarmed by the piercing shriek of a soldier without, who had been nearly cut in halves by one of the *Carolina's* balls.

All day General Jackson sat at his upper window, unable to see the enemy's position and marvelling at their inactivity. It was so obvious to *him* that their only chance was an immediate attack, that he began to fear they might have some deeper scheme for getting around his position than he, a soldier of the backwoods, could divine.

General Pakenham was not idle. The moment he reached the camp and had received the report of the general in command, he proceeded to examine the position. He determined, first of all, to destroy the *Carolina*. By the evening of December 26, after twenty-four hours of strenuous exertion, nine field-pieces, two howitzers and a furnace for heating balls were brought from the fleet and placed in position on the levee opposite to where the *Carolina* was immovably fixed. During the night everything was made ready; the guns were placed, the shot were heated.

At dawn on the twenty-seventh of December, the British opened fire on the *Carolina*. The second shot, white hot, penetrated her side and lodged in the main hold, where the fire could not be reached nor quenched. The contest was fierce while it lasted, but it was over in half an hour. The crew of the *Carolina* were forced to abandon her, and she blew up with an explosion which shook the earth for miles around and was heard in New Orleans. The *Louisiana* escaped; her crew, in boats propelled by oars, towing her to a place of anchorage, close in shore, opposite General Jackson's headquarters.

The American army lamented the loss of the little vessel to which they owed so much, and experienced a brief discouragement. The English were correspondingly elated. They were now for the first time able to form a battalion on the plain, or eat their dinner, or sleep at night, without danger of disturbance from the *Carolina's* aggravating balls. This gave General Pakenham an opportunity to test the fighting power of the Americans which he was not slow to improve, and which General Jackson welcomed with the belligerent alacrity that he always displayed when anticipating the festivity of battle.

CHAPTER XXII.

GENERAL PAKENHAM TESTS THE FIGHTING POWER OF THE AMERICANS—GETTING READY FOR THE FINAL STRUGGLE.

General Pakenham's next operation he styled a *reconnoissance*. He had not yet seen the American position, and could not see it without the cooperation of a large force. The whole of December 27 was employed by both armies in laborious preparation for a movement which had now become possible. The crew of the *Carolina* were stationed in the Lines to serve the heavy artillery. From daylight till dark the whole American force labored at the embankment and the canal, a work of peculiar and always increasing difficulty from the scarcity of soil. The British spent the day in bringing up stores and heavy guns from the ships, as well as field-pieces, of which, before night, they had ten at the front. General Jackson gave them no peace, night or day. As "The Subaltern" says:

"The Americans harassed our pickets, killed and wounded a few of the sentinels, and prevented the main body from obtaining any sound or refreshing sleep. Scarcely had the troops lain down when they were roused by a sharp firing at the outposts, which lasted only till they were in order, and then ceased; but as soon as they had dispersed and had once more addressed themselves to repose, the same cause of alarm returned, and they were again called to their ranks. Thus was the entire night spent in watching, or at best in broken and disturbed slumbers; than which nothing is more trying, both to the health and spirits of an army."

Soon after dawn, on December 28, General Jackson was aware that the enemy were about to approach his Lines. He was ready for them. His forces had been greatly increased, his Lines strengthened. The *Louisiana*, saved the day before by the skill of her commander, Lieutenant Thompson, was only waiting for the word to let out her cable and swing into position.

General Pakenham accomplished his purpose of viewing the American position. His army marched in two columns, and presented an appearance as compact and orderly as if on parade, giving the raw troops behind the American Lines, for the first time in their lives, a spectacle of military pomp and circumstance. The muskets of the British troops glittered in the morning sun, and their various uniforms, red, tartan, grey and green, were brilliantly displayed upon the brown stubble of the Delta. The nature of the ground and the situation of the plantation houses were such that the British did not come in view of the American position until they were fully exposed to the American fire. Artillery and small arms began at once their deadly work. The great guns were aimed by the same men that had yesterday manned the *Carolina*, and they were now assisted by the band of the Lafittes from Barataria. The British officers record that scarcely one cannon-ball passed over their heads or fell much short of their line, but nearly every one struck into the midst of their ranks, causing terrible havoc. Moreover, at the very crisis of the advance, the plantation houses, which had veiled the American position, were set on fire, and blazed up as if full of combustibles. This greatly added to the embarrassment and peril of the English troops. While the cannonade mowed down their ranks, the fire of two large *chateaux* and their villages of outbuildings scorched some of the troops and blinded most of them with smoke. At the right moment, too, the *Louisiana* had joined in the fray, and swept the level field with heavy shot continuously from nine o'clock till three.

This movement though styled a *reconnoissance*, was not so regarded by the British officers who have left a record of it. They expected to sleep in New Orleans that night, but, as " The Subaltern " informs us, before they had got near enough to General Jackson's canal to form a conjecture of its breadth or depth, the order came for the men to halt and to shelter themselves as best they could. " Long before noon," he says, " all thought of attacking was for this day abandoned, and it now only remained to withdraw the troops from their present perilous position with as little loss as possible." It took all the rest of the day to accomplish this. During the long afternoon, the Peninsula heroes lay low in wet ditches, or crawled away behind fences, huts and burning houses, the cannon-balls occasionally " knocking down the soldiers and tossing them into the air like old bags." An officer explored one of the elegant houses near their line of march, the hall of which was floored with variegated marble and adorned by two large globes and an orrery.

"On entering a bedroom," he remarked, "lately occupied by a female of the family, I found that our advance had interrupted the fair one in her study of natural history, as a volume of Buffon was lying open on her pillow."

He also observes that, "in spite of our sanguine expectation of sleeping that night in New Orleans, evening found us occupying our negro hut at Villeré's; nor was I sorry that the shades of night concealed our mortification from the prisoners and slaves."

Commodore Patterson reports that the *Louisiana* was exposed to the enemy's cannonade that day upward of seven hours, during which she fired eight hundred shot, and yet had but one man slightly wounded. His men, he says, were all picked up from the streets of New Orleans, "and yet I never knew guns better served or a more animated fire."

The repulse of the British inspired General Jackson with new ardor in the defense of his post. Besides planting more cannon where this action had shown them to be necessary, and extending his breastworks farther into the swamp, he began a new line of defense two miles nearer the city, in case he should be driven back. He requested Commodore Patterson to plant cannon on the opposite bank of the river, and there the indefatigable commodore, aided by Major Latour, established a battery of heavy guns. The streets of New Orleans were searched again and again to man the new works, and the general urged the ladies to examine once more their houses and to send to the front every musket and pistol and even every flint and ramrod that they could find. Men kept coming in from the upper country without arms and almost without clothes, and there were many already in the Lines who had nothing resembling a weapon except the pickaxe and the spade with which they worked.

Sir Edward Pakenham called a council of war after the great repulse of the twenty-eighth. Its conclusion was to regard General Jackson's Lines in the light of a fortified place, to be taken by a regular approach. They resolved to construct a line of works parallel to his, at a distance from it not exceeding three hundred yards. During the next three days, thirty pieces of heavy cannon were brought up from the fleet with prodigious labor. On the last night of the year 1814, as soon as it was quite dark, one-half the British army marched forward to a line about three hundred yards from that of the Americans, and there they spent the night throwing up a chain of batteries. The night was very dark, and the soldiers were ordered to work in perfect silence. They soon experienced the same scarcity of soil which had induced General Jackson to employ bales of cotton. The English had no cotton within reach, but every storehouse and barn about them was filled with hogsheads of sugar, the crops of the last two years. These were rolled into position in immense numbers, and they gave at least a comforting appearance of strength to the British works.

New Year's Day dawned slowly upon this novel scene, for a dense fog had overspread all the plain. During the night, a suspicious sound of hammering had been heard in the direction of the enemy's camp by the American sentinels; but after daylight all was silent. As late as nine o'clock, no sound was heard and no movement was perceived. General Jackson therefore allowed, for the first time, a brief respite from the intense toil of the last eight days.

The English, too, were inactive, waiting silent within their works; but waiting only for the lifting of the fog to open a simultaneous fire from their six new batteries. Suddenly, toward ten o'clock, the fog dispersed, so as to reveal clearly the American position, and even the sun shone forth, diffusing a welcome warmth and brilliant light.

"We could perceive," wrote "The Subaltern," "all that was going forward in the American Lines, with great exactness. The different regiments were upon parade, and being dressed in holiday suits, presented really a fine appearance. Mounted officers were riding backward and forward through the ranks; bands were playing and colors floating in the air. In a word, all seemed jollity and gala."

He might have added, if he had known the fact, that General Jackson's horse was standing saddled near headquarters, and that the general himself, with a portion of his staff, was about to mount and ride out for a New Year's review of the troops.

At that moment the whole of the thirty pieces of artillery in the British batteries opened fire upon the regiments so gayly parading. The sky was filled with hundreds of Congreve rockets. Such was the violence of the fire that during the first ten minutes one hundred balls struck General Jackson's headquarters, and it was marvelous that himself and his staff escaped from the building without serious injury to any one. His troops were about ten minutes in getting back to their guns and opening fire. Then was seen the wisdom of the measures taken during the last three days. Commodore Patterson's battery, on the opposite bank, poured a fearful fire into the very midst of the British position, while the direct fire from Jackson's Lines was maintained with a force and vigor far surpassing that of three days before. Fifty pieces of artillery of large calibre were concentrated upon the British position for an hour and a half. The smoke was then so dense that nothing whatever could be seen, and several of the guns were so hot that it was no longer safe to charge them.

About noon the order was given to the American batteries to cease firing. Slowly the smoke rolled away from the plain, and the result of the fire was gradually disclosed. While no serious impression had been made upon the American fortifications, the six batteries of the British, which had presented such a formidable appearance in the morning, were almost level with the earth. The guns were all overthrown. The sailors who had manned them were seen running to the rear, and all over the plain were descried indications that the British troops had again taken to the ditch, and were hiding behind huts and heaps of stubble.

Those hogsheads of unsalable sugar were the cause of this swift destruction of the British batteries. The sugar had afforded no protection whatever against the American fire. The balls went straight through the hogsheads, not perceptibly impeded. It had been better if the English artillerymen had been exposed to view without this semblance of defense. On this day, too, General Jackson discovered the insufficiency of cotton-bales. They were knocked about by the heavy cannon-balls in an alarming manner, and some of them caught fire, making an intolerable smoke. They were all quickly removed, and their places supplied with the black and spongy soil of the Delta.

The great superiority of the American artillery fire astounded the British. The unusual skill of American riflemen had long been conceded; but the English had believed that in an artillery contest the Americans would be no match for them. The discovery that their raw, uncouth foes could shoot almost as accurately with cannons as they could with rifles, had a depressing effect upon the British. They were now, for the first time, seriously and generally disheartened. The spirit of the rank and file was broken. Twice they had marched toward Jackson's Lines only to be frustrated with every circumstance of painful discomfiture, and it was hard to convince them that they were not fatally overmatched. They had nothing to eat but the salt provisions they had brought with them; the sharpshooters gave them no rest at night, and they were now exposed to a fire of eighteen guns from the opposite side of the river. It was not, as one of the British officers remarked, that the men wished to escape from a disagreeable situation. They were like chained dogs, that see their enemy but cannot reach him, and can only growl and gnash their teeth.

This second repulse took place on Sunday, January first. Four days then passed away, with no movement on the part of the British which General Jackson could discern or guess. He was strongly inclined to believe that a soldier of such experience and celebrity as General Pakenham would not make a third attempt to accomplish the impossible. He even wrote to the Secretary of War that, in his opinion, the Lines he then held would not be again attacked. Having reached this conclusion and waited four days, he became intensely anxious with regard to General Pakenham's next scheme. He expected him to withdraw from his present false position, and, perhaps, make his appearance suddenly in some other part of the Delta.

General Jackson had not forgotten the lessons of war which, while a boy of fourteen, he had studied through his knot-hole in the prison fence at Camden, thirty-five years before. He remembered that a few hours' relaxation of discipline and vigilance had led to General Greene's disastrous defeat by an inferior force of the enemy. He was determined that no disaster should occur to his troops or to the enterprise entrusted to him, through lack of precaution on his part. He sent spies in every direction. He watched the enemy's position with unslumbering vigilance. He had men floating down past it in the night, and a few spies succeeded every day in bringing a semblance of news from the British camp. He passed many hours of acute anxiety while appearing to be intent upon nothing but strengthening his Lines, which he firmly believed to be impregnable against the force arrayed against him.

Toward the close of the week it became evident to General Jackson that a more formidable advance of the enemy than he had yet withstood was about to be made upon his Lines, simultaneously with an attack upon his new works on the other side of the Mississippi. He believed that this movement would bring on the closing struggle between the Americans and the invaders, and he was ready for it.

Meanwhile, the electric news of his success in thus far holding his ground against an expedition so formidable was spreading through the land, and gradually fixing all minds, in blended hope and apprehension, upon what he and his brave men were doing in the Delta of the Mississippi.

CHAPTER XXIII.

PRELIMINARIES OF THE GREAT BATTLE—GENERAL JACKSON READY FOR THE FIGHT.

At one o'clock on Sunday morning, January 8, 1815, General Jackson was asleep at his headquarters, in his old-fashioned and threadbare uniform of buff and blue. Precisely at that hour, as the custom was, the troops in the Lines, consisting of half the force, were relieved by the other half, and for a few minutes every man in the army was in motion. All was done in silence. Not the flash of a lantern was permitted, nor a sound that could be avoided; and very soon all was still again. Then a messenger from Commodore Patterson arrived at headquarters. The sleeping general was aroused and listened to the messenger's report. It was to the effect that Commodore Patterson and General Morgan, from personal observations made by them during the afternoon and night, were assured that, while a feint would soon be made by the enemy on General Jackson's Lines, their main attack would be delivered against the works on the other side of the river; wherefore, General Morgan requested that reinforcements should be sent to him immediately.

"Hurry back," replied General Jackson, as he sat upon the lounge on which he had been sleeping, "and tell General Morgan that he is mistaken. The main attack will be on this side, and I have no men to spare. He must maintain his position at all hazards."

The messenger, who was B. D. Shepherd, a patriotic merchant, withdrew and returned with all speed to the other side. General Jackson had patiently considered this very danger, and felt acutely his weakness on the other side of the river; but, in truth, he had not a man to spare, and if he had had men, he had not weapons to place in their hands. To hold his own Lines and batteries, extending a mile across the plain, he had but about three thousand two hundred men, and he expected at daybreak an attack of twelve thousand veteran troops. This was the prevailing estimate of the enemy's force at headquarters.

There was no more sleep for General Jackson. When Shepherd was gone, he looked at his watch, and finding that it was past one, he said to his slumbering aids:

"Gentlemen, we have slept enough. Rise. The enemy will be upon us in a few minutes. I must go and see Coffee."

There was not much to be done in the way of preparation, on the American side, for either officers or men. By four o'clock, every company was at its post in the Lines, very much as usual, for few of the troops yet suspected that the final attack was about to be made upon them. General Jackson and his immediate circle were sure of it, but before he had lain down upon his lounge the evening before, he had performed every act which he could think of to make his preparations for the contest complete. One of his last measures proved to be of great value. The day before, after finishing his final inspection of the Lines and batteries, he had turned to his companion, General Adair, of Kentucky, a recent arrival, and said:

"Well, what do you think of our situation? Can we defend these works or not?"

"There is one way," replied General Adair, "and but one way in which we can hope to defend them. We must have a strong corps of reserves to meet the enemy's main attack, wherever it may be. No single part of the Lines is strong enough to resist the united force of the enemy. But with a strong column held in our rear, ready to advance upon any threatened point, we can beat them off."

General Jackson accepted the suggestion, and ordered Adair himself to act with his Kentuckians as the reserve, giving him ample discretion as to the selection of his post. And thus it was that General Adair, at a quarter past four on the decisive morning, with a thousand Kentucky riflemen, marched down to a point fifty yards behind the portion of the works which a deserter, the day before, had correctly informed General Pakenham was the weakest part of the American position. Adair's selection of the spot was one of the fortunate circumstances of the great day. In combination with the deserter's report to the British commander, it resulted in the leading of the main column of the invading army into a trap, from which it escaped only in defeat and with horrible slaughter.

General Pakenham, too, was up betimes. He rose full of hope. He was supposed to be the ablest commander of his age—thirty-seven—then living.

He was a handsome, noble, chivalric gentleman, animated by a lofty sense of duty, and as generous as he was brave. He little thought, as he mounted his horse that morning, that the shadow of death was already beginning to envelope him. He was in the saddle at two o'clock, and rode at once to the bank of the river to see how it had fared with the force of fourteen hundred men who were to cross the Mississippi, and make a simultaneous attack on the opposite shore. All had gone badly with them. There was a low stage of water, and eight hours had been lost in dragging boats through a canal, dug by the troops from Lake Borgne to the Mississippi, and launching them into the river. Instead of fourteen hundred men, scarcely five hundred reached the other shore, and, instead of getting there early in the evening of January seventh, it was daybreak on January the eighth before they stood upon the bank, and they had been carried by the swift stream a mile and a half below the point at which they were to have landed.

Pakenham heard the story of this mishap, but he could not rectify it. Like General Jackson he thought of the other side of the river with much apprehension; but he had done all that was possible for it, and he rode away toward the front. He was afterward blamed for not awaiting the result of the attack on the western bank of the river, before beginning the assault on General Jackson's Lines, inasmuch as the issue of the impending battle would perhaps wholly depend on the success or failure of the attack on General Morgan's works.

At four o'clock in the morning, the main body of

the British army was already drawn up in three principal columns of attack. On the high road near the river and parallel with the levee stood a column of light troops, one thousand in number, under Colonel Rennie, who were to attack the strong works defending the road. Next to them, two hundred yards distant, was the regiment of praying Highlanders, as they were called, under the command of Colonel Dale, who were to go to the assistance of Colonel Rennie if he should require assistance. All these troops were subject to the orders of General Keane, who commanded in that part of the field. Four or five hundred yards beyond the Highlanders was the main column, three thousand strong, under General Gibbs, who were to assail the Lines where they were supposed to be weakest. This column was to be headed by an Irish regiment, the Forty-fourth, carrying fascines to fill the ditch, and ladders upon which to mount the breastwork. Beyond them and close to the Cypress Swamp was a regiment of colored troops from the West Indies. There were various other corps and detachments, some of which were lost in the dense darkness of that foggy morning and did not succeed in reaching their posts. A mile in the rear was the reserve column, consisting of two newly arrived regiments, under General Lambert, who had accompanied them. Altogether, there were about eight thousand British troops under arms that morning in front of General Jackson's Lines which were defended by three thousand two hundred men.

The British troops were not in good spirits. Being veterans, they had discovered that the Americans were handled by a commander who thoroughly understood his business. They had also learned what deadly marksmen the Americans were, with cannons as well as with rifles. In all their battles, they had never before encountered such destructive fire. So deep was the impression which their encounters with the Americans had made upon them that Colonel Mullens, of the Forty-fourth regiment, that had been detailed to carry the fascines and scaling ladders at the head of Gibbs's column, said: "My regiment has been ordered to execution. Their dead bodies are to be used as a bridge for the rest of the army to march over." The lion-like Colonel Dale, of the praying Highlanders, on being asked "what he thought of it," when news of the delay of the attack on the western bank of the river was spoken of by the physician of the regiment, simply handed the physician his watch and a letter and said: "Give these to my wife; I shall die at the head of my regiment." But General Pakenham did not share these feelings. He and many of his troops had assisted in driving the French out of the Spanish Peninsula. They had never been defeated. It was inconceivable to him that such troops could be beaten by a horde of American militia, commanded by a general whose name was unknown to the military circles of Europe. He had his lesson to learn, and it was written for him in the blood of brave men, including his own.

The peculiar darkness of the morning hindered every operation of the British troops and caused some serious errors, delays and omissions. As late as six o'clock, General Pakenham received intelligence that the fascines and ladders had not been taken to the head of the main column. He sent an order to rectify the error; but when the rocket pierced the fog at six o'clock, which was the signal to begin the assault, he was not absolutely certain that the regiment assigned to this duty had reached its post. But the signal had been given; daylight was just beginning to pervade the mist, and the British columns were slowly advancing.

At length the heavy fog which had covered the Delta began to yield to the influence of the rising sun. It lifted a little here and there, then settled down again as densely as before, then broke into huge masses, between which distant objects could be discerned. Hundreds of the American troops had been peering into the mist and straining their ears to catch any unusual sound. General Jackson had cast many a look beyond the Lines. Adair had thrust his head above the parapet and gazed. Carroll and Coffee had taken their turn, but seen nothing. About seven o'clock, Lieutenant Spotts of Battery No. 6, nearest the Cypress Swamp, discerned through a rift in the fog, but only for a moment, General Gibbs's massive column of redcoats. They seemed far away and as near to the Swamp as men could safely march. The thunder of Lieutenant Spotts's great gun terminated the suspense in every part of the scene of operations and on both sides of the river. It informed every man in both armies that the hour had come.

The mist closed again and the gun was silent. General Jackson walked along the Lines toward the point that seemed directly menaced, speaking to each corps as he passed: "Don't waste your ammunition. See that every shot tells. Let us finish the business to-day." Not a word was spoken in reply, for the order imposing absolute silence was still in force. Soon the fog, as the way of the fog is in that region, broke into dissolving masses and suddenly rolled away, disclosing to the view of the Americans the whole plain, apparently covered with advancing troops, and affording to the sharpshooters of the backwoods, for the third time, the spectacle of a splendid military pageant moving toward their position. At this moment the band of the Battalion d'Orleans struck up "Yankee Doodle," changing in due course to other patriotic airs, and never ceased to play until the main action closed.

The heavy column of General Gibbs was marching with perfect steadiness toward the Lines at a distance of perhaps three-quarters of a mile. No one who has seen a heavy column of British troops advancing to an attack can forget the majesty of its appearance or the impression it gave him of seemingly irresistible power. Christopher North spoke truly when he said that the spectacle of a British army, in the full panoply of war, advancing upon its foes, presented a symbol "of the right hand of the power of God." Let us give due recognition to brave men.

As the magnificent column of General Gibbs came steadily on, the Americans awaited it in silence. They saw that it was composed of gallant and determined men, but they did not fear its onset. They keenly felt that the coming battle was to be decisive of the campaign. They had reasonable faith in themselves; they had absolute faith in their commander, and they welcomed the imminent deadly struggle with grim exultation. They knew they would have terrible work to do. They did it.

CHAPTER XXIV.

THE BATTLE OF NEW ORLEANS.

When General Gibbs's column came within half a mile of the American Lines, the three batteries furthest from the river opened fire upon it—at first, with little effect; but, as the column came nearer, throwing balls into the very midst of it, and bringing it more than once to a temporary halt. As it came still nearer, the huge cannon balls, as an eye-witness reported, cut great lanes in the column, tossed men into the air and hurled them to the right and left. But it still advanced with little pause and no haste, until it came within range of the sharp-shooters of Tennessee and Kentucky, massed at the very spot toward which it was directing its march. Including Adair's Kentuckians, there were four lines of riflemen, one behind the other, most of them men accustomed from boyhood to depend in part for their subsistence and their safety upon the accuracy of their aim and the rapidity of their fire. At the right moment, when the enemy were within two hundred yards, Carroll gave the word "Fire!" and at the same moment, as it chanced, Commodore Patterson, from the other side of the river, opened fire with a portion of his artillery.

The discharge of the small arms from this part of the Lines was as steady, as continuous and as deadly as it could have been from a row of accurately pointed Gatling guns, and its effect upon the heavy column of the British was most murderous. Nevertheless, it continued its steady, unflinching, even-paced approach, with General Gibbs at its head, until the mounted officers in advance caught sight of the wide ditch in front of the American works. The fascines and ladders were nowhere to be seen. "Where are the Forty-fourth?" cried an officer. "If we get to the ditch," he said to his general, "we have no means of crossing!" At this moment General Gibbs shouted: "Here come the Forty-fourth!" and a portion of that regiment really was struggling along with ladders and fascines. Relieved by the shout of their commanding general, the column still pressed on, until the foremost rank was within one hundred yards of the ditch.

But mortal men could do no more! And there really appeared no motive for going forward, for there was no sign visible to the troops of an adequate supply of the means of getting over the ditch, and still less of scaling the works behind it. Every mounted officer of the advancing column had fallen except the general commanding it. One-half the troops were disabled, and the rest were falling fast with every step they took. The front ranks hesitated, halted, and thus threw the column into disorder. General Gibbs ordered them with passionate earnestness to re-form, but it was manifestly impossible. To the American riflemen, as one of them afterward said, the column appeared to reel like a red ship in a stormy sea. Soon it broke to pieces, and the men ran headlong to the rear, many of them excusing themselves by saying that not a ladder or fascine had been brought to the front.

General Pakenham rode up and cried: "For shame! Recollect that you are British soldiers! *This* is the road you ought to take," pointing to the American Lines. He soon came up to General Gibbs, who said to him: "I am sorry to have to report to you that the troops will not obey me. They will not follow me."

Upon hearing this, General Pakenham took off his hat, rode to the front into the worst of the fire, urging on the troops by orders, entreaties and gesticulations. A ball shattered his right arm while it was raised aloft, and it fell to his side. The next moment his horse was killed. One of his aids dismounted from his pony, upon which Pakenham, as if unconscious of his broken arm, mounted again and followed the column, which was still in retreat, beseeching them to halt and re-form. While he was so doing, a handful of gallant British troops made their way to the ditch, plunged across it, and fell as they were striving to climb the slippery breastwork.

A second time the main column advanced, Gibbs on its right, Pakenham on the left, seemingly still unconscious of his broken arm. They marched at a quicker step than before. As they came within range, a thirty-two pounder, loaded to the muzzle with balls and scraps of iron, poured its contents into the very head of the column, disabling, as it was afterward estimated, two hundred men. The American riflemen continued their fire with the same deadly effect as before. Pakenham turned to one of his aids and said: "Order up the reserve!" then, catching sight of the praying Highlanders, he cried out, waving his hat with his left hand: "Hurrah! Brave Highlanders!"

He never spoke again. At that moment a discharge of grape-shot struck the group of officers by whom he was surrounded. One of the shots gave him a bad wound in the thigh and killed his horse. Captain McDougal caught his general in his arms, drew him away from the dying animal, and was supporting his head, as he lay upon the ground, when he was wounded for the third time, and was happily deprived of consciousness. They carried him to the rear, placed him under an old live oak-tree, which was standing a few years ago, and there in a few minutes he breathed his last. A minute or two after the fall of Pakenham, Gibbs was mortally wounded, and, almost at the same time, General Keane was wounded twice, although not mortally. The great column of three thousand men, after twice advancing to the charge, disappeared from view, and the Highlanders, who had marched with solid step to their relief, stood helpless in front of the American Lines until five hundred and forty-four of their number had fallen. No braver or better men ever stepped upon a battlefield, or fell before the fire of a foe.

The attack at other parts of the line fared no better. Colonel Rennie, posted on the river road, did indeed capture by the headlong rapidity of his assault, the outlying redoubt, but held it only for a moment. Three brave men, Colonel Rennie,

Captain Henry and Major King, reached the summit of the rampart close to the river, and Rennie cried: "Hurrah, boys, the day is ours!" At that instant, the three heroes fell dead into the ditch below. Their troops were instantly driven from the redoubt, and the whole British army sought safety, some in flight, and more by hiding wherever there was a chance of shelter.

Of all that host of valiant men only one, Lieutenant Lavack, got over the top of the American parapet unwounded, though with two bullet-holes in his cap. Another officer of the main column, Major Wilkinson, fell mortally wounded upon the summit. The American troops, admiring his courage, carried him tenderly to the rear, where Major Smiley, of the Kentucky reserve, said to him:

"Bear up, my dear fellow; you are too brave a man to die."

"From my heart I thank you," said the dying hero. "It is all over with me. You can render me a service; it is to communicate to my commander that I fell on your rampart, and died like a soldier and a true Englishman."

Lieutenant Lavack was taken alive and unharmed. When he found himself a prisoner, he looked behind him, wondering the troops had not followed. "But," as he used to say, in telling the story, "the two leading regiments had vanished as if the earth had opened and swallowed them up." Lieutenant Lavack was the hero of the hour, and the whole army afterward vied with one another in doing him honor.

An equally interesting and more touching event

occurred at the other end of the Lines, near the river. As Colonel Rennie's column advanced to the attack, their bugler, a boy of fourteen or fifteen, climbing a small tree within two hundred yards of the American lines, straddled a limb and continued to blow the charge with all his power. "There he remained," says Major Latour, in his history of the campaign,* "during the whole action, whilst the cannon-balls and bullets plowed the ground around him, killed scores of men, and tore even the branches of the tree in which he sat. Above the thunder of the artillery, the rattling fire of the musketry, and all the din and uproar of the strife, the shrill blast of the little bugler could be heard, and even when his companions had fallen back and retreated from the field, he continued true to his duty, and blew the charges with undiminished vigor. At last, when the British had entirely abandoned the ground, an American soldier, passing from the Lines, captured the little bugler and brought him into camp, where he was greatly astonished when some of the enthusiastic creoles, who had observed his gallantry, actually embraced him, and officers and men vied with each other in acts of kindness to so gallant a little soldier."

What a singular—what an incomprehensible creature is man, in whose heart are intimately mingled the most terrible passions for vengeance and destruction with the manliest admiration of his foemen's valor and the tenderest sympathy for those whom he has slain in the rage of battle!

* Jackson and New Orleans.

The battle of New Orleans lasted twenty-five minutes. One-half of the American army did not fire a shot, for the battle was fought at the two ends of the line. During that brief period seven hundred British troops were killed, fourteen hundred were wounded, and five hundred were taken prisoners, or were soon to be taken. On the American side the loss was eight killed and thirteen wounded. Two men were killed in repulsing the column of General Gibbs; two in the redoubt on the high-road; four in the swamps, pursuing the colored troops.

When General Jackson looked over the Lines after the smoke had cleared away, he saw the space in front of Carroll's position, for the distance of two hundred yards, apparently covered with fallen soldiers. The course by which the Gibbs column had marched, resembled a broad red streak, so closely did the red-coated slain lie together. In conversing upon that glorious and terrible hour, General Jackson would say:

"I never had so grand and awful an idea of the resurrection as on that day. After the smoke of the battle had cleared off somewhat, I saw in the distance more than five hundred Britons emerging from the heaps of their dead comrades, rising up all over the plain, and still more distinctly visible as the field became clearer, coming forward and surrendering as prisoners of war to our soldiers. They had fallen at our first fire upon them, without having received so much as a scratch, and lay prostrate as if dead until the close of the action."

The scene had every element of horror that can

be conceived. Notwithstanding the brilliancy and importance of the victory, the prevailing sentiment among the American troops, who were as generous and sympathetic as they were patriotic and brave, during that day and the next, had in it as much of compassion as of exultation.

But the day was not yet won. By the time General Jackson had walked along the line congratulating the troops upon their success, he began to look across the river with some anxiety. He mounted the breastwork near the levee, with General Adair by his side, and soon discovered that a British column on the opposite shore was advancing vigorously to the attack of General Morgan. He called for three cheers for the American soldiers. While his men were cheering, he saw Morgan's troops abandon their works, and their retreat drew after them the entire force on that side of the river. In other circumstances this mishap might have been fatal, but the strength of the British expedition was broken. General Lambert, upon whom the command of the English had devolved, clearly perceived that it would be impossible for him to hold the western bank of the river, and on the following day he withdrew the troops. Then General Jackson felt a reasonable confidence that he had defended New Orleans. He said to his staff:

"They *may* try it again, but my private opinion is they will not; and if they do, we shall be able to give a good account of ourselves."

For a time the daring general was all but resolved to take the offensive, and "drive the British into the sea;" but on reflection he concluded "to let well enough alone," and quietly but vigilantly awaited developments.

Ten days later, General Jackson and his staff, from the upper story of their headquarters, were spying the English position three miles below. Nothing seemed changed. But when the veteran General Humbert was handed the spyglass and asked his opinion, he looked at the British camp, and said: "*They're gone!*" "How do you know?" asked General Jackson. Humbert pointed to a crow that was flying so close to one of the supposed sentinels as to show that it was only a dummy, and not well enough made to deceive even a crow. And so it proved. They were gone, leaving eighty wounded men, who could not be moved, to "the humanity of the American commander." These men were all most tenderly cared for, as well by the American soldiers as by the families of New Orleans.

Upon returning from a visit to the abandoned British camp, General Jackson prepared to lead his victorious army back in triumph to the city they had defended. First of all, he asked Abbé Dubourg, the head of the Roman Catholic clergy in Louisiana, to celebrate a public thanksgiving in the cathedral, "in token of the great assistance we have received from the Ruler of events, and of our humble sense of it." He wrote numberless letters, addresses and reports, in which the services of every corps, and of every man who had distinguished himself, were specially noticed. He concluded his address to the army with these words:

"This splendid campaign will be considered as

entitling every man who has served in it to the salutation of his brother-in-arms."

On the morning of January 21, this glowing address was read to the army, a competent reader being designated for every regiment. Then the general led the troops back to the city, where the entire population received them with heartfelt acclamations. Two days later occurred the solemn service of thanksgiving at the cathedral, with every circumstance which could enhance the festal and grateful joy of the occasion. In the evening the city was illuminated. For once, discipline was relaxed, while both soldiers and people gave themselves wholly up to conviviality.

Meanwhile the people of the United States were wrought up to a high pitch of anxiety with regard to the struggle at New Orleans. The slow mails of that period carried the news of Jackson's night attack of December 23; then of the repulse of the British on January first, accompanied by the news of the arrival of General Pakenham with greatly overstated reinforcements. The hopeful ones believed that Old Hickory would defend the city and defeat the invaders; the desponding ones felt sure that the British force was irresistible, and that it would not only drive Jackson from his defenses, but conquer the whole western country. At last, on February 5, 1815, twenty-eight days after the battle which irretrievably shattered the power of the British expedition, *The National Intelligencer*, of Washington, gave the great and joy-giving news under the heading, in its largest type:

"ALMOST INCREDIBLE VICTORY!"

Never before had an Administration been so gloriously relieved from such an agony of suspense, or the American people so deeply stirred with gratitude and exultation. The name of Andrew Jackson spontaneously became a beloved household word to the remotest bounds of the Union, and the people rejoiced all over the land with exceeding great joy. When the great news crossed the Atlantic, Americans in Europe rejoiced even more than Americans at home. They could once more hold up their heads with national pride. "Now," said Henry Clay, when the news reached the negotiators of peace at Ghent—"now I can go to England without mortification."

In his account of General Jackson's Southwestern Campaign, Mr. Adams disparages the importance of the victory at New Orleans, while in other portions of his history he unconsciously gives ample evidence of its immeasurable value to the country. He informs us that a malignant and powerful movement was on foot in the Eastern States to dissolve the Union and form a New England Confederacy; that in the belief that the British had captured New Orleans, the New England Commissioners were on the way to Washington to impose their terms on the discredited and helpless Government. Under date of January 23, 1815, Mr. Adams gives a letter to a co-conspirator from Timothy Pickering, a few years before a Senator of the United States from Massachusetts, and then one of the leaders of the disunion party, in which Mr. Pickering exultingly says: *

"If the British succeed in their expedition against New Orleans—and if they have tolerable leaders, I see no reason to doubt of their success—I shall consider the Union as severed. This consequence I deem *inevitable.* I do not expect to see a single Representative in the next Congress from the Western States."

Lord Castlereagh, in discussing American affairs with the King of France several weeks before Mr. Pickering wrote his letter, is reported to have said: †

"Sire, I expect that at this time most of the large seaport towns in America are laid in ashes—that we are in possession of New Orleans, and have command of all the waters of the Mississippi and the lakes; so that the Americans are now little better than prisoners at large in their own country."

Pickering and Castlereagh, and a great deal more in Mr. Adams's eighth volume, show what incomputable consequences were involved in the result at New Orleans, so far as human prescience could forecast them. Mr. Adams relates that as the emissaries of disunion were on their way to Washington, they were brought to a halt by the news of General Jackson's success at New Orleans. In truth, they instinctively knew that their schemes were frustrated by this unexampled victory, and concealing their nefarious intentions as well as they could, they sneaked back home amid the enthusiastic rejoicings of a victorious and united people.

* Adams, VIII, 300.

† Parton I, 566.

Mr. Adams repeatedly sneers at General Jackson's generalship, and indulges in much censure and disparagement of his defense of New Orleans. The most competent authorities differ with Mr. Adams.

"The Subaltern," who wrote so graphically the history of the British expedition against New Orleans, and lived to be ninety-one years of age, in 1885 (three years before his death) wrote to his friend General James Grant Wilson of New York, about Jackson's New Orleans campaign, in these words:

When I look back upon the means which General Jackson adopted to cover New Orleans, and remember the material of which his army was composed, I cannot but regard his management of that campaign as one of the most masterly of which history makes mention. His night attack on our advanced guard was as bold a stroke as ever was struck. It really paralyzed all our future operations, for though unsuccessful it taught us to hold our enemy in respect, and in all future movements to act with an excess of caution. The use also which he made of the river was admirable. Indeed, I am inclined to think that to him the generals who came after him were indebted for the perception of the great advantages to which the command of rivers may be turned. And do not let us forget that he had little else to oppose to Wellington's veterans fresh from their triumphs in Spain and the south of France, except raw levies. Altogether I think of Jackson as, next to Washington, the greatest general America has produced.'

CHAPTER XXV.

AFTER THE BATTLE—GENERAL JACKSON ARRESTS A JUDGE—THE JUDGE FINES GENERAL JACKSON—THE GENERAL PAYS THE FINE—UNPRECEDENTED HONORS.

When the battle of New Orleans was fought on January 8, 1815, peace had been concluded at Ghent between Great Britain and the United States, fifteen days. The ship that bore the glad tidings was still on the ocean. It did not seem probable that so powerful an armament as the British expedition would abandon the attempt against the Gulf coast after one failure. In the mind of General Jackson the question was where the next blow would fall; and as he wrote to the Secretary of War, he was "but too sensible that the moment when the enemy is opposing us is not the most proper to provide for them."

Therefore, after the festivities at New Orleans on January 21, military duty was resumed, and everything went on as before the departure of the hostile army. Martial law was maintained in all its inconvenient rigor. The Lines were still manned by day and by night. The wet and unhealthy camp behind the Lines still consigned many men every day to the hospital and some to the grave. The situation was alleviated as far as possible, and the incredible hardships were borne without complaint, as belonging to warfare.

So passed twenty-nine days after the flight of the enemy. Then Edward Livingston, who had been arranging the exchange of prisoners, returned to the city, bringing news, certain enough for most purposes, but indirect and unofficial, that the treaty of peace had been signed at Ghent, fifty-seven days before. The homesick army and the people of the city were thrown into an ecstasy of excitement. Unhappily, the package which the British admiral had received from Europe contained only a newspaper announcement of the intelligence, which neither commander could practically regard. Jackson at once published an address to the troops, explaining the impossibility of his accepting or acting upon a newspaper paragraph, and exhorting them to a patient continuance in duty for a little while longer.

The address did nothing to soothe the swelling discontent, to which the press soon gave strong expression. The business men detained in service were in a fever of impatience to sell their cotton and sugar and get them loaded on board the departing ships. The legislature sought in various ways to interfere. The French consul, attempting to shield and set free non-naturalized Frenchmen, General Jackson ordered him out of the city, not to return until the news of peace was officially published. He also ordered away all Frenchmen who were not citizens of the United States. Against this order Mr. Louis Louaillier, a distinguished and wealthy member of the legislature, published an able article in one of the newspapers. General Jackson sent an officer and a file of soldiers to arrest and consign to prison the offending member. Mr. Louaillier's counsel applied to Judge Dominick A. Hall, of the United States District Court, for a writ of *habeas corpus* in his behalf. The judge granted the petition. General Jackson replied by the following order:

"NEW ORLEANS, March 5, 1815.
Seven o'clock, P. M.

"TO COLONEL ARBUCKLE, *Headquarters Seventh Military District:*

"Having received proof that Dominick A. Hall has been aiding and abetting and exciting mutiny within my camp, you will forthwith order a detachment to arrest and confine him, and report to me as soon as arrested. You will be vigilant; the agents of our enemy are more numerous than was expected. You will be guarded against escapes.

A. JACKSON,
"Major-General Commanding.

"Dr. William E. Butler is ordered to accompany the detachment and point out the man.

A. JACKSON,
"Major-General Commanding."

An hour after the reception of this order, Colonel Arbuckle obeyed it, and that very night Judge Hall and Louis Louaillier were prisoners in the same room at the barracks. Other persons of less importance were also arrested for conduct tending to excite insubordination. A few days after, General Jackson caused Judge Hall to be conducted by "a discreet non-commissioned officer and four men" of a cavalry troop, beyond the lines of General Carroll's command and there "set at liberty."

The next day, March 13, sixty-four days after the battle of the 8th of January, arrived from Washington a packet giving official information of the treaty of peace and the cessation of hostilities. The glorious news was instantly published by the general officially, and with it he proclaimed a full pardon and immediate release of all persons who had offended against martial law. The next day he dismissed the volunteers of Tennessee, Kentucky, Mississippi and Louisiana, with an eloquent address of Jacksonian warmth and force.

Martial law having been abrogated, and the civil law having resumed its prerogatives, Judge Hall seized upon the occasion to give a signal proof of his judicial power. He summoned General Jackson to court to answer for his disregard of the writ of *habeas corpus.* On the appointed day the general appeared in court, attended by a numerous crowd, who were strongly disposed to disturb the decorum of the proceedings. He stood upon a bench and reminded them of the duty and respect owed by all citizens to a court of justice. He declined to apologize to the court or to explain or defend his conduct. He told the judge that in a paper presented the day before by his counsel he had given a full explanation of the reasons for his rejection of the writ and the arrest of the judge. The court had refused to receive the paper, and he had no other defense to present.

"Under the circumstances," said he, "I appear before you to receive the sentence of the court, having nothing further in my defense to offer."

Here was the typical American hero, statesman and citizen. In war, a lion; in policy, a sage; in peace, obedient to the law. It would be gratifying to be able to add that he was as tractable in disposition as Franklin, and as considerate as Washington in dealing with his fellow-citizens.

By a very little forbearance and concession on the part of General Jackson, the whole trouble might have been avoided. It should be remembered, however, that it is much easier for a person in good health, writing of these affairs under comfortable circumstances, to exercise a spirit of forbearance and concession, than it was for a sick commander-in-chief, racked with pain, harassed with anxiety and irritated by numberless annoyances, to subordinate his convictions of military duty to the amenities of civil life.

The judgment of the court was that "Major-General Andrew Jackson do pay a fine of one thousand dollars to the United States." He was borne back in triumph to his headquarters, the horses being removed from the carriage. Upon reaching his desk he sent back an aide-de-camp with a check for the amount of his fine, and there the matter ended for the time. President Madison, who was a weak and irresolute man, did not approve General Jackson's robust proceedings, and requested him to "observe a conciliatory deportment" toward the Legislature and people of Louisiana. The general explained to the Administration his reasons both for proclaiming and for maintaining martial law, to which no formal reply was made, and the disagreeable episode was soon forgotten in the indescribable joy and exultation of the time.

Nothing now remained to be done but to settle the pecuniary account of the defense. General

Jackson paid for the immortal cotton bales at six cents a pound, net price of cotton on the day the bales had been taken from the vessel and placed in the Lines. Mrs. Jackson arrived with their little adopted son, and the ladies of New Orleans made much of both.

General Jackson had a triumphal welcome home from almost every organized body in Western Tennessee. A procession of students, soldiers and citizens met him on his approach to Nashville, where, in the public square and in the court-house, he had an overwhelming reception, to which he responded with his usual simplicity and tact. His neighbors and friends met him near the Hermitage, to which he now returned after an absence of twenty-one months, during which he had broken forever the power of the Creek Indians, prepared the way for the acquisition of Florida, and defended the Gulf coast against the most formidable military and naval expedition which has ever approached the shores of the United States with hostile intent.

All the world could appreciate the brilliancy of the late campaign; but to Tennessee General Jackson had rendered a service so peculiar that it could be realized in all its extent only by her own yeomen, who now, for the first time since the settlement of the country, could sleep in absolute security against the savages whom they had displaced. Nothing could ever long disturb or seriously diminish the affection they felt for their heroic benefactor. It was simply true, as was often said in Tennessee, that "the popularity of Andrew Jackson could stand anything." This overwhelming popularity spread from Tennessee throughout the Union. All the preceding failures of the war seemed but to enhance the luster of its closing achievement, which restored the Nation's mortified self-respect and healed its wounded self-love. The masses of the people never forgot Old Hickory's transcendant services at New Orleans. Years afterwards, when he was a candidate for the Presidency, the thrilling shout "Hurrah for Jackson!" coming hot from their hearts, attested their appreciation of the work he did for his country in that memorable campaign.

After four months' rest at the Hermitage, General Jackson made a journey to Washington. The army had now been reduced to ten thousand men, commanded by two major-generals—Jacob Brown, in the northern division, and Andrew Jackson, in the southern division—both of whom had entered the army during the late war from the militia service. Jackson's visit to Washington on this occasion was in obedience to an order from the Secretary of War, the ostensible object being to arrange the distribution of the southern division of the army.

Perhaps the real object was to afford the victorious general a national triumph, and the whole journey did indeed resemble a triumphal progress. Escorts of mounted men went out to meet him from every large town, and accompanied him far beyond its borders. At Lynchburg in Virginia there was a grand banquet of three hundred persons, one of whom was the ex-President, Thomas Jefferson, who toasted the Defenders of

New Orleans in these words: "Honor and gratitude to those who have filled up the measure of their country's honor." General Jackson volunteered a toast: "James Monroe, late Secretary of War." It was a well-chosen sentiment for him to offer, for Mr. Monroe had pledged his whole estate in dispatching the two boat-loads of muskets, the arrival of a portion of which had made it possible to arm in time the volunteers from Tennessee. It was signficant also, because James Monroe was the Democratic candidate for the Presidency, and the election was to take place in a few months.

At the city of Washington, General Jackson was an unparalleled lion. He seems to have won all hearts by the unexpected gentleness of his manners, and the quiet dignity of his bearing.

Returning homeward early in 1816, he made an extensive tour among the Indian tribes, the Creeks, Cherokees, Chickasaws and Choctaws, holding treaties here and there, quieting some claims by money, others by negotiation. He had great success in dealing with Indians, particularly at this time, when the prestige of recent victory was added to the authority of his rank. In this journey he opened a vast extent of country to pioneers who were anxiously waiting to enter it. Again the saying arose thoughout the State that General Jackson never returned home without having done some great thing for Tennessee.

To complete his felicity, he was now enabled by his salary as major-general to pay off the last of his debts and build a modest house of brick for the gratification of his wife. For his own part, he had been well content with his double log-cabin, for as yet he had known in his whole life no other kind of home. About this time, too, his wife having become a member of the Presbyterian church, he built for her an exceedingly small brick church on the Hermitage farm. The general never failed in his attendance at this little church, and it was at his house that the clergymen were usually entertained. General Jackson always treated clergymen with respect. His own reverent nature would incline him to do so; it gratified Mrs. Jackson to have him extend the most generous hospitality to her favorite guests; and he never forgot his revered mother's ardent desire that he himself should become a minister of the Gospel.

Peter Cartwright, the noted pioneer preacher, relates an anecdote that is characteristic both of himself and General Jackson. Cartwright was in the habit of preaching very plainly, without regard to the official or social dignity of any of his hearers. His motto was: "Hew to the line, let the chips fly in whose face they will." On a certain occasion he was to preach in a church in Nashville. The pastor of the church was a time-serving sycophant, who dreaded the Reverend Peter's homespun rhetoric and plainness of Gospel inculcations. Just as Cartwright was about to begin his sermon, he felt some one pull his coat, and heard his fastidious and nervous brother whisper: "General Jackson has come in!" The hiss of the whisper was admonitory, and plainly said: "Now, Cartwright, be on your good behavior!" Indignant at what he considered an exhibition of unmanly sycophancy on the part of

"An Ambassador of Christ," the old pulpit hero turned to the congregation and roared out: "Who is General Jackson? If he don't get his soul converted, God will damn him as quick as he would a Guinea negro!"

The effect of this outburst was overwhelming, with respect to everybody except General Jackson, who stood leaning against a post, in plain view from the pulpit, with a smile of amusement playing over his grim countenance. When church was over, the fastidious pastor predicted that "General Jackson would chastise the preacher for his insolence." On the contrary, the next day in Nashville the general advanced to meet Cartwright in the street, told him that he was a man after his own heart, that he highly approved his independence, and that "a minister of Jesus Christ ought to love everybody and fear no mortal man." The soldier of the United States and the soldier of Christ had many traits in common, and they became fast friends for life.

CHAPTER XXVI.

POLITICAL MANŒUVERING—INDIAN TROUBLES IN FLORIDA—GENERAL JACKSON AGAIN IN THE FIELD.

During the winter of 1816–17, General Jackson had a very interesting and elevated correspondence with James Monroe, who had triumphed in the recent Presidential election. He gave the incoming President much good advice; urging him, among other things, to rise superior to party feelings in the administration of the government. Mr. Monroe replied in the same lofty strain, and was able to live up to it during his whole Administration. This correspondence had a powerful influence on the fortunes of General Jackson.

In March, 1817, after Henry Clay had declined the War Department, Mr. Monroe was about to nominate Andrew Jackson for the same post, when he received from the general a private request that he would refrain from doing so.

As commander of the southern division of the army, General Jackson was chiefly occupied with Indian affairs. He had no very serious trouble with the savages of Alabama, Mississippi and Georgia, for they were clearly within his jurisdiction, and also within his reach. As the year 1817 went on, his attention, and that of the whole country, was gradually drawn to the Spanish province of Florida, thinly inhabited, weakly governed, and furnishing unequaled opportunities for irregular enterprise. Its untrodden wilds and everglades became the refuge of runaway slaves, discontented Seminoles and hostile Creeks who had refused assent to the treaty of Fort Jackson. The English Colonel Nichols reappeared there and gave fallacious hopes to his late defeated allies. Adventurers from other lands resorted thither upon various pretexts, and the Spanish governor was wholly unequal to the repression of disorder in a province which is to this day the largest State east of the Mississippi River.

The negro runaways, who had no friends, either white or Indian, English, Spanish or American, built a fort on the Appalachicola, and occupied it with three hundred and thirty-four inmates. A single red-hot shot, heated with difficulty in the galley-fire of a United States gunboat, blew the fort into the air, killed two hundred and seventy negroes instantly and mortally injured nearly all the rest. Only three men escaped from the ruins unharmed. This event destroyed the power of the negroes in Florida, and gave a brief period of repose to the other inhabitants.

Strange to relate, the destruction of the negro fort only inflamed the passions of the Seminoles, and excited them to more active hostility. They readily obtained supplies both of ammunition and weapons from the neighboring Bahama Islands. Filibusters from abroad misled and excited them still more. In November, 1817, there had been robbery and murder both by whites and red men in the border counties of Georgia and Florida, and a growing alarm had spread through all the region. Some

Georgia militia were in the field. United States troops, under the command of General Edmund P. Gaines, occupied Fort Scott, near the junction of the Chattahoochee and Flint rivers. In Georgia, near Fort Scott, was an Indian village called Fowltown, containing forty-five warriors, whose chief had set up the red war-pole, around which the warriors danced in the evening. General Gaines, on hearing this intelligence, sent for the chief, who refused to come. Then he dispatched a force of two hundred and fifty troops, under the command of Colonel Twiggs, with orders to bring to him these forty-five warriors and their chief, peaceably if they could, forcibly if they must. The detachment reached Fowltown just before the dawn of day, November 21, 1817. The warriors fired upon them. The troops returned the fire, upon which the Indians fled, leaving behind them two men and one woman slain, besides several wounded. Colonel Twiggs, on searching the town, found in the house of the chief a red coat of the English uniform, a pair of golden epaulets and a certificate in the handwriting of the British Colonel Nichols that the chief of the Fowltown warriors had always been a true and faithful friend of the British. Colonel Twiggs remained near the town, which was burned on the following day by the order of General Gaines himself.

On December 1, 1817, an open barge, containing forty United States soldiers, seven wives of soldiers and four little children, was slowly ascending the Appalachicola River, a few miles below Fort Scott, in Georgia. Not an Indian had been seen by the party. Suddenly, as the boat was warping close in shore, past a swamp covered thick with cane and trees, a large party of Indians lying in ambush poured a volley of musketry into the boat, killing or wounding nearly every soldier at the first fire. The savages rose from their ambush, leaped into the boat and completed the massacre, with all the aggravations known to savage warfare, even to the dashing out of the brains of infants torn from their mothers' arms. Only two men escaped unharmed. One woman was spared, who was carried away captive.

Having tasted blood, the Seminoles raged about the Georgia frontier, killing, destroying and plundering. All Georgia was in terror. Homes were laid waste and hundreds of cattle driven off. Before Christmas, Fort Scott, at the junction of the Chattahoochee and Flint, was threatened, and the garrison was short of provisions.

In Florida, as General Gaines computed, there were but 2,700 warriors, but rumor exaggerated their numbers tenfold, and their hostile proceedings seemed to the people of the Gulf States almost as formidable an outbreak as the one which had preceded the Creek War of 1813-14. It had also its peculiar difficulties, because these Indians came forth from a Spanish province, a foreign land, and as soon as the work of destruction was accomplished, sought and found protection under the Spanish flag.

On January 11, 1818, six weeks after the massacre of the barge party by the Seminoles, late in the evening, a messenger from Mr. Calhoun, Secretary of War, reached General Jackson's abode and placed in his hands a dispatch ordering him to the frontier to quell this alarming disturbance, and authorizing him to call upon the governors of adjacent States for all the men he needed. Before he slept that night, the general had decided upon his plan of operation, which was to call out his old and well-tried volunteers of Tennessee and Kentucky, and swoop down upon the savage foe, wherever they might be, without regard to boundary lines.

So thought, so done. That was Andrew Jackson's way. It is doubtful if there ever was a historical character who more instinctively realized that "the flighty purpose never is o'ertook," or that "the firstlings of his heart" should be "the firstlings of his hand." The governor of Tennessee, as it chanced, was absent from Nashville and could not be reached. General Jackson "took the responsibility." Eleven days after the receipt of Mr. Calhoun's order he left Nashville with a guard of two companies, amid the acclamations of the whole population, and started for Fort Scott, four hundred and fifty miles distant, leaving a thousand of his comrades at the rendezvous nearly ready to follow him.

Before leaving home, General Jackson wrote a private letter to President Monroe on the delicate matter of boundary lines and the Spanish flag. The substance of it was: Why not seize the whole of Florida and hold it as an indemnity for the outrages of Spain?

"This," he added, "can be done without implicating the government. Let it be signified to me through any channel (say Mr. J. Rhea) that the possession of the Floridas would be desirable to the United States, and in sixty days it will be accomplished." What confidence in his ability! And the results always showed that his confidence was not misplaced.

Mr. Rhea was an aged member of Congress from Tennessee, and much in the confidence of General Jackson. Now it so chanced that at this very time Mr. John Quincy Adams, Secretary of State, was entering into negotiations with the Spanish minister for the peaceable acquisition of Florida by purchase or otherwise. To promote this negotiation General Gaines had been ordered to treat the Spanish governor and the Spanish flag with the most scrupulous respect. He was not to cross the boundary unless the occasion was irresistibly urgent, and on no account whatever was he to pursue a hostile party into a fortification over which waved the Spanish flag.

Nevertheless, Mr. Monroe, from a sick-bed sent for Mr. John Rhea, showed him General Jackson's letter, and requested him to inform the general that the President *approved of his suggestions.*

General Jackson received this vague reply when he was within a day's march of Fort Scott, and he accepted it as an unequivocal sanction of his proposal to seize and hold as much of Florida as he thought best. The Secretary of War had given him large discretion, and this letter, as he always maintained to his dying day, authorized him to conduct the war absolutely according to his own judgment. This should be remembered in order that the reader may understand the far-reaching consequences which resulted from General Jackson's just and rational interpretation of the authority given to him.

It should also be remembered that he was not informed of the negotiation with Spain for the purchase of Florida.

Thus authorized, and thus imperfectly informed, General Jackson paid not the slightest attention to boundary lines. He attacked the Seminoles wherever he could find them, and he pursued them whithersoever they sought refuge. The rapidity of his movements so forestalled the combinations of the enemy, that no considerable body of Indians was ever encountered. Many villages were burned. In one of them the soldiers found the red pole of war near the council-house, from which were suspended fifty fresh scalps, some of women and infants. In a house near by, there were old scalps of three hundred men. A thousand head of Georgia cattle were recaptured in the wilds of Florida.

General Jackson pushed on to the Spanish fort of St. Marks, at the mouth of the Appalachicola River. Discovering incontrovertible evidence that hostile Indians had found refuge within its walls, he wrote very politely to the Spanish commandant, informing him that "to prevent the recurrence of so gross a violation of neutrality," he deemed it expedient "to garrison that fortress with American troops until the close of the present war."

Upon receiving from the Spanish commandant a reply denying that Indians hostile to the United States had found refuge within the fort, and refusing to surrender, General Jackson instantly marched into the fort, removed the Spanish flag, substituted the stars and stripes, and garrisoned the fort with his own troops. He continued to treat the Spanish governor with politeness and consideration. He informed him that he would furnish transports "to convey himself, his family and his command to Pensacola." The United States navy cooperating, he assumed the control of the commerce of the port, and in all other ways comported himself as became a conquerer who had brought St. Marks into the possession of the United States.

Other Indian villages were captured. In a few days, so far as was known, there was not a hostile body within the bounds of Florida. On his homeward march, he received from the governor of Pensacola a "solemn protest" against these proceedings, and a threat that, if he did not at once retire from the province, he should be compelled to do so by force. He replied to this document by marching for Pensacola, then garrisoned by three hundred Spanish troops. He opened fire upon the fort with one nine-pounder and five howitzers, and was about to order an assault, when the place was surrendered.

In Fort St. Marks, under the protection of the Spanish flag, General Jackson found a Scottish trader named A. Arbuthnot, who, he had reason to believe, had been intriguing with the Indians and inciting them to hostility. Another British trader was taken with one of the Indian parties in the field. His name was R. C. Ambrister. He wore a British uniform, and had done his utmost to arouse the Indians to resist the Americans to extremity. These two men were put into close confinement at St. Marks. A court-martial was ordered to try them for "exciting the Indians to war," "acting as spies" and "inciting the Indians to murder." The court consisted of Major-General E. P. Gaines, president, and thirteen commissioned officers. Both men, after a two days' trial, were found guilty. Arbuthnot was sentenced by the court to be hanged; Ambrister to receive fifty stripes and to be confined with ball and chain for twelve months. General Jackson approved the sentence dooming Arbuthnot to die, but disapproved that of Ambrister. He ordered Arbuthnot to be "suspended by the neck with a rope until he is dead, and Robert C. Ambrister to be shot to death." The sentences were executed on the following morning, after General Jackson had resumed his homeward march. Attempts were unjustly made to cast odium on General Jackson for the execution of these men; but he never wavered in his belief that they were the immediate cause of all the massacre and woe which had been caused by the Seminole outbreak. "They were spies, sir; they were spies," he would say. And what else could he say or think when fourteen commissioned officers, after a thorough trial of the case, had pronounced them guilty of the offenses charged?

CHAPTER XXVII.

GENERAL JACKSON'S PROCEEDINGS IN FLORIDA CAUSE A WORLD-WIDE COMMOTION—THE POLITICIANS EAGER TO MAKE USE OF HIS POPULARITY.

General Jackson left Florida in possession of the forces of the United States. There were garrisons of American troops both at St. Marks and at Pensacola, and no flag was seen at either place except the stars and stripes. Nashville received him on his arrival, as so often before and so often after, with enthusiastic approval. A public dinner was given him. One of the toasts was:

"Pensacola—Spanish perfidy and Indian barbarity rendered its capture necessary. May our government never surrender it from the fear of war!"

General Jackson volunteered the following toast:

"Our Country: Though forbearance is her maxim, she should show to foreign nations that, under a pretense of neutrality, her rights are not to be outraged."

When the information of what General Jackson had done in Florida reached Europe, it occasioned a profound sensation. The Spanish ministry at Madrid was amazed and confounded. In Great Britain, the administration of Castlereagh was at its wits' end between its reluctance to resume the burdens of war, and the clamors of the people for revenge upon the slayers of Arbuthnot and Ambrister. Every cabinet in Europe discussed the dilemma.

The vast preponderance of American opinion sustained General Jackson. The negotiation with Spain for the cession of Florida was, of course, disrupted, seemingly never to be resumed. President Monroe and his cabinet discussed the whole subject almost daily during July and August, 1818. Mr. Calhoun, the Secretary of War, gave it as his opinion that General Jackson had exceeded his orders and that his conduct ought to be formally investigated. Mr. Crawford thought that, in taking the Spanish forts, General Jackson believed and had reason to believe he was doing what the President wished done. The President himself, though he denied all recollection of the Rhea letter, had no choice but to agree with Mr. Crawford,

In these critical circumstances, John Quincy Adams, the Massachusetts baby of Andrew Jackson's natal year, now Secretary of State, came to the rescue of the Administration, of the North Carolina baby, now the famous and embroiling General Jackson, and of the imperiled peace o the world. He said, in substance:

The case is so complicated that, whatever course we adopt, we shall do some wrong. We must stand by General Jackson, while frankly admitting that he has done some unauthorized acts. His taking of the Spanish posts, although it was his own act, was just and necessary under the circumstances. Mr. Adams advised that both Pensacola and St. Marks be restored to Spain. With regard to the execution of the British traders, he accepted the verdict of the court-martial, as well as the presentation of the evidence upon which the verdict was founded. His reply to Senor Pizarro, the Spanish minister, was a document of torrent-like power and audacity. It concluded with a threat to the effect that if ever *again* an officer of the United States should be compelled to march into Florida and seize the Spanish forts, the United States would hold them and the province itself as a permanent possession.

Never had a diplomatic paper more immediate and striking success than this. Besides quieting the conscience of the American people, it more than half convinced the Spanish government. It had its effect on Lord Castlereagh, and essentially contributed to the preservation of peace. It satisfied even General Jackson, though he made an exceedingly wry face at the surrender of the forts.

It remained for the Congress of the United States to pronounce its judgment upon the disturbing events in Florida. Upon that judgment, too, the electric dispatch of Mr. Adams had its effect.

General Jackson, at the Hermitage, was watching the course of events with an eagle eye. One evening in January, 1819, he dropped in upon his neighbor, Major William B. Lewis. They had met earlier in the day, when the major had shown his general an overcoat fresh from the tailor's. General Jackson had tried it on, and pronounced it a good coat. On entering Major Lewis's library in the evening, and seeing the overcoat still hanging over a chair, he took it upon his arm, and said:

"Major, there's a combination in Congress to ruin me. I start for Washington to-morrow morning. My overcoat is rusty; I want you to get another made for yourself and charge it to me, and let me take this one with me."

The general gave further explanation of the supposed combination and took his leave. The next morning before the dawn he was on horseback again for a twenty days' ride to Washington. At the capital he refused all invitations until Congress had pronounced its verdict. Day by day he was closeted with the President, with members of the Cabinet, with members of Congress, showing documents, making explanations, and in general conducting the campaign. The debate in the House of Representatives lasted nearly a month. Henry Clay was General Jackson's chief opponent in the House, as Mr. Calhoun had been in the cabinet. They all belonged to the same political party. Clay and Calhoun were already strenuous aspirants to the Presidency. As John Quincy Adams and Colonel Benton informs us, Clay and Calhoun snuffed danger to their own aspirations in General Jackson's overwhelming popularity, and naturally wished to deal him a blow that would so diminish his popularity as to render him innocuous as a rival. Hence their efforts to crush him on this seemingly favorable occasion. But they made a fatal mistake—a mistake that was fatal to their own political aspirations, and resulted in raising an impassable barrier between them and the Presidential chair. February 8, 1819, the resolutions of censure came to the vote. The execution of the two British traders was sanctioned by a vote of 90 to 54; the seizure of the posts was justified by 91 to 65. Congress sustained General Jackson.

He next took the verdict of the people. He left Washington February 11, 1819, for a visit to the northern cities. His four days' stay at Philadelphia was a continuous round of festivities and receptions. Whenever the public could catch a glimpse of him he was greeted with the most enthusiastic cheers. At New York, the Common Council conferred upon him the freedom of the city. He dined with the Mayor and a brilliant company of guests. Tammany Hall gave him a public dinner. The newspapers bestowed upon him almost unmingled eulogy. What surprised the gentlemen who were nearest him was the unvarying tact of his demeanor and his responses, as well as the soldier-like dignity of his bearing before the public. At Philadelphia he gave as his toast "The memory of Benjamin Franklin;" at New York, "Governor DeWitt Clinton." At Baltimore and Washington, on his return, similar attentions were paid him, and as he approached his home, it appeared as if all Tennessee united to give him an unequaled welcome.

Meanwhile, Mr. Adams continued his triumphant diplomacy. While General Jackson was dancing at the New York ball, Feb. 22, 1819, the Spanish minister had signed the treaty which ceded Florida to the United States. There were some delays in surrendering the country, but on the same day in February, 1821, all difficulties being removed, the treaty was finally ratified, and Spain announced her readiness to surrender the province.

The army being now greatly reduced, General Jackson resigned his commission. President Monroe immediately appointed him Governor of Florida, and Commissioner to receive the Territory from the Spanish officials. He held his office in Florida but four months. He resigned in disgust, and early in November, 1821, he was at home again. He was then fifty-four years of age, and hoped to spend the evening of his life in cultivating his farm on the banks of the Cumberland. The new Hermitage was completed—a two-story brick house, with a double piazza in front and behind. It was neither a handsome nor a spacious edifice, but it was then the finest house in the county. Behind it was a well kept garden, and around it one of the best cultivated farms in Western Tennessee. General Jackson had no expectation whatever of reentering public life. Civil office he never relished, and the cession of Florida seemed to have removed all danger of foreign war.

It was in vain, however, that General Jackson dreamed of passing the remainder of his days in rural quietude and in the felicities of domestic life. Such an overshadowing reputation as his, such unparalleled popularity as he enjoyed, were possessions too valuable to his party and to politicians to be permitted to go unused. As one of his admirers said: "Never since the days of Washington has any man held such winning Presidential cards as Old Hickory has in his hand." That, of course, settled it. "The good of the country" demanded that General Jackson should give up his personal desires and permit his private interests to be sacrificed in behalf of the public welfare.

At first, General Jackson resisted all appeals

THE HERMITAGE.—*See Page* 272.

made to him to become a candidate for the Presidency. But there has never been a popular citizen of the United States who could elude the machinations of astute party leaders who had resolved that he should serve his country as a Presidential candidate. General Jackson's scruples were overcome. He consented to enter the field as a candidate; and, on entering the field, he took his personal characteristics with him. The result was interesting. As soon as the old hero got into the fight, not only his opponents, but also his supporters, were astounded at the ability he displayed in this new field of warfare. I say new field of *warfare*, because such it was. Whenever Andrew Jackson went into a contest of any kind, warfare accompanied him.

CHAPTER XXVIII.

THE ART OF PRESIDENT-MAKING—GENERAL JACKSON A CANDIDATE—NO ELECTION BY THE PEOPLE—HENRY CLAY DECIDES THE CONTEST IN THE HOUSE OF REPRESENTATIVES.

The early Presidents of this Republic were nominated in a very quiet, expeditious, inexpensive and pleasant manner. In January or February of the year of a Presidential election, a notice, of four or five lines, was issued by each party, inviting its members of Congress to meet in the Representatives' chamber at the Capitol, at seven o'clock in the evening, for the purpose of "recommending candidates to the people of the United States for the offices of President and Vice-President." At the time appointed, the caucus met, organized, balloted; and, behold, the great business done! Usually it was all over by nine o'clock in the evening, and the nominations were accepted by the rank and file of each party without audible demur.

In this simple way the man who had the strongest claim to be considered the head of his party, was very likely to be placed at the head of the Presidential ticket. But the Congressional caucus stood in the way of all personal ambitions that were beyond the recognition of the leaders of the two parties at Washington assembled. In 1824, there were five statesmen, of national prominence and great talents, who had some hope of being presented as candidates for the Presidency to the rank and file of the dominant party: William H. Crawford, of Georgia, Secretary of the Treasury; John Quincy Adams, Secretary of State; John C. Calhoun, Secretary of War; Henry Clay, Speaker of the House of Representatives, and De Witt Clinton of New York.

But there was a group of men in Tennessee who had set their hearts upon the elevation of Andrew Jackson to the Presidency. The most resolute and zealous of these was Major William B. Lewis, who had served under Jackson in the late war, and had rendered him at critical times extremely important service. Major Lewis was a wealthy Tennessee planter of the old school, absolutely destitute of political ambition, but most warmly attached to his old commander, whom he believed to possess a military capacity equal to that of Alexander, Julius Cæsar or Napoleon Bonaparte. He believed also that he was capable of administering the government on the principles avowed in his correspondence with Mr. Monroe in 1816, of which the major possessed a copy. His home was on the road which the general always traveled on his way from his farm to Nashville, and there had grown up between the two families a familiar, confidential and affectionate friendship.

The general had returned from Florida in November, 1821, a private citizen for the first time in ten years. Then it was that Major Lewis entered upon the task of placing him on the road to the Presidency. Many other men cooperated in the work; many things were done in many States; but the animating spirit of the movement in its earlier and doubtful stages was Major Lewis, who was probably the most adroit wire-puller and consummate political manager of that time.

First, the Nashville *Gazette*, in January, 1822, placed the name of Andrew Jackson conspicuously before its readers as a Presidential candidate, and the movement was seconded by the press of the State generally. In July, 1822, the Legislature of Tennessee adopted a series of resolutions formally nominating General Jackson as a candidate. In 1823 it devolved upon the Legislature to elect a United States Senator to succeed Colonel Williams, a highly popular gentleman opposed to General Jackson's election. Major Lewis now adopted a bold measure. To use his own language: "As nobody else could be found to beat Colonel Williams, it was proposed to beat him with the general himself." Andrew Jackson was accordingly elected a Senator of the United States. A movement in favor of the general was also started in Pennsylvania, where at every assemblage of the people the name of Andrew Jackson proved to be irresistibly attractive.

King Caucus was dethroned. The Congressional caucus met, indeed, in 1824, but only sixty-six members attended, and the nomination by it of Mr. Crawford carried but little weight.

General Jackson's conduct at Washington as a member of the Senate, was everything which his most prudent friends could have desired. He buried the tomahawk extremely deep. He had had a quarrel with Winfield Scott; he now made friends with him. He became reconciled to Henry Clay, dined with him, invited him to dinner, and rode with him in the same carriage. Strangest of all, he and Colonel Benton became cordial friends, though the general still had in his arm a relic of the Benton affray in the shape of a bullet. His votes in the Senate were such as commended him to conservative business men, and some of them were well pleasing to the Federalists. He wrote a letter favoring a moderate and "judicious" tariff. He voted for several internal improvement bills.

A masterly movement of Major Lewis's was the timely publication, in 1824, of the dignified and patriotic correspondence which had taken place in 1816 and 1817, between General Jackson and President Monroe. The calm and elevated tone of this correspondence had the best possible effect in winning to the general's side the solid citizens, who care nothing for party triumphs, except so far as they promote the welfare of the country.

It is evident from the records of the time that General Jackson was the most brilliant and captivating personage in Washington. The season itself was one of exceptional interest. The eighth of January was celebrated all over the country with unusual fervor. The general figured in many attractive pageants and ceremonials. Mr. Custis, of Arlington, presented him with General Washington's pocket telescope. Mr. Robinson, of Sudley, Va., gave him the pair of pistols which General Washington received from Lafayette during the Revolutionary War. With Lafayette himself the general had many pleasing interviews, for this was the year of Lafayette's triumphal progress through the United States. Here is a passage from one of Mrs. Jackson's letters:

"We are boarding in the same house with the nation's guest, Lafayette. I am delighted with him. When we first came to this house, the general said he would go and pay the marquis the first visit. Both having the same desire, and at the same time, they met on the entry of the stairs. It was truly interesting. The emotion of revolutionary feeling was aroused in them both. At Charleston, General Jackson saw him on the field of battle; the one a boy of twelve, the marquis twenty-three. He wears a wig, and is a little inclined to corpulency. He is very healthy, eats hearty, goes to every party, and that is every night."

Incidents of this kind exhibited the candidate to the country in a captivating light, and made him a favorite theme of the newspapers. His demeanor both in public and in private was all suavity and grace. As Daniel Webster said, in one of his letters to his brother Ezekiel, "General Jackson's manners are more Presidential than those of any of the candidates. He is grave, mild and reserved. My wife is for him decidedly. . . The truth is, he is the people's candidate in a great part of the Southern and Western country." Several observers of the period report that, of all the candidates, he was the ladies' favorite in Washington.

But these attractive qualifications did not suffice on this occasion. The people failed to elect a President in 1824, and it devolved upon the House of Representatives to choose one of the three leading candidates, Crawford, Jackson and Adams. As Jackson received the vote of more States and of more people than any other candidate, it was natural that his friends should look to the House to gratify the desire of so commanding a plurality. Henry Clay, then at the most effective and brilliant period of his long career, forty-seven years of age, had been for many years Speaker of the House of Representatives, and had acquired in it so great an influence that he now held the gift of the Presidency in his hand. He left his home in Kentucky fully resolved not to vote for Andrew Jackson in any circumstances whatever; first, because, to use his own language, Jackson was "a military chieftain," and, secondly, because, as a military chieftain, he had shown an arbitrary cast of character—reasons, it may be remarked, which would have prevented Mr. Clay from voting for George Washington for President. No doubt Mr. Clay had persuaded himself that these were the true reasons for his opposition to General Jackson; but deep in his heart was the actual reason, namely, an unconquerable personal dislike of Andrew Jackson, generated by the clear perception that of all men he was most to be dreaded as a political rival.

Crawford, who had been prostrated with paralysis, was equally out of the question; and, therefore, by a kind of self-imposed necessity, the Speaker threw the whole weight of his name and influence in favor of John Quincy Adams. A long contest had been expected in the House, and the hall was crowded with excited spectators. On the very first ballot Mr. Adams received the votes of thirteen States, then a majority, and Daniel Webster, one of the tellers, announced to the astonished and breathless multitude that John Quincy Adams had been chosen President of the United States. The announcement was received with faint applause and some hisses. The galleries were cleared and the House soon after adjourned.

The defeated candidates gave no outward signs of disappointment, least of all General Jackson, who could be, when the occasion required it, a consummate histrionic artist. That very evening, four or five hours after the vote in the House, he met his successful rival face to face in the East Room, at President Monroe's last levee. We have a graphic account of the meeting of these North Carolina and Massachusetts babies, now grown so great, from the pen of S. G. Goodrich (Peter Parley):

"Mr. Adams was by himself; General Jackson had a large, handsome lady on his arm. They looked at each other for a moment, and then General Jackson moved forward, and reaching out his long arm, said:

"'How do you do, Mr. Adams. I give you my left hand, for the right, as you see, is devoted to the fair. I hope you are very well, sir.'

"All this was gallantly and heartily said and done. Mr. Adams took the general's hand, and said, with chilling coldness:

"'Very well, sir. I hope General Jackson is well?'

"It was curious to see the Western planter, the Indian fighter, the stern soldier who had written his country's glory in the blood of the enemy at New Orleans, genial and gracious in the midst of a court, while the old courtier and diplomat was stiff, rigid, cold as a statue."

A few days after this meeting, Mr. Adams offered

the post of Secretary of State to Henry Clay. The Kentuckian consulted his friends, thought the matter over for a week, and accepted the offer. It was an act which a skillful politician would not have done. Mr. Clay did it, however, and did it apparently without anticipating the interpretation which would be put upon it by his antagonist.

General Jackson heard this news from Colonel R. M. Johnson, of the Senate, and instantly attributed the appointment to "bargain and corruption;" or, as he wrote to Major Lewis, "The *Judas* of the West has closed the contract, and will receive the thirty pieces of silver. His end will be the same. Was there ever witnessed such a bare-faced corruption in any country before?" The same idea, though expressed more moderately and at greater length, was spread over the country by means of a letter from Jackson to Major Lewis, both of whom lived and died implicitly believing in the truth of the charge.

In another long letter to Samuel Swartwout, of New York, Jackson descanted with masterly force and tact upon Henry Clay's objectionable phrase, "military chieftain." A better letter for a political purpose has never been written, and it had the additional merit of being substantially true. He sketched briefly his career as a soldier, showing that it was the peril of his country which alone had ever called him into the field from civil pursuits; to which he had gladly returned when no foe menaced its borders.

"Mr. Clay," he added, "has never yet risked himself for his country. He has never sacrificed his repose, nor made an effort to repel an invading foe."

This long and powerful letter, published in hundreds of newspapers, was almost enough of itself to elect the author of it to the Presidency at the next opportunity.

The general's homeward journey to Tennessee was a triumphal progress. If he had been the President-elect he could not have been more enthusiastically welcomed.

Soon after General Jackson's arrival at home, occurred General Lafayette's memorable visit to Nashville. There was a pageant of many days, during which it was impossible to determine which was the popular hero of the occasion; the French or the American general. At the Hermitage, General Jackson had the pleasure of showing the French gentlemen over his farm, where, as one of them recorded, "we everywhere remarked the greatest order and the most perfect neatness."

CHAPTER XXIX.

THE PRESIDENTIAL CAMPAIGN OF 1828—GENERAL JACKSON TRIUMPHANT—SUDDEN DEATH OF MRS. JACKSON—ITS EFFECT ON THE GENERAL—THE INAUGURATION.

The Presidential campaign of 1828 began on the day of Mr. Adams' election by the House of Representatives in 1825. Four years of pageantry and tumult followed. But it was not all tumult and festival. The "bargain and corruption" cry had its effect. Henry Clay did not submit in silence to the charge of bargain and corruption. He personally met the charge, and gave as complete a refutation of it as the case admitted. But, unfortunately, although the charge was undoubtedly false, it was, nevertheless, one of those charges which can only be denied, not refuted, at least, so far as political opponents are concerned; and it was used with damaging effect. Mr. Clay's adherents carried the war into Jackson's own county, even into his own family. The whole life of Andrew Jackson was ruthlessly raked over, and commented on with partisan rancor and unscrupulousness. His duels, his feuds, his personal affrays, his hanging of deserters and his execution of Arbuthnot and Ambrister were made the most of.

The campaign was distinguished for the envenomed animosity displayed on both sides. Adams was accused of numberless political crimes, and also of personal dishonesty. Every one of the accusations was doubtless untrue; but Adams was so cold-hearted, so regardless of the obligations of comradeship, so steeped in that odious bogus public virtue which always strengthens the opposition and from which a friend can never derive any benefit, that the masses of the people loved to believe whatever was said against him, and he had but few zealous personal defenders. Jackson, on the other hand, was so chivalric and warm-hearted, and it was so well known that he never turned a cold shoulder to a friend, his supporters rushed to his defense with that self-sacrificing devotion which seldom encounters defeat.

Of all the floods of vituperation and calumny that were poured upon him, nothing moved General Jackson except the attacks made upon his revered mother, and the revival of the ancient scandals concerning his marriage, which also keenly wounded Mrs. Jackson. Major Lewis, besides organizing a committee at Nashville to investigate and refute false charges against the general, undertook personally the congenial task of defending Mrs. Jackson. He devoted six months to this object, traveled thousands of miles in search of evidence, and performed his duty so well that the vindication of Mrs. Jackson was complete. Only the basest and most malignant of mankind could thenceforth lend a hospitable ear to the slanders against her.

An Irish refugee named Binns, who was in favor of Adams, and edited a Philadelphia paper called the *Democratic Press*, brought out a number of campaign hand-bills which attracted much attention. One of them, called the "Coffin Hand-bill," attained great notoriety. I have a copy of it before me. It is adorned with six intensely black coffins, on each of which is the name of a soldier who was hanged for desertion, at New Orleans. A blood-curdling account of the hangings is given, and it is intimated that should Jackson be elected President of the United States, some of his opponents would meet with a like tragic fate.

There had never been so much talent, whether political or literary, employed in a Presidential campaign as in this one on behalf of General Jackson. Much of the writing was done with a high degree of ability, and a number of the general's friends gave themselves up, without reserve, to the work of electing him. On the other hand, the attacks upon him were often delivered clumsily, and recoiled upon the accusers. There was a lumbering pamphlet, for example, in which General Jackson's combats and duels were presented in the form of a numbered catalogue, from one to thirty-six. This labored work called forth the following paragraph:

> "COOL AND DELIBERATE MURDER.—Jackson coolly and deliberately put to death upward of fifteen hundred British troops on the eighth of January, 1815, on the plains below New Orleans, for no other offense than that they wished to sup in the city that night."

So adroit a sentence as this, in the crisis of a Presidential election, neutralizes the effect of many pamphlets. For those who could not read there was the hickory pole in thousands of villages and towns, the erection of each of which furnished an opportunity for an interesting procession and plenty of campaign speaking.

Imagine, too, General Jackson's visit to New Orleans to celebrate the eighth of January, 1828. A magnificent procession of steamboats descended the Mississippi and swept past the city on the morning of the great day, General Jackson standing on the upper deck of one of them, his head uncovered, visible to the countless multitude. Eighteen steamboats of the largest size steamed round the crescent and descended as far as the battle-field, where imposing ceremonies took place. This grand demonstration was ridiculed by a portion of the opposition, while others used it for the purpose of trying to make the people believe that if Jackson were elected President he would overthrow the liberties of the country and establish a military despotism.

Everything seemed to work in favor of Jackson. President Adams himself wrought for him by his exasperating disregard of his obligations to his political friends. Binns attempted to give him a few hints on the subject, but was coldly informed that the President would not make any removals of office-holders for political reasons. Binns bowed respectfully, and remarked that the consequence would be that the President himself would be removed as soon as the term for which he had been elected should expire. In reporting the incident Binns said : " This intimation [of his removal] gave the President no concern, and assuredly did in no wise affect his previous determination."

Election day came around at length. Andrew

Jackson was elected President of the United States, and John C. Calhoun was reelected Vice-President. Out of 261 electoral votes, Jackson received 178 and Mr. Adams 83—less than half the whole number. All New England, except one district in Maine, voted for Adams and Rush. New York gave them sixteen electoral votes to twenty for Jackson and Calhoun. New Jersey, Delaware and Maryland voted for Adams and Rush. Every other State voted for Jackson—Pennsylvania, Virginia, both Carolinas, Georgia, Kentucky, Ohio, Alabama, Mississippi, Missouri and Illinois. As for Tennessee, in the whole State Adams and Rush obtained less than three thousand votes, and in many towns every vote was cast for Jackson and Calhoun. A distinguished gentleman of North Carolina told Mr. Parton that he happened to ride into a Tennessee village on the evening of the last day of election. He found all the men in the place engaged in hunting down two of their fellow-citizens. He asked what the obnoxious men had done. He was told that the village had set its heart upon giving Andrew Jackson a unanimous vote, but these two men had frustrated this desire by voting for Adams and Rush. When the whiskey flowed freely in the evening, the exhilarated majority proposed to tar and feather the two independent voters, who, however, fled to the woods and so escaped.

When the news reached the Hermitage, it created no particular sensation, because the close calculators had pretty clearly anticipated the result. Mrs. Jackson quietly remarked:

"Well, for Mr. Jackson's sake, I am glad. For my own part, I never wished it."

But the people of Nashville received the tidings with the enthusiasm that was usually aroused among them by any event which nearly concerned General Jackson,and they resolved to celebrate the victory by a banquet that should surpass anything known in the annals of their city. The day appointed for the dinner was December 23, the anniversary of the first attack upon the British below New Orleans. General Jackson had accepted an invitation to the banquet. While the gentlemen of Nashville were making arrangements for the festival, the ladies organized themselves into sewing-circles for the purpose of preparing a sumptuous wardrobe for Mrs. Jackson to wear after she had taken up her abode in the Presidential mansion. But alas! she was never to wear those sumptuous garments! The shroud was to take the place of the White House robes.

The morning of December 23, 1828, the day appointed for the grand banquet in honor of the election of Andrew Jackson to the Presidency, broke auspiciously upon Nashville. Soon after sunrise the various committees were completing the work of preparation. The setting of the long tables and the decoration of the dining-room were nearly finished. The officers and men of the troop who were to escort the President-elect from the Hermitage to the city were dressing for their long ride. Country wagons and wayfarers were beginning to come in, and the roads far and near were filled with people on their way to the capital.

In the midst of these festive preparations, a horseman arrived from the Hermitage with dreadful news: Late in the evening before, Mrs. Jackson had died suddenly of heart-disease. She had been ill for several days, but had recovered sufficiently to be seemingly out of danger. These facts were not known to the public, and the shock caused by the news of her death was paralyzing. The grief of the people was beyond portrayal. Every one felt, and felt most poignantly, that the death of Mrs. Jackson was a personal affliction and a national calamity.

All the festive preparations were immediately abandoned. A handbill was printed countermanding the previous arrangements, and requesting the people to observe the day of the funeral by abstaining from their ordinary business and causing the church-bells to be tolled.

At the Hermitage, the blow had fallen with terrible force, with crushing weight. For a long time the bereaved husband clasped his wife in his arms, refusing to believe that she was dead. He sat by her side all through the hours of the night, inconsolable, occasionally feeling her pulse and placing his hand over her heart, still hoping that she might revive. Major Lewis, who had been immediately sent for, arrived just before daylight, and found him still sitting there speechless, the image of despair and woe. At the funeral he was supported to the grave, at the bottom of the Hermitage garden, between General Coffee and Major Rutledge, and he needed their help at every step of the short distance. At the sight of this pitiful spectacle, the vast concourse which had assembled from all the country round manifested uncontrollable emotion. The general seemed to have grown aged and helpless in a night, and when some old friend seized his hand and uttered words of sympathy, he was unable to make an audible response. He rallied somewhat in a few days, but it was remarked by all his nearest friends that he was never the same man again.

The acuteness and depth of his sorrow had important consequences to the nation; at least, so many of his friends imagined. He believed that the scandals of the late campaign had hastened the death of his wife, if they had not caused it, and he knew that they had embittered the last months of her life. For some years Mrs. Jackson had been revered by a large circle in Tennessee as an eminent saint, a woman exalted more by her virtues, her boundless benevolence and her religious devoutness, than by her connection with the most popular man in the nation. No doubt this circumstance sharpened to her the bitterness of the attacks upon her good name, and more hotly inflamed the just indignation of her husband. In his own mind, he held the leaders of the opposite party responsible for the cruel charges and insinuations which their newspapers had promulgated. He knew his own power over his adherents, and he imagined that Mr. Adams or Mr. Clay had but to express a wish to the editors of their party organs to silence them on any topic. So decided were his convictions on this subject, that he never forgave Henry Clay, and when he went to Washington to be inaugurated, he refused to call on, or have any intercourse with, Mr. Adams, the outgoing President.

One shrinks from probing the state of mind and heart which the agony of his bereavement and his conviction as to the cause of his wife's death engendered in General Jackson; but in order that we may understand certain future events, it is necessary for us to have a true conception of these facts; for the death of Mrs. Jackson had an influence upon the political history of the United States, and effects of national consequence issued from her grave. Unless one gives his best consideration to the subject, it is difficult, perhaps impossible, to measure the depth, the poignancy of Andrew Jackson's bereavement, which was in exact ratio to the extent and quality of the love which he cherished for his wife. All the unparalleled earnestness, intensity, chivalry, tenderness, devotion and reverence of his nature were concentrated in his love for her. When he became her husband he in no wise ceased to be her lover. His love was of that dignity that it went hand in hand even with the vow he made to her in marriage. Instead of suffering the least eclipse, his gallantry, his devotion, his respect, his admiration, his love grew with his growing years. As I have already said, the chosen of his heart was to him no less sacred than his God, and in the words of Holy Writ, he could truly say: "'I have loved thee with an everlasting affection; therefore with loving kindness have I drawn thee.'"

Nor did Andrew Jackson's love cease with his wife's death. He mourned her to the last day of his life, and was guided by what he supposed would be her wishes in all matters in which he thought she would have taken an interest had she been alive. In the last year of his life, as he was sitting near her grave, talking with Major Lewis about certain provisions in his last will, the major suggested that his entire estate should not be given to his adopted son, but that a portion of it should be settled on the son's wife and children. After a long pause, the general said: "No. If *she*," pointing to the tomb in the garden, "were alive, she would wish him to have it all, and to me her wish is law."

The Honorable Nicholas P. Trist, President Jackson's private secretary, relates an affecting incident which occurred while the President was on a visit to the Rip Raps in Virginia. Mr. Trist had retired for the night and so had the President. At the last moment, the secretary remembered certain letters about which he wanted specific instructions. "As the letters were to be sent off early the next morning," Mr. Trist says, "I returned to his [President Jackson's] chamber-door; and tapping gently, in order not to awake him if he had got to sleep, my tap was answered by 'Come in.' He was undressed, but not yet in bed, as I supposed he must be by that time. He was sitting at the little table, with his wife's miniature—a very large one, then for the first time seen by me—before him, propped up against some books; and between him and the picture lay an open book, which bore the marks of long use. This book, as I afterward learned, was *her* prayer-book. The miniature he always wore next to his heart, suspended round his neck by a strong black cord. The last thing he did every night, before lying down to rest, was to read in that book, with that picture under his eyes."

It is not to be expected that a man who loved his wife, living and dead, with such loyalty of affection,

MRS. ANDREW JACKSON.*—*See Page* 292.

* From a photograph by Thuss, Nashville, Tenn.

with such immutable devotion, and who believed that her death had certainly been hastened and probably caused by the calumnies of her detractors, would permit the wrongs done to her to go unredressed. Perhaps it would never have been possible for Andrew Jackson to ignore personal considerations in the bestowal of office, so powerful in him was the noble instinct of providing for honorable, capable men to whom he felt himself to be indebted for services done for him and for the country. To this instinct, so natural to the natural chieftain and the idolized leader of men, was now added an equally natural and commendable desire for retribution upon those who, as he believed, had wantonly violated the sanctity of his home and profaned the name of the gentle and affectionate wife who had made it home to him for so many happy years.

It was a month's journey then from Nashville to Washington. On a Sunday afternoon, in the middle of January, 1829, General Jackson left Nashville, accompanied by his nephew, A. J. Donelson, who was to be his private secretary, and by Mrs. A. J. Donelson, who was to preside in the White House. Major Lewis also went with him, and a few other friends, and the general carried in his pocket his inaugural address, which had been written at the mansion of Major Lewis. The party descended the Cumberland in a steamboat to the Ohio, and steamed up the Ohio to Pittsburg, a voyage of many days, during which the boat scarcely passed one log-cabin without receiving the best salutations its inmates could offer. At the larger towns immense multitudes gathered to cheer the general on his way.

On reaching Washington and settling at the Indian Queen Tavern, the President-elect received hundreds of visitors every day, and it was evident that a large number of the people who were flocking to Washington, had come with the expectation of being appointed to office. As Daniel Webster wrote, in his humorous way, Feb. 19, 1829: "A great multitude, too many to be fed without a miracle, are already in the city, hungry for office."

There was a strange excitement among the people, many of whom, as Mr. Webster remarked, "really seem to think that the country is rescued from some dreadful danger."

Never before had there been such a crowd at an inauguration. At the moment when the multitude caught sight of General Jackson's erect, imposing form, as he issued from between the columns of the well-known portico, every hat was removed and ten thousand radiant human faces shone upon him. "The peal of shouting," as a gentleman present has written, "rent the air, and seemed to shake the very ground." During the stillness that followed, though every ear was attentive, not a word could be heard of the inaugural, except by the group immediately around the speaker. There was a tumultuous crowd at the White House afterward, and in the evening a general illumination. It seemed in the exhilaration of the hour as if all parties and all men joined heartily in the cry, "Hurrah for Jackson!"

CHAPTER XXX.

PRESIDENT JACKSON LOOKS OUT FOR HIS FRIENDS —THE MRS. EATON COMPLICATION—WASHINGTON LADIES ON THE WAR-PATH—SINGULAR RESULTS OF THE SCANDAL.

Great apprehensions had been inspired among office-holders by General Jackson's elevation to the Presidency. During the interval which elapsed between his election and his inauguration, the opposition newspapers had been industriously predicting that he would turn all his opponents out of office to make room for his friends; that, in fact, "a clean sweep might be expected." Consequently, every act of the new President was scanned with a searching scrutiny, such as terror sometimes inspires.

The announcement of the new Cabinet did not disturb public tranquility nor add to the terror of the office-holders. With the exception of Martin Van Buren's nomination as Secretary of State, every Cabinet appointment was interpreted as a direct blow at Henry Clay. Samuel D. Ingham of Pennsylvania, Secretary of the Treasury, had taken the lead in spreading abroad in his State the "bargain and corruption" calumny. Three other members of the new Cabinet had voted in the Senate against the confirmation of Henry Clay to the office of Secretary of State, in 1825, namely: Major J. H. Eaton of Tennessee, Secretary of War;

John M. Berrien, of Georgia, Attorney-General, and John Branch, of North Carolina, Secretary of the Navy. Mr. Van Buren, who was in the Senate in 1825, voted in favor of Mr. Clay's confirmation. The new Postmaster-General, W. T. Barry, of Kentucky, besides being a prominent herald of the "bargain and corruption" cry, had taken the lead in the movement which had turned Henry Clay's own State against him in the late election. Other appointments bore the same peculiarly anti-Clay interpretation.

The significance of these appointments excited little remark at the time, and Mr. Clay himself did not publicly notice it. But before his departure from Washington, a panic began to spread among the office-holders in that city, many of whom had been appointed or promoted through his recommendation. The question was discussed among them with bated breath, What did the President mean, when he said in his inaugural address that the people had called him to "the task of reform," "the correction of abuses," and "the counteraction of those causes which have disturbed the rightful course of appointment, and have placed or continued power in unfaithful or incompetent hands?" They were not long in discovering what these phrases meant. They meant a clean sweep, or, as the new President called it, "a complete renovation of the public service." About as fast as the business could be done, the incumbents of nearly all the good places under the control of the President were removed, to make room for men who had combated the slanderers of his wife and conspicuously helped to bring his Administration into power. Those who were removed had themselves helped to swell the torrent of slander against Mrs. Jackson, or else were the "minions" of Henry Clay or some other political leader, whom President Jackson looked upon as an instigator of the attacks upon the good name of his wife.

An office was half-forced upon Major William B. Lewis much against his wishes. As soon as he had witnessed the triumphant result of his six years' toil, in the inauguration of his old commander and friend, he announced his intention of going home to superintend the labors of the planting season. "Why, Major," said the President, "you are not going to leave me here *alone*, after doing more than any other man to get me here?" Major Lewis could not resist the plea, and it was finally agreed that he should become one of the auditors of the Treasury, and retain his abode in the White House.

A great outcry was raised by the ousted office-holders and their friends, and by the entire opposition party, on account of President Jackson's "complete renovation of the public service." He was vehemently charged with "corrupting the civil service," and to this day many people believe that the charge was true. But Professor Sumner, who, from his point of view, very properly says as little as possible in favor of Jackson's proceedings, remarks:* "It is a crude and incorrect notion that Andrew Jackson corrupted the civil service. The student who seeks to penetrate the causes of the corruption of the

* Sumner, 147.

civil service, must go back to study the play of human nature under the dogmas and institutions of the States named [New York and Pennsylvania.] He cannot rest satisfied with the explanation that 'Andrew Jackson did it.'"

Andrew Jackson always believed in an honest and capable man, no matter to what party he belonged, and he opposed all schemes to plunder the Treasury which came to his knowledge. In his day it was customary, as in our day it is customary, for hordes of politicians and interested speculators to combine to further each other's interests at the public expense by means of special legislation and otherwise. Of all the Presidents, Jackson was the only one who had the courage to face this almost omnipotent interest and defy it. "Jackson affronted the whole interest. He was not able to put an end to the abuse, but he curtailed it. He used the exceptional strength of his political position to do what no one else would have dared to do in meeting a strong and growing cause of corruption. He educated his party, for that generation at least, up to a position of party hostility to special legislation of every kind."*

During the progress of his "complete renovation of the public service," the President was personally occupied with an affair which only confirmed him in his already passionate conviction that "the minions of Mr. Clay" were men of such atrocious baseness that no duty could be clearer than the expulsion of them from the public offices. A few weeks before the inauguration, Senator Eaton, of Tennessee, had

* Sumner, 194.

married Mrs. Timberlake, a pretty and vivacious widow, with whose good name the gossips of Washington had been busy for many months. She was the daughter of William O'Neal, the landlord of the old Indian Queen Tavern in Washington. She had grown to womanhood in that hostelry, and was known to its frequenters as Peggy O'Neal. She married Purser Timberlake, of the Navy, and became the mother of two children. During her husband's absence at sea calumnious gossip made free with her name, and when, on board his ship in the Mediterranean, Purser Timberlake cut his throat after a drunken debauch, the Washington gossips accepted the theory that he had taken his life on hearing of his wife's misconduct at home.

When the news of Purser Timberlake's death reached Washington, Major Eaton was, as he had been for some years, an inmate of the Indian Queen Tavern, and not indifferent to the agreeable qualities of the landlord's daughter. He now wished to marry her, but as he was about to become a member of General Jackson's Cabinet he began by asking the general's opinion of the project. The President-elect had been acquainted with the O'Neal family for thirty years, and the Indian Queen Tavern had always been his home in Washington. Mrs. Jackson had been there with him, and she became warmly attached to the family, and particularly so to Mrs. Timberlake and her sprightly children. So General Jackson answered: "Why, yes, Major; if you love the woman, and she will have you, marry her by all means." The Senator reminded his chief of the scandals which had been afloat concerning the lady and himself. "Well," said the general, "your marrying her will disprove these charges and restore Peg's good name."

The marriage occurred in January, 1829. A month later, when it was known that Senator Eaton was about to be appointed Secretary of War, the ladies who in that case would be expected to call upon Mrs. Eaton (formerly the Widow Timberlake, and, before that, Peggy O'Neal), and even concede to her a certain precedence in society, were deeply moved.

For some weeks, the scandal was confined to the circle more immediately interested; but at length it was brought to the notice of President Jackson himself, through the agency of Rev. E. S. Ely, a distinguished Presbyterian clergyman of Philadelphia. He was one of the oldest friends of the President, and he could not endure the thought of his giving any countenance to "a dissolute woman." Dr. Ely had received his information from the Rev. J. N. Campbell, pastor of the church in Washington which Mrs. Jackson and her husband had attended. He wrote a long letter to the President, informing him that the ladies of Washington would not speak to Mrs. Eaton and detailing a number of accusations of the most atrocious character, which need not be repeated. He solemnly called upon the President, for his own sake, for the sake of his departed wife, for the sake of his administration, for the honor of the government and of the country, not to visit, receive or recognize "such a woman."

General Jackson speedily replied to Dr. Ely, defending the lady with a fervor and adroitness not often equalled. He related the history of his own familiar acquaintance with the O'Neals, and showed the absolute improbability of the shameful stories about Mrs. Eaton. Mingled with his gallant and admirable defense of his friend's daughter were characteristic manifestations of his fervent antipathy to Henry Clay. Among other things, he said: "I have not the least doubt but that every secret rumor is circulated by the minions of Mr. Clay for the purpose of injuring Mrs. Eaton, and through her Mr. Eaton; but I assure you that such conduct will never have my aid."

The President's defense of Mrs. Eaton did not convince his old friend, Dr. Ely, nor his pastor, Mr. Campbell, nor the ladies belonging to the families of the other members of the Cabinet. Neither Mrs. Calhoun, nor Mrs. Berrien, nor Mrs. Branch, nor Mrs. Ingham would call upon Mrs. Eaton; nor would Mrs. Donelson, the mistress of the White House, visit her, though obliged to receive her. "Anything else, uncle," she said, "I will do for you, but I cannot call upon Mrs. Eaton." The President replied: "Then go back to Tennessee, my dear." She went back, and her husband, the private secretary, went with her, and they remained away six months. The wives of the foreign ministers were equally prejudiced against Mrs. Eaton, and were equally resolute in their refusal to associate with her. They, of course, were beyond the reach of the President's indignation, as he could not send their husbands home for such a reason.

In 1848, I met scores of persons in Washington who professed to know all about "the Mrs. Eaton

Scandal." A majority of the ladies with whom I conversed on the subject believed that Mrs. Eaton was "a good-for-nothing creature," but the gentlemen usually spoke in her favor. The person with whom I talked most on the subject was the son (then twenty-two years old) of one of the "Cabinet ladies" who would not associate with Mrs. Eaton. He had heard his parents and their friends discuss the subject hundreds of times, and he said they were still in the habit of talking about it. The impression made on his mind by what he had thus heard was that Mrs. Eaton was a bad woman; at any rate, his mother "hated the very sound of her name." This was not unnatural, as his mother's behavior toward Mrs. Eaton had led to his father's removal from the Cabinet.

It so chanced that Mr. Van Buren, the Secretary of State, who was a widower without daughters, having been detained by business connected with the governorship of New York, which he had just resigned, did not arrive in Washington until three weeks after the inauguration of President Jackson. Being thus free to act according to his own convictions, and satisfied of Mrs. Eaton's innocence, he called upon her as a matter of course, and treated her with the particular, the marked, the emphasized respect which he felt to be due to her as a victim of atrocious slander.

It also happened that Mr. Vaughn, the British minister, a particular friend of Mr. Van Buren's, and Baron Krudener, the Russian minister, were both unmarried men. Each of these three gentlemen made parties expressly for Mrs. Eaton, at which they exhibited for her every possible mark of esteem. They did not succeed in overcoming in the slightest degree the repugnance of the Washington ladies, but they did succeed in gratifying General Jackson to the utmost degree. Mr. Van Buren, in particular, completely captivated the President, and did this, as all who knew him intimately would readily believe, without being guilty of the slightest insincerity. He thought his friend's wife had been foully maligned, as doubtless she had been, and he gladly seconded every effort of the President to vindicate her good name. In doing this, besides winning the President's warmest regard, he pleased and won Major Eaton, the President's special friend in the Cabinet; also Mrs. Eaton and her mother, both old friends of General Jackson's. He also gave great satisfaction to Major Lewis, who lived in the White House, the constant companion of the President, and who was nearly connected with Major Eaton by marriage.

The friendship of all these influential persons drew with it all the more particular and intimate adherents of the President—the inner Jacksonian circle, notably Amos Kendall, of Kentucky, and Isaac Hill, of New Hampshire. Daniel Webster's amusing comment upon these events and signs of the times was very far from being a jest:

"Mr. Van Buren," he wrote in January, 1830, "has evidently quite the lead in influence and importance. . . It is odd enough, but too evident to be doubted, that the consequences of this dispute in the social and fashionable world are producing great political effects, *and may determine who shall be successor to the present Chief Magistrate*."

Mr. Webster's prediction was far more prophetic than even he supposed it was when he made it.

CHAPTER XXXI.

THE WAR UPON THE UNITED STATES BANK—FORESHADOWING OF NULLIFICATION—PRESIDENT JACKSON READY FOR ANYTHING.

"The United States Bank War," though a bloodless contest, was one of the bitterest wars that ever raged on the American continent. It convulsed society, as well as business and politics, from one end of the Union to the other. Millions of people verily believed that it would be impossible for the country to get along without a United States Bank. "Destroy the Bank and you destroy the country," was an adage of the time.

The first Bank of the United States was chartered in 1791, and was to continue till March 4, 1811. There was much contention on the subject, and Andrew Jackson became strongly prejudiced against a United States Bank. An effort was made to re-charter the old Bank in Febuary, 1811, but the bill was defeated in the Senate by the casting vote of Vice-President Clinton. During the War of 1812, the finances of the government and of the country got into such a deplorable condition that a new Bank of the United States was suggested as a remedy. A bill chartering the second Bank of the United States was passed by Congress in 1816. The Bank went into operation January 7, 1817, and was to continue till March 3, 1836.

In 1829, when Andrew Jackson succeeded to the

Presidency, the United States Bank, situated in Philadelphia, with twenty-five branches in other important centers of business, was an important and imposing institution. Its capital was thirty-five million dollars. The government balance of public money deposited in the Bank averaged nearly seven millions; the private deposits more than six millions. Its bank-note circulation was twelve millions. It discounted notes to the amount of forty millions a year, upon which it made a profit of three millions. At the parent Bank in Philadelphia there were a hundred clerks, and each of the branches had its president, cashier and board of directors, besides employed persons in the twenty-five branches to the number of four hundred, the greater part of whom were men of standing and influence, enjoying compensation which was liberal for that day. The notes of the bank were current everywhere without discount, and often commanded a small premium at remote cities, such as Calcutta, Canton, St. Petersburg and Cairo. The stock of the Bank was considered an investment highly desirable and perfectly safe. The Bank was governed by twenty-five directors, five of whom were appointed by the President of the United States. Besides the national character thus imparted to it, the Bank received and disbursed the whole revenue of the nation. Its president was Nicholas Biddle, a man of highly attractive personality, fluent with tongue and pen, of honorable and generous sentiments, and abundantly competent to manage the Bank in ordinary times.

The ancient opposition to any United States Bank,

well-founded and sufficient as it was, appeared to have exhausted itself in 1829, and Andrew Jackson himself seemed to have outlived his former prejudice against it. It is absolutely certain that he came to Washington with no thought or purpose concerning the Bank in his mind. The charter had still seven years to run.

The first dealings of the Administration with the Bank were unusually cordial and satisfactory. The Bank went out of its way to oblige the Secretary of the Treasury, who thanked it for the accommodating spirit it had shown, and this he did with very marked emphasis, and more than once. In a word, despite theoretical objections and old prejudice, the new Administration accepted the United States Bank as part and parcel of the governmental system of the United States, just as they did the post-office and the consular service.

Nevertheless, during this first summer of the Presidential term, a storm was brewing against the Bank in far-off New Hampshire, unnoticed, which proved to have in it the elements of a cyclone of irresistible and destructive force.

Editor Isaac Hill, of New Hampshire, then Second Comptroller of the Treasury, was a person high in the confidence of the President. He had a rooted hostility against Jeremiah Mason, the president of the Branch of the United States Bank at Portsmouth, New Hampshire. The president of every bank is compelled by his position to make enemies, because he is continually obliged to discriminate among business men and to say *No* to persons whose prosperity and solvency may depend upon his saying *Yes.* Isaac Hill and his party friends charged and believed that Jeremiah Mason had conducted his Branch Bank in a manner that was "partial, harsh, novel, and injurious to the interests of the Bank, destructive to the business of Portsmouth and offensive to the whole community."

These and other accusations coming officially to the knowledge of Nicholas Biddle, he went to Portsmouth, spent six days in the investigation of the charges, and satisfied himself that they were groundless. He was also convinced that Mason was in all respects a model bank president. Mr. Biddle concluded a letter to the Secretary of the Treasury on the results of his investigations at Portsmouth with a foolish passage which the Administration interpreted and accepted as a defiance. The directors of the bank, he said, did not "acknowledge the slightest responsibility of any description whatsoever to the Secretary of the Treasury touching the political opinions and conduct of their officers, that being a subject on which they never consult and never desire to know the views of any Administration." He further intimated, with sufficient plainness, the intention of the directors to manage the bank according to their own judgment, and not to permit any "interference in the concerns of the institution confided to their care."

How repeatedly have disastrous consequences flowed from seemingly insignificant circumstances! This foolish rhetorical flourish of Mr. Biddle's too facile pen was the proximate cause of the destruction of the United States Bank.

From the days of Alexander Hamilton, Andrew Jackson had had a strong antipathy to a United States Bank, which had slumbered during recent years; but on reading the voluminous correspondence between Mr. Biddle and the Secretary of the Treasury, his antipathy instantly awoke, never to slumber again as long as the Bank existed. He was surrounded, too, by men whose opposition to the Bank was only less decided than his own.

In his next annual message to Congress, the President began the war on the United States Bank which did not cease until that overshadowing institution was destroyed. The contention led to many important political changes; among others, to the election of Isaac Hill as United States Senator from New Hampshire; to the deserting by the *United States Telegraph* of the Administration, of which it had been the organ, and to the founding of the *Washington Globe* as the new organ of the Administration, with Francis P. Blair as its editor. Mr. Blair, one of the most powerful political writers of that time, was brought on specially from Kentucky to take charge of the new organ, which he conducted with consummate ability. The *Globe* was surprisingly successful from the issue of its first number, and gave the Administration a skillful and powerful support, which was of incalculable value.

As an offset to this important acquisition, Henry Clay, in 1831, returned to the Senate. The brilliant orator at once provided Mr. Blair with inexhaustible editorial topics. It was Henry Clay who induced the Bank to apply for the renewal of its charter in 1831, so that it should enter as an issue into the Presidential election of 1832. The wisest friends of the bank said: "No; let us keep it out of the Presidential contest; let us wait until we have a friend in the Presidential chair." The impetuous Clay, never a tractable nor a skillful politician, thought otherwise. Pennsylvania, as he truly remarked, had been and still was the stronghold of the Jackson party, and the Bank was located in Pennsylvania. Congress would certainly pass the bill renewing the charter. If the President vetoed it the great controlling State of Pennsylvania would unquestionably abandon him. If he should sign it, he would be fatally weakened in the South and West. The mistake in this reasoning was in supposing that Philadelphia and Pennsylvania were politically synonymous; whereas they had very little in common, and there was even some political antipathy on the part of the great body of Pennsylvania farmers to the chief city of their commonwealth.

The impregnable strength of Jackson rested on his honesty and the soundness of his financial views. Biddle's financial theories were unsound, and the distressing exigencies of his situation led him to deviate into unsound practises. He countenanced enormous issues of drafts by the Branch Banks, which were to be and were used as currency. They were in fact the counterpart of bank-notes. They were drawn on the parent Bank for even sums ($5, $10, or $20,) by the cashier of any branch, to the order of some officer of the Branch Bank, endorsed by the latter to bearer, and then circulated like bank-notes. The amount of these drafts at one time amounted to seven millions four hundred thousand dollars. A high authority says: "Great consequences hung on the strait into which the branch drafts had pushed the Bank, and this measure of relief to which Biddle had recourse. Biddle was too plausible. In any emergency he was ready to write a letter or report, to smooth things over and present a good face in spite of facts. Any one who has carefully studied the History of the Bank, and Biddle's statements, will come to every statement of his with a disagreeable sense of suspicion."*

Biddle asserted that the Bank stood between the country and financial ruin. "The whole policy of the Bank for the last six months," he wrote in 1832, "has been exclusively protective and conservative, calculated to mitigate suffering and yet avert danger." As Professor Sumner says: "He sketches out in broad and bold outlines the national and international relations of American industry and commerce and the financial relations of the Treasury, with the Bank enthroned over all as the financial providence of the country. . . However, it was all humbug, and especially that part which represented the Bank as watching over and caring for the public. . . If the Bank had been strong, Biddle's explanations would all have been meretricious; as it was, the Bank had been quite fully occupied in 1831–32 in taking care of itself, mitigating its own sufferings and averting its own dangers."†

* Sumner's Life of Jackson, 269. † *Ibid.* 270, 271.

The bill rechartering the Bank of the United States, after a debate of great ability and occasional violence, and an excitement out of doors seldom created by a financial measure, was passed by the House of Representatives, July 3, 1832, by a vote of 109 to 76. It had previously passed the Senate by a vote of 28 to 20. It was presented to the President for his consideration on the Fourth of July. Six days after he returned it to Congress, vetoed. He accompanied the unsigned bill with one of the longest and one of the most ingenious messages ever sent to Congress. Never did a public document have such a strange fortune as this message, for it was circulated by each party as a campaign bombshell that would be fatal to the opposition. It was viewed by some of the leading partisans of Mr. Clay with the most sincere and complete contempt, as a vulgar explosion of ignorance, prejudice and hate. Nicholas Biddle, the president of the bank, appears to have been as truly delighted with it as he said he was. In reply to Henry Clay, who had asked him what he thought the effect of the Veto Message would be, he replied that it was working as well as the friends of the Bank could desire.

"It has all the fury of a chained panther biting the bars of his cage, and my hope is that it will contribute to relieve the country from the dominion *of these miserable people*. You are destined to be the instrument of that deliverance, and at no period of your life has the country ever had a deeper stake in you."

On the other hand, the message was circulated through the agency of the office holders in every part of the country, and everywhere it came with convincing power to the farmer and the artisan. Everything that was done by either party helped to make the people familiar with the message, and the more familiar with it they became, the more powerfully it drew them to the support of President Jackson.

During this Presidential term, the great debate took place between Mr. Webster and Colonel Hayne, of South Carolina, on the nature of the Constitution of the United States and the fundamental character of our Government. It was in that debate that the great parliamentary battle between Secession and Unionism was fought. Extraordinary interest was imparted to the debate by the magnitude of the vital issues involved, and the unexampled power and splendor of Webster's argument. No President ever followed the proceedings of Congress with keener interest than Andrew Jackson. No matter how late the House sat, he would never go to sleep until Major Lewis or his secretary had returned from the Capitol, and given him the substance of the proceedings. He was deeply stirred by this famous discussion. His personal sympathies were with Colonel Hayne, the brother of the excellent and valiant soldier who had served under him in the Creek War and at New Orleans; nor did the President yet believe that the nullifiers had a serious purpose. As the debate went on he felt more acutely the fallacy of some portions of Mr. Hayne's argument.

"Well," said he one evening to Major Lewis, "and how is Webster getting on?"

"He is delivering a most powerful speech," said

Lewis. "I am afraid he is demolishing our friend Hayne."

"I expected it," said the President.

And soon after, when the State-rights men had their grand banquet, ostensibly in honor of Thomas Jefferson's birthday, two remarkable and ever memorable toasts were given; one by the President of the United States,, and the other by Vice-President Calhoun. The President gave:

"Our Federal Union: it must be preserved."

Mr. Calhoun offered the following:

"The Union: next to our liberty, the most dear; may we all remember that it can only be preserved by respecting the rights of the States, and distributing equally the benefit and burden of the Union."

CHAPTER XXXII.

PRESIDENT JACKSON'S CHOICE OF A SUCCESSOR—RUPTURE WITH CALHOUN—PRESIDENTIAL ELECTION OF 1832—ANYTHING TO BEAT JACKSON—HIS TRIUMPHANT RE-ELECTION.

Like other Presidents-elect, Andrew Jackson went to Washington in 1829 expecting and intending to serve but one term. He was then sixty-two years of age, a sick, infirm, bereaved and suffering man, consoled and sustained chiefly by the presence of his Tennessee relations and neighbors.

At that time there were two friends of his, of eminent note and long public service, who might rationally indulge the expectation of being preferred by him as a successor. These were Mr. Calhoun and Mr. Van Buren, two of the babies born in 1782, and both now in the prime of their years. To both of them it must have been apparent that the preference of a President so intrenched in popularity as Andrew Jackson would go far toward deciding who should take his place in 1833. This was more apparent when the offices throughout the whole country had been filled with Jackson men.

Before any one had given much thought to the matter the Eaton scandal had divided the new cabinet into two hostile parties, equal in number—three to three. Van Buren, Eaton and Barry sustained Mrs. Eaton; Ingham, Berrien and Branch, all married men, owing to the hostility of their wives to

Mrs. Eaton, could not avoid the appearance of siding against her. Mrs. Calhoun, too, refused to call upon the lady, which involved the Vice-President himself in the affair; and it happened that the three anti-Eatonians, Ingraham, Berrien and Branch, were Mr. Calhoun's political friends and allies.

At once, therefore, before the first few weeks passed by, the President cooled toward Calhoun and warmed toward Van Buren. As time went on the coolness became hostility, and the warmth kindled into a decided and even passionate preference. Van Buren was a singularly bland and good-natured man, and understood perfectly the art of "getting along with" a masterful and fiery spirit like Jackson, who soon became perfectly at home with him. He began to speak of him to his familiar friends as "Van," and was heard sometimes to address him as "Matty." He liked and relished his company to an extraordinary degree.

Moreover, as an old-fashioned Democrat reared in the school of Jefferson, the Secretary of State was in perfect accord with the President on the Bank question, and agreed with him in opposing all the movements and doctrines that gave any semblance of strength to the nullifiers. Calhoun, on the contrary, was ominously silent on the Bank, and was openly hostile to the protective tariff, which he had so warmly supported in 1816. He would not hear of any tariff compromise. When he was asked as to the disposal of the surplus revenue, on the near extinguishment of the public debt, his only reply was that there should be no surplus. The tariff must be reduced until the surplus had disappeared.

During the whole of the year 1829, the excitements of his new situation told severely upon the long ago weakened health of the President. In December, Major Lewis, his familiar and constant associate, almost despaired of his life, and the President himself felt how slight a hold he had upon existence. The two old neighbors conversed upon this subject with the utmost freedom, not without reference to the alarming prospect that, in case of the President's death, he would be succeeded by a Vice-President who was opposed to his policy on every leading point. Major Lewis, too, took the deepest interest in having Mr. Van Buren succeed General Jackson, and he talked frankly upon this subject also to the President.

"It occurred to me," he once wrote, "that General Jackson's name, though he might be dead, would prove a powerful lever if judiciously used, in raising Mr. Van Buren to the Presidency. I therefore determined to get the general, if possible, to write a letter to some friend to be used at the next succeeding Presidential election (in case of his death) expressive of the confidence he reposed in Mr. Van Buren's abilities, patriotism and qualifications for any station, even the highest within the gift of the people."

The general consenting, such a letter was written to Judge John Overton, of Tennessee (Jackson's second in the Dickinson duel), who, however, lived and died without knowing the purpose for which this letter was written. It extolled Mr. Van Buren as the "dear friend" of the President; a man, open, candid and manly; republican in his principles, and a true friend of the people. The President wished he could say as much for Mr. Calhoun, but he could not, and he had a right to believe that "most of the troubles, vexations and difficulties I have had to encounter since my arrival in this city, have been occasioned by his friends." Moreover, Mr. Calhoun was factiously opposed to the special objects of the Administration. This letter had all the appearance of a private and casual communication, but carefully attested copies were made of it and put away among the private papers of Major Lewis.

The President rallied during the early months of 1830. His health was so greatly benefited by the bracing winter of the capital that the Overton device passed out of memory, as the question of the succession became more interesting. Upon one point the President was now fully resolved, that neither Clay nor Calhoun should ever occupy the Presidential chair, if he could prevent it. There appears to have been an unrecorded programme arranged, that extended far beyond the next Presidential election. It was an "understood thing" between the President and his most confidential friends, that he should be succeeded by Martin Van Buren, and Van Buren by Colonel Benton, which it was thought would carry the matter beyond the public life of Clay and Calhoun.

The first steps toward the execution of this programme were taken as early as March, 1831. A series of adroit political manœuvres followed, by which, in due time, Andrew Jackson was placed before the people as a candidate for re-election to the Presidency in 1832.

A few weeks later occurred the momentous rupture between the President and the Vice-President. At a dinner-party in the White House, given in honor of ex-President Monroe, Major Lewis chanced to learn that, in 1819, it was Calhoun, not Crawford, who had expressed the opinion in the Cabinet that General Jackson's conduct in the Seminole War ought to be submitted to a court of inquiry. A long correspondence between the President and Vice-President followed this discovery, in which Mr. Calhoun vigorously but inaptly strove to avert the serious blow to his ambitious hopes, with which he saw himself menaced. The President, already estranged from him, would not be appeased, and ended the correspondence by announcing that their friendly relations were at an end.

In 1831, the Vice-President published the correspondence in a voluminous pamphlet, accompanying it with temperate explanatory remarks, in which he appealed to the people of the United States as their common judge, or court of last appeal. The President retorted by retiring to private life Mr. Calhoun's three political allies in the Cabinet; a change which he effected by a series of adroit and audacious movements. First, Major Eaton *resigned*, alleging that he had accepted the office of Secretary of War only in deference to the wishes of the President, and but for a short time. As everything was now going on so prosperously, he thought the time for his withdrawal had come. The President accepted his resignation with cordial expressions of gratitude and esteem, and appointed him Governor of Florida. Five years later the Eatons went abroad, Mr. Eaton having been commissioned to represent the United States at the court of Spain.

Mr. Van Buren resigned next, in an elaborate letter, which was replied to by the President with affectionate warmth. Mr. Van Buren went abroad ere long as Minister to England. The President then asked for the resignation of Messrs. Ingham, Berrien and Branch, on the simple ground that he deemed it best to "entirely renew" his Cabinet.

Edward Livingston, Senator from Louisiana, who had been notified beforehand of these events, and had agreed to accept the place of Secretary of State, now received the appointment. Louis McLane, Minister to England, was recalled and placed at the head of the Treasury. Levi Woodbury was made Secretary of the Navy, and Lewis Cass, so long governor of Michigan Territory, was appointed Secretary of War. Roger B. Taney, of Maryland, a lawyer of great eminence, was appointed Attorney-General. This change in the Cabinet, a thing which had never before occurred in the midst of a Presidential term, since the formation of the government, created an excitement throughout the country difficult for us now to imagine, and soon after the long-smothered scandal concerning Mrs. Eaton burst into publicity.

The acute disappointment of Mr. Calhoun produced peculiar and ominous excitement in South Carolina. In the course of the summer of 1831, Mr. Calhoun published an address of inordinate length, avowing himself a believer in the doctrine of nullification. Threatening paragraphs accompanied and followed it, to the effect that, unless the protective tariff were promptly modified, South Carolina would refuse to pay it on goods imported in her harbors.

As had often happened before, the President's action in changing his Cabinet gratified many of his opponents, and somewhat alarmed his more timid adherents. We find Mr. Clay writing of it in this manner:

"Who could have imagined such a cleansing of the Augean stables at Washington, a change almost total of the Cabinet? Our cause cannot fail to be benefited by the measure. It is a broad confession of the incompetency of the President's chosen advisers, no matter from what cause, to carry on the business of the government. I think we are authorized to anticipate confidently General Jackson's defeat." Daniel Webster was not so confident, and he proved to understand the situation better than his popular colleague.

Early in the following session of the Senate, the nominations of the new Cabinet officers came before it for confirmation, and they were all confirmed without serious opposition. But when it came to that of Mr. Van Buren for Minister to England, Clay, Webster and Calhoun united in a movement to defeat it. Mr. Calhoun erroneously attributed to Mr. Van Buren the intrigue which had resulted in the President's hostility to himself. He believed, also, that the dissolution of the Cabinet was wholly Van Buren's contrivance. Clay and Webster were of opinion that Van Buren was the author of the alleged new policy which conferred the public offices upon members of the dominant party. This, also, was an error. At that time there was no man living who had the Roman courage and virtue requisite for the thorough enforcement of such a system except Andrew Jackson. A pretext was found for rejecting Mr. Van Buren in one of his dispatches to the Secretary of State, and he was rejected accordingly.

Fifty-one days, as Colonel Benton records, were spent in the preliminary intrigue, but the debate upon it lasted but two days. It was in this brief discussion that Governor Marcy, of New York, used an expression which has never since been forgotten, and is not likely to be. He was defending Van Buren from the charge of having incited the President to conduct the national government on the principles long practiced in New York.

"The politicians of New York," said Marcy, "boldly preach what they practice. When they are contending for victory they avow their intention of enjoying the fruits of it. If they are defeated, they expect to retire from office; if they are successful, they claim as a matter of right the advantages of success. They see nothing wrong in the rule that *to the victor belong the spoils of the enemy.*"

Mr. Van Buren found many able and brilliant defenders on this occasion, both within and without the Senate chamber. When the vote rejecting his nomination was announced, Colonel Benton turned to a friend and said: "You have broken a minister and elected a Vice-President." On the day that the news reached London Mr. Van Buren was a guest of Prince Talleyrand, who then represented the King of the French at the British court. Lord Auckland, an experienced politician said to him: "It is an advantage to a public man to be the subject of an outrage." Colonel Benton reports a remark of Mr. Calhoun's on the event which shows how imperfectly the great Nullifier comprehended the political situation at the time.

"I heard Mr. Calhoun say," records Benton, "to one of his doubting friends: 'It will kill him, sir, kill him dead; he will never kick, sir; never kick.' And the alacrity with which he gave the casting votes on the two occasions, both vital, on which they were put into his hands, attested the sincerity of his belief and his readiness for the work."

Seldom has even an ambitious politician been more mistaken than Mr. Calhoun was in this matter, for this rejection by the Senate strengthened Mr. Van Buren's position very greatly and in every way. It became from that hour the President's ruling object to secure his elevation, and the whole Jackson party embraced his cause with renewed earnestness. The consolatory letters which reached him by every mail gave him opportunity for highly effective replies, by which he contributed almost as much to the triumph of his chief as to his own.

The question at once arose by what machinery of politics Mr. Van Buren should be presented to the people as a candidate for the Vice-Presidency. The device selected was that of a national convention, which accordingly was held at Baltimore on May 21st, 1832. Three hundred and twenty-six delegates were present at this convention, the great majority of whom were office-holders, or friends representing office-holders. Judge Overton, of Tennessee, had been selected as the permanent presiding officer, but he was prevented from attending by his infirmities. The business of the convention was done with the utmost ease and dispatch. On the first ballot, Martin Van Buren received 260 votes; P. P. Barbour, 40; R. M. Johnston, 26. The convention then adjourned without publishing any platform of principles, or issuing an address to the people. The nomination was truly the act of the President. Major Lewis personally informed Mr. Parton, that, on learning by chance at the last moment that one of the delegates (Major Eaton), just arrived from abroad, intended to oppose the nomination, he wrote to him "warning him of the danger of such a course, *unless he was prepared to quarrel with the general.*" Major Lewis adds that this delegate fortunately received his letter "in time to save himself, and perhaps Van Buren, also."

Thus the Democratic candidates presented were Jackson and Van Buren. Those of the Whigs, as the opposition were beginning to be called, were Henry Clay and John Sergeant. The anti-Mason party nominated William Wirt, of Maryland, and William Ellmaker, of Pennsylvania. It is a curious instance of the blindness of political leaders that Henry Clay felt more apprehension on account of the supposed popularity of this new party than he felt from the party which supported Jackson and Van Buren.

Clay belonged to the school of statesmen who

believe in "paternal government," and think they can do better for the people than the people can do for themselves. That is to say, at bottom, instead of wishing for "a government of the people, by the people, for the people," those paternal statesmen want government of the people, by statesmen, for statesmen. Clay's arrogance in this respect repeatedly gave offense to the masses, and the Jacksonians took good care that it should do him as much injury as possible.

The Presidential campaign of 1832, which was in some respects the most important election of the kind that had ever occurred, called forth an amount and variety of effort probably never equaled in a similar contest. The Jackson men again employed the popular device of erecting hickory poles, which called together vast concourses of enthusiastic voters. The Whigs gave sumptuous banquets and made eloquent speeches. The Anti-Masons sought to congeal the blood of the people by their portrayals of the alleged secret horrors of Free Masonry.

The real issues of the struggle were by no means overlooked. The United States Bank, the necessity of modifying the tariff in order to reduce the revenue, the threats of Nullification in South Carolina, the removal of the Cherokees beyond the Mississippi, and the President's vetoes of internal improvement bills, were discussed with sufficient coolness and ability to make it plain to the dispassionate voter, that, all things considered, it had become a necessity of the time to sustain Andrew Jackson, in order to secure the welfare of the country, and perhaps to save the Union from destruction. And Andrew Jackson was re-elected President of the United States by a majority which exceeded the anticipations of the most sanguine Democrats. Out of 288 electoral votes (then the whole number) he received 219, leaving only 69 for distribution among the opposing candidates.

Having been thus overwhelmingly sustained by the people, President Jackson entered upon his second term more resolute than ever to settle firmly and sternly all the issues between him and his opponents. The result was that his second term was the most exciting and eventful Administration which the United States had ever known.

CHAPTER XXXIII.

THE RISE AND FALL OF NULLIFICATION.

The second term of Andrew Jackson's Presidency was exciting and eventful. Public affairs had never before absorbed so continuously the attention of the people. It seemed as if all eyes were directed toward the capital, where the antagonists of the President gave him abundant opportunities of exhibiting all his strongest and some of his most attractive traits. There were times when he appeared to have conquered all opposition and stood forth in the eyes of the people as the manifest savior of his country.

First of all, Calhoun and the nullifiers of South Carolina drew his fire. In 1832, the public debt having been so nearly reduced as to make it certain that during the next two years the last payment would be made, the necessity of reducing the revenue was obviously becoming imperative. The moment the last year's payment was completed, the public revenue would be more than twice as great as the needs of the government, then about thirteen millions per annum. There were three plans of relief in 1832 before the country: 1. Henry Clay's bill to abolish the duties on raw material, while preserving the protective system otherwise intact. 2. The President's plan, which was to do all that Mr. Clay proposed and as much more as the case required, or nearly as much, and to divide the surplus revenue, if there should be any, among the States. 3. The demand of John C. Calhoun, which included the total abandonment of the protective principle, as unconstitutional, oppressive and, in the long run, injurious to business.

Mr. Calhoun's ground was one which a reasonable statesman could stand upon if he supported it in the republican method and spirit by argument alone. But Calhoun accompanied his argument with threats. He gave the country to understand that, if the duties were not promptly reduced to the revenue standard, South Carolina would *nullify* the acts of Congress imposing them, refuse to pay the duties, and import her merchandise from foreign countries at her own ports free of all duty.

The State-rights theory, from which Mr. Calhoun sophistically deduced "the constitutional right of nullification," has its origin in desires and aspirations which are inherent in the nature of man. Every human being wishes to be free, and to enjoy his inalienable right to life, liberty and the pursuit of happiness with the least possible interference by society or the State. This trait of character, this passion of the human heart has always been strong in the British people—English, Scotch, Welsh, and Irish—by whom the thirteen original States were colonized. The descendants of the original colonists inherited their love of personal and political liberty, and cherished it with passionate devotion; they fought for it; for it they risked their lives and fortunes and staked their sacred honor. For a hundred and fifty years they contended for it against British kings, British parliaments and British courts. They suffered much from kingly tyranny, from parliamentary tyranny, from judicial tyranny, and were therefore keenly jealous of executive power, of legislative power, and of judicial power. So sensitive had they become and so deep and unchangeable were their convictions on this vital subject that, although they thereby imperilled their success in the Revolutionary struggle, they refused to give the Continental Congress or the old Confederation sufficient executive power to carry its own legislation into effect. It could recommend lines of action to the States, but it could not enforce its recommendations.

It may be expedient to remind readers whose memories have become rusty as to these matters, that after weary years of trial and experiment the States discovered that, under the Confederation, they could not unify their independent powers and bring them to bear with sufficient effect to command the respect of foreign governments and protect their commerce against foreign aggression; that they could not satisfactorily adjust their internal commercial relations or any inter-State interests which were drawn into dispute; that the people could not enjoy life, liberty and the pursuit of happiness on strictly State-rights principles except within the boundaries of their respective States, although it often happened that inhabitants of one State had to pursue their happiness into another State, where, being aliens, they had no State rights, and therefore could not enforce their happiness. They discovered, in short, that they were encumbered with an inadequate government, under which they could not form a more perfect Union, establish justice, ensure domestic tranquility, provide for the common defense, promote the general welfare, nor secure the blessings of liberty to themselves and their posterity. The pressure of this deplorable condition led to the calling of the Constitutional Convention in 1787, for the purpose of instituting, if possible, a Federal Government which, without trenching on the rights of the States, should have sufficient delegated power to perform all those general governmental functions which its creators (the several States) should assign to it. But as soon as the Convention got under way it was found that the formation of such a government was seemingly impossible. The States were so jealous and tenacious of their rights that rather than part with enough of them to give supreme power to the Federal Government which they were trying to create, they preferred to go on as best they could, as disunited States, without a Federal Government. Little by little, however, their jealousies and prejudices and fears were overcome. With what difficulty this result was attained can be learned only by studying the proceedings of the Constitutional Convention and the discussions which followed the submission of the Constitution to the people for adoption or rejection.

In considering this subject, it should be remembered that every one of the original thirteen States was an independent sovereignty or nation, completely endowed with national rights and powers; whereas, the Federal Government which they wished to create for certain specific and limited purposes would have no powers whatever, and in the nature of things could not have any powers whatever, except such powers as its creators (the sovereign States) should delegate to it. Those delegated powers were to be exercised, not for the benefit of the Federal Government and in accordance with its own arbitrary will, but for the equal benefit of the sovereign States which created it, and in accordance with the terms of the Constitution whereby and wherein those powers were delegated. The powers delegated to the Federal Government comprise such governmental functions as the States themselves could not separately perform. For example: It was essential that money should be coined which would be legal tender in every State. No State could coin such money, so the power to coin it was delegated to the Federal Government. It was necessary that navigation laws regulating foreign commerce and also inter-State commerce should be enacted. No State could enact such laws; therefore the power to enact them was delegated to the Federal Government. It was necessary to negotiate treaties with foreign nations which should bind all the States and be of equal benefit to all; it was essential to form a more perfect Union, to provide for the *common* defense, to promote the *general* welfare, and as no individual State could do any of these essential things, power was delegated to the Federal Government to do all of them.

Any State could supervise its own internal affairs, relating to marriage, divorce, the collection of debts, the punishment of violators of its State laws, etc. The States needed no Federal Government to attend to such matters for them, and they reserved all power over such matters to themselves; the Federal Government having no power to meddle with such State rights any more than the government of Great Britain, France or Russia had. This feature of our government was illustrated during the discussion of the massacre of Italian assassins in New Orleans (March, 1891.) The Italian Prime Minister demanded that the Federal Government should interfere and punish the persons who killed the Italians; whereupon, the American Secretary of State instructed him that it was impossible for the Government of the United States to take any action on the case, inasmuch as it had no jurisdiction over the police or criminal affairs of individual States.

In evolving and formulating the Constitution great efforts were made to guard the indefeasible rights which the States reserved to themselves against the possibility of encroachment or interference on the part of the Federal Government; but when the Constitution was complete and submitted to the people of the States for adoption or rejection, it was fiercely assailed on the ground that the reserved rights of the States were not sufficiently protected.

After a prolonged, critical and exhaustive discussion of the subject, a majority of the voters in the several States were persuaded that the Federal Government which was to be instituted under the Constitution could not exercise any powers except those which had been specifically granted to it; and this being the general understanding, and because it was the general understanding, the Constitution was adopted. But as soon as the Federal Government went into operation, it began to exercise "implied" and "derivative" powers, on the plea that without the exercise of such powers no efficient government was possible; that as a matter of course and as it was understood from the beginning the Federal Government must and would exercise whatever powers were necessary to carry into practical operation and effect all the powers which had been specifically granted to it. Unless this were done, it was argued, those specific powers had been granted in vain, and in vain had the people of the United States ordained and established their Constitution. Webster subsequently demonstrated that that was sound legal and constitutional doctrine; nevertheless, if the people had suspected that such implied and derivative powers lay concealed in the Constitution and could be logically and lawfully evoked from the Constitution, they would not have adopted it. Indeed, had the interpretation of the Constitution and of the powers of the Federal Government which Webster presented and established beyond the possibility of logical contradiction in his reply to Hayne in 1830, and to Calhoun in 1833, been made in 1788, it is doubtful if one State would have voted for the adoption of the Constitution.

It should be remembered that at the time of the formation and adoption of the Constitution, the love and appreciation of the Union which exist to-day were as impossible as the present physical condition of the Union was then impossible. Then the different sections were remote from one another in time as well as in space, and a man could pass from one section to another only at great inconvenience and often at the risk of his life. Now, the Union is physically bound together by railroads along whose iron arteries the currents of travel and traffic ceaselessly flow, and is still more closely conjoined by the electric telegraph which, like a vast nervous system, brings every part of the country into immediate touch and sympathy. Furthermore, since Webster demonstrated the incomputable value of the Union and the impossibility of perpetuating American liberty without it, the appreciation of it and the love for it have been constantly growing, until now the preservation of the Union is both seen and felt to be of more importance than any other consideration which can be presented to a patriotic mind. But in 1788, and for several years thereafter, there was very little Union sentiment among the people of the United States. They cared vastly less for the Union than for their idolized State rights. Such regard for the Union as they had was of a practical, not a sentimental nature. "What is the Union doing for us? What is the Union going to do for us?" were the questions which the people asked. Unless the Union should prove to be practically useful to them, and useful in a way which they could appreciate, they did not care for it. Therefore, the assumption by the Federal Government of implied and derivative powers aroused the State-rights instinct and brought on the contest which subsequently assumed nullifying and secession phases. Thomas Jefferson was the first nullifier, was in fact, the father of nullification. In his original draft of the famous Kentucky resolutions of 1798, there occurred (in the 8th resolution) these words: "Where powers are assumed which have not been delegated, a *nullification* of the act is the right remedy." So far as I have been able to learn, that was the first time the word nullification was used in our political literature. Jefferson also took the ground in another resolution that the States should concur in declaring the Alien and Sedition laws "void and of no force," and that each State should "take measures of its own for providing that neither of these acts shall be exercised within their respective territories." The Kentucky legislature struck all this out; but in 1799 it passed a resolution suggesting that, "A *nullification* by these sovereignties (the respective States) of all unauthorized acts done under color of that instrument (the Constitution) is the rightful remedy." Thus the seed of nullification planted by Jefferson germinated and bore fruit in actual legislation, and in the course of time grew into such a mighty tree that all the birds of secession and disunion lodged in its branches—a upas tree which was not rooted up until Lee surrendered to Grant at Appomattox. And yet, who ever connects Jefferson's name with nullification or disunion? "Nothing" says Professor Sumner, "is more astonishing in American political history than the immunity enjoyed by some men, and the unfair responsibility enforced against others. Every school-boy is taught to execrate the Alien and Sedition laws and John Adams bears the odium of them, but no responsibility worth speaking of for nullification attaches to Jefferson. He was the father of it and the sponser for it, and the authority of his name was what recommended it in 1827."*

From the day that Jefferson planted the seed of nullification in his Kentucky resolutions there was no lack of nullifiers and disunionists. Kentucky and New England led off in these matters, but every section of the country took its turn. Whenever a law of Congress pressed sorely upon any particular class or section, threats of nullification and disunion were heard. The abolitionists and freesoilers were violent disunionists just preceding the war. They did all they could to nullify the fugitive slave law, and were ready to dissolve the Union rather than be made slave-catchers for the South. The truth is that men are governed by a desire to promote their own welfare and by the passions engendered in defending their rights. There has seldom been a community or a party, whether political or religious, which would not violate any of its principles to preserve its own existence, to secure what it believed to be a vital advantage, or to avert unendurable oppression. When a government persistently inflicts upon a large portion of its citizens what they believe to be and feel to be an intolerable wrong, those citizens become willing to let the oppressive government go and are ready to seek for a government more considerate for what they believe to be their rights. It is not at all strange, therefore, that the Southern State-rights party took that course when they were so sorely aggrieved by the tariff of 1828. Their action was unquestionably unwise and unpa-

*Sumner, 215.

triotic, but it was neither unnatural nor unprecedented. New England had set them the example twenty odd years before when Jefferson's embargo was destroying the commerce of the Eastern States and reducing many of their once affluent citizens to beggary; but Massachusetts acted with less passion and more discretion than South Carolina. "The grievance of the South in 1828," says Professor Sumner, was undeniable. . . . Their interests were being sacrificed to pretended national interests, just as, under the embargo, the interests of New England were sacrificed to national interests. In each case the party which considered its interests sacrificed, came to regard the Union only as a cage, in which all were kept in order that the stronger combination might plunder the weaker. . . The more thoroughly the economist and political philosopher recognizes the grievance of the Southerners in 1828, the more he must regret the unwisdom of their proceedings."*

The tariff of 1828 which spurred South Carolina into nullification in 1832, was known as the "Tariff of Abominations," and was probably as unjust a tariff as could be imposed upon the country; but its unjust provisions were not due to its friends; they were forced into the bill by its enemies for the purpose of defeating it altogether. Against the indignant protestations and the earnest efforts of its friends the bill was so loaded down with odious provisions that its defeat was believed to be assured. But when it came to the final vote on the passage of the bill, it was passed, to the utter consternation of

* Sumner, 210.

its opponents. The protectionists accepted the bill, outrageous as it was, rather than have no tariff at all, and so caught the freetraders in their own net. The dilemma of the Southern opponents of the tariff was deplorable, and the means they took to remedy it made it still worse. If they had patriotically obeyed the law, yet lawfully sought to have it repealed or modified, they would have won the sympathy of the country and gained their end. But when they changed the issue from the upholding of a tariff to the upholding of the Union, and challenged the supremacy of the Supreme law of the land, they threw away their advantage and invited defeat. Their first overthrow occurred in the Senate, in January, 1830, when Webster, in his reply to Hayne, established forever the legal and constitutional supremacy of the Union, and demonstrated that the alleged constitutional right of nullification or secession is a chimera of an illogical mind. The parliamentary overthrow of secession was enthusiastically welcomed by the people, but it did not arrest the proceedings of the nullifiers. Their threats grew louder and more defiant from 1830 to 1832, and at last Mr. Calhoun gave notice, as has been related, that unless the tariff was so modified as to reduce the duties to the revenue standard, South Carolina would *nullify* the acts of Congress imposing them, take her commerce with foreign countries into her own keeping, and regulate it to suit herself.

Calhoun's demand that the tariff should be reduced to a revenue standard was made in accordance with the intepretation of the Constitution by the

State-rights party, which contended that the Federal Government "had no power to lay a tariff except for revenue only." It was admitted that in laying a tariff for revenue, the Government might adjust the duties so as incidentally to protect American manufactures; that is to say, the object of laying a tariff should be to raise revenue, and protection should be only an incident. That was the prevalent doctrine prior to the war of 1812. During that war, American manufactures expanded to such an extent that they became nearly equal in importance to agriculture or commerce. As a matter of course, when the war closed, the vast manufacturing interest sought to protect itself by securing tariff legislation in its favor. It succeeded so well that the result, as Benton says, "reversed the old course of legislation—made protection the object instead of the incident, and revenue the incident instead of the object; and was another instance of constitutional construction being made dependent, not upon its own words but upon extrinsic, accidental and transient circumstances. It introduced a new and a large question of constitutional law, and of national expediency, fraught with many and great consequences."*

One of the many and great consequences generated by this constitutional contention as to the powers of the Federal Government to impose a tariff for the specific purpose of protection, now confronted the country in the guise of nullification. Congress made great efforts to avert the threatened disturbance. Mr. Clay's bill was passed as a pacifi-

* Benton, I,3.

catory measure in June, 1832, by which the revenue was reduced three millions, and the President signed it, as being a step toward the right system. The nullifiers in South Carolina derided this effort to appease their indignation, and proceeded to execute Mr. Calhoun's threats. A Convention of the people, authorized by the Legislature, met at Columbia, in November, 1832, a few days after the Presidential election, and adopted, without one dissentient voice, the Ordinance of Nullification, declaring the tariff law "null, void and no law, nor binding upon this State, its officers or citizens." It further decreed that no duties enjoined by it should be paid or permitted to be paid after February 1, 1833.

According to the provisions of this tyrannical "Ordinance," no appeal to the Supreme Court was to be allowed, and even an attempt to appeal should be held as criminal. If the government of the United States should try by force to collect the duties, "the people of this State will thenceforth hold themselves absolved from all further obligation to maintain or preserve their political connection with the people of the other States, and will forthwith proceed to organize a separate government, and do all other acts and things which sovereign and independent states may of right do."

The governor and legislature, with the utmost possible emphasis, adopted and commended this Ordinance, and the governor was authorized to accept the services of volunteers, organized like the Minute Men of the Revolution. There was open preparation for war throughout the State. Men, women and children wore the blue cockade, with a palmetto button in the middle of it. Medals were struck bearing inscriptions hostile to the Union. In December, 1832, Mr. Calhoun resigned his office of Vice-President. A vacancy was created in the Senate for him, to which he was at once elected. When he left his home to take his seat in the Senate, the State of South Carolina was in a universal ferment.

During all this year, 1832, whether he was at Washington or at the Hermitage, the President of the United States watched the proceedings of South Carolina and her ruling spirit with a keenly attentive eye. He viewed them merely as the treasonable devices of a morbidly ambitious and acutely disappointed man. His contempt for the movement was unbounded. He said to General Sam Dale, an old Indian fighter, who had served under him in the West: "If this thing goes on our country will be like a bag of meal with both ends open. Pick it up in the middle or endwise and it will run out. I must tie the bag and save the country. They are trying me here; you will witness it; but, by the God of Heaven, I will uphold the law!" Upon hearing these words, the old soldier expressed a hope that, after all, things would go right. "They *shall* go right, sir!" the President exclaimed, with sudden vehemence, dashing his pipe down upon the table and breaking it to pieces.

He had a few devoted friends and adherents in South Carolina, of whom Joel R. Poinsett was the most active and the most competent. Poinsett kept the President promptly advised of every movement, and he on his part quietly took all possible precautions. He stationed General Winfield Scott at

Charleston, and placed some regiments and parts of regiments of regular troops where they could be of immediate use in an emergency. The naval force in Charleston was increased, and five thousand new muskets were deposited in Castle Pinckney. He sent a confidential messenger to Charleston to play the part of an intelligent traveler, and carefully inspect the forts, islands, revenne cutters and defensible points. He came to an understanding with the governors of adjacent States, and made it a sure thing that, in case of an overt act of treason, he could place fifty thousand men in South Carolina within forty days, to be followed in another forty days by fifty thousand more. In these days of peace, it is appalling to think with what a tempest of war he would have overwhelmed the Nullifiers if they had had the courage to push their movement into treasonable collision with the government.

Recently, we have had published the secret correspondence of those months between the President and Mr. Poinsett, in which Andrew Jackson shows, as on many other occasions he exhibited, the heart and mind of a natural master of men. His first and strongest desire was to turn South Carolina loyalty against South Carolina treason, and so confine the turmoil to the limits of that rebellious State. Failing in this, he waited only for the perpetration of an overt act of treason to arrest Calhoun with his principal adherents and put them on trial for that capital crime. In his letters to Poinsett, he applied to the case in hand the precise interpretation of the law of treason, which in 1807 he heard luminously laid down by Chief Justice Marshall at the trial of Aaron

Burr. He dwelt particularly on these two points: 1. There is no treason until an overt act is committed; 2. When an overt act is committed, all aiders and abettors are equally involved in the crime. "The first act of treason committed," he wrote in January, 1833, "unites to it all those who have aided and abetted in the execution of the crime."

While thus quietly preparing for emergencies, the President was taking measures to arouse the patrotic feeling of the country. As soon as the Ordinance of Nullification reached him, he began to compose a proclamation by way of reply to it, in which he refuted the doctrines of the Ordinance with a rare blending of logic, tact and fire. He reproduced, in Jacksonian language, the unanswerable argument made by Webster in his reply to Hayne. It is said that his favorite pen was a steel implement of such vast size that his friends were wont to say that when it needed mending he sent it to a blacksmith to have it repaired. This pen shed ink profusely. In writing the proclamation against the nullifiers, the President dashed off page after page with such rapidity that a friend who came into the office found fifteen or twenty pages scattered over the large table to hasten the drying of the ink.

In response to the nullifiers' assumption that when, in the judgment of any State, the General Government transcends the powers granted to it by the several States, it breaks the "constitutional compact," and justifies an aggrieved State in nullifying the offensive law, and in seceding from the Union and resuming the independent position it enjoyed before the Union was formed, the President said: "I consider the power to annul a law of the United States, assumed by one State, incompatible with the existence of the Union, contradicted expressly by the letter of the Constitution, unauthorized by its spirit, inconsistent with every principle on which it was founded, and destructive of the great object for which it was formed."

Had this expression of opinion been uttered by Webster in the Senate, the nullifiers would have disregarded it; but coming from the President of the United States who, it was well known, would back it up with the whole power of the Government, it compelled the respect of some of the most radical South Carolina statesmen sufficiently to make them pause in their reckless career.

The response of the people to the proclamation was electric and overwhelming. Enormous meetings were held in the open air in New York, Boston, Philadelphia, as well as in every State outside of South Carolina.

Congress meanwhile was once more engaged with the chronic difficulty of the tariff, trying to reconcile irreconcilable interests, with the inevitable result of disappointing many and satisfying none. The Verplanck bill, favored by the President, was the most radical, since it proposed a large and sudden reduction of the tariff. Mr. Clay's compromise was less displeasing to the manufacturers, since it reduced duties gradually—ten per cent. per annum until all should be reduced below twenty per cent.; his object being to accomplish the unavoidable reduction with the least possible shock to business, while saving as much as possible of the protective policy.

Mr. Calhoun supported and voted for the bill of Henry Clay, rather than for that of Mr. Verplanck which was more in accord with his own position. No doubt, there was a compromise all around, in effecting which the unrecorded action of the lobby was mightier than the legislation of Congress. There were concessions on every side, to avoid civil war, to avert from an erring sister the ruinous consequence of her own rashness, and to save the neck of John C. Calhoun.

As soon as Congress adjourned, the chief Nullifier travelled southward night and day, and reached Columbia in time to prevent South Carolina from committing or permitting an act of treason. To quote the authorized biography of Mr. Calhoun by his friend Jenkins:

"Some of the more fiery and ardent members of the Convention were disposed to complain of the Compromise Act as being only a half-way, temporizing measure; but, when Mr. Calhoun's explanations were made, all felt satisfied, and the Convention cordially approved of his course. The Nullification Ordinance was repealed, and the two parties in the State abandoned their organizations and agreed to forget all their past differences."

Strange to relate, all the promoters of this compromise appeared to be gainers by it. Mr. Clay, who visited New York and New England in the course of the summer, was hailed with enthusiasm in the manufacturing centers, and not less in the great cities along the coast. Daniel Webster, too, reached the highest point in his career as the man who had refuted the fallacies of nullification with such brilliancy and power as to render his argument a permanent national possession. General Jackson was warmly attracted toward Mr. Webster, paid him marked attention, sending his own carriage to convey him to the Capitol when an important debate was expected. Even Mr. Van Buren, sitting tranquilly in the chair of the Senate, acquired additional strength in his character of candidate for the succession.

CHAPTER XXXIV.

THE PRESIDENT'S NORTHERN TOUR—RECEPTION AT HARVARD COLLEGE—SERIOUS DIFFICULTY WITH FRANCE--PRESIDENT JACKSON'S LAST MESSAGE—HIS EXTRARODINARY POPULARITY —HE GOES HOME—HIS FINANCIAL AFFLICTIONS.

The man who gained most by the contest with the nullifiers, and by the compromise which enabled them to retreat from their false position, was President Jackson himself. His visit to the North and East during the summer of 1833 occasioned such an outpouring of popular enthusiasm as the cities of New York and New England had never before witnessed. His most inveterate opponents were captivated by his elegant manners, his majestic bearing and his genial courtesy. In his "Figures of the Past," Josiah Quincy, who had been detailed by the Governor of Massachusetts to accompany President Jackson through that State, tells an amusing incident which occurred at Attleboro, where the Presidential party stopped for breakfast after leaving Rhode Island. After breakfast they visited the manufactories of jewelry for which Attleboro was famous even at that early day. As they were going through one of the factories the superintendent of the establishment said: "You have been interfering with our business, Mr. President, and should feel bound in honor to take these buttons off our hands," at the same time exhibiting many cards of buttons stamped with the palmetto tree. These, he said, had been ordered by the Southern nullifiers as distinguishing badges; but they had been rendered worthless by the President's proclamation. Mr. Quincy says that the President "seemed greatly amused at the discovery that treason in South Carolina had its commercial value in Massachusetts."

President Jackson frequently said, in speaking of nullification, that the tariff had been a mere pretext of the nullifiers; that they wanted to break up the Union, and that their next pretext would be the slavery question—a prediction that proved prophetic.

The President's reception at Harvard College was unexpectedly cordial and enthusiastic. Mr. Quincy's father was then president of that institution, and was delighted to find their distinguished guest to be such a high-toned gentleman. The College Federalists had taken pleasure in thinking and speaking of General Jackson as a backwoods ruffian, full of fight, destitute of brains, and utterly wanting in manners befitting cultivated society. In the teeth of this prejudice, as Mr. Quincy says, "his appearance before that Cambridge audience instantly produced a toleration which quickly merged into something like admiration and respect. The name of Andrew Jackson was indeed one to frighten naughty children with; but the person who went by it wrought a mysterious charm upon old and young."

Singularly enough, John Quincy Adams was bitterly opposed to Harvard's conferring the degree of LL.D. on President Jackson. The Massachusetts baby evidently began to be jealous of the matchless success of the North Carolina baby. But the degree was conferred nevertheless; and Mr. Adams unbosomed himself to his diary by recording that "time-serving and sycophancy are the qualities of all learned and scientific institutions."

While the government was grappling with nullification, a serious difference arose with France, the ancient ally and benefactor of the United States. During the Bonaparte wars many vessels of the United States had been unlawfully detained, fined and confiscated by the French government, for which the United States had been ever since vainly demanding compensation. In 1830, Louis Philippe came to the French throne. He was a cordial friend of the United States. He remembered with peculiar pleasure his travels in Tennessee when Andrew Jackson was a pioneer lawyer there, and cherished for him a particular esteem. Lafayette, too, again gave to the American negotiator the powerful aid of his popularity and of his interest with the king. The negotiation proceeded so prosperously that, on the Fourth of July, 1831, the king of the French signed a treaty agreeing to pay the United States five millions of dollars in six annual installments, the first to be paid February 2, 1833.

Mr. Rives, who represented the United States in the negotiation, came home in triumph, and the affair was supposed to be happily settled. Quite as a matter of course, Congress passed a law providing for the appointment of three commissioners to divide the money among the claimants, and, as the treaty bound the United States to reduce the duties upon French wines, a law to that effect was passed. So certain was the Secretary of the Treasury of receiving the money on the day appointed, that a draft for the amount was sold to the Bank of the United States, and its proceeds placed to the credit of the government. The bank sold the draft to bankers in England, who presented the same at the French treasury for payment. Imagine the surprise and the embarrassment of all parties concerned, when the French minister of finance notified the bearers of the draft that, as the French Deputies had not appropriated any money for the purpose, it could not be paid. The Deputies had simply neglected to make the appropriation, as the bill was introduced late in the session, and was not made what was then called "a ministerial measure."

President Jackson was so disconcerted and in so many ways offended by this failure, that he accepted the resignation of Edward Livingston as Secretary of State, and sent him as minister to France in a national vessel to see what was the matter. He was accompanied by his son-in-law, Thomas F. Barton, the husband of his beautiful daughter Cora, who had played about General Jackson's knees and brought him his rice at New Orleans in 1815. But neither Mr. Livingston nor the French ministry nor King Louis Philippe could succeed in inducing the French Assembly to vote the money. The king gave Mr. Livingston a confidential hint on the subject. Let the President of the United States, said he, insert a few lines in his next message to show our dilatory Deputies that he is in earnest in the matter, and means to insist upon payment.

General Jackson acted on this suggestion; but his idea of a friendly hint differed somewhat from that which prevailed in the diplomatic circles of Europe. In his message of 1834 he recommended that, in case the money should not be voted at the next session of the French Chambers, a law should be passed "*authorizing reprisals upon French property.*" On reading the message, as Mr. Barton used to relate, the king of the French was much surprised, but more amused. Upon the whole, he was well pleased with the message, because he thought it would actually induce the Deputies to vote the money. But as soon as the words of the message were printed in the French newspapers, with extracts from Mr. Livingston's confidential correspondence, showing that the king himself had suggested the warlike tone of the message, the entire French people seemed to be thrown into a paroxysm of excitement and indignation. The French minister resident at Washington was at once recalled, and Mr. Livingston was informed that his passports were ready. The Chambers were appeased for the moment by a notification from the king that diplomatic intercourse between France and the United States had been suspended.

Mr. Livingston's conduct on this occasion was eminently diplomatic and wise. Instead of at once applying for his passports, he determined to wait until he could hear from home. Being a master of the French tongue, he addressed to the ministry a frank and eloquent explanation of the misunderstanding, in which he showed that the President's message was designed to avoid hostile measures and was written wholly in the interests of peace. Dispatches, however, soon arrived from Washington which compelled him to take his departure, and finally Mr. Barton, the Secretary of Legation, who had been left in charge of the American mission, was ordered home.

On Mr. Barton's arrival in the winter of 1836, he found the President so inflamed with indignation against the French that it was with great difficulty he told his story, and he was obliged at length to say to the President that he could not explain the situation in France truly unless he were allowed to speak without interruption. "Right, sir," said the President; "go on, sir." He then explained that all France was in a frenzy on the matter. The king, the ministry and all persons capable of reflection lamented this, and earnestly desired a restoration of all the old friendship with the United States. Mr. Barton's clear explanation allayed the President's excitement. Nevertheless, he said to Congress that, as the French were evidently preparing for war, it would be only prudent on the part of the United States to make similar preparations, such as the increase of the navy and the completion of the coast defenses.

By this time the American people were roused almost to the degree of excitement prevailing in France. Even John Quincy Adams in the House of Representatives supported the action of the President in a speech so spirited and powerful that the tradition of its effect remains until this day. As Mr.

Seward records, "the very walls of the Capitol shook with the thundering applause it called forth."

At this alarming crisis the government of Great Britain offered to mediate between the two estranged nations. The offer being promptly accepted, the President had the pleasure, on the tenth of May, 1836, to inform Congress that "the four installments, due under our treaty with France, had been paid to the agent of the United States, and that no proper exertions of his should be wanting to restore the ancient cordial relations between the two countries."

The excitement subsided, and all parties, particularly Louis Philippe himself, united in applauding the vigor and firmness of President Jackson. The happy news came a month after the payment of the last installment of the public debt, an event which was celebrated by a banquet in Washington, at which Senator Benton presided, and a hundred patriotic toasts were offered.

One more conflict remained to be fought out by this most combative and victorious of men, one that he had been waging with unabated zeal from the early months of his first term—that with the United States Bank. He destroyed the Bank at last, and thereby did his country an inestimable service; but it was unfortunate that a safe and sufficient substitute for the Bank was not provided before that dangerous institution was overthrown.

On the 30th of January, 1835, an attempt was made to assassinate President Jackson. He, with members of his Cabinet, had attended the funeral, in the hall of the House of Representatives, of Hon. Warren

R. Davis, of South Carolina. The procession had moved out with the casket containing the corpse. The President (with Levi Woodbury, Secretary of State, aud Mahlon Dickerson, Secretary of the Navy) was issuing from the door of the rotunda, that opens on the portico, when a man stepped forward into a little open space about eight feet in front of General Jackson, leveled a pistol at his breast, and pulled the trigger. The cap exploded with such a loud report that it was supposed the pistol had fired. Colonel Benton said he heard it at the foot of the steps, some distance away, and with a great crowd intervening. But the pistol did not go off. The man dropped it instantly, and leveled another pistol, which he had held ready cocked in his left hand, and pulled the trigger again. The cap exploded without firing the pistol. The President instantly rushed upon the man with his uplifted cane; he shrank back; Secretary Woodbury aimed a blow at him: Lieutenant Gedney, of the Navy, knocked him down; he was secured by the bystanders, and handed over to the officers of justice. His name was Richard Lawrence. He was an Englishman. It was found, on examination, that he was of unsound mind, and had conceived it to be his divine mission to shoot the President, so as to relieve the country from the business depression under which it was alleged to be suffering.

The pistols were examined and found to be well loaded. On being recapped, "they were fired without fail, carrying their bullets true, and driving them through inch boards at thirty feet distance; nor could any reason be found for the two failures at the door of the rotunda. . . . The circumstance made a deep impression upon the public feeling, and irresistibly carried many minds to the belief in a superintending Providence, manifested in the extraordinary case of two pistols in succession—so well loaded, so coolly handled, and which afterwards fired with such readiness, force, and precision—missing fire, each in its turn, when leveled eight feet at the President's heart."*

The last message of President Jackson contained a warning note as to the growing surplus. He took the ground that there should be no surplus and no taxation beyond the legitimate needs of the government. To the last hour of his second term he retained his popularity in full measure. Gifts and congratulations rained upon him, and when he appeared, an infirm old man, at the inauguration of Mr. Van Buren to the Presidency, he was the central figure, the commanding personage of the occasion. For once, in the history of governments, the setting outshone the rising sun. For once, the people, who are usually rated as fickle and ungrateful, turned on their god when he set the same look that they turned when he rose. As the vast concourse looked their last upon the feeble but still majestic old man who from his boyhood had served his country with such heroism and devotion, many of them shed tears, and their final "Hurrah for Jackson" came fervid from grateful hearts.

The admiration of the people of that generation for General Jackson and their unparalleled devotion

* Benton, I. 521.

to him, have been looked upon by his enemies as among the worst evils that ever befell the United States. In their opinion, Andrew Jackson's elevation to the Presidency was a national misfortune. They cannot deny that he accomplished much that was of advantage to the nation; but they maintain that for whatever good came out of his administration the country was indebted to an overruling Providence. It is useless to argue against convictions which are founded on prejudice and hatred; and the more honest and sincere the holders of such opinions are, the less possible it is to modify them. It is conceded that the foreign diplomacy of President Jackson was very successful. The most amicable relations were sustained with great Britain; useful commercial treaties were made with several countries, and expiring treaties were renewed with others; indemnities for spoliations on American commerce were obtained from France, Naples, Spain and Portugal, and the United States for the first time took its equal station among the nations of the earth. President Jackson's domestic administration was correspondingly successful. The Creeks were removed from Florida and the Cherokees from Georgia; the public lands were thrown open to the people at nominal prices; the United States Bank was overthrown; the gold currency was largely increased; the national debt was extinguished; nullification was crushed, and Union sentiments were made paramount throughout the land. The people appreciated these national benefits; they believed in President Jackson's honesty and patriotism; they admired his courage and his purity of life and character, and they spontaneously condoned his faults of temper and his summary mode of dealing with obstacles.

Moreover, it was understood and felt in all parts of the country that General Jackson's sympathies were with the people—with poor and struggling men; that he wished for a sound currency with which the wages of the workman should be paid, so that when the laborer received a dollar for his day's work it should be a dollar, and buy a full dollar's worth anywhere. When the favorite hero of a free and enlightened people exhibits qualities so popular and valuable as these the devotion he evokes may sometimes seem to be fanatical, but it is none the less genuine.

The ex-President's homeward journey was a continual triumph. No President going to Washington to assume governmental power was ever so honored as was this old man who had taken leave of public life for ever. He was seventy years of age, his hair as white as snow. The infirmities of age, greatly emphasized by his continual ill-health from boyhood, subdued the rugged energy of his manner and softened the leonine expression of his countenance into an engaging gentleness of aspect and deportment which gave an additional attractiveness to the habitual majesty of his demeanor. The inhabitants of Nashville gave him an enthusiastic welcome home. Among the vast assemblage was a large company of boys. The Hon. Andrew Ewing, then a very young man and the spokesman for the boys, thus describes the scene: "The day of his [General Jackson's] return was to me one of the most memorable of my existence. We met him in the cedars near Lebanon. The old men were ranged in front, the boys in the rear. He got out of his carriage. * * * He then drew near us. I stepped forward, spoke a few words of kindness, and wound up by saying 'That the children of his old soldiers and friends welcomed him home, and were ready to serve under his banner.' His frame shook, he bowed down his head, and whilst the tears rolled down his aged cheeks, he replied: 'I could have stood all but this; it is too much, too much!' The crowd gathered around, and for a few moments there was a general outburst of sympathy and tears. I may live a hundred years, but no future can erase that scene from my memory."*

Soon after his arrival at the Hermitage, he wrote to a friend: "I returned home with just ninety dollars in money, having expended all my salary and most of the proceeds of my cotton crop; found everything out of repair; corn and everything else for the use of my farm to buy."

It was necessary, therefore, for him to resume at once his labors as a planter, and by the sale of a piece of land, to raise money for a working capital.

*Parton's Life of Jackson, III: 630.

CHAPTER XXXV.

ANDREW JACKSON'S LAST YEARS—HIS CONVERSION—HE JOINS THE CHURCH—HIS CLOSING HOURS—HIS DEATH.

On his extensive farm the ex-President found abundant and congenial occupation during the last years of his life. At this time he possessed about a hundred and fifty slaves, to whom he was an indulgent and considerate master, as well as a steadfast friend in time of trouble. He loved to look upon a well-cultivated field of cotton or grain, and he still had the keenest enjoyment in the finer breeds of sheep, cattle and horses.

Chaplain Milburn, the Blind Preacher, then a keen-sighted boy upon his father's Western farm, remembers the general's viewing some superior animals just imported from England. He remembers, too, how the old man's face glowed with pleasure as he gazed upon them, and eagerly pointed out the blending of beauty and strength in their forms. "Never," said the preacher, "shall I forget the impressive appearance, the tall, spare figure, the glittering eye and the commanding presence of the erect old man." He showed as a farmer the same qualities that gave him success elsewhere; vigilant watchfulness, forethought, careful calculation, unslumbering attention to the duties in hand.

He was still a busy politician. The mail-box at his garden-gate was a large receptacle, but often it was not large enough to hold what the mail brought him. As long as he had strength to sit at his desk, he answered with his own hand every letter that required an answer. He wrote often to President Van Buren, and gave cordial support and applause to his calm and sagacious dealing with the financial embarrassments of his term.

As usual, his house was well filled with visitors, some of whom recorded their conversations with him. He was a man much given to maxims, some of which were his own, such as: "Take all the time for thinking the circumstances allow; but when the time for action has come, stop thinking." Alluding to his early history, he would quote Shakespeare's "tide in the affairs of men," adding, "That's true, sir, I've proved it during my whole life."

One great grief and disappointment afflicted him during the last years of his life. His adopted son, named by him Andrew Jackson, was not successful as a man of business. His misfortunes so reduced General Jackson's available resources, that in 1842 he was obliged to borrow ten thousand dollars, and asked Mr. Blair of the *Globe* to lend him the money. Blair and Rives, now enriched by the public printing and the prosperity of the *Globe*, desired to make this loan on General Jackson's personal security alone, meaning thereby to make it, if possible, a gift. The old man saw through their generous scheme; it affected him to tears; still he would not permit them to carry it out, but secured the loan by a mortgage on his estate. Soon after, the fine imposed upon him at New Orleans in 1815 was refunded, principal and interest, by act of Congress, Mr. Calhoun voting for it. This gave him twenty-seven hundred dollars additional, and it came at a very good time.

In 1842, when he was seventy-five years of age, he fulfilled, at length, the promise he had made to his wife many years before, that when he had done with politics he would follow her example and join the church. A protracted meeting was held in the little church on the Hermitage farm, all the services of which were attended by the family, General Jackson himself being always in his accustomed seat. At the last of the meetings, on Saturday afternoon, the Reverend Doctor Edgar of Nashville, who personally told the story to Mr. Parton, was the preacher; his subject, "Providential Interposition." He observed, as he proceeded with his sermon, that his distinguished auditor was singularly attentive, and on the spur of the moment he gave the discourse a personal bearing. He sketched the career of a pioneer who had escaped the perils of the wilderness, the wiles of the Indian, the dangers of war, the conflicts of politics and the attempts of the assassin. "How can such a man," exclaimed the preacher, "pass through such scenes as these unharmed, and not see in it an Omnipotent Hand?"

At the close of the service General Jackson asked Doctor Edgar to visit him; which, however, the clergyman could not do until Sunday morning. The aged warrior found it a hard matter to come into the kingdom, and he spent the greater part of the night in reading the Bible, in prayer and in conversing with his daughter-in-law, who intended to join the church the very next day. As the Sunday morning was dawning, he obtained relief, and met Doctor Edgar with joy and triumph in his countenance. He announced his desire to join the church that morning, with his daughter. The clergyman, after asking the usual questions and getting satisfactory replies, spoke as follows:

"General, there is one more question which it is my duty to ask you. Can you forgive all your enemies?"

He was silent for a good while. At length he said:

"My political enemies I can freely forgive; but as for those who abused me when I was serving my country in the field, and those who attacked me *for* serving my country—doctor, that is a different case."

Doctor Edgar, however, insisted that the forgiveness must be entire and embrace the whole family of man. After a considerable pause, the candidate got so far as to say that he *thought* he could forgive even the men who had made his defense of his native land a pretext for assailing him.

The scene in the little church that morning was never forgotten by any who witnessed it. Besides being crowded to the very uttermost, the windows were darkened by as many black faces as could get near enough. At length the general and his daughter stood up to make the usual public profession. He leaned heavily upon his walking-stick with both hands, and his face was wet with tears. When finally he was pronounced a member of the church, the feelings of the congregation, which had been restrained during the ceremonial, burst forth in sobs and cries, and the clergyman himself was unable to speak. Some one started a familiar hymn, and in singing this the feelings of the excited company at last found both expression and relief.

What an encouragement in faithful well-doing it should be to all pious mothers thus to learn that Andrew Jackson's early religious instruction, given in his humble home in the old Waxhaw settlement, at last bore its legitimate fruit and in spirit brought him back, after all those years, a childlike old man, to his mother's knee and his mother's prayers. The memory and the influence of his mother's teaching, of her example and her prayers, had never entirely left him. Like soft-whispering angels, they had perpetually and lovingly hovered over him and around him even in his most wayward steps, and in later years the powerful influence of his wife's religious character and pious wishes, had been added to them. To a friend who spoke to him in 1839 about the calumnies as to his skepticism with which he had been assailed during his Presidential canvasses, General Jackson responded with great emphasis:

"Yes, sir! For thirty-five years before my election to the Presidency, I read at least three chapters of the Bible every day, which is far more than any of my detractors could say with truth, in this respect."

From the day he joined the church he spent most of his leisure hours in reading the Bible, and in studying Scott's Commentaries. He read prayers every evening in the presence of all his family and servants. A few weeks after they wished to make him a ruling elder of the little church, but he said: "No; I am too young in the church for such an office. My countrymen have given me high honors, but I should esteem the office of ruling elder in the church of Christ a far higher honor than any I have received."

During the last two years of General Jackson's life, after he had been an invalid for thirty years, his malady took the form of consumption, which was much aggravated by dropsy, a constantly recurring diarrhœa, and other painful symptoms. Few old men have more acutely or more continuously suffered, and no one could ever have borne such sufferings with more fortitude or more patience. That unparalleled character of his—"the impossibility of being displaced or overset"—which had borne him so triumphantly through all manner of trials and impediments, now stood him in stead during his protracted and agonizing illness. Mr. Trist, who has already been quoted as to General Jackson's character, says: "There was more of the woman in his nature than in that of any man I ever knew—more of woman's tenderness towards children and sympathy with them. Often has he been known, though he never had a child of his own, to walk up and down by the hour with an infant in his arms, because by so doing he relieved it from the cause of its crying; more, also, of woman's patience and uncomplaining, unnoticing submissiveness to trivial causes of irritation. * * * As regards patience I have often seen his temper tried to a degree that it irritated mine to think of, by those neglects in small things that go so hard with an invalid—as he always was at the period when I knew him—and which are so apt to test one's temper. But things of this kind passed off without so much as a shade coming over his countenance."

Mr. Blair, of the Washington *Globe*, who visited General Jackson toward the close of his life, witnessed an exhibition of his patience and tenderness, when one of his little nephews, a vigorous boy six years of age, ran against him as he sat in his chair silently enduring one of his agonizing headaches. The suffering old man turned deadly pale and fell back in his chair breathless. When he had recovered a little, he spoke to the boy in the tenderest way, and as though caring more for the feelings of the alarmed child than for his own suffering: "Oh, my dear boy, you don't know how much pain you have given your uncle!" Indeed, it seemed as though over this long perturbed, fiery, untamable spirit the Lord had thrown a mantle of peace, the spiritual garment of the soul, woven out of regenerated integrity, purity and courage, through patriotic deeds unselfishly performed, and unwavering trust in divine mercy and redeeming grace. "Thou wilt keep him in perfect peace, whose mind is stayed on Thee."

During every interval of relief, the general still loved to converse on his old topics. About six weeks before his death, Dr. Edgar asked him what he would have done with Calhoun and the nullifiers if they had persisted. To this question he replied, with remarkable energy:

"Hanged them, sir, as high as Haman. They should have been a terror to traitors to all time."

To the last days of his life he was pestered by office-seekers, who besought him to sign their recommendations. They invaded and pervaded his dooryard, his piazza, and sometimes his sick-chamber. What is there in the way of obtrusiveness, intrusiveness, invasiveness, pervasiveness, meddlesomeness or crookedness of etiquette to which the office-seeker will not with alacrity resort? And yet this pestiferous creature has one Christian virtue; if you smite him on one cheek, he will meekly turn the other to you, also—if he has not already obtained your signature. The human race is divided into men, women and office-seekers. It was so in the beginning. In the Garden of Eden, as Milton informs us, there was a man, a woman and an office-seeker who had been kicked out of heaven for offensive office-seeking. That original office-seeker played the devil in Paradise, and made life an everlasting burden to the descendants of that unfortunate pair who were so foolish as to sign his recommendations. And, worse still, he had descendants—has always had them—has them now. They were more troublesome to the sick and dying old hero of the Hermitage than all his Indian and foreign foes had been. He could slay his Indian and foreign foes, but, unfortunately, there were obstacles in the way of his meting out justice to the office-seekers who so ruthlessly annoyed him. " I am dying," the worn-out old man said one day— "I am dying as fast as I can, but they will keep swarming upon me in crowds, seeking for office—intriguing for office."

The last national subject which occupied his attention was the annexation of Texas, or "the *recovery* of Texas by the United States," as he put it. He was greatly rejoiced when the work was accomplished.

The venerable ex-President suffered on through weeks and months; but finally the time drew near when that indomitable character which no earthly power had ever been able to displace or overset was to be subdued by the power of death. His last day on earth was June 8, 1845. It was Sunday—a warm, pleasant day. He was seventy-eight years old. It was known that his end was near, and all day long crowds of his servants and slaves thronged about the house, filled the piazza, and looked in at the doors and windows, sobbing and wringing their hands. They all loved him, for he had always been a kind and just master, and also their faithful friend. He spoke to them affectionately at intervals.

"I go a short time before you," he said, "and want to meet you all, white and black, in Heaven." He repeated, with emphasis, "*white and black.*"

The very last words he spoke were addressed to his sobbing slaves: "What is the matter with my dear children?" he tenderly asked. "Have I alarmed you? Oh, don't cry! Be good children, and we will all meet in Heaven."

He died at six o'clock in the evening. His last look was affectionately fixed upon a portrait of his wife that hung opposite to his bed. His old comrade, Major Lewis, closed his eyes. The funeral, which took place on June 10th, was attended by thousands of people from Nashville and all the country round. He was buried in the Hermitage garden, by the side of his wife, of whom he had spoken with characteristic loyalty of affection not long before he died, saying: "Heaven will be no Heaven to me if I do not meet my wife there."

The tablet which covers his remains bears this inscription:

GENERAL

ANDREW JACKSON,

BORN ON THE 15TH OF MARCH, 1767,

Died on the 8th of June, 1845.

THE TOMB OF ANDREW JACKSON.—*See Page* 368.

INDEX.